LEONARDO'S BICYCLE

NOVELS OF PACO IGNACIO TAIBO II
IN ENGLISH TRANSLATION

AN EASY THING
THE SHADOW OF THE SHADOW
SOME CLOUDS
NO HAPPY ENDING
FOUR HANDS
LIFE ITSELF

LEONARDO'S BICYCLE

PACO IGNACIO TAIBO II

Translated by Martin Michael Roberts

THE MYSTERIOUS PRESS

Published by Warner Books

A Time Warner Company

Originally published in Mexico as *La Bicicleta de Leonardo*
by Joaquin Moritz

Mysterious Press books are published by Warner Books, Inc.,
1271 Avenue of the Americas, New York, NY 10020.

A Time Warner Company

Printed in the United States of America
First U.S. printing: September 1995
10 9 8 7 6 5 4 3 2 1

Library of Congress Cataloging-in-Publication Data

Taibo, Paco Ignacio, 1949–
[Bicicleta de Leonardo. English]
Leonardo's bicycle / Paco Ignacio Taibo II : translated by Martin
Michael Roberts.
p. cm.
ISBN 0-89296-589-4
I. Roberts, Martin Michael. II. Title.
PQ7298.3.A58B5313 1995
863—dc20 94-44506
CIP

This book is for those caretakers of my moral stubbornness, my old pals Jesús Anaya, Mariano Rodríguez, and Jim Adams, and for two writers whom I love very much: Jerome Charyn, the vampire of Manhattan-Paris, and Justo Vasco, Patito Travels representative in Havana.

LEONARDO'S BICYCLE

When heavy substances fall down through the air, and the air moves upward to continually fill the space left behind . . .

—Leonardo da Vinci

FIRST SECTOR

Bicycle

There would be no point in opening his eyes if he were paralyzed . . .

—Ross Thomas

Leonardo (I)

Why are preparatory sketches often much more beautiful than the finished object, and always much more interesting? Why is there more power in these unfinished strokes, in outlines, in hazy ideas, than in the final product that the painter comes up with some time afterward?

There can be no doubt that the attraction of the unfinished sketch is to be found in the literary framework within which the painting is depicted, starting with its feeble beginnings, because at such a time drawings are ideas floating around before clutching at the final lifeline. Doubtless sketches have a narrative of the future painting within them, but there is also a bridge between the painting and the ideas that beget it, the threads of reality that will have to be knitted together to make it. Therein also lie the relationships between the painter and his material. Sketches are better than the finished product because they reveal the experiment, because they illustrate the quest, because within them lies an array of alternatives and variations stemming from which there will doubtless be a one and only, a unique, final result.

They are better, because as well as foreshadowing the final result, there is a quest to be found within them.

There then, that feeling of: *the finished work is here, and not in the mural-to-be that will never be painted*, is probably what stirred up the emotions of the Magus himself, the native of Vinci, when faced with the sketches of horses with which he had spent years preparing the general layout for the mural that was to be called *The Battle of Anghiari* and that today, now that Leonardo is food for worms, are partly to be found in Windsor, Great Britain (identified by the codes 12326, recto, and 12327, recto), and Madrid, Spain, in the National Library as part of the Madrid Codex II.

Those were not his only horses. Years before, he had lost sleep over the equestrian statue of Francesco Sforza. That was a project for a monumental horse made out of bronze that never came to be cast, as the 156,000 pounds of metal intended for it went to Ferrara to be turned into cannons.

Now they were faces of moving horses (*Do horses have faces? Which feather is it that steers the flight of angels? Which way do the ripples spin when you drop a stone into smooth waters?*), distant and with ferocious expressions, as if the battle had possessed them, too, and as if they harbored the same feelings of hate as their riders. Wicked horses distorted by fury, to the extent that one of them is transfigured by the pencil into a roaring lion.

When Gonfaloniero Soderini commissioned him to paint one of the murals in the Council Chamber in the Palazzo Vecchio, Leonardo probably had the intuition to realize the fate that awaited the painting and nonetheless, as against his bad habit of forgetting the art of painting in the name of other curiosities and obsessions (after all, it should not be forgotten that Leonardo was brought up without a mother to imbue him with the vice of formality), he spent weeks and months preparing the mural that, for his employers, was to commemorate the battle of Anghiari, the one in which an obscure *condottiere* had led the Florentines to victory against the Milanese a hundred years before (it might as well have been five hundred, with its being as far away then as it is now), but that would symbolize the bestiality of war for Leonardo.

Leonardo arrived at Florence in that year of 1503, while running away from himself, one of his bad habits, and also running away from his usual obsessions and setbacks. For three years he had been military engineer to Cesare Borgia and had looked askance when the Duke de Valentinois, the Cardinal of Pamplona (with a papal permit for fornication), wove plots, bought and sold *condottieri*, peddled arms, set up deadly intrigues, sent his now useless old cronies to the gallows, and waged minor wars, pulling them out of his handkerchief and the poison bottle. It all made for quite a sensation, albeit a bit harrowing, seeing the architect of evil unfurling his tunic. Nonetheless, Leonardo had looked askance, while he was surveying the Urbino villa in order to fortify it, suggesting military options for the defence of Piombino, or drawing maps of Imola with military objectives. He looked askance, turned a blind eye, with a feeling of *lèse-humanité*, of alienation. He looked, instead, toward the flight of birds (*the lightest feathers are situated below the most resistant ones, and their ends are turned toward the bird's tail. It is thus because the air below flying objects is thicker than that which is above and behind them*). The maestro Leonardo had looked askance a lot in order to avoid being infected with moral plague.

Now in Florence there were horses, and he was changing patrons and commissions: a wall to paint a battle on and a project to channel the River Arno. It was then that his notebooks filled up with steeds with human faces, and maps.

First there was a host of studies, drawings, sketches, of common people glimpsed on the Florentine streets and transferred to paper, the faces of paupers and beggars hired in the alleyways who, to the outrage of the nobles, were to have their expressions go down in history. Finally, on Friday, June 6, 1505, he began painting a large piece of paper, whose end result would then be transferred to the wall.

And so, by a twist of fate, the Vincian version of the battle would end up in the mural, that in Leonardo's design had the fight over a battle standard as its focus, but whose real centerpiece was a narrative of madness, a point of brutal contact, where armed men and riders were ensnared, with infantrymen covering themselves with shields, lances seeking bodies, sabers hacking at flesh, and, under the hooves of a horse (which had worried him so much), one man stabbing another.

The mural was begun amid strange omens: *On Friday at the thirteenth hour, I began to paint in the palace, and as soon as I set the brush down, the weather began to get worse and bells began to ring, calling men to work. The painted paper was torn, the water began to spill out of the broken jar where it had been, and it suddenly began to rain cats and dogs, and so on, until dusk, the day being like night.*

And the world, wide and outlandish, was in those very days bringing forth voyages of Portuguese boats loaded with cargoes of African slaves bound for the Americas, a peasant war in Germany disguised as a religious war, three popes succeeding each other in just one year, and the Jews being expelled from Spain. The world, gone mad, was taking little notice of a private madness like Leonardo's.

Birthday

He deceived the concierge by telling her he was fifty-two on the day he turned fifty-three. A pickup truck with loud-speakers passed by below his apartment window, beginning the election campaign. He left the faucets open so that the water would run for some time while he was shaving himself, as if the year he had pilfered would go down the drain along with the dirty shaving foam. Throughout the morning he had listened to dire old and scratched records by the Glenn Miller Orchestra, pretending to work on a new novel. He ate canned tunafish with mayonnaise, and some whole wheat bread that was slightly moldy.

It was only when, alone, he switched on the TV to see a ladies' basketball game from the U.S. college league that José Daniel Fierro found the peace he had lost and felt he had discovered a worthwhile way to celebrate the ominous birthday that was bringing him closer to old age.

His liking for American lady basketball players was the result of a succession of accidents, all with marked soap-opera-like overtones, admissible in the case of people unlike him, those who always emerged unscathed from harsh reality. If he had not broken his ankle while walking down the steps in the National Film Theater one night after a film lecture . . . If he had not installed cable television in his apartment in order to keep his plaster cast company . . . If he had not spent three months struggling with the writing of a novel that, frankly, did not exist. If it were not for these twists of fate, he would never have discovered his latest sexual perversion. Because faithfully following women's basketball games from the American college league—or the ladies, as the commentators preferred to call them—was not a sporting passion, much as José Daniel tried to fool his puritan subconscious, saying that if some liked boxing, horse racing, or sumo wrestling, then he . . .

It was sex pure and simple and, moreover, it was sporting sex, platonic, long-distance, and minority sex. In a country where there are so many majority sports obsessions, being in love with a lady American basketball player was a minority sporting passion, a tacky one really, without any allies to call on the phone to comment on the games, and that seemed to reduce everything to a masturbation substitute.

The imagination that José Daniel could not put down on the pages of his novel overflowed from him now, drowning the sound from the TV, as he commented out loud:

"And now, the blond piece from Oklahoma, sweating profusely, with hairy armpits, brushes her left tit against the referee . . ."

His broken leg was the pretext. But José Daniel had

gotten used to not needing pretexts for any solitary act during this past year of his life. Furthermore, he was preparing to turn his private perversion into public literary virtue: he made notes of the strange things that turned him on, that he did, or that occurred to him: "letting melted ice cream run out of the corner of my mouth . . . the marvelous smell of lighter fluid, benzine, that soaks into your lips and mustache when you suck it . . . the glory of taking a piss sitting down" (the last was something to do with his broken foot, or so he thought). And the notes were usually musings spoken out loud, thanks to a tape recorder, because he found himself talking more and more to himself.

"And you can see Jackie O'Brien's D-cup when she reaches out to catch the rebound . . . And you can even see her pubic hairs when she makes that tremeeeeendous leap in the air."

It was sex-at-a-distance. Three weeks previously, the commentators in Houston, who José Daniel admired at a distance, had picked the Texas Longhorns as their favorite team, and he had followed them intently from that moment on.

"And slipping as she loses her balance, we see twenty-year-old Ludmilla Washington landing with her ass against the basket uprights . . . And she likes it! Ladies and gentlemen, she likes it!"

Thanks to the discovery of the Texas Longhorns, José Daniel began to write down the times of all the games on TV and, faithful as could be, while buses went by on the street with their exhaust pipes open and the sweet-potato sellers' carts whistled past, he would drag his broken leg over to the brown chair his ex-wife left behind, put a six-pack of Tecate to one side, and begin to watch the American college girls.

"And just as Eloisa Waterfront throws the ball while she

closes in on the enemy's turf, she sets up a terrible wobbling in her crotch, with her vaginal fluids lubricating the fabulous pace that brings her up to the basket, alternately lifting her buns up, one-two, one-two, bringing her to the edge of orgasm, and making her give the ball away, while she concentrates on coming, ladies and gentlemen, but she takes no notice, she does not care . . . That's how you *get to heaven*, baby. Thirty-six to twenty-nine, you stupid bitch."

The Texas Longhorns were a marvel of extramural and (José Daniel added in his spoken journal) uterine fury. Passion, pure and simple. They fought for each ball as if their lives depended on it, they argued with referees as if they were permanently suffering from premenstrual tension, they celebrated each basket with howls of enthusiasm, made fun of their opponents, blew kisses to their acne-faced adolescent fans in the front rows, missed easy shots, and scored impossible ones.

He adored them.

But that day, his damned birthday, with fifty-three years weighing him down, he was about to see a sight that would change the next few months of his life and, to a certain extent, his whole life (as José Daniel would like to have said in a novel, writing like Victoria Holt). First, the phone rang. Then Karen Turner entered the fray, and the cameras gave the writer, who rose hobbling from his chair, a big close-up of her freckled face.

And then, as José Daniel Fierro hesitated between answering the phone and sitting down again, drawn by the electromagnetic pull of the new player's face, the writer, condemned to the loneliness of his room by a broken foot, watched the girl smiling at him, and went completely crazy. As an old soap opera had once said: "He lost his powers of reason over an illusion."

Leonardo (II)

Ambitious people who are content with the gift of life and the world's beauty suffer the penitence of ruining their lives without ever possessing the usefulness and beauty of the world.

What did the fifty-year-old painter mean? That it was necessary to renounce change, discoveries, quests, that he was obliged to renounce the vocation of denial? No, not he. Any other thinker whose biography did not refute the facts, but not he.

What then?

Finally, the original painting on paper—which was to be transposed to the mural to be called the *Battle of Anghiari*—was finished and put on display for a few days, eliciting admiration and surprise. Meanwhile, Leonardo, who had already become bored with the project just as he got bored with everything because he always moved quicker than the act of consummation, because he thought more quickly than it took to carry things out, because the idea anticipates the act, stole away from his duties and went back to studying the flight of birds, obsessed with finding the key that would allow him (*Air moves like a river and carries clouds along with it, just as running water drags along anything that floats on it*) to rise above the rest of men by using a machine.

At last, on January 28, 1505, Leonardo's assistants began to set up wooden boards and trestles to mount the scaffold, and made up the complex mixture of ingredients that would constitute the base on which the mural would be painted: six hundred pounds of plaster, ninety pounds of resin, and eleven pounds of linseed oil. Throughout the month of March and half of April, while the mixture was drying out, Leonardo went obsessively back to the flight of birds (*When heavy substances fall down through the air, and the air moves upward to continually fill the space left behind . . .*).

When summer came, it seemed that the mural was on the point of being finished, with ferocious horses and the standard captured, and only the final coat needing to be done. Leonardo had pondered the matter and, instead of using the fresco technique, tried a method he had read about in Pliny. A big coal fire was lit in the hall in order to heat it up. The heat of the fire dried the walls out and evaporated the fluid parts of the ingredients. Apparently, everything was working well and the lower part of the fresco had just dried, when the upper part began to melt.

The men's helmets, the steeds' heads, melted into droppings, awful blobs, irrelevant remains; everything vanished into globules of paint . . .

Telephones

José Daniel Fierro had a slightly paranoid relationship with telephones. For that reason, during those months of torrential rain that make the Mexico City telephone network, already badly damaged by the earthquake in 1985, the rats, and old age, break down completely, he gazed at the receiver with more and more mistrust.

It was a shitty phone, bought in a Radio Shack in New York by his ex-wife, in the shape of a turtle shell and with a malignant, almost unreal, pink color, part of the heritage of distressing bits and pieces left behind after the divorce: a pink telephone, a salad-drier, a double album by Julio Iglesias, all of Mishima's novels, a Swiss cuckoo clock, some really tacky artificial silver cutlery, an album of high school photographs (*her* high school, not the glorious First District High School), and a first-aid box full of medicine whose precise use was unknown.

Each time he picked up the phone there was a maelstrom of sound: lines always getting crossed, shrill whistling sounds that made you hang up, shoving the receiver aside as if it were a leprous baby, numbers that would not let themselves be dialed, whole hours with the lines down, the writer's voice coming back to him as a distorted echo, as if he had already turned fifty-five; interruptions in the middle of a call where an anonymous voice would identify itself as a Telmex, the Mexican telephone company, operator, and ask him to repeat his surname slowly along with the seven figures of his phone number; strange sounds, like birds in agony . . .

It was election year, and his paranoid sensitivity conflicted with his hard-boiled reason. José Daniel Fierro argued out loud with his computer screen and told it that if they wanted to tap his phone then there was no problem; on the contrary, it would work perfectly well then; but he argued back that those bastards were a bunch of con men to begin with. Why would they want to tap his phone anyway? What the hell had he done lately? Sign a petition protesting against university bureaucracy. Crap. Write a novel, another one, about police corruption. Blowing bullshit populist tunes on his own trumpet. He had spoken at a rally for the Democratic Revolutionary Party. Nothing, within the system's logic. He was one more intellectual. Or rather, a goddamn citizen. At its height, the Mexican state would have contemplated historic alternatives—either exile in the Islas Marías islands or the embassy in Istanbul—but time had devalued writers and their ilk in the state's perverse logic. Now, they set up museums and scholarships, strange 30,000-new-peso prizes if you were on one side, nonexistence or certificates of oblivion if you were on the other.

That is what logic decreed, but when you have been active for ten years in the catacombs of the pre-1968 Left, when you have lived through experiences like the Santa Ana commune and the eleven months in jail that came afterward, you cannot help having an unpleasant paranoid aftertaste, based on the absolute certainty that the Mexican state's primary function was to fuck your life up, that its only purpose was to screw its citizens.

Anyway, the writer ended up eyeing the phone with a look full of distrust, with dark suspicions. But it was a big step to cut the cables with the scissors he had on top of his desk, and one he could not bring himself to take.

When the phone's ringing came together with the vision of Karen Turner, all his unpleasant aftertastes regarding telephones came back to him like waves thrashing around in his head. Without being able to take his eyes off the television screen and the face of the relatively short girl (she could not have been more than six three) with the freckles and the cropped mop of hair, he stood as if frozen for a second, then picked up the phone as if it were a dog turd.

"Issa Tropea here, you dope. Io sono your publisher, but iffa you don havva book, whadda fuck I print?" said a voice that he knew, speaking to him in *cocoliche*, that strange mixture of Italian and Spanish that had been invented in Argentina.

"I'm writing it, you jerk. Don't you know you can't put writers under pressure? It's a sin!" José Daniel said to his Italian publisher.

"Tu sei like Leonardo, you no finish niente, nothing, nothing at all, niente," Tropea answered him, laughing.

But he only devoted a corner of his concentration to the pink phone. The rest of it was still absorbed with the glorious image of the Turner girl that had just disappeared. He tried to pick her out of the group. The ball was in the opposing team's hands, some college girls from New Mexico, with a mixed appearance of chicanas, Watusis, and Swedes.

"What's you goddamn book about, then?"

"About lady basketball players, jerk. What else is there to write about in Mexico? Lady basketball players and my grandfather, who was a terrorist in Barcelona. In times like these, he needs to be vindicated. In Barcelona, they're painting his turf pink. To celebrate the Olympics, pal. And he wasn't even a Stalinist. He was an anarchist and, what's more, the Stalinists hated him and even tried to kill him during the Spanish Civil War, but he gave them shit anyway . . . Well then, it's about lady basketball players."

"Tu sei talking serious, my friend? You won't sell one copy of that shitty book in the States. Lady basketball players and anarchists?"

Where had the freckle-faced girl come from? She was not one of the team's regular players. For a few seconds, her name flashed on the screen, superimposed underneath her face: *Karen Turner*. José Daniel tried to listen to what the American commentators were saying, but his Italian publisher kept on at him:

"When you senda you book?"

"Next month, old man. I swear by the Virgin of Guadalupe. Don't you trust me? When the hell have I let you down?" said José Daniel, hoping the publisher would not answer him.

And suddenly, the freckle-faced girl reappeared on the screen, grabbing a rebound from one of the lanky black girls from New Mexico. She stole across under the basket and way out of shooting range, she jumped and threw the ball, making a showy corkscrew movement in the air, until it reached the hoop and went down, brushing the basket as it went. An impossible basket. The crowd roared. José Daniel cheered, holding the receiver under his chin.

"Whadda you cheering for, dork?"

"I'll tell you tomorrow, man. Ciao, Marco. This is very important. Tropo importante, pal." And he dropped the phone as he painfully dragged himself along, limping, back to his chair.

The Turner girl was celebrating the shot, as if it were the first one in her life, darting a glance of hate to the crowd and baring her teeth. José Daniel was nonplussed. How come he had not seen her before? Afraid of missing a thing, anything whatever, he hobbled backward over to the kitchen with his eyes glued to the television. He made himself a chicken sandwich with bell peppers and Dutch cheese, and went back to his chair. The Turner girl had missed an easy ball; to get it back she fouled a black beauty by grabbing her shorts.

Where had she come from? Little by little, he picked up the thread from bits and pieces of the commentary. Damned sportscasters, they did not seem to care. Had they not seen her? She was a rookie, a freshman, someone who had recently arrived from Boondocks High School in the asshole of the world. She was not part of the first team, she came on now and again from the bench, and her entry onto the court did not matter to the commentators. Neither was she a star followed by the college crowd. But José Daniel Fierro, who was not a detective story writer for nothing, and saw a lot deeper into human passions and characteristics than commentators, horoscope writers, and psychiatrists, saw something in her right from the start, that magic touch that . . .

For example, and without getting in too deep, the peculiar

way the sweat made a lock of her hair stick to her temple, and the way she kept trying to brush it off. For example, the way she stared off into space in the middle of a vital move and suddenly snapped back into the game mentally. She hated with a passion, and managed to pull off brilliant moves now and again. Only now and again.

In that first stint, she did not last more than three minutes in the game. The camera did not close in on the look of rage on her face when she was sent off. She came back on at the end of the third quarter and scored two three-pointers, more or less one after the other, then missed an easy basket and got sent off for a stupid technical foul. She would not play anymore in that game. José Daniel Fierro held his breath for ten seconds. Then he went toward the television and switched it off.

"Damn," he said out loud, staring at the screen.

Leonardo (III)

Fate could have had worse things in store for *The Battle of Anghiari*. As if it were not enough that the work on the wall had been destroyed, Leonardo had fallen victim to one of his frequent attacks of ennui, and was not very keen on finishing it, wrapped up instead in umpteen obsessions. To such an extent that even the persistent Florentine bureaucrats, who had threatened to fire him if he did not finish the job, ended up giving in and forgetting about him, while the painter went off to Milan.

Not only was the mural ruined and not only would the painted wall be covered over with plaster by orders of the Medicis in order to wipe out all traces of work done under the republic; it was not enough that the empty space be assailed by new frescoes as time went by; nor that the remotest traces faded away and that not even modern ultrasound investigations could find any remains of the old murals; as if this were not enough, the paper on which the mural had originally been set out had faded away.

But the mural with the horses and the battle for the standard was not condemned to complete oblivion. Fortunately, the layout had been copied many times and there are reproductions that give a clear idea, at least of what would have been the central part of *The Battle of Anghiari*. One of these copies can still be seen in the Casa Horne in Florence, another in the Rucellai Palace in the same city, yet another in the Uffizi Hall, and one even exists outside Italy, the one drawn by a young Flemish man called Peter Paul Rubens, who had visited Italy a century after the events recounted here and, fascinated, had copied the central motif, the part known as the "struggle for the standard"; this copy is to be found in the Louvre.

Leonardo's work was not only condemned to quasi-disappearance, but as often happens, to the realm of myth. Because of this, and thanks to those copies and the sketches and preparatory drawings, it is possible today to speak of a mural that does not exist as if it did. A metaphysical mural, you might say.

And this is a permanent and absurd feature of Leonardo's story. Once again he had brought his life to an impasse of incomplete works, of unaccomplished projects, of things unfinished. *The Battle of Anghiari* was bound for the attic of dreams, to the coffer of illusions, along with the *Horse*, the equestrian statue of Sforza, whose bronze was melted down into cannons . . . and this strange injustice seemed to follow him after death, making his most famous paintings disappear, like *Leda and the Swan*, or the portraits that he did for Branconi, so that they can only be studied through copies made by his contemporaries. A long line of metaphysical works.

There no doubt exists a Vincian curse on things unfinished, disappeared, unaccomplished, or lost. Perhaps it was for this reason that Leonardo, in his will, requested that sixty beggars, each with a candle in his hand, should go down to his grave with him, and that they should be well paid for this send-off. So that his death could be public testimony. So that his disappearance from the scene could be attested to by the beggars and lit up by the candles. So that the proof would at least be grounded on that. But Leonardo was not capable of foreseeing that none of his sixty wretches was capable of writing, and so, with the death of the candle-bearers, even Leonardo's funeral faded away, as if it had been drawn with ephemeral materials. For this reason there are no accounts of Leonardo's last journey, the entombment of the painter, military engineer, researcher into the tides, and the flight of birds and men. We speak here of sixty paupers with candles. But some authors say that they were candelabra, others that they were small candles, and the rest that they were flaming torches, that the sixty (and some say they were forty-two, and others none at all) wretches hired for the night carried in their hands, to keep the body company on its way to the grave.

It is just as well, as injustice tends to balance itself out in the inertia of the human world. If there really is no written testimony of the funeral, nor drawing, picture, or account, then legend has taken care of it just as it was meant to be; the painter's definite intention to finish something off, to finish the unfinishable, to keep hold of the unaccomplished, to hang on to what would end up being lost.

The candles whose wicks wafted in the nighttime breeze

in the French city of Amboise, wafted in legend—lighting up the Magus's physical departure from us and his entry into the coffers of reserves, loves, mysteries, and usefulness that we, his successors, have created.

Love Affairs

Karen Turner threw a hateful stare at him from the television screen, although she could not have been consciously aware of her admirer's existence, and José Daniel Fierro, previously known to the inhabitants of Santa Ana as *Chief Fierro*, democratic sheriff, detective story writer, and fifty-something, started drooling and was verging dangerously on orgasm.

Karen bared her teeth with rage when the Texas Longhorns' coach threw a towel at her, which she limply tossed over her shoulder as she slid onto the bench, her long pair of legs floating between her body and the action.

They were losing 13 to 7, the game was just starting, and Karen had had an unlucky break: an exchange of elbows with the shooter from the Something Tigers that ended up with her enemy getting away and scoring, and a foul, which meant that the other team got an extra point.

José Daniel felt distress, then fury: "You should have really fucking laid into her with that elbow, you should have knocked that bitch's tit into her ribs," he said, and finished off what was left of the beer.

His thing about Karen Turner, after only four weeks of watching her play, had gone beyond a good man's love and had turned into derangement and complicity.

The Turner girl seemed to feel for him and looked for him in the seats without finding him, looking at the cameras and spectators as if searching for him. Two weeks before, she had had a superb game, scoring twenty points and catching unreal rebounds. But the week before, after only playing for five minutes, she had really fucked up, biting one of her opponents and spitting on the referee when he called a technical foul.

She was calmer today. The game was not up to anything else. The Tigers from who-knows-where were a nothing team who kicked their own ass, shooting from halfway down the court with no style, and it was only a question of minutes before the Texas Longhorns took control of the game and imposed their combination of fury and rhythm to walk all over them on the scoreboard.

Karen came on in the second quarter and scored an impossible three-pointer, jumping up with her back to the basket and turning around in the air to aim. Then she let them clap and did nothing else, except exchange murderous looks with a black girl with thick lips some eight inches taller than her, who had gone out of her way to try to block the shot.

It was then that Karen Turner looked over her shoulder for one last time, her expression was picked up by the camera zooming in on her, and José Daniel knew she was saying goodbye to him until next week.

Leonardo (IV)

Leonardo da Vinci was, for Sigmund Freud, the patient he could never get onto his couch. Even so, he tried. Freud started with a painstaking study of the painter's biography, if such a thing is possible with a biography so full of gaps and subsequent rewriting. Then he began to speculate on the displaced libido of a man who had a relationship of disgust and remoteness with women and whom he could only re-create when separated from them by a canvas. A personality who in his daily love life practiced a platonic homosexuality.

Good old Sigmund, who was a fiend when it came to getting to know others, went on looking until he hit on one of the few phrases that Leonardo wrote about his childhood in his notebooks.

Freud started with the following dreamlike memory of Leonardo's:

Finding myself in my cot, a vulture came close to me, opened up my mouth with its tail, and repeatedly hit me with it between the lips.

With such scarce, but for Freud so significant, material, the analyst began a large chain of logical and psychoanalytic extrapolations: tail for penis, a simulation of fellatio, a transferal of the act of sucking the maternal breast; elements relating to Leonardo's history of having been born the bastard son of a notary, abandoned by his peasant mother at a tender age to be brought up in his paternal grandfather's house . . .

And Freud carried on, embellishing the story: the obsession with the flight of birds, a derived fantasy. The scattering of his work, an obsessive curiosity. Displaced sexual energy . . .

But to analyze the Magus from Vinci was to enter the blind alley of Leonardo's insatiable peeping, his manias, his unceasing reflections and curiosity, his ravings and erratic changes of direction. One wandered off from his geometric obsessions to come to his research into the flight of birds, the anatomical studies, his calculations about sfumato, or his household accounts in which he worked out how many eggs were eaten by the group he lived with in Florence, made up of his disciples, assistants, and the rest.

Freud developed a theory about Leonardo's latent homosexuality, expressed in his asexuality. Nonetheless, he started off from a badly translated phrase and from absolutely insufficient information. Whether Leonardo was homosexual or not, active or passive, platonic or practicing, few facts in the Magus's hazy biography could confirm. Some find the proof in the incident during his youth in which he was accused of sodomy along with three others, although the defenders of Leonardo's heterosexuality could find proof to the contrary in the result of the trial, which absolved him. Some would say there was no better proof of Leonardo's homosexuality than the lengths that eighteenth- and nineteenth-century biographers took to conceal it. If there is smoke, and a lot of screens trying to hide it, then there must be fire, too. Some find the definite and almost inarguable proof in that Leonardo, painter and man of all the sciences, native of Vinci, on April 8, 1503, while he was painting *The Battle of Anghiari*, lent his assistant (disciple, companion, lover?) Giacomo, better known as Salai or Salaino, three gold ducats so that he could have some pink breeches made. Few will then notice after this forceful argument what comes next, in which Leonardo notes down: *I still owe him nine ducats, but for his part, he owes me twenty, seventeen that I gave him in Milan, and three that I gave him in Venice.*

What Freud did not do was connect his proposed interpretation of Leonardo's homosexuality with the inventions he produced in those days following the disaster with the mural. Whether Leonardo's repressed libido looked for an outlet in ways that sex could not offer, whether it was because of the evident disaster of the mural, *The Battle of Anghiari*, whether the Magus was trapped in a century that did not have much to offer when it came to technology, the fact is that Leonardo invented the bicycle in those days and his invention vanished.

And Leonardo's homosexuality is as good an explanation as any for understanding why, at that point in his life, Leonardo, in love with the impossible, drew a sketch of a two-wheeled vehicle four hundred years ahead of his time, with a saddle, rear pedal-drive, and chain-wheel, that doubtless proved to be what we would call it long afterward: the bicycle.

Cable Television

When a novel just will not come out; when the world surrounding the novelist is becoming dominated by entropy in all its chaos; when you lose the umbilical cord with the essential narrative subject, and in this case you were dealing with a whole city (with all its underpasses, fruit sellers, domestic squabbles, polluted clouds with copper-colored edges and poisoned sparrows dying with pathetic expressions, and rivers overflowing with fecal excrement, where the remains of Columbian caravels sailed along), the novelist is overwhelmed by a severe distaste, a pathological grudge, along with hoarseness, tiredness, muscular pains in the neck, and a renewed obsession with suicide.

Exterior signs abound; your nails grow, infectious spots come up underneath your chin, the hearing in your left ear gets worse, you forget to put your name on the electoral roll, you begin ten novels and do not finish a single one, you lose your sense of smell, your eyes begin to stream and you are never sure whether this is due to emotion or atmospheric pollution, and as if that were not enough, you pick up habits that you would be better off not to remember.

The novel seemed to be about his grandfather, Angel del Hierro, and the streets of a Barcelona that José Daniel had never known. It was also about a dubious baron, spy, and cardsharp, with a life story that seemed to be a pack of lies, and a lover, who in her day had the unlikely name of René Scalda, and who José Daniel imagined to have heavy thighs; and there was the possibility that all of this, Barcelona in the 1920s, the city that had become "the house of death," the grandfather, the Baron, the big-assed lovers with lilac garter belts, would in some way be connected with the owners of an everyday grocery store in the Condesa district (dateline for this second narrative line: last week). The book had been provisionally entitled *The Ballad of the Stars*, because of the fact that the pistols the anarchists in Barcelona used between 1920 and 1923 were Star-brand pistols, and José Daniel wanted to push a review of the relationship between romanticism and violence in the novel, a meeting of gunshots and love affairs. The Baron's son could be polygamous and the grandson might be an acquaintance of his who smuggled liquor and was mixed up with some very disreputable federal agents from Toluca.

But the book just could not get past the first draft, beyond the sixty pages of supposedly finished paragraphs, together with the notes that led nowhere. The characters came together in anecdotes, but could not make atmospheric links between revolutionary Barcelona and Mexico fucking City. Maybe because the novel had stubbornly or lovingly dug its heels in modernist Barcelona and did not want to make its way through time and travel to the very Mexican Condesa district. And he put it down to the pollution and the narrative distance, to the lack of acquaintance he had with one city and the abundance of superficial knowledge he had of the other. José Daniel had lived through something similar while he was writing *Pancho Villa's Head*, but memory is a short-lived thing and each novel tends to turn into a new and different torment that seems like the first one in your life, although it is not.

In the midst of all this chaos, José Daniel Fierro was getting old, and the definite proof (the gray hairs in his mustache were just a physical accident) was his growing racism. He was becoming more intolerant with each passing year and there was no anti-racist rationality, no humanitarianism, that could rectify his feelings. His Catalan friends from Lérida gave him a pain in the ass when they spoke in that tone which, to a Mexican ear, is pure insipid arrogance; he could not stand blank expressions in the faces of Byelorussians, nor the way that most women from Toulouse (at least the ones he had seen one afternoon) wanted to be beautiful without being so; and above all, a gum-chewing gringo poisoned his soul. No matter what he did to avoid prejudice, all this garbage had found its way into his life.

On top of the enormous Packard Bell television set that served as an altar in the remains of his home, he had lit three candles, praying that Karen Turner would not be part of the cud-chewing legion, would not speak like people from Lérida, or be of French or Byelorussian descent. These were his last hopes. Up till now, the freckle-faced girl had given no sign of being anything other than a savage, who allowed her emotions to hold sway over her concentration and her technique, but there were no indications that she chewed gum. In any case, José Daniel Fierro was living in a dangerous situation, whether the temperamental American basketball player he was deeply in love with chewed gum or not.

Not only was he turning into a racist and becoming ashamed of his stupid emotions, of his senile intolerance; as if that were not enough, the woman who washed his clothes had not turned up for the last two weeks. Doña Euge must have fallen back into one of those marital crises that often immobilized her. Something was happening in the streets that escaped him. There were student demonstrations again. The prices of newspapers and cigarettes were going up. He was at least a month behind on his correspondence. His novel was not coming out.

José Daniel Fierro rummaged through a pile of dirty clothes and found a pair of creased-up socks that did not stink too much, and a Zacatecas State Penitentiary soccer team sweatshirt. He bundled them up and covered the distance between the bathroom and his bedroom shivering with cold. As he went by the table, he picked up two envelopes from the pile of mail that contained something that might be a check.

He was sleeping in in the mornings, watching television in the afternoons, and writing by night. Without going out of the apartment. Confined between four walls. He was becoming aware that any jail tends to turn into a universe, as one of his teachers, Philip K. Dick, well knew. And any routine then, as comfortable as it may appear, could be dangerous.

The telephone squawked. A secretary announced that Joaquín Díez-Canedo wanted to talk to him.

"If you look in the pile of packages that have come to you in the mail these last months, you will find some proofs, with the covers and all, for *Return to Santa Ana*. If you open the wrapping and look over the galleys, and give me the okay, you can even read the corrections over the phone, and I can send it off to the printers. But if you don't do it in the next two minutes I'll take it as if you said yes and I'll send it off to be printed anyway."

"Okay. I swear I'll do everything you say," said José Daniel, and hung up.

He sat down in front of the television set and looked through the control panel for the American channel that broadcast ladies' basketball games. There was an hour to go before the encounter between the Texas girls and their rivals from a private university in Miami. He spent it zapping, keeping well clear of news programs and cartoons.

The phone rang a couple of times, and he did not bother to answer it. He limped his way into the kitchen: There were a couple of bottles of Mundet pear juice left over from Ojeda Stores' last delivery, a couple of cans of Mexican tunafish that tasted of Chilean clams and dolphin. The bread was green. He threw it away. The fridge was full of lemon Jell-O and beer, and the freezer was full of frozen strawberries. The mayonnaise had been used up. An old brown lettuce looked up at him. He opened a pair of cans and put them on a plate. He had to wash a fork to be able to eat. He cut the edges of one of the packets of strawberries with a scissors and poured them into a miraculously clean dish and left them to thaw out. There was a two-month-old newspaper on the kitchen table. He glanced at it. The news seemed fresh to him.

He fell back into the chair just in time to see the Texas Longhorns come out on to the court.

"Fuck me dead, your mother's cunt!" he said, in a mixture of Mexican and Chilean, under the influence of the clams.

Something strange was going on. The Turner girl was not playing today. He waited with his fingers crossed until the cameras showed the Texas bench. She was not there. He lost interest in the game and was only concentrating on whether he had not made a mistake, or if the object of his obsessions had come out of the locker room late. It was odd. The bench was short-handed. Five on court, only four on the bench. Neither Karen Turner nor Jackie O'Brien, the Longhorns' highest scorer, a tall and plain blonde.

The game was a washout.

He was a washout. What the hell was going on? You couldn't believe in illusions anymore. Not even prefabricated illusions that came by satellite through a cable to the Roma Sur district in Mexico City.

Leonardo (V)

After his death in France in 1519, Leonardo's manuscripts were handed over, according to the express wishes laid out in his will, to his disciple Francesco Melzi, who took the bundle of notebooks, loose leaves, notes, and unclassified bits of paper back to Milan with him. Melzi had taken charge of the chaotic treasure and tried to put it in some sort of order, compiling a primitive catalogue in the villa at Vaprio, and numbering documents and loose sheets.

After the disciple died, almost fifty years later, Leonardo's voluminous paraphernalia began to be hived off into legacies to which not much importance was attached, and were sold off in bits and pieces. Lesser larceny followed loss and looting, damp pieces of paper were thrown away, and notebooks lay forgotten in chests of old clothes.

Scattering the work around meant that some notebooks

ended up in Spain. Many others traveled along a strange road, imperial piracy in most cases, and ended up in several English libraries and museums. In the course of the next three centuries, an occupation known as that of "Vincian fanatic" sprang up. Whole lives were dedicated to the hunt for Leonardo's manuscripts, to searching for and finding them, to purchase or theft. Four English Lords (Arundel, Lytton, Ashburnham, and Leicester) devoted themselves obsessively to reconstructing Leonardo's legacy. Neo-Platonists and esoterics, Rosicrucians and scientists, art lovers and fanatical collectors, mystics and harbingers of human flight, threw themselves into the task of recovering Leonardo da Vinci's papers and bringing them together in a peculiar hagiography. Several Italian religious personages, Spanish librarians, and French esoterics devoted a large part of their existence to the quest for Vincian material. They resolved to find signs of the Magus's adherence to the worship of the Virgin Mary in their findings, of his love for plants, any sort of occult reference, any premonition of the key to eternal life. In spite of a real legion of searchers and devotees joining in the hunt, several notebooks were lost.

For the purposes of what is to be told here, the fate of only five of Leonardo's codices need interest us. We refer to Atlanticus Codex, Notebook A in Paris, and the famous Madrid Codices I, II, and III.

In the sixteenth century, Pompeo Leoni bound many of the loose papers that were part of Leonardo's legacy into a huge album in order to prevent their being scattered, and this later became known as the Atlanticus Codex. The rear side of some of the sheets of sketches, drawings, engravings, or notes remained hidden in most cases, and only now and then would Leoni open up a gap in the enormous notebook, whenever a particular matter seemed overwhelmingly important to him, in order to see the reverse sides.

The Atlanticus Codex was obtained in a not entirely legal way by Cardinal Borromeo, founder of the Ambrosiana Library, who left it in their custody after renouncing ownership. Napoleon and his looting hordes got hold of a great part of this material. The Atlanticus Codex was returned to Milan at the end of the Napoleonic wars, but the rest of the manuscripts remained in France or were scattered.

Just a few years ago, during one of the codex's many restorations, while the restorers were trying to uncover the backs of the sheets hidden by the binding, some pornographic drawings (of a type known in Mexico as "little English rooster") were found within folio 133, where Leonardo had drafted an architectural plan of a round fortress. Far more importantly, there was also what undoubtedly appeared to be a bicycle. The porno drawings, sexual organs turned into little animals by dint of putting a beak, tail, or paws on them, were not really important, but the bicycle attracted the attention of specialists and experts. A whole host of debates and voices of doubt was aroused by the sketch, hidden for three centuries; even so, as Augusto Maroni, a professor from the Catholic University of Milan, well established, the drawing of the bicycle was not done in Leonardo's hand, and neither were the little English roosters. They had all been made in the sixteenth century, more than three hundred years before the bicycle had been invented, and three hundred and fifty years before the bicycle reached the degree of sophistication of the design that was uncovered.

It was evident that the bicycle and the little English roosters could not have been made after the manuscript had been bound.

The experts saw the hand of one of Leonardo's assistants in the drawings, one of the adolescents who hung around him, probably Jacopo dei Crapotti, better known as Salai, who had committed all kinds of mischief throughout his life at the master's side since the age of ten, as witnessed by Leonardo in his diaries and the notebooks themselves.

The experts then pointed out that the drawing was probably a poor copy of an original design of the vehicle produced by Leonardo himself, who was very accomplished in designing all types of machinery. The teenager had probably copied it from the Magus's papers onto the back of a piece of paper with other designs on it. Who else but Leonardo could have designed a bicycle four hundred years before technology could make the invention possible?

Nonetheless, confirming these hypotheses was made impossible by the absence of nearly eleven notebooks accounted for by Melzi in his inventory that had slipped away over the years from the mass of the original legacy, where it may have been possible to find the earliest design of the two-wheeled vehicle.

There were two or three notebooks among the lost papers that were acquired by Philip V, King of Spain, at the beginning of the seventeenth century, and belonged to the Spanish crown from that time on. They were then transferred to the National Library in 1830, where they mysteriously vanished into thin air. For 135 years, the notebooks were given up as lost and their disappearance was put down to theft but, in 1965, a furious combing through the library in Madrid, instigated by the librarians' Milanese counterparts, tracked the manuscripts down. They were originally catalogued as Aa 119 and Aa 120 but, due to some mix-up, had been recatalogued as Aa 19 and Aa 20, and then became so many more leaves in a forest of immense and forgotten archives, hidden between thousands of other manuscripts. The third notebook never showed up.

The rediscovery of the two notebooks, swiftly christened Madrid I and Madrid II, had the effect—among other things—of reopening the contemporary debate over the Vincian bicycle between Leonardo fanatics and experts. The designs of gears for chain-driven traction could be seen on page 5, top, and page 10, top, forming part of the copied design, and proved beyond any doubt that Leonardo was almost four hundred years ahead of his time in inventing the bicycle.

Cockroach

José Daniel Fierro watched the cockroach slowly crawling up the cream-colored wall toward the ceiling. It was not the first one he saw, but it was special; it was an unusual cockroach. Since he had broken his leg, his hunting instinct had been sparing. Did cockroaches believe that ceilings were the forecourt to heaven?

The house had been going downhill, and he along with it. The last remnants of control had withered away during the week. He did not order groceries to be delivered by phone, he did not lean out his window to order things from the mobile market; he stopped answering the doorbell; he often forgot to eat . . . On Friday he sat in front of the television an hour and a quarter before the game was due to start, and he spent the time daydreaming drowsily.

He took no notice of the voice-overs by the American

commentators, as he was used to substituting his own running commentary for that of the game itself, but the pictures made him go up to the television and turn the volume up.

A minute's silence was being observed. The Texas Longhorns were wearing black ribbons, in mourning. The stadium was unusually quiet. The girls from both teams were lined up in the middle of the court, waiting for a sign from the referee. Then the normal uproar began.

José Daniel Fierro took stock of the situation by listening to what the commentators said: The O'Brien girl was dead, the minute's silence was for her. But what about Karen Turner? Where was that freckle-faced girl?

He went over to the phone. He dialed the area code for New York, and then slowly dialed the number. He waited fifteen seconds until a voice he knew said, "Hello."

"Where's the University of Texas? Which university, which town are the Texas Longhorns from?" he asked Willie Neuman, his American translator.

"Chief Fierro? You're absolutely crazy, my friend. Since when have you wanted to study at an American university?"

SECOND SECTOR

The Worst Thing About Horror

The worst thing about horror
is that there is no horror.
—Leonid Andreyev

K's Story (I)

Well I'll be fucked if I change what I said first time, pal. I'll be fucked, like I said, and I'll kiss the cross, all for the ghost of Saint Pedro Infante.

They came out of the hotel on their own, a bit high on the booze, laughing and gabbing with each other in that foreign crap, as if they were half shit-faced. Gringas celebrating. So what? There's a shit-pile around here, more than enough for anyone who wants them, and so many that even little dark girls are back in demand; the ones with tight pussy, that is. But these were two blond pieces a guy really gets off to look at, really huge, pal. Fucking enormous gringas. What a pair of bitches, come down from the sky, they had to duck down in the doorway, these gringas, to get through. And that's where I lost sight of them, until I came out like everyone else after hearing the goddamn screaming. But like everyone else, I wasn't the first, one of the last, because I mean, if they were killing someone it was no friend of mine, because I was cruising on my own, without waiting for anybody. And it was out of curiosity, and everyone was going along, like you do, out of some bullshit curiosity to see what you can get out of it. And get nothing. One of them was laid out, the blondest one, laid out on the ground, in front of the hotel, with one hand on the grass in the median and her body dumped on the street, in a puddle and with her legs on show, with her skirt up. And there was some jerk there they call the Blind Man shouting that she'd been kicked to death, except he isn't blind, just that he gets that way sometimes with all the junk he shoots into his stupid body. And I said to myself, you can't die from being kicked, they can work you over, give you a broken rib, a loose elbow, a jaw knocked to hell, but dying, like I mean fucking dying, no way. Nobody uses boots with toe caps around here anymore, they're out of fashion, just crappy moccasins, and with those it's a bitch to kick someone to death. Shut the window, will you, because the rain gets in and I'll get sick. And so the gringa is laid out there, sprawled all over the place, with blood coming out of her mouth and her forehead, a whacking great gash about two inches big. And then someone makes his way across and says: *I am a doctor, gentlemen*, as if he wants to show off to the chick he's got with him, because this jerk sure isn't so much as a vet, and he walks up and we make a ring around him, and he says: *She is not dead, but almost. She must have an internal hemorrhage. Call an ambulance*. That asshole of a doctor giving his orders. And then some guys got out of the way, because even if your sainted mother dies you don't want to wait for the law to come, even if you won a car in a raffle, if there's Federal

Police around. No, they're not like regular cops you're used to. Can't you close that goddamn window, pleeease? You see, and some of us must have asked inside, what about the other one? Because the other gringa wasn't around. And then the Blind Man must have realized, because he said, without anybody asking him, *They took the other one off in a pickup*. No, I decided it was time to split, but when the bartender told me to come back and pay the tab, Mariano, quit farting around, I went back in. Other guys who weren't such jerks as me just kept going; one of them, Suspenders, who plays drums in a salsa band and deals grass, said to him: *Look for it yourself in the mirror, asshole, I'll bring you the shit tomorrow, because right now I'm kind of short*. And the gringa out there with her eyes wide open and, as far as I was concerned, seeing God in the raw. Whatever that jerk of a vet said, she was a real stiff. Well, if I'm doing this the way I should, why the hell am I here, soaked by a goddamn hose and with the goddamn windows open? Shit, have they left the windows open so I can commit suicide? I'll get a cough, dammit. No, I know, it's all nice and friendly. I just wonder how they got her into the pickup if she was so big, it must have been sideways. And then some guy, making like he was elegant, says to the Blind Man: *Did you get the license plate number, sir?* He must have been some goddamn creep from Guanajuato or Mexico City, who thinks blind people can always see and not only when they want to. And the other guy realizes everyone's looking at him, and he caught on, he really did, the penny fucking dropped, that he'd been screwed, for sucking cocks in the hotel doorway when some bastards came along and kicked one gringa to death and threw the other one into a pickup. And then he says to him: *License plates, friend? What plates? Here in Ciudad Juárez everyone has plates from across the border, and you can never see them because it gets so dark. And I didn't see no goddamn plates in my goddamn life.* And to talk of something else, could you take that bit of metal off my balls and close the window, because I'll get a cold in my dick, and it's not supposed to be that way when you come to make a voluntary statement, and I've even got a bag from the supermarket with two bottles of brandy in it, so you can see I just dropped in to tell you some goddamn story about a dead gringa and another some absolutely, absolutely unknown assholes took away. You got that down?

Jerry in Saigon (April 28)

More than once in the years to come he surprised himself by saying those had been the three worst days in his life, when he knew full well that was not true. But through force of habit, because repeating that viewpoint made him agree with the rest, made him the same and did not attract suspicious glances, it ended up being one of his biographical details, a fact, a piece of information.

The three worst days in Jerry's life: "Monday, April 28, 1975, Tuesday the 29th, and Wednesday the 30th." *Three awful days, my friend.* But he well knew the story behind that story was not like that; that they had been three marvelous days when you did not have to look over your shoulder, you never excused yourself on bumping into someone, and there was not a single palm-reading Gypsy woman in the world could tell you what would happen in the next few minutes. Three godless days. Three days of redemption. Three days of collapse in which he had burned two million dollars in twenties with lighter fluid, had killed two men and women without having to worry about filling in forms, had missed a flight and several appointments, and had had croissants and *café au lait* for supper without anyone trying to charge him for it.

Those days: with the bloodstream full of adrenaline, a feeling of immortality that would be with him from then on along with a load of other bits and pieces that were stuck in his memory, like dizzy images, memory banks of lost emotions, dreams.

For the first time in a long while, they were days in which no manual was any use, in which the rules went to hell in a handbasket, and no obligatory regulations had to be observed. For a man like Jerry, April 28 had been the first day of freedom he could recall since that distant childhood he had no interest in remembering. And things simply happened like that, like dusk slipping underneath pink clouds in a mackerel sky. There were neither orders nor intent. Nobody said to him, "Jerry, as of four o'clock today you are free, you can do what you want, you can kill who you want, you can smoke what you want, even here, in the office. You can even kick the ambassador in the balls. If you want to, of course." Nobody said anything like that, the words were never spoken. Just that when the mortar shells began to fly, Jerry appreciated that everything had changed and said to himself, "There is no God, anything goes. It is the end of the world, and everything is allowed." And he acted accordingly.

The U.S. embassy in Thong Nhut Street was covered with a concrete hood that was hardened against direct hits from mortar fire. It was any modern architect's nightmare designing that sort of reinforced concrete canopy, but after the attack on the embassy in the Tet offensive, in 1968, the architects had nothing left to say about the embassy's aesthetic appeal. The first three floors were given over to the apparent normality of routine work and to the bureaucrats; the fourth to sixth floors belonged to the CIA. At the beginning of 1975, it was the biggest station anywhere in the world, outside the headquarters in Langley. Sixty Marines usually looked after the building, along with two hundred drivers, a restaurant-bar, a recreation area, and twenty-one gardeners.

Jerry was coming out of one of the inner elevators and onto a corridor on the sixth floor when he felt the panes in one of the windows shaking and the dry thud of mortars in the distance. It was a cold morning, with fog too, a rare thing in Saigon. Jerry looked curiously through the windows and watched the small columns of smoke on the other side of the Saigon River.

"They're here already," he said out loud to a secretary pouring water into a vase. Some of the station's operatives were running along the corridor; somebody went to a closet behind the small fridge and took out an M-3.

His immediate superior took him by the arm as he rushed along the corridor. Lehrman had a lopsided walk that ended up being a slight skip.

"The sons of bitches have taken one end of the New Port Bridge. There was an attack by VC commandos at dawn and the Arvins ran off. Now there's a helicopter counterattack under way, but they won't get them out of there."

"We saw it coming, though, didn't we?" Jerry asked him. "The only ones who didn't are General Ky, the fat girl with the cables, and Ambassador Martin."

"They want an assessment. Right now."

"And why me?" Jerry pulled up in front of a water cooler in the corridor, making his boss trip up.

"Because someone has to be the idiot who gives them the bad news. Someone has to tell them that there are North Vietnamese units breaking through on Highway 4, and that they must have a whole division finding its way into the southern suburbs."

"Why don't the military guys from the attaché office do these assessments? They just leave us with the political disaster stories, and rumors of how the French want to get back into Vietnam, and how Minh is talking to the VC about making a pact."

"You tell them everything, and don't let the military forget," said his chief, before limping away. When he came to the code-room door, he stopped while holding the doorknob and stared at Jerry.

"As soon as you've finished with the ambassador, come back home, my boy, there's a few things I want you to do."

Jerry went up to the window and felt the panes of glass shaking with the shock waves from the mortar shells going off. A secretary was crying. It wasn't bad, paradise was going to shit and nobody could do anything to stop it. At bottom, he was even thankful to the VC and the North Vietnamese for the final assault; it was no bad thing that the units that had been defeated in the Delta had been cut off from Saigon and could not get into the city. That would prevent a war fought by bandits, well-armed deserters gone mad, looting and shooting at anything that moved . . .

Nobody took much notice of his report or his assessments. The ambassador was still convinced that if they changed the president for someone more innocuous, the North Vietnamese would be disposed to negotiate a truce. Nobody wanted to listen. Jerry was not bothered very much, either. When he managed to get back to his office, in the middle of an atmosphere verging dangerously on hysteria, Lehrman had vanished, but he had pinned a note to his door with instructions for him. Jerry took a short-barreled .38 complete with holster from a drawer and hung it from his shoulder.

When he went out into the street a heavy downpour had started, lasting for as long as it took Jerry to find a raincoat. Jerry looked at the sky, the clouds had disappeared. It was magic rain coming from nowhere, with no clouds. God did not exist, he was able to confirm. In the parking lot they handed his car over to him, a green Mustang. He heard the sound of mortar fire. *They're leaning on us, but they could lean a lot harder. They're obviously giving us time to evacuate, so we can clean up the city without bloodshed on their part. They don't want a massacre.*

Three blocks away from the embassy a police officer was changing clothes, taking his uniform off and putting on a checked shirt with a torn sleeve. Right in the middle of the street. A few hours before, several police officers had been promised that they would be evacuated by sea, and their families in barges down the Saigon River, if they could keep the harbor safe. As far as could be seen, this guy had not heard and had decided to cross over to civilian life without any further bureaucratic delays.

Jerry saw a few soldiers piling up sandbags in the entrance to the CIO headquarters, the Agency's Vietnamese affiliate. Even so, security controls were so lax he could get in by showing a Saigon Tennis Club card to a soldier who was nervously watching the street. Bill Johnson had proposed that they evacuate eight hundred of these guys, and there was even a list of officers who might be useful to the Agency in case of a total collapse. The list was buried in the bureaucratic mess somewhere.

Jerry wandered along the corridors toward the liaison office. The day before, General Binh, the National Police chief, had left Saigon on a hush-hush flight, and the son of a bitch had made himself busy running around the jewelers' stores picking up farewell tributes (although they asked for the money as "a contribution to the final defense of Saigon"), as well as giving the order to burn the lists of stool pigeons and double agents. But it was all Polgar's fault; the great moron was afraid that ordering the destruction of the files could be interpreted as a symptom of despair and spread panic amongst the allies.

The office was empty, a vase full of water had been spilled over the papers on the table. He went across the corridor to look for Colonel Mai. When he opened his office door, he saw the CIO's man in charge of public relations put a .45 under his chin and blow his brains out, splattering blood all over Jerry's trousers just as he went in. Jerry jumped backward and knocked a coat rack over, and then tried to stop his hands shaking. On his way out, he picked up the beer the dead man had been drinking.

In the file room he found an army captain who formed part of Binh's advisory staff.

"You have to burn the files on double agents and stool pigeons. You have to do it."

"Binh left no orders," the man said, with a glassy-eyed stare.

"If the VC get hold of this, they'll cut the heads off all your friends who cannot get out. You have to give the order."

The officer, with his face covered in sweat, continued to stare at him. He held a pistol in his hand and moved it one way and another, as if not sure what to do with it. Jerry got worried and slowly raised his hand to the butt of his revolver in the shoulder holster. Finally, the man went out of the room. He came back in ten minutes.

"It is done."

"Do you know where Mai is?"

"Where he always is . . . are you going to get us out of here?"

"There's a plan, isn't there? Billy took charge of that one. You have to go to a place where they'll pick you up in some buses and from there they'll take you to some helicopters and airplanes. Isn't that right? It's all taken care of. But nice and easy does it, don't panic. Polgar doesn't want everything to go under because of hysteria."

Jerry went out of the room. It would be the last time he would see the guy, whose name he had not even remembered. Nonetheless, he would never forget the look of hate the CIO captain gave him as he left. For a while he felt it digging into his back.

The waitresses from the bar next to the embassy had vanished, someone had decided to send them to Guam the day before. Jerry helped himself to a sweet vermouth. Vinh was at another table across the way, by a window.

"They didn't want to let me in to see you. They don't want to let gooks in . . . yesterday we weren't gooks, but brave allies, the anti-communist bastion of Southeast Asia . . ."

Jerry thought Vinh was full of shit, but did not tell him even so. If anything was going now, then Vinh could complain about anything he wanted to, be a virgin again, make speeches . . .

"They said you were looking around for me . . . outside," Vinh said, after a moment of silence.

He pointed vaguely to the street, where the sounds of ambulances mixed with the permanent noise of North Vietnamese artillery and mortar fire, which was now shelling the air base. He was chewing gum and wearing dark glasses that would not let you see what he was thinking.

"I have very strict orders. We have to burn your factory down. A delicate matter."

"Are you crazy?" he said, but did not continue. He stared at his hands in silence for a bit and then he asked:

"Already, so soon?"

Jerry looked at him and stared him down. Vinh couldn't take it for long. He let his head drop down to his chest.

"I have to fetch something. Have you got time to move something?"

Jerry nodded.

They went out, walking slowly. Jerry realized that nobody was going to be able to complain if he took the glass of vermouth away in his hand, and he walked off with his arm around Vinh. They got into the Mustang and went down to Cholon, the Chinese quarter. As they went over the bridge on the Saigon River, a woman showed them her son, a baby covered in rags, lifting him up with her arms. The Mustang had its windows rolled up so they could enjoy the air-conditioning. Jerry stepped on the gas. What had she wanted to say to them? Did she want to hand the baby over to them?

"There's sharpshooters in the city."

"No, they're madmen from the regular forces who are shooting at building windows. Running amok, you know?"

The cookie factory was in an alleyway in Chinatown, a two-story building painted dark green. Two native Meo guards brandishing Soviet AKs came out of the entrance booth. One of them was wearing a short-sleeved shirt with palm trees on it. Vinh barked some orders at him in a dialect that Jerry could not understand. It was getting dark.

"Will you take me?"

Jerry nodded.

Half an hour later, the two men came out of the factory on a small fork-lift truck and began to load thirty-four three-kilogram bags of heroin into the Mustang's trunk. One hundred and two kilos of H. A fortune worthy of Rockefeller. With this he could buy a good part of Air America's fleet, which would surely be up for sale in a couple of weeks.

Jerry went into the factory and planted the explosives just as he had been told to do. Then he pushed a red button and began to count down from 120. The countdown made him remember a song by Elvis, so that he broke off counting and began to hum. Somewhere between 85 and 80 he was sidetracked and lost count. He waved to Vinh and the two of them walked out. The Vietnamese guy said goodbye to his bodyguards, giving them fistfuls of money he did not even count. They exchanged hugs. The two guys went off down the alleyway with the AKs still between their hands; when Jerry got down from 37 to 35, 34, he and Vinh got into the Mustang and reversed fifty yards down the street. Then they went up it again. 8, 7, 6 . . .

The explosion did not wait for the countdown to reach zero; the blast of air scorched their faces. Vinh watched tongues of flame flickering up to the sky. The air was filling up with black smoke and acid; chemicals were burning. The blaze cleared away the shadows that were being cast over the alleyway, already crowded with inquisitive people going up to see the fire.

Jerry took his pistol out and shot the Vietnamese man in the back of the neck. His body fell to the floor as if it had been covered with cement. Jerry looked around to see if anyone had seen him. There were no witnesses, a dozen onlookers watching the fire with their backs to him and the corpse. It wasn't that important anyway.

When Jerry got back to the embassy, he saw that a lot of locals had gathered in the recreation area behind the building waiting to be taken to the airport. The majority of them worked for agencies associated with the embassy. He drove the green Mustang into one of the security areas and took the trunk keys off the key ring and put them in his pocket. A guy was pissing into the swimming pool.

The ground-floor incinerators were blazing away with burning paper, and there was ash floating in the air.

Lehrman questioned him with his eyes. Jerry nodded. Then his boss told him about Ambassador Martin's "opium dreams." He was still expecting a cease-fire at any minute. The guy had a terribly harsh pneumonia, and refused to have his wife, Dotty, air-lifted out of the place.

The journalists had also gone crazy. Jerry felt that for once they would like to have armed themselves, gone out onto the street with a machine gun, some hand grenades, and a knife between their teeth, instead of cameras with enormous telephoto lenses. The press boys would like to have been someone else. None of them were saying, for example, "I told you so." In Jerry's mind, nothing brought these idiots together like a disaster.

Someone had told him, while shitting himself in one of the corridors, that it had been decided to evacuate Bien Hoa Airport and then bomb it, but a countermanding order had been given for some reason. The North Vietnamese had it surrounded in any case, but were not attacking.

Jerry was witness to half a dozen strange situations as the day drew to a close. A foreign officer cheering when he heard that there had been a changeover in the presidency, that Minh had taken Huong's place and that peace talks were being considered. Some low-flying planes. Memories of the attack on the presidential palace a few days before provoked a false alarm, the embassy's proximity made more than a couple nervous, guns were appearing from everywhere, and you could hear rifles being cocked; one of the secretaries became hysterical and began to pray out loud. Polgar was very worried and asked Jerry to sound out whether Ky was plotting a military coup. Jerry confined himself to grabbing the phone and asking the *Miami Herald* correspondent. He said no. He gave the answer to the station chief, who seemed to be satisfied.

Jerry decided not to go back to his apartment to sleep. He thought it over several times. *The carpet in the map room, or the back seat of the Mustang.* Given what he was carrying in the trunk, he plumped for the first option. In any case, he could see the parking lot from the map room.

The end of the world was turning out to be more fun than he could have hoped.

K's Story (II)

No, no way. Here in this hotel's parking lot we've got two guards and a twenty-four-hour-a-day watch. Here, pardon my language, that kind of shit doesn't happen, it was in another hotel, a flea-pit, on East 23rd Street, where they went. Here they just dumped the other gringa, the one who stayed alive, at eight in the morning the day after, well not right after, but the one after that, after the night they kidnapped her and kicked the other one to death. And they dumped her there during my shift, gentlemen.

One of the boys from the parking lot came to tell me about it and I told Marisa to call the police and the Red Cross and I go out there, and yes, the girl was laid out right there, on top of the grass they have there between the lobby and the parking lot. And no, she didn't look anything unusual, just that she was really pale, like plaster. And the boy said to me: They threw her off a black pickup truck, and he gave me the license plate number. A gringo he tells me; a gringo and a little guy who looks as if he's from around here. And I stared at him, because what the fuck do you do in a case like that? No, I didn't know it was that gringa basketball player that had been kidnapped, I'd even been in her room when the police checked it over and I spoke to the gringo from the newspaper in El Paso who showed me some photos of her dressed in her college uniform, and I knew they'd come here to celebrate after a game they'd won and all that, but looking at her just dumped there, she just looked like the girl from next door, didn't she? Like the really big girl from next door, poor blond thing. I mean, because even before I felt sorry, when the doctor said they'd taken a kidney out of her, I got really mad, because you just can't do that, after you beat some stupid bitches in a game, you come here on vacation and then some assholes come along, kidnap you, and rip your kidney out.

The Red Cross guy said she was in shock, real bad, and to tell the truth, was at death's door, and if she wasn't it was because the paramedic realized straight off and gave her a transfusion and who knows what else, and half saved her. She was pale, real pale, the blond girl, poor thing, so tall and so helpless. Well, I mean to say, if they took your kidney out, what would you be like? And look, taking her kidney out just for going out in the middle of the night. And even then, she was okay compared to her friend. The police said that, and the papers too, that it was the first time it had happened.

But there's so many fucking bastards around here lately that it certainly won't be the last time.

Jerry in Saigon (April 29)

Jerry Milligan, almost the same name as the saxophone player, got a phone call at four in the morning. He'd fallen asleep half an hour before. They asked for Lorenz, he identified himself as Milligan. He half listened to the words, distracted because he had tangled himself up with a blanket and because the sound of the shells bursting was more worrying than anything they might be saying to him on the phone. Mortars were falling on Tan Son Nhut Airport, mortars and .130 caliber artillery shells. That was the sound that had followed him into his dreams. They must have been at it for a few hours now.

"The time has come. They're on their way," said the voice on the phone.

"Thank you, you're very kind," said Jerry, with the tone of a British butler.

The voice on the other end of the phone vanished into thin air.

Lehrman appeared in the doorway.

"There's an order to stick together in the embassy. If the North Vietnamese decide to fire their .130s at the city, then it's a real snafu."

"It's four in the morning," Jerry complained.

"Don't tell me that. There's just been a meeting. The ambassador wasn't there, the evacuation plans were gone over. Nobody spoke about *us* . . . I can tell you it has been decided to evacuate, but 150 embassy personnel will have to stay behind, an operative group of *tough guys*. Fifty from the station looking after a hundred white-collar men from the State Department. Who's going to be the mother hen?"

Jerry wandered around the corridors. What was he going to do with the contents of the Mustang's trunk? It would not be of any use in Saigon, unless Uncle Ho's nephews were going to go into the dope business on a big scale. He was going to leave millions behind him.

The hours were running past. Before he realized it, he was in the middle of a baroque and absurd discussion, and his opinion was requested. Polgar wanted to cut down a tree in the middle of the yard, to allow the big Huey helicopters to land. The ambassador, offended, did not want to show signs of panic: to chop down a tree in the embassy, and right in the middle of the morning, seemed to him an act of barbarity and despair.

Jerry took a submachine gun from the top of a table and went out into the parking lot. There were a lot of people, on one side and another. They must be organizing Option 4, the general departure order for all U.S. citizens still in Vietnam by helicopter, an order wired at 22:51 Washington time, but received during the Vietnamese morning because of the time difference. The lines of people indicated that they had reached phase one; petty bureaucrats were waiting their turn to be evacuated by the Air America helicopters and buses that would take them to Tan Son Nhut air base. But the rumor had it that the base was increasingly unstable.

It was all so hellishly theatrical, and if it were not for the sound of the helicopter blades and the dry roar of mortar and artillery fire, you could think in terms of a trial run, the filming of a disaster movie whose cameras were extraordinarily well hidden. An intelligence clerk from the wire office whispered to him that since nine o'clock in the morning Vietcong commandos had begun finding their way into the confines of the air base, and sporadic gunfire had been heard.

Jerry, who had yet to make up his mind between an earthquake movie and a musical comedy with a script by the Marx Brothers, sorted out the extras from the chaos and made his way to the parking lot. He got into the Mustang. Strangely, the car was full of dust. He went along the avenues at half speed, looking for the port. On the radio he heard the old Platters' version of "Only You." Through the open side window he looked at streets he knew and whose location, even so, escaped him. He was lost, as if the map of the city he usually carried around in his head had disappeared, as if it had been hidden in a fold in his brain.

He stopped the car at a traffic light. A few yards away, two Vietnamese soldiers were arguing over an upturned cart that was yoked to a dead donkey. The soldiers were arguing with guns in their hands, one of them was bleeding from the forearm. The street was deserted. In the same abrupt way in which they had probably begun their squabble, the soldiers stopped and came over to the Mustang. Why had he braked? It was not the ideal moment for obeying traffic lights that flashed from red to green for nobody. The soldier pointed his gun at him and shouted something. His companion distracted him by grabbing his shoulder. Jerry took out his gun and fired at almost point-blank range, aiming at the face that was now turning back toward him. He stepped on the gas.

Sweating adrenaline, he alternated between streets that were deserted and crowded. People seemed to be congregating haphazardly, looking for a way out. Hundreds of Vietnamese were waiting outside the USIA offices for their turn to be evacuated.

The Chinaman sat on the floor on a small mat, in a room that Jerry remembered as full of objects and was now surprisingly empty.

"I do not know you. I have never seen you," the Chinaman said to him.

Jerry did not know what to say.

"You do not exist anymore, reality does not exist. We are not in this room. There is no 'now,' " said the Chinaman in a monotonous voice. He had glassy eyes.

Jerry felt he could get nothing out of the wrinkled man, who, until three days ago, had been Saigon's heroin baron.

He listened, over the apple-green Mustang's radio, to some declarations by General Minh asking soldiers not to desert. Jerry smiled, knowing the general had a Vietnamese Air Force DC-6 on standby, surrounded by a dozen of his personal guard, with its departure for the Philippines scheduled for the early afternoon.

A strange sort of madness had taken over in the embassy. People were moving awkwardly and at the same time in a rush, like the victims of a badly worked out choreography. Jerry had the misfortune to run into Ambassador Martin, who ordered him to take charge of six Marines who were carrying green sacks over their shoulders.

"Burn it. Make sure it's all burned," said Martin, as he rushed away from the scene.

Jerry nodded and led his strange command toward the yard, wondering what it was that had to be burned. Two big empty gasoline drums were waiting for them and the soldiers began to empty the sacks' contents into them. Hundreds of twenty-, fifty- and hundred-dollar bills fluttered in the air. One of the soldiers came up with a big can of lighter fluid and began to squirt it over the wads of cash, while another two cocked their M-2s and looked darkly at those who were coming their way: two Vietnamese secretaries, a cook in uniform, and three onlookers from the consular section. Then they looked at Jerry, as if waiting for him to do something.

"What's all this?" Jerry asked the sergeant who seemed to be in charge of the Marines.

"Two million dollars from the embassy's emergency funds, sir."

"And it has to be burned?"

The sergeant looked at him and threw him a smile. He was a young black guy. He seemed to be as willing as Jerry to do it. At that moment Ambassador Martin came along in a snit, with a military escort, the lowest ranking of whom was a three-star general.

"Burn it! What are you waiting for? I have authority from the Treasury Department."

Jerry got a lighter and lit the edge of a hundred-dollar bill, and Ben Franklin's face disappeared into the flames. He threw it into one of the drums and the blaze made him step back a few yards. He repeated the operation. The sergeant checked the sacks over to make sure they were empty.

Jerry stood back to watch the most absurd bonfire he had ever seen. If they had wanted to burn something so badly, he could have swapped them the contents of the Mustang's trunk for the two million. It was not a fair deal, but in these circumstances, he did not mind losing a bit . . . A helicopter hovering less than fifty yards above made some burning notes fly out of the drums, then the bills were sucked up by the updraft from the helicopter rotor blades. The soldiers ran after the burning bills, butterflies of fire, among them some bits of green paper that did not seem to have been touched by the blaze. The sergeant tried to stop them. Jerry gave him a sign to leave off.

As he came out of the elevator on the sixth-floor, he saw a secretary throwing two typewriters down the stairs.

Through the windows he could see the helicopters beginning to take personnel on board. Civilians with attaché cases were lining up in the yard. Jerry went out to look around while he searched in the recesses of his mind for an escape route for those little bags.

Madness ruled outside the embassy gates. The Marines had shut them up; the neighborhood was considered unsafe. Rumors that sharpshooters were on top of the roofs in the district had everybody hysterical. A grenade that accidentally landed three hundred yards away sent hundreds of people into a pandemonium. It was not possible to organize the unorganizable. Thousands of Vietnamese, Koreans and Filipinos, Chinese, war babies, began to cling to the gates hoping the promise to evacuate them would be kept. Everyone was terrified, civilian clerks in various government agencies; military personnel who had stripped their uniforms off ten minutes before; soldiers' lovers, drivers and waiters, whores, lottery-ticket sellers, weekend wives with their mixed-race babies in their arms.

In the office, Lehrman handed him a cable. Jerry read it carefully.

"It's a lie. They just want to put us under more pressure."

"And if it were true?"

"It isn't," Jerry answered. "We ought to know the difference between a hoax and a bulletin. That's our job, isn't it?"

"If this bunch outside get to know, they'll get even more hysterical," said Lehrman, crumpling up the piece of paper: an intercepted North Vietnamese message saying that the center of Saigon was going to be bombed in the next few hours, with the palace as the main target.

"The ambassador wants us to let them know through all the channels that we are getting out already. Everybody, including the 150 I told you about. Can you do that through the Hungarians, or the Germans?"

Jerry went into the Cercle Sportif, the glare bouncing off his dark glasses. The restaurant-club was empty. He went up to a coffee machine that was still working and poured himself a *café au lait*, picked up a pair of stale rolls from a tray beside it. He began to chew slowly, trying to make the bread go down a dry and sticky throat. Christo Mandajsiev turned up a few minutes later, his face covered by enormous green spectacles. The Bulgarian—wearing a white shirt that was too small for him and through whose buttons you could see his potbelly and sweaty undershirt—had a nose for unexpected situations; he went up to the coffee machine quickly and served himself a double with cream and a Danish pastry. The Bulgarian diplomat doubtless doubled as a spy; Jerry had followed him for a couple of months in 1974. There was nothing to lose, so Milligan gave it to him straight.

"I'll give you a green Mustang."

"Haven't you got a Chrysler?" the Bulgarian said, laughing.

"I've got a few million dollars in heroin in the trunk."

The Bulgarian took off his glasses, revealing a pair of big sad eyes with bags under them. "Today's full of surprises."

"If you get it to Thailand in a couple of months, I'll give you a million dollars."

The Bulgarian chewed his pastry and carefully weighed the situation. No, Milligan was not joking. No, it was not a CIA trap. No, it was not a bad deal. With a million dollars you could buy a movie theater on Broadway.

"Can you buy a movie theater on Broadway with a million dollars?"

"More. Two or three, a chain of them," answered Jerry, who did not have the faintest idea.

K's Story (III)

No, I'm no jerk. They kidnap a gringa, they bring her back thirty hours later, without a kidney. The doctors say it was a professional operation. They stole her kidney, dammit. Shit, you go out to chug a few beers and they mug you, kick your friend to death, kidnap you, throw you into a tacky hospital, operate on you, take a kidney out of you, leave you a few hours in a postoperative room, and then dump you in the street with postop shock. Well then, you go back to brass tacks.

I may be a hick journalist, but I'm no jerk. Do they do kidney transplants in Ciudad Juárez? In which hospital? Was there an emergency case a week ago for which there wasn't a donor? There's no call for that sort of thing around here. Texas stuff? Then what the fuck do they kidnap on this side for? A kidney transplant isn't any old shit, you need a surgeon, a complete medical team, a dialysis machine, and some training. And why is she alive? Because the doctors settled for taking her kidney out, but not killing her. That right? And if it was in Texas, why do they come and kidnap her over here? On top of all that other shit, they've got to cross the border twice. Well, I'm no jerk, and what's more you get goose bumps on your skin thinking about shit like that. What happens if next time they want a dick transplant and they grab you on your way out of the cantina?

All right now, it was here then, in a hospital hereabouts. Come on. Then they go and tell me that they don't do kidney transplants in Ciudad Juárez, that that's high technology, stop fucking around, when have we done that sort of thing in the Third World, pal. And I say: It can be done but they don't do it? Or it just can't be done and never has been? And a pal of mine who's a doctor with Social Security says to me: Don't be a jerk, pal, yes they used to do them, but they don't anymore. Can't you see the shit that's going down? If anyone ever did one, then they've forgotten how.

Jerry in Saigon (April 30)

The navy helicopters flew all night. The city was lit up in flashes, like it was being photographed by demons. What with the chopper blades and the noise of mortar fire and the .130 batteries the VC were using to shell the northern access route to Saigon, it was a booming nightmare.

Jerry woke up on the carpet in the code room in a cold sweat. He had forgotten to tell the Bulgarian that the final evacuation was fixed. Was it important? Would they start bombing? No, nothing like that. It was obvious. On his return to the embassy, the news and pictures gave full account of the mass exodus. Nguyen Cao Ky, the government's vice-presdent, had left Vietnam on a helicopter to an American aircraft carrier, the USS *Midway*, that was waiting for refugees in the South China Sea. A busload of journalists looking for the missing link that would take them to the airport through the streets of Saigon was held up time and again by crowds who banged on the doors and windows.

Parachutists from the South Vietnamese army were exchanging gunfire with the Marines outside the Defense Attaché Office. Air America had broken off picking up future evacuees from rooftops until half-past six at night. The CIA helicopters were short of fuel and the darkness made the operation increasingly dangerous. On top of the wall overlooking the railings closing off the embassy gates, the CIA head in Vietnam, Thomas Polgar, was picking out a few Vietnamese. Those who tried to force their way in were pushed back by the Marines. Someone tried to climb the wall and was kicked down by CIA agents or Marines, now acting as violent doormen for the escape route, the gateway to heaven. Rumors said that the Vietcong and the North Vietnamese had started to march at about midnight toward the city center. The airport was no longer being bombed.

But that had been a few hours ago. What now? Jerry tried to stand up, his arms aching. He went down to the parking lot; somebody offered him a bulletproof vest on the way. It was 1:45 in the morning. He got into the car and tried to make his way through the crowd; he had to ram about a hundred Vietnamese who were pushing hard on the embassy gates. Behind him he heard gunfire, probably sentries firing warning shots. He drove through the pitch-dark night, lit up now and again by explosions. In front of the park, the Bulgarian was waiting for him, smoking those awful cigarettes that left acrid smoke in the air around him.

"See you in Thailand, my friend. Go and pick out some movie theaters on Broadway," he said by way of a goodbye as he took the car keys. Jerry gave him the papers, and in turn got a set of keys hooked on to a fake silver key ring with a hammer and sickle on it. He got into an old Polish Lada that he dumped two blocks from the embassy. Then he walked and mingled with the crowd, which surprisingly made way for him up to the vicinity of the gates, where it thickened and turned into a wall that would brook no arguments. Jerry drew back to smoke a cigarette and take it all in from a distance.

There can be no hell without spectators. Nothing can quite have any real existence without onlookers.

A little later he tried again. He tried to make his way through the crowd. Although shouts, pushing and shoving, and kicking abounded, a part of the crowd made way, as if expecting something from him, as if identifying with his distress. By the time a black Marine corporal grabbed him by the shoulder and made some way for him at gunpoint, backed up by two of his men, Jerry's shirt was torn to shreds and his nose was bleeding. Two Korean soldiers tried to get in with the group, but the corporal smashed them in the face with his pistol butt.

He arrived in time to watch the Marines escort Ambassador Graham Martin onto the embassy rooftop and into a navy helicopter. The ambassador had the American flag folded up under his arm. Seconds later, another helicopter took Polgar, the CIA chief, away, along with his group. It was around two in the morning.

As if somebody had noticed the imminence of the total evacuation, the last exit, a different sort of livid chaos reigned in the vicinity of the embassy. The Marines were scarcely able to control the entrance and had fired several times above the crowd's heads. There were constant clashes in the gateway and on the wall. Blows, attempts to get over to the yard, gunfire: bayonets glinted, babies were lifted up in despairing mothers' arms, shrieking men held up papers that nobody was interested in reading.

Half an hour later, the mist began to clear slowly. In the milky clearness of dawn, Jerry went up onto the embassy roof. From there he climbed a metal spiral staircase and got onto the last helicopter, miraculously still waiting on the landing pad. The last transport for nonuniformed personnel.

If immortality is a photograph taken in a unique moment, if immortality is in black and white, only in black and white, in a gray photograph that records the dance we do with the stars for a hundred twenty-fifth of a second, if that's the way it is, then it was a Reuters photograph that made Jerry Milligan immortal.

Sax-Lagrange was the one who took a series of photos from the embassy yard, using an 800mm, f8 telephoto lens mounted on a Minolta, in which Jerry stepped onto that last helicopter taking off from the landing pad in the U.S. embassy, holding his arm out to an old Vietnamese lady, a .38 blatantly sticking out of the back of his waistband, and a fox terrier under his other arm. One of those photos went around the world and nearly all the readers of the planet's main newspapers could see Jerry's sangfroid in a city that felt it was on fire, although it was not; a city that said it was on the verge of being wiped off the face of the earth, although it was not to be. Jerry, reaching out for the old lady's arm, smiling, carrying the dog. The last of the Mohicans, the last of the knights of the Empire. There was elegance, savoir faire in Jerry's gesture, bare-backed and with one of his sleeves ripped; a touch of danger provided by the image of the .38's butt sticking out of his belt and over his shirt. Jerry looking over the horizon, while two Marines with machine guns leaned out of the rear hatchway of the helicopter, waiting for the hordes that were not coming.

But . . .

a) It was not the last helicopter. Rather, it was the last helicopter transporting civilian personnel, although that was not important and the caption under the photograph was to forget that small detail. Other helicopters were to pick up the Marines who had undertaken the last holding operation, holding that crowd back from the embassy gates, eager to leave and made up of widows and one-day wives; secretaries; cast-off agents; collaborators; two or three hundred from the CIA's Vietnamese sister, the CIO; Chinese black marketeers; native personnel from the thousand and one bureaucratic structures the Empire had set up in South Vietnam, and that were now sinking like paper boats in a raging river.

At about half-past seven in the morning, the last squad of Marines, who had been holding the crowds back at the embassy gates, made their way into the bunker and closed off the access to the rooftop by throwing grenades at the elevator machinery, went up floor-by-floor throwing incendiary bombs, and, at 7:53 in the morning, got on board the last helicopter, which rose from the embassy landing pad and which would land on the aircraft carrier a few hours later. Thousands of Vietnamese who had collaborated with the Americans were left waiting for the evacuation they were promised.

b) Jerry, even though the contrary seemed to be the case, was not helping the old lady onto the helicopter; he was trying to shove her off. And when the helicopter soared away, crammed with excess weight, he tried to throw her out over the Saigon River. And only a mad-eyed Marine, born in Tulsa, stopped him by sticking the barrel of his

M-2 in his ribs, screaming that Jerry would feed the fish in the river if he threw the old lady off.

c) Jerry did not throw the old woman off; she got safe and sound to the aircraft carrier *Coral Sea* in the South China Sea and, being the mother of the former head waiter in the defunct embassy, ended her life happily several years later in Lima, Peru, minding some of her grandchildren and a garden. Jerry threw the fox terrier into the ocean instead, in a gesture of absurd brutality that did nothing to improve the helicopter's stability. The dog vanished barking into the air. Just a long growl fading away.

d) The English photographer took refuge in the Reuters office and there, with the door bolted and blocked with two desks and several chairs, waiting for the Vietcong to arrive, locked himself in the darkroom and sent half a dozen photos off afterward. The Reuters picture editor in Bangkok picked out Jerry's photo and quickly relayed it to London. That same photograph was first to be published in the London *Evening Standard* and later went around the world, thanks to Associated Press's wire service. The caption did not mention Jerry by name; it just said he was a CIA agent, the last of the Americans, the unfortunate Graham Greene character, the last son of the Empire that was pulling out with pathetic grace.

A photo.

SECTOR THREE

Desperately Seeking Karen

The Ballad of the Stars
(Part One)

The first being a personal novel
trying to merge with the second novel,
which has no hope of being published,
and both written by

José Daniel Fierro

For Cindy Pérez, a nurse at the
Ciudad Juárez General Hospital

What one has lived through and what is recounted afterward are easily confused.

—Sigmund Freud

The E.T. of the Wild Frontier

I might let all the ashtrays fill up to overflowing: the blue one on the bedside table, the gray one with birds on top of the fridge, the 35mm film can full of gray dust putting the finishing touch to a pile of books in the living room. I might leave them filling up with cigarette butts, apple cores, ash, plastic cigarette wrappers, canceled checks torn to shreds, half-burned matchsticks, photos of a trip to the beach with another woman, taken many years ago. When they are all filled up, I might throw the double-barreled shotgun they gave me in Santa Ana into a canvas bag along with two packs of cartridges, four bank cards, a wad of traveler's checks and half a dozen socks, a "Patito Tours" T-shirt, a gray turtleneck sweater I happen to like a lot, in spite of the elbows being worn through, and I might go out, leaving thc door ajar and all the faucets open, with water gushing out everywhere. Being in a rush does not usually give you time to get nostalgic. That comes later. And if nostalgia is a latecomer, sadness takes even longer. I might hobble to the elevator and I might hang around there, pondering my indecisiveness; *look before you leap*. Then I might go back to my apartment to shut the faucets. The flood would be well under way, the bathroom carpet soaked through. I suppose that there would be remnants of an orderly citizen in my soul, that I would have second thoughts, that the idea of flooding the apartment with all my books in it would terrify me: Quevedo floating in the garbage, the entire set of Howard Fast's novels wallowing in chaos, the complete works of Pío Baroja swelling up, the novels of Inspector Maigret floundering on my goddamn recent past and tossed overboard. But apart from the rational second thoughts, I might leave "Black Magic Woman" by Santana playing full blast. And I might leave it jammed, so it will carry on playing for ever and ever, until they cut the electricity off, until there is an earthquake, or until they drop the Bomb on Mexico City . . . It could be my decibellicose monument, a record player replaying the counterpoint and bass line in the percussion section forever. José Daniel Fierro was here, and he left blackmagicwoman drumming away. JDF, who went away from this city, because this city did not love him anymore.

There is only one type of revenge, that which you take out on your own past.

In the doorway to the apartment building, I might stop to think up a farewell greeting with good taste, a well-wrought phrase with a certain literary quality to it, while my neighbors' lights would be turned on, roused by Doug Rauch's congas, José Chepito Areas's kettledrums, Michael

Shrieve's drums, and Carlos Santana's guitar. I would not be able to come up with anything.

There would no longer be any streetcars in my old street, they will have done away with them years ago in a show of premonitory ecological genius. The Mexico City mayor's office would have decided to save electricity, and one out of every two streetlamps would be out of service, because of which I will be moving in the dark, and on foot. And while limping along División del Norte Avenue, I might hear the click of stoplights. The definitive sound of nighttime loneliness.

And if hell is within us (and I could not even say whether I could claim to have coined that phrase), the only way of escaping hell is to put some distance between one and oneself. Or to put it more bluntly: to go to where the others are.

So for that reason, on that future night with the darkness blazing, the only one of the "others" who might interest me will be a freckle-faced girl basketball player who used to defiantly stare at the audience, picking me out from all of them, at the enormous electronic distance of a flickering TV screen, like a lone bedside lamp, the only candle on a birthday cake, in a sick writer's room, in the middle of the Del Valle district in Mexico City.

And then I might feel that it is for real, that I would be burning bridges, setting fire to memories, wiping out the past, drying farewell tears, saying goodbyes, as I hobble along like good old Chester in *Gunsmoke*. I might walk up to a taxi stand, the start of the journey, to end up at the Northern Bus Station. The place for definite goodbyes.

I might see Mexico City fading into the distance through the bus window, and on going past the enormous concrete pillars in Ciudad Satélite with their pastel shades, it could start to rain, with which my passion for the city I would be leaving behind might assert itself, and that would provide me with a grandiose goodbye speech. Saying goodbye in torrential rain.

I could take six days to get to Ciudad Juárez, sleeping with broken dreams, leaving buses and stopping off in hotels, giving the broken leg a rest in gas stations, hating the narrow seats in buses that go north on the Pan-American highway, taking me along to madness. And the journey might be a transition, I suppose: from fear to fear; passing through euphoria. A revolution in my circuitry, playing around with hell. I will hate myself to distraction, loathing my craving for a cigarette in the no-smoking buses; I will be living in a state of confusion, with certainty vanished, and the latent panic that rolls along with the wheel of fortune. But all the while I am putting the miles down between myself and the other me I might be getting smart, sharp, I might let the rare feeling of apprehension get ahold of me—not to get me down, but to charge me up with energy. And then I might recall the last few months some other way, I might get the jitters, I might become obsessed with the last images of the basketball game, with those pathetic teenage American women basketball players, the girls, the *ladies*, keeping a minute's silence, all quiet and scared, in their black ribbons for mourning on their uniform sleeves.

I could be another José Daniel Fierro, as I go along growing a beard that, due to the lack of mirrors, I would only be able to appreciate by touching it, and in which I would not be able to see the gray hairs. I might be a new character, I might be José Daniel Fierro, a writer grown old but not with shit for brains; a whole new José Daniel Fierro. Your goddamn phoenix, assholes. Nothing more, nothing less, I am somebody new, I might be saying to myself in the outskirts of Ciudad Juárez, when the dunes are eating into the asphalt on the highway, watching tumble-weeds rolling along in the middle of the desert and neighboring trails going nowhere. I might be the very same Get Me Fierro (GME), the Lone Writer, the Ideological Gun, the .45 Caliber Typewriter, the Sumbitched Peg-Leg, the E.T. of the Wild Frontier.

Fuck you, brother!

A Phony Corpse

Lenin never was in Barcelona in the spring of 1920; Trotsky was not there either, no matter what the *American News* articles datelined in the Catalonian capital might have said, as they certainly used to tell lies a great deal. On the other hand there was a Cuban magician there who called himself Leonardo Padura Buenaventura, because the same day in which the story of the Bolshevik leaders was published in the daily *El Diluvio*, it also spoke of a Cuban having done the rounds of the music halls without much success, and there was an article about his failed attempt to make a nude dancer disappear. What is more, if we are to go by what reports given in the newspapers were saying, on that same day the doctor-poet Casimiro Pérez Arce drew up a brief note telling of how he had cured the aforesaid magician from the French pox, using sulfur drugs.

And Mike Gold, that ultra-left-wing young Jewish man from the Lower East Side, would not have been in Barcelona writing a play set during the Mexican Revolution called *Fiesta*, and neither would a young Pinkerton agent called Dashiell Hammett, who was beginning to write detective stories at night, have been in Barcelona, much as he would have liked to. On the other hand, Angel Samblancat, the poet and journalist in a jacket with worn-out elbows and trousers whose folds were full of dirt, was writing in Barcelona:

Those who speak of the street and its tenderness have never found themselves naked and on the cobblestones at twenty.

And Dr. Svengali, the film-maker and seductive hypnotist, was not in Barcelona either, but instead there was that man with a bloated neck that was just about held in by his collar, the one who left a smell of cologne and Havana cigars around him and called himself the Baron.

The dismal glow of the gaslight from the streetlamps was reflected in the port's dirty water; the ebb tide washed up pieces of driftwood on the dockside, along with bits of newspaper and oil stains. Beneath the slimy pale color of that light you could see the aquiline yet bloated profile of the Baron, a callous bird of prey.

His features had been getting sharper over the years. He was losing his hair and acquiring that bland appearance that will do just as well for a policeman as for a butcher, for a brothel-owner as well as for a tavern-keeper. He appeared in the photos that were held by allied spying agencies as being more rounded, powerful, ruddy, with a little Tyrolean hat—as if he were a model on vacation advertising Swiss chocolate, as if he were a half-witted aristocrat, as if he were a sly trickster taken from the story of *Pinocchio*. As if that were what he wanted to be.

His assistant was skinny, with very long arms and a fierce look, a jailbird called Antonio Soler, alias the Majorcan, who regarded the Baron with a mixture of fear and contempt.

By the flickering light from the streetlamps, these characters were handling something in a skiff a few yards from the quayside. A sack? A rag doll? No, a dead man, a limp corpse, still bleeding. A bit further off, you could hear the bustle and the music coming from Chinatown, the symphony of a vice-ridden binge.

Barcelona was the house of death, and as such, death was sometimes disguised as festival. In Barcelona, fortunes were staked every night on the roulette wheel and more wretched people than millionaires were born; in Chinatown you could find whores from twenty-one countries who would ask you the time in Spanish, and at least fifteen brands of phony champagne. You could get a man killed for twenty-five pesetas and get him beaten up for thirty, because it's harder to beat a man up than to kill him. After the crazy bonanza of the war years in Europe there came the depression. The same Catalan industry that filled its coffers during the war selling blankets, fuses, binoculars, mortar, canned food, flour and biscuits, pistols, and mattresses to both sides, now had its warehouses filled up. A few months before, the city had been immobilized by the biggest general strike since the Bolshevik revolution and the German uprising, and that had opened up a hole in the heavens to come as big or bigger than the one that you could see in the listless clouds on a winter's night. The Baron and Soler had managed to sit the dead man up in the skiff and get back to the pier. They were now waiting for the plot to thicken. The Baron smoked a small and twisted Havana cigar. Soler cleaned his fingernails with a knife.

And then the boards of the dock squealed, making way

for a cloaked figure who carried a flashlight. Soler and the Baron exchanged a swift and knowing look as the figure came up to them.

"The corpse is awaiting you, Your Lordship," said the Baron, in his guttural accents.

"Good and dead, just like you wanted, eh?" Soler added, putting his knife away.

The cloaked figure, face shadowed by a hat with an unusually wide brim, walked to the edge of the pier and lit up the dead man's smashed face with his flashlight. He stepped into the skiff, approached the corpse and appeared to touch it. His cloak fell open and revealed a pearl-gray waistcoat with silver buttons. He moved back onto the dock. "Did he say anything before he died?"

"Pardon me, sir, but he said he would shit on Your Lordship's whoring mother. He'd guessed on whose orders we were acting," said Soler.

"Fine," said the cloaked figure, and handed an envelope to the Baron. He took hold of it with two fingers, as if it were some very ceremonious act, and put it away inside his sports jacket. Then he gave a signal to Soler, who cut the line that bound the skiff to the pier.

"So long, Señor Del Hierro," said the henchman, sending the corpse on its way. When the floating coffin was drawn into the ebb tide, it would be carried out to the end of the harbor. A dull glow came from the skiff as it was lit up for the last time in the lamplight. Then it vanished into the dark.

The Baron watched as the cloaked man went off into the night, and later heard the unmistakable sound of a Studebaker firing up. Then he turned to Soler.

"Who would think that that gentleman has an aristocratic title, and his family are Spanish grandees?"

"He got his hands wet with the blood. Did you notice?" said Soler, tossing his cigarette into the water.

"The bit about shitting on his mother was good, very imaginative, Soler."

"Thanks, boss."

"Well, I hope Del Hierro never turns up again in Barcelona; then we will have our hands clean of this business," said the Baron, summing things up in his own special way.

"As you will. If he turns up around here, we'll kill him again."

"Just so, a second time. Now get the message to the newspapers." The Baron cut him short, and gave a slightly forced laugh. Del Hierro made him panic, even as a phony corpse.

The Telmex Runaway

As for the goddamn phone bill, I said to myself, leaving my Mexico City apartment, you can get your whoring mother to pay it, because I'm going away and yes, I'll leave the phone there for you, all for you, so you can take it and stick it up your ass. If I left my Leonard Cohen records, then I'd damn well leave that tacky pink phone, that I wouldn't even wish on the mayor of Mexico City as a birthday present, and I might as well leave you the bill, too, with its six calls to Austin, Texas, seven to Ciudad Juárez, one to New York, and a two-hour talk with the *Notimex* correspondent in Chihuahua, and another one for an hour and a half with the editor of *La Prensa*. Let Father Hidalgo pay you for it, and so what if you cut me off.

But I would wake up in a cold sweat. Why the hell should I argue with the manager of the *Teléfonos de México* branch office in the Mixcoac district in Mexico City? I would not be in Mexico City anymore. And this would not be Mexico City, this would not be then. I might be in a motel in Ciudad Juárez, and when I am drying the sweat off the nape of my neck with the edge of a sheet, the name of the place might come back to me in an instant: *Motel Camelias*. And on the bedside table there could be a box of chocolates with soft mint centers and the name of the hospital in which Karen Turner might be.

It could be a new routine. It might consist of two levels, the first one to do with getting an old routine back together: opening my eyes, lighting a cigarette, trying to get the last phrase from the first dream out of the recesses of my memory, drink a beer. Second level: exercises for the leg with the cast on it. Type of exercise: none. It is in a cast. So, I could watch the little old sun that does not warm you up and, meanwhile, I might find myself lighting up another Delicado and walking over to the bathroom.

In a room in the Ciudad Juárez General Hospital, a ridiculous interview might await me:

"No, sir, the young lady cannot talk to you or to anybody. She's in a coma."

"But I can see her. Even if it's from a long way off. Right?"

"Are you a relative, sir?"

"No," I might say to the nurse, who is gazing at a nonexistent spot a few inches above my shoulder, watching my lateral biomagnetic aura, because if she wanted to look at my florid beard she would treat me better.

"Well then, even less so," the Scientologist nurse would say, who would have taken a course in personability and customer service with the state employees' Social Security Agency, but having skipped the last two classes, the awesome and important ones, *güeñísimas*, because those were the ones where they explain that it's a sin to spit on people who ask questions, she would not look at my beard but a spot in space where my spaceship might be waiting for me.

"No, I'm a . . . you know, a writer, who's doing some work . . . as you might say, you know, on a story . . . my name is José Daniel Fierro . . ." I might say beaming, as who could deny the E.T. of the Wild Frontier and a runaway from Telmex a shot at the truth?

The senior nurse's face would be transformed and I would almost die from the goddamn fright, modesty, and shame:

"You mean the one who wrote *Pancho Villa's Head*?"

"Well, I mean, yes . . ." I would say, cowering with all the shyness of glory. Because I would certainly have run into the only nurse in all of Ciudad Juárez who has read a book of mine. And I would have to forget having cast aspersions on this wonderful and cultured assistant of Galen and accusing her of being a Scientologist.

"The very same."

And then the doors might open.

Karen could be real. Connected to a life-support system, as pale as the sheets she lay on, in which the color of her hands will not show up, her face distorted by an oxygen pipe, her freckles faded away.

"Poor thing. Right? The blonde. Been like that for six days," the nurse might say behind my back.

And I would know very well why, because the point of reference is obvious and direct, I would remember a song by Procol Harum that was a hit in the 1960s, and I would leave the room quietly and go down the hospital corridors humming it softly, so as not to bother the patients.

When would electric light have gotten to Barcelona? What was gaslight like? It would be necessary to see photos to measure the distance between the lampposts, above all in the port area. Would the pitch not be a little bit like in a serialized story in a newspaper? Something more direct, less artificial. Those serialized stories had their good points, but . . .

A Rampaging Baron

Little Antonio Amador entered the editorial offices at *El Progreso* mid-morning with a mean disposition: a rotten bitterness, a blind fury that gnawed away at his spleen, a feeling of leaving things half done, unfinished, that for a meticulous man like him was unbearable. And on top of all of this he had a fever that went up and down, upsetting him, making him sweat profusely or shiver like a naked child. *That is what malaria was like for characters in novels*, he thought. His entrance was heralded by a fanfare of coughing that made him tremble. On getting to the desk he shared with the theater critic, he wiped his lips gently with a red handkerchief, making the other journalists shudder and feel obliged to turn away, and making the secretaries commiserate and suddenly discover they had a lot of work to catch up on.

"Before you continue with that shit we'll never be able to publish, I need you to write me a piece on that dead man they found in Barceloneta, who must have been one of your crowd," the editor-in-chief said to him in passing.

Amador answered him with a dry cough that made the bosses' mouthpiece hurry on along. It was bad luck to run into a dead man in the morning.

Antonio "the Flea" Amador was a living corpse for more than one reason. Dr. Heredia, who practiced in the Modelo prison on behalf of the Confederation, the CNT, the federation of labor unions, had given him up for dead two years before because of an attack of tuberculosis, swearing he would never get through the winter; but the first winter had come and gone, the second had slipped by quickly, and the third one was under way, although the fevers and the sickness tenaciously hung on to him. He was a wonder of survival, a freak of nature, a miracle of stubbornness. The hired gunmen of the bosses' organization had condemned Antonio Amador to death along with the other editors of *La Soli*; he was in love with a tall woman with rosy cheeks who pretended not to notice; he had passed half a dozen of the last twelve months in prison; there was no uninvolved person in Barcelona who would sit down to eat lentil stew at the same table as him for fear of getting shot; there were three charges for offenses against public opinion hanging over him in which he would surely be found guilty on all counts; he slept with whores who were friends of his, in run-down boarding houses, going from one mattress to the other and picking up the lice the last client had left behind; he rocked his friends' lonely and whining children to sleep; he drank *café con leche* at dawn in the corner bars; and he had a wretched job at *El Progreso* that moreover would not last long. A job for which he got half pay and was forced to write under a pseudonym—otherwise the bosses' organization would remind the newspaper's proprietor that it was forbidden to employ people who were blacklisted. If such a letter should arrive, the editor would be best off firing him because the bosses' organization could boycott the newspaper, withdraw advertisements, or cut down on their paper quota. Antonio Amador was a sort of wounded bird, bringing ill omens.

He nodded at the editor's words, which had been left hanging in the air, but instead of going through the partition where the editor-in-chief's office was he stormed off through the common room, looking threateningly at the journalists and a pair of office boys who were making packages in the enormous hall full of desks and chairs, *where typewriters flourished like the roses of wisdom*. He picked up the remains of a Danish and ate it then and there with a few sips of *café con leche* left by the Lizard, the bullfighting reporter, who had hidden away in the outhouse because the Flea had threatened him with death a couple of times, *for being servile and a liar, for kissing the asses of the bosses' organization*. He had sworn that the next time he met him face-to-face he would slice off one of his testicles with a razor.

When he had finished his walk, Amador went up to the desk he shared, took his jacket off, put it on again with a shiver, and took a little black-bound notebook out of his pocket. The tuberculosis was wearing him down, the death threats by gunmen had shattered his nerves and had given him a strange nervous tic—his left shoulder twitched and he looked behind him almost all the time—and in general the portents of death disagreed with him, put him out of sorts, giving him nightmares during his sleepless nights.

He typed while standing, with the typewriter propped up on two volumes of an encyclopedia, leaning against the wall with his waistcoat loose, open enough to show the .32 caliber seven-shot Star revolver he had stuck in his waistband and that rested on the root of his sexual organ.

He typed for ten or fifteen minutes, frequently consulting his notebook. He had almost gotten the beginning right:

There are characters who appear to be caricatures of evil. Their childhood is a foreboding of their future destiny. They kill street dogs when they are scarcely more than babies and end up killing workers in Barcelona, charging so much a head; they deceive their mothers on their deathbeds and cheat their private doctors. Characters like Baron von König, whose biography will seem to readers to be like a fairy tale for sick old people, although it is not, where shamelessness, greed, and lust are gathered together along with organized crime; and it would be just that, a fairy tale, if Baron von König were not in Barcelona at the very moment you are reading this article, planning to deceive or even kill some innocent person.

To put his life story together from the bits and pieces that frightened informants had passed on to us, or thanks to the access to archives we have been allowed by officials in the Ministry of the Interior, has been difficult. Baron von König is a man who moves about by stealth as well as by arrogance, who is conspicuous in his search for employment but then hides behind dozens of disguises. In his circle of intimate friends he has created a sinister reputation by spreading not a few rumors about his own past, as if to make himself more attractive to the scoundrels who hire him, and who turn out to be, as we shall see, no more and no less than the pseudorespectable forces of social order, the moneyed and titled aristocracy in this martyred Barcelona.

One day the Barcelona bosses' organization's secret ledgers will be opened, and this shadowy story will be complete, and we hope it will be over the shriveled-up corpse of that murderer of Catalan workers, Baron von König. And then blood shall become literature, as you cannot make literature from blood.

Antonio Amador knew that the newspaper could not publish anything like that, not even a toned-down version of the article on the Baron's gang he was writing, but it was all a game of bluff. He was not writing it for the newspaper, but for a manifesto he had been commissioned to do by the Confederation and that in good time would be published by *España Nueva* in Madrid—which was not subject to such strict censorship as in Barcelona—and through which *El Progreso*, in all innocence, could publish it in a toned-down version, quoting the Madrid newspaper as the source.

The second part gave him more trouble; Amador's first draft was swarming with his doubts and uncertainties:

After being thrown out of Berlin, Rudi Colmann, the name our leading player went by in those days (What kind of a faggot's name was that? thought Amador), *he then called himself Federico Stagni* (ditto above), *went to Venezuela, where he persuaded a Jew to lend him a small fortune* (no, that was in Buenos Aires, and they lived in the same boarding house), *and with the proceeds* (or more likely with other money, or whatever he had left over from the Jew's money if he had gone to Buenos Aires first), *he set up a gambling house.*

But that is just one version. In others, he had been married to a certain Mademoiselle Lemoine in Buenos Aires, as well as living off Miss Lemoine while going by the name of Albert Collman, engineer by profession and native of Alsace. He swindled a Polish Jew by the name of Heinrich Meyer (shame it was not Mannfred, that sounded much better) out of fourteen thousand pesos, *a fellow guest at a hotel, convincing him to go into a partnership to start up a gambling house.*

And just what was this Rudi-Federico character doing in

Buenos Aires around 1908? And why was he originally from Berlin in both versions, Amador wondered. He went back to work, changing the Jew's name to Mannfred by the stroke of a pen. If journalism was to be one of the exact sciences, then you could not go about calling people by six different names. Mannfred would stay where he was. Anyway, the Argentinean Jew from Venezuela (or the Venezuelan Jew from Argentina) was not going to complain.

And he went back to work. "*And in Berlin, because . . .*" just to stop again a moment later, because what had happened in Berlin?

The first Berlin story. The Baron's background. It was all about a young man obsessed with gambling, a compulsive gambler, *quickly acquiring great agility and skill in handling cards, dice, and the roulette wheel.* And off he went to play in Berlin.

Just what the hell did people play in Berlin? Marbles? Toy soldiers? Amador wondered, who had never traveled outside Spain, and who had left his adopted city just a couple of times since he came to Barcelona from Zaragoza six years before, to go to a Confederation congress in Madrid, and to Zaragoza to give a lecture. He only knew Berlin from a few film clips and a couple of novels.

Second Berlin story (or maybe only the second part of the first story): *According to some in that German city, at about the turn of the century the famous Baron ripped off an army captain to the tune of 25,000 marks, cheating him while gambling, for which he was found guilty of subversion and sentenced to six years in jail for fraud. And that was where his escape began, which would take him to Venezuela, passing through Argentina on the way.*

But he was not a Berliner. *The one who would later be known as Baron von König* and here there was the temptation to turn the draft into something more than a few notes, *must have been born in 1867 or in 1874* (well, give or take seven years), *in Potsdam, Cologne, or Hanover* (there you go, he was definitely German), *his original name was Friedrich Stallman or Rudolph Stallman, but he might also have called himself, before or after he was born: Julius Rudolph von K., F. von Rosbdel, Federico Stagni, or Albrecht Colmann.* Marvelous, simply marvelous.

Although wherever it may have been that he was from, and whatever his date of birth, he certainly was not born a baron, he was not christened Rudi, and his surname was not what was to be his favorite alias: von König.

There was something missing. There was only one fact about his father, whose money boxes he must surely have plundered, whom he must have poisoned to claim the insurance money, doubtless cutting his finger off in the paper cutter. What a ruthless bastard!

As far as his relationship with his father, a baker or rather a butcher in Alsace, is concerned, we are only in possession of one fact; when his father died, König moved to Brussels (where from?) *and opened up a cabaret there, with gaming tables where cocaine flowed freely, a drug that was very much in fashion in Germany at the end of the century.* If anyone was capable of reading this story, then they deserved to have Baron von König as an adopted son.

But it seems that he got to Brussels beforehand. Was that after the Berlin business? And in Brussels he was only a waiter in a beer hall; and only after his father's death did he feel motivated to start a cabaret, which he definitely transferred a year later. But the Berlin business could have been after all of this, because K was in jail in 1910.

Then when was it that they threw him out of the casinos in London and Amsterdam? And when was he the boss of a gang of professional confidence tricksters on the Côte d'Azur? He would have to write out a new draft of this rigmarole.

Worn out by the story, Antonio Amador left the rough draft of that dubious biography of Baron von König right there and started to ponder what the actual person himself looked like, whom he had obviously never met face-to-face. He imagined him selling fake lottery tickets in a picture-postcard Vienna, with snow on the pavements, the *Blue Danube* playing and fat whores drinking champagne out of ballet shoes. And he imagined him as being stout, with waxed tips to his mustache and a knife with a six-inch blade in his garters as he prowled through the mist in London. He also imagined him in knickers and a Prussian helmet, so thin you could hardly see him, with sharp features, in Roman hot baths surrounded by opera singers.

Stimulated by the strength of these musings, Amador pounced on his typewriter again and wrote:

And as if all these exotic details were not enough, along with wax-tipped mustachios and passports emblazoned with colors and various names, this character crosses the ocean one day and turns up in Caracas, Venezuela, going by the name of Federico Stagni, and passing himself off as a representative of the Monte Carlo casino. That pose did him wonders when it came to starting a branch of the casino in a run-down neighborhood in Caracas. A former inspector with the Barcelona police has told us the following:

"The business they did in that sleazy dive was marvelous. Let it suffice to say that their concessionaires cleared about a thousand pesos a day each and that the best part of the money gambled in that den of iniquity was wrongly, horribly come by: loot from robberies, bloodstained money, money from fraud, money from embezzlement, and petty thieving."

But the business must have been so scandalously fraudulent that the very same authorities that had previously granted the license got fed up with him and took him to the border . . .

Amador paused at this point and checked the manuscript over. He changed the police inspector to a *police inspector from Bilbao* so they could go and fuck with someone other than his informant, he added the adjective *tropical* to Caracas, to give a little bit of color to the affair, and walked over to the corner of the editorial office to where there was a map of the world to find the frontier where they had escorted the Baron to. Colombia, he decided.

He went back to the typewriter and battered away furiously, sweating more and more profusely.

After a brief stay in Colombia, it seems that he went across Africa and some say that he ended up in Asia and stole diamonds in the Transvaal on the way.

The anonymous historians seem to agree that in 1914, as war broke out, he set himself up in Paris, offering his services to the French secret service. There he managed to combine his spying activities with one of his more usual frauds, while he went under the name of Louis Foulier, for whom an arrest warrant was issued by the Paris police. He left the unearned reputation of being a skillful dice player behind him.

This lover of outlandish pseudonyms and the easy lifestyle came to Spain in 1915, to begin a new and no less long and hazardous trek. And here we can offer the reader a combination of very precise facts and very hazy stories:

a) He crossed the border at Irún and set himself up at a summer retreat for the Madrid aristocracy, called Fuenterrabía.

Amador hesitated a second, delved into the nearest ashtray until he found a normal-sized butt which he quickly lit. Was it a matter of talking about the decadent Spanish nobility who went to soak their asses on northern beaches in the summer? He decided to stick to his story.

b) It seems that he almost immediately undertook an operation for the French secret service, tricking the barman in the station cafeteria, Antonio Calvo, into crossing the border on any old excuse, where the French authorities were waiting to accuse him of being the organizer of an escape network for German prisoners of war. Calvo was shot after a very summary trial. Whether the barman was the organizer of that network, or the fake baron made it up to get some money out of the French, was never made clear.

c) K set himself up in Fuenterrabía. He soon acquired a Mercedes-Benz motor car, a chauffeur, a lover, and a daughter (of the lover). He handed out money to the poor, presented the town hall with five hundred pesetas for the needy, and he was nominated director of the casino in Fuenterrabía. He hung around there until 1917, when he was thrown out by Governor López Monís for having ruined the good name of a provincial family casino, where suicides had never used to proliferate after a night at the roulette wheel.

And König vanished, disappeared. Rumors later filled in the gaps and it is said that as a common tourist he went along, embezzling his way through Bilbao, Palma de Mallorca, Cartagena, Seville, Cádiz . . . It is said, because saying does not cost anything, that he worked indiscriminately for Février, head of the French secret service, as well as for Hortwig, head of the German spy network.

And finally, he got to Barcelona at the beginning of September 1918. It had to be Barcelona, where the sea was churned up by the war and the greed of the bosses had raised up the mud from the murky depths and had drawn in all the hustlers, the scum of capitalism, turning it into a mecca for crooks and the dregs of humanity.

In Barcelona he set himself up at No. 25 Rambla del Prat with his lover, whose initials were C.J., and lived a double life, switching between one Conchita and his partner, René Scalda, with whom he lives to this day in the Maison Meublé in Santa Ana Street. It seems our main player is broadminded and has a somewhat flexible morality, as his legal wife went to live with a pimp, a former butcher (and with K's full consent, who had it in mind to embezzle him) by the name of A.P., at No. 85 Enrique Granados Street. And it seemed to end up as a very suitable ménage à trois, as the man ended up helping them out with their business. The three of them cheated out of sixty thousand pesetas a French jeweler called Margarite Bernadine, who had a mole on her left buttock.

Sparks were flying off the typewriter when he stopped. Amador himself seemed to be overwhelmed by some electrical phenomenon. What a load of crap! He decided to cross out the bit about the mole on the French lady's bottom, so as not to compromise his friend Jorge Fernández Font. Just as he was preparing himself for a third bout of key bashing, a new fit of coughing came over him, making him feel as if his body were being cut in half. Tears streamed from his eyes and a few drops of blood trickled out of the corner of his mouth.

"What the hell's going on, I told you to come and see me, that somebody has got to take care of this," the editor-in-chief said to him, throwing the competition's newspapers at him. In all of them there was a small item telling the same story, give or take a few words, which had been underlined.

"And what's this?" Amador asked, trying not to make it sound like a death rattle and covering his lips with a red handkerchief.

"That's just what I'm asking myself. Since when do newspapers come out with a story about a body before the body has even been found? Because, as far as I know, the blood-stained dinghy is over there, in the harbor, but when they picked it up, there was nothing in it but some hose and a few stains. No corpse at all."

Antonio Amador carefully picked up the typewritten sheets of his rough draft and put them away in his pocket. He eyed the newspapers with a look that he hoped would denote a mixture of wisdom and experience.

A few hours later, Amador left the *El Progreso* offices hidden behind a few bundles of back numbers of newspapers that were being taken away in a truck. The drivers were union members, and often awestruck as far as the journalist's comings and goings were concerned. On some occasions he left on the back seat of the editor's car, with the complicity of the boss's chauffeur; on others he climbed out of a basement window, or dressed in a motorcyclist's goggles and in the sidecar of the messenger's bike. The best routine was a lack of routine. And as he went out he also came in. The only difficult thing was to find a suitable disguise. When you are five feet nothing, the best thing to be is a dwarf. There was not a false beard or mustache, there was not a Seville woman's dress under which he could hide, nor a mechanic's overalls, nor a bullfighter's suit, if we are going to be exotic about things, that could hide him from a deliberate stare. If they wanted to find him, they would end up finding him. Better later than earlier, he said to himself, patting his gun and biting off half a mouthful of Spanish omelet the driver had given him.

And it was there, while reading old newspapers, while a heavy downpour fell on the back part of the truck, that he learned that Lenin was going around Barcelona incognito, and that the magician Leonardo Padura Buenaventura had made a cabaret artiste friend of his disappear (friend of Amador, that is, not the magician) that same night in the Pompeya Music Hall, to make amends for his failure the day before, and that Mike Gold, the playwright who was opening a play about the Mexican Revolution, had also written a novel where a wonderful phrase leaped out of the pages: *The rose of syphilis flowers in the streets.*

The Chinese Detective

"They found the pickup truck, the same one, with the same goddamn license plates, dumped over there, on the way to Las Cruces. They'd stolen it across the border a week before, in some crummy town in Texas. So there's nothing around here. These dudes are professionals. A lot of goddamn setting up for the job and all. A lot of shit . . . two gringas dead in Mexico and just like that, not even a trace of them."

In the newspaper editorial offices there was nothing new to find out. In editorial offices they just rehash what you know already. A land of certainties and assurances. In editorial offices wisdom is confirmed but you do not find information. I might think, listening to the journalist who would give me his version, that it is almost the same as my version, although he is talking about Karen, whom I would be visiting religiously, day after day, like a dead girl.

"And now every goddamn doctor in Ciudad Juárez—from hospital manager or head surgeon up—has forgotten about one thing, the fucking kidney. Nobody knows about operations anymore and even the word 'dialysis' is like a curse. Now they've taken it out of the textbooks, bunch of asslickers."

But not every doctor would have forgotten. I might find one, the key man, the one who performed a kidney transplant in 1991. But that would be much later.

So then I would turn my eyes toward Karen's silent body. I would listen to the sound of the artificial respirator, the gentle bass rhythm with which Santana might start a number, "Oye Como Va," for example, by the great drummer Tito Puente, recorded in 1970 in the Wally Heider studios in San Francisco. And then the recurring image of Karen spitting at the referee at a crucial moment in the game might come back to me, as Carlos Santana strums his guitar and Rico Reyes sings the lines "*Oye como va mi ritmo, bueno pa' gozá, mulata.*" A musical image, wild, ideal for a slow-motion playback, so different from the gentle sight of pale Karen struggling to survive in her hospital bed.

And the E.T. of the Wild Frontier would spend hours looking at the unconscious blond girl, trying to guess her wishes, trying to get inside the head of someone at death's door, remembering scenes from games and joyful expressions. That brutal elbow jab with which she slammed an opponent from Illinois into the bench; that expression of contempt and defiance when she scored a basket behind her back without seeing the backboard. And then the deathly pallor again.

Forced into a routine by hospital hours. Forced into a routine by other routines. Doubts and hospital visits in the mornings. Unease and fruitless investigations in the afternoons. Doglike loneliness and the novel by night.

And at all times of the day and night, I would walk around the city, feeling the sticky asphalt on the soles of my shoe and the metal support of my plaster boot scraping the sidewalks, looking for a doctor who might know something more; speaking to young journalists who would call me "sir" and would say they have read my books, who would wear wire-rimmed glasses and drive Chevrolets with Texas and Arizona license plates on them. Doing the rounds of this so un-Mexican city, so cut off by distances, denied to pedestrians, so dried out and dusty; where I would only have my cult of the memory of Pancho Villa in common with the natives.

And between a Karen dead in life and the loose dirt in the alleyways behind the hospitals, I might go around cooking up material for nightmares, and at times, in the loneliness of my room at the *Motel Camelia*, I might write the novel I'm never going to finish about my grandfather and the evil Baron, thinking about another city, one with a sea to it, a Barcelona as mythical and unreal as this dried-up Ciudad Juárez, sleepless, crazy, talking to myself, murmuring nonsense, thinking that things that have been happening will have to happen.

And the Baron, in any case, would turn out to be like the heavy in the Sergio Leone movie, that Lee Van Cleef guy. Just like him. Because in the chaos of searching for Karen's attackers, having a central character just like Lee Van Cleef wouldn't matter too much to me. Well, yes, it would matter for one thing: Rudi Colmann, the baddest of bad guys, would have found his alter ego over the years in a Hollywood gunman.

And I might be like a Chinese detective: an unreal asshole. Dopey and phantasmagoric at the same time. A Chinese detective who fills in gaps left by answers with questions. The Chiang Kai-shek of information technology looking for a black pickup truck, offering some dough, some greenbacks, some bucks, a few bills, to whoever says he's seen a guy with silver-tipped boots who goes around kidnapping gringas, and another shorter Mexican guy, who to give you more of an idea does the same thing. A nosy Charlie Chan inquiring if anyone has seen a multicultural cross-frontier hit squad.

And one day I might be looking at the black pickup truck that would turn up in the Guadalupe district. So shiny and polished because they've cleaned all the fingerprints off, the law might say, in the voice of a uniformed sergeant from the local police. A black Toyota stolen in El Paso a month back, whose backseat covers the Mexican forensics are scraping. They might be able to find some traces of dried blood that might or might not belong to Karen.

And for all that I might go around and around the turf, looking at my own bloodshot eyes in the black paintwork, nothing would occur to me, I would not see clues the others would miss, nor would I guess anything. Not even the Chinese detective that I would have become would be able to come up with a brilliant move, nor would the border country have any answers on offer. And the dust in the air, the abandoned truck that would already have had its windshield and three tires ripped off by looting vultures, will give me a burning thirst, a feeling of stupidity that all the beer in Ciudad Juárez, Chihuahua, won't be able to defeat.

And I might go and see Karen in the hospital, to tell her by telepathy that if she does not wake up and come back to me we'll never be able to find the motherfuckers who kidnapped her. That if she does not give me any more facts, if she does not tell me what happened, I will keep on doing the sleepless rounds of the avenues and alleyways, asking dumbass questions. A ghost haunting the Avenida de las Américas that turns into Lincoln Avenue and finishes at the Cordova Free Bridge, over the Río Bravo. A writer is just a writer, who creates fiction but does not perform miracles. I might be defeating myself, as much as I love her, as much as I want to get her revenge for her, as much as I share her unbridled hate for all authority, including basketball referees.

The Ballad of the Stars

Barcelona had nearly a dozen daily newspapers in 1920: *El Progreso*; *La Lucha*; *El País*; *La Soli*, organ of the Confederation, the CNT, when it was not banned; *La Veu*; *La Publicidad*; *El Correo*. As well as these there were two Madrid newspapers, *El Sol* and *España Nueva*, that had a significant Catalan organization that allowed them to compete in the city. Amador read nearly all of them out of stubbornness (except *La Soli*, which was, of course, banned once again), and not just the ones that the editor-in-chief placed on his desk. He just had to read the small note about the death of an anarchist in the harbor, but in passing he took time to glance at the kitchen recipes, an account of the happenings in Mataró, an interesting debate about whether French roulette wheels should be allowed in Barcelona gambling houses, two articles by a doctor in favor of a vegetarian diet, and all the information that could be found about a strike in Bilbao. Reading newspapers was a vice, he had decided, while his colleagues hammered on the bathroom door that he had locked himself behind an hour before in order to find out about harsh reality. He came out, drying his hands on a towel embroidered with lilac-colored flowers and, without paying any attention to his detractors, put a first summary together:

In four Barcelona newspapers a small article had appeared that, give or take a few flowery touches, repeated the same story about the corpse of Angel del Hierro, a well-known active anarchist and member of shock groups sympathetic to the CNT, who had been found dead in a boat drifting in the outer reaches of the port. Del Hierro had been killed by a series of blows to the head, probably inflicted by an iron bar that was found in the same boat. His death was put down to a confrontation between the shock groups themselves. No way, said Amador to himself, you can pull that one on somebody else.

Later on that day, Antonio "the Flea" Amador, perhaps the best journalist in that crazy, deceptive, and bloody city, a fiend for the truth, a knight of the Holy Grail for information, wandered around the harbor, asking questions here and there. Later on, his erratic movements would bring him to the editorial offices of several newspapers, where he cautiously undertook his own investigations as to how that strange item came to be published.

Angel del Hierro had been a quiet man, to whom was attributed, in some very narrow and very reserved groups of anarchists on the fringes of the Confederation, the assault that had caused the death of Bravo Portillo, ex-head of special services in the Barcelona police. That marvelous assault, occurring in early September of the previous year, had caused not a few bottles of bad champagne to be uncorked in working-class neighborhoods and had made Amador write that day: *The witnesses, who today as always are not entirely reliable, say that it happened on the corner of Santa Tecla. Whether they followed him from the platform of a streetcar, whether there were two or three people responsible for the attack (one of whom was wearing a cap that he would lose during the assault), they shot him through the back, wounding him. On hearing the first shot Bravo tried to hide in a doorway, and drew his gun. And then the versions differ again as to whether he fired back or not. More shots were heard. A coalman and his wife, at dinner, came to the door and saw the moment in which Bravo came tumbling down. The accounts slip into inaccuracy once again, and some turn the coalman's wife into another coalman named Rafael Barajas. "The policeman had his hand on his crotch from which blood was streaming," and as Bravo was falling he said, "They have betrayed me and killed me," and in the memory of other witnesses this becomes a "They have shot in betrayal" or a "I am a swine and a traitor," with which we can confirm the theory that you cannot believe the "famous last words" of a dying man. In the unreliable account of the witnesses, it can be surmised that between fifteen and twenty shots were heard.*

That story was to bring Amador three more death threats.

Manuel Bravo Portillo, the murderer of workers, a police official who worked simultaneously for the German spymasters, a pimp, seller of safe conducts for workers traveling abroad, protector of drug traffickers and murderer of Pablo Sabater, had danced the waltz of the Stars, the waltz of the .32 caliber Stars.

He was picked up and taken to the dispensary, where he

died ten minutes after arrival. He left a life insurance policy to his wife, having been covered for the astronomical amount of 120,000 pesetas.

Amador was convinced that one of the two executioners who killed Bravo, the foul beast of the Barcelona police, had been Angel del Hierro, but all his conviction stemmed from no more than two very fragile rumors, scarcely discerned from the morass of calumnies, disinformation, and drivel that inundated Barcelona. Obviously the police did not have the least idea, and were a long way from being able to identify him. Not even the network of informants that the bosses' organization's hit squads maintained had gotten close to the matter, not by a long way, not even a sniff of it; if they had, Del Hierro would not have been able to continue openly acting as a representative of the CNT in the streetcar and automobile assemblers' strike during the last few months of the year. Amador could even remember having seen him at a soccer match two weeks before. Alone, as ever. With a pair of empty seats around him that he used for spitting out the hulls of the sunflower seeds he chewed quite calmly, without worrying about the other spectators.

Amador went over the few things he knew about Del Hierro on the fingers of his right hand: he was tall, thin; originally from some shitty Castilian town, like him; no more than twenty-five years old. Or was it thirty, and it was just his faraway look that made him seem younger? He was very deaf in his left ear, it made him turn around in an odd way when the coversation turned to his comrades on that side of him. He knew everything about foreign countries and flags, and even national anthems. He was capable of recalling what the national anthem of the old Ukraine was and explaining that the Scots had their own flag, or what coinage was used on the coast of Senegal all the while smiling; he had an open and easygoing smile. This was nothing unusual in that strange world of encyclopedic anarchists, with their strange and obsessive erudition.

Amador himself spoke medieval Italian fluently and had read Boccaccio in the original, could hop along in Latin and give a good account of himself in French. But Del Herrio, whom he had not seen more than . . . he counted the number of times on his fingers, remembering: four times? He was a remarkable man among remarkable men, because Del Herrio was always followed by the murmur of short phrases spoken in a low voice, a faint halo that at times seemed to glow like a rainbow, looks of admiration from some and lack of recognition from others. The most interesting nameless man in a Barcelona that was already fascinating by itself as far as characters went. It was said that the first time he had been run into jail was for having pissed in the baptismal font in the Santa Coloma church, as the ultimate anti-clerical act; and not content with that, he had broken the priest's jaw with a tremendous blow, after having accused him of sexually abusing the orphans placed in his care.

But watch out, these tell-mes and let-me-tell-yous made Del Hierro seem like an earnest fellow, but Amador remembered him as a joking and satirical character—full of obsessions, but capable of laughing at them.

Once, a woman whom Amador shared with Del Hierro, who was also given to protecting and going around with prostitutes, told him that the thin man was very skillful at darning his clothes and had once even stitched up a polka-dot dress for her.

And Del Hierro was dead? Amador continued his inquiry with the same intensity that he seemed to put into everything, breaking off only to eat some tiny fried fish, more bones than anything, that a barman had given him in the Barceloneta district. And from there, with the feeling of not having eaten anything and his stomach rumbling due to the unfulfilled promise, Amador wandered off to ask more questions around the harbor.

A bloodstained dinghy had been found drifting, a Basque proprietor smoking on the stern of his steamship had towed it in; and yes, in the dinghy they had found a bloodstained hose. So that was that. But the dinghy had been found in the morning when the news was already being passed around in the newspapers. What kind of shit was that?

Amador continued his wandering. A rain cloud had come to rest above the harbor and was beginning to drip all over the little journalist. Going up the Ramblas he entered the Ensanche district, trying to escape from the rain, but the rain kept up with him. In the newspapers the affair was clearer, or more obscure. The bulletin had ended up, in every case, in the hands of journalists who were closely linked to the bosses' organization. And Amador's inquiry produced more than one wary glance. Who would want Del Hierro's corpse to turn up before it turned up? Who needed the corpse to be identified at once? In that Barcelona of nighttime gunshots and the light of deadly flares, it was clear-cut: the news confirming the death of Angel del Hierro only mattered to someone who wanted to charge for the work he had done.

They murdered him, they put him in a dinghy, and then passed on the article so as to be able to hand over the bill. But the dead man had slipped overboard and was now feeding the barracudas in the middle of the Mediterranean. Was the story quite like that? Were there barracudas in the *Mare Nostrum*? If it was like that, whoever had passed the note on to the scab journalists was the murderer. Shit, they had killed Del

Hierro. Another one of the legion of those who had fallen in this last year. Amador rubbed the butt of his pistol and promised to find out more about the matter. If there was something he hated more than the bosses' organization's hit squads, more than the lovers of Spanish noblemen, and lottery ticket sellers (the latter because they induced faith in a false paradise), it was journalists who had sold out: the worst whores of them all, who had infiltrated the most noble occupation in the world.

The Boy Scout of Nonexistent Cities

Nobody would know then how many inhabitants Ciudad Juárez might have. How many it used to have, how many it had had. A city of alluvial soils and passes, flat and outstretched, in which they say there's around a million people, and the figures swing between 800,000 and 1,200,000, and then I would have to leave it at that, in that "nearly a million" which I will like for being a round and imprecise figure.

In the first few days I might want to change my attire, to hide what would be odd about me. I might then buy a pair of cowboy boots in a closeout sale from some factory, in front of which there would be a line of cars and pickups, because the merchandise would go in a matter of hours, and then everything would have vanished: dust thou art . . . They would not be any old boots, they would be phony

Texan boots, or rather Mexican boots, with a high leg, and I would be unduly using the plural because boots, no way, a left boot, and that would be it.

A blind man's cane, for somebody who cannot walk, and dark glasses for somebody who gets lost in the light of so much blindness. Boot(s), polarized glasses, white flexible cane that whistles in the air whenever you move it; two of the inevitable red and blue checked shirts, black jeans, and a thick leather belt with a big buckle with two tin buzzards on it. I would believe in characterization. In *mise-en-scène*. I would have the appearance of an investigator. There might not be any answers. There would be unsolved petty details, like where to put the boot that would be left over. Tie it with some twine to my belt? Hang it over my shoulder? Petty details, you know.

Are there any precedents for this anywhere? A kidnapping with surgery and postoperative treatment thrown in? On the other side of the border? Traffic in organs? Rumors. Eyes bought here. Babies bought there. Rumors.

In the loneliness of the night, while I read Carlos Fuentes's latest novel, the rumors would not be able to console me. Someone up there might have offered me the chance to give some lectures in the cultural center. I must be over the hill. The only thing that would be left for me would be to write a review in the *Diario de Juárez* newspaper, sign a contract to make a film or autograph books in Sanborn's.

And even so, I am a sucker for rumors and I would have a wall in my motel room covered with them like tattoos, mixed up with notes for a novel that just does not want to be written. I would have pinned up photos, notes, and newspaper cuttings with thumbtacks. If anyone knew how to read tattoos, then they might be able to decipher the ones covering the walls of my motel room. You could write two novels with them:

Here a cutting from a Ciudad Juárez newspaper uproariously demanding the electric chair for the kidney snatchers. Below a pink card with a rough map of the streets parallel to the Ramblas that go up from the Catalan harbor. There a note picking up the rumor that a guy nicknamed "the Viking" was going around the parking lot in Azucenas Street saying that *he* knew . . . there a strange note about the two girl basketball players having spoken that afternoon with a couple of guys in the snack bar at Sanborn's about how they ought to go for a tour of the colonial missions. Beside all this, three postcards of the places they might have visited, the three oldest churches in Texas: Socorro, San Elizario, the Isleta mission, also known as Our Lady of Mount Carmel, islands on the frontier that in the seventeenth century served as refuges for tame Indians and Spanish people scared of an uprising by the real Indians . . . Just by the mirror where I would be able to see the beard that I would refuse to shave morning after morning, a photo of the American girls taken in the street and never collected; both smiling, carrying two six-packs of beer and wearing yellow pants. There a hurried note picking up the rumor about the kidnapping of babies. Here a note to myself wondering why Antonio Amador never had any money, despite earning half pay at *El Progreso*. There a journalist's phone number, or the address of a grade-school teacher who said he knew what was happening, and did not know a damn thing. There a card from a restaurant where you could eat excellent charbroiled steak. On the table lamp, a physical description of my grandfather, the Black Angel of Barcelona. He was not like Amador remembered him, neither was he like the memory of him I would invent years later. Thin, deep-set sad eyes in contrast with a beaming smile, a mop of black hair that covered one side of his forehead. In the corner, two Polaroid photos of Karen in her hospital bed.

And if I cannot dig around in the depths of Ciudad Juárez, then I would not be able to in Barcelona either, although the two cities have me in their clutches and are wearing me out.

I would like that deadly, crazy Barcelona and I would like to describe it. Small shops and art nouveau, proud metal, locomotive rails building up aerial frameworks for enormous exhibition halls full of machinery. A lot of red bricks and shiny steel. And the Palacio de La Pedrera where the Baron would have had his offices, not in Rambla de las Flores, but in the middle of the nouveaux riches' part of Barcelona, the ones who shock the older rich with their architectural outspokenness and their art nouveau full of Indian exoticism.

What the hell had I missed in Ciudad Juárez?

I would begin to miss Mexico City.

Dying Naked with a Sailor's Cap On

Antonio Amador, taking advantage of his size and the fear he inspired in most people, emerged into the *El Progreso* editorial offices from the ladies' toilet, having entered the building through the bathroom window. His smoldering cigarette, together with his outlandish entrance, drew disapproving glances from the secretaries.

"He is going to die, and so young, too," said an unwashed young blond girl in hushed tones, from behind the counter where they sold subscriptions and announcements per word. She was hopelessly in love with the little journalist, and tried not to let it show; she did it so well that he had no idea of the burning passions he had brought about.

Amador walked directly over to the editor-in-chief's desk and said to him without further ado:

"There was a dead man, but I don't think it was the one

they said it was, because it takes more than a bunch of queers to kill my friends. And as for the papers that got the news item, they got it well before the police found the dinghy. So, those who killed the dead man were the ones who passed on the news item, and they were up to something, and Del Hierro disappeared from his house and his job four days before the bloodstained boat turned up. All of that leaves me with two sheets and ten lines of copy, and let someone else take care of the answers to all the questions I'll have thrown up. Else you can wipe your ass with the copy. All right?"

The editor-in-chief nodded, overwhelmed.

Amador wiped the sweat from his brow with the same handkerchief he used to wipe away the blood he coughed up, in spite of the fact that in the office the winter temperature could not have been much more than forty degrees. It was clear that he was burning up, a human stove, a feverish oven although he never took his jacket off; something he never did because a) he was a gentleman; b) he did not want his pistol to be too conspicuous; c) the right sleeve of his shirt was torn.

Smoking slowly and fearful of swallowing the smoke, he put the two sheets and ten lines of copy together (which despite the outspoken remarks turned out to be a dozen when typed), and theatrically placed them on the editor-in-chief's desk before going back to his unfinished manuscript about König's gang, whose following chapter began with the following phrase:

What is heaven for some people is hell for others.

Now and again he turned out well-rounded phrases like that. Maybe, just maybe, if he managed to get through the winter, he could turn into a novelist, and that only by the grace of God, who was surely a count in this rotten Spain, by the grace of the Baron and Arlegui, the Barcelona police chief.

Baron von König makes four or five thousand pesetas a month through bribes, blackmail, and payment for killings and beatings, while in Barcelona, the monthly wage of a textile weaver is scarcely 120 pesetas, and a bricklayer does not even get as much as ninety, and that after a successful strike last November.

The shitty-assed Baron was a shadow who could only be guessed at through his actions, who never let himself be seen. Was it really like that? Or was Amador scared to stand face-to-face with him and look him in the eye? Stand face-to-face with him and look him in the eye, Antoñito. Shit, damn, and hell! The whole curse, the little journalist said to himself, remembering the patient tutoring in profanity from his long-gone mother and father, and carried on piecing his facts together.

It would seem that during the general strike, the apocryphal Baron got himself introduced by a Belgian to Bravo Portillo—at that time chief of the Barcelona police's Special Brigade and now sadly deceased—who was very taken with this character, in whom he recognized a mirror image of himself, an equal, and to whom he offered a part of the take, setting him up in an office in No. 71 Vallirana Street to receive informers. These were turbulent times for Bravo Portillo's gang, which was in the public eye thanks to a journalistic campaign, and for which reason the relationship between K and BP was not up to much.

Was that part true? He got that from a hoarse chorus girl, Armegnol's sister, he being the one the woodworkers' union had condemned to death if they ever saw him in Barcelona. It was lacking in substance. No one else spoke about the connection between K and BP, the two black monsters of the bosses' organization's gangs; the most probable thing was that they had never met each other. He decided to leave that part as it was and blend it in with something he knew for certain. Well, *si non è vero, è ben trovato.*

It was very much in keeping with the Baron's character that on BP's death he turned up at the offices of the Barcelona Bosses Federation saying the murdered policeman was like a brother to him, and that he wanted to avenge his death.

Thinking the Baron might be an agent provocateur, they quickly got rid of him. It must be remembered that at that time there were serious tensions within the bosses' organization and that the dominant inclination was to negotiate a truce with the CNT, with the government as a mediator. König was not put off. Thinking he could fry other fish in that fiery situation, he went to the organization's treasurer, Miró i Trepat, and spun a long yarn that, in brief, said, "He had already been collaborating in that most important and delicate task that the dead police officer (with whom he was linked by bonds of the most sincere and cordial nature) was in charge of." It seems that Miró took the bait and was captivated by this character, entrusting him with putting the gang back together using money from reserves belonging to the bosses' organization's slush fund.

K was then renting a ground-floor office at No. 6 Rambla de las Flores and began to reorganize the remains of BP's gang, which had broken up after their leader's death, having been dangerously thrown into the light and were unprotected. K, who was no innovator, set up the same structure that Bravo Portillo had tried and tested: paid informers, infiltration of the unions, a network of the dregs of society, and a well-used army of gunmen. He did not turn his nose up at buying off a few policemen who might be useful, like Inspector Luis León. To these characters he added anything he could dig up in the sea of mud thrown up by the social ferment.

The Baron kept such right-hand men by his side as Antonio Soler, alias "the Majorcan," who oversaw the gunmen; López

Crespo, alias "the Blond" (Amador hesitated here, because according to his notebook, he also had to take account of Epifanio Casas, but he had fallen out with the Baron for having put the blame on other members of the group); *a resurfaced Bernardo Armegnol, who on Bravo Portillo's death had fled from Barcelona and had spent two months in the shadows in Valencia; Manuel Grau, informer; Conrado Gimeno, a classic type from the pages of the criminologist Lombroso, who was thrown into jail for selling a secret letter belonging to the chief of the Vidal militia for a bottle of wine; the former jailbird Julio Laporta, alias "the Billy Goat"; the famous "Mirror," Mariano Sanz* (putting his notebook to one side, Amador interjected another detail here); *the shameless homosexual, Gonzalo Jubilate; Pedro Torrens, baker and police informer; Antonio Jilletes; Julio del Clot; Manuel Martin; and the former policeman Jerónimo Batanero* (and here Amador wrote a questioning remark beside the former policeman's name; had he not run away from Barcelona two months ago?).

With the gang back together, König went around to Miró i Trepat's office every Friday (Amador remembered the treasurer of the bosses' organization and hesitated over whether to put a few more details down, like his being the owner of a mattress factory, a man with a vinegary face, as if he suffered from permanent indigestion, and that he had a lover who cheated on him with a bullfighter) *to deliver reports, receive orders and collect wages.*

It was getting late. The little journalist got up from his chair, put the newly typed sheets into his jacket pocket, and went out as he had come in, through the ladies' bathroom, taking the breath away from a secretary who was taking a piss, her bottle-green knickers around her ankles.

He went wandering around Chinatown and ended up trying to get warm in a bar called El Rápido, which was frequented by friends. There were no faces known to him, but a prostitute acquaintance of his made signs for him to come over to the bar.

"Coffee, Antonio?"

Amador nodded. He only came up to her chin; if he got too close he'd run the risk of sinking into the husky-voiced woman's chest.

"They want me to strip and dance for them dressed up as a sailor boy," she said.

"Who?"

"Some clients."

"But if you strip, how are you going to dance for them dressed as a sailor?"

"Only with the cap, my boy. You seem a bit slow at times. In this weather, with just a cap on . . ."

"Maestro Amador, a cigarette please," said a soft voice. Amador lifted his eyes and saw a teenager stretching his hand out to him.

"I'm Joaquín, from *La Soli*, the copyboy. We're colleagues."

"It's not your day, sonny. I haven't got so much as a match on me."

"You have to take what you can get, Antoñito," said his friend with the husky voice, cutting the conversation short.

"Take no notice of them. Let them mind their own business."

"And where will you and I sleep tomorrow, my boy?" she answered back, walking toward the door as she shrugged her shoulders.

Amador followed her out with his eyes. She had an exquisite heart-shaped ass. She was a good girl, too; she wanted to save up to start a bar in Oviedo. A bar without whores, which would have a library of social-interest novels at the end of the counter, free for whoever wanted to read them. Looking at her, he saw the two guys who had come through the door. The one in front wore a white cravat and was drawing a revolver from beneath his waistcoat: the Monkey. Amador's hand went to his waist and he went behind the bar. The first shot shattered the woodwork on the counter and bounced off a spittoon beside him as he crawled.

There were shots everywhere; bottles were smashed, chairs and tables went down amid the screaming, bull-fighting posters were torn from the walls, drunks keeled over headfirst.

Amador was dragging himself around the back end of the bar, drawing his pistol, when he noticed that the shots had finished. He slowly stuck his head out. Neither of the two gunmen was still in the tavern. The Monkey was a bricklayer who had defected from the union and worked with Soler, the Majorcan. The whole thing had been fucked up. Bit by bit, the rest of the crowd gathered around the tables again. A teenager was stretched out on the floor, in a pool of blood; the one who had asked him for a cigarette a short while before. The journalist kept looking at the wide-open eyes that saw no one. He helped himself to a piece of sausage from the tapas bar, shook the sawdust from his trousers, and walked quickly over to the door. The police would not take long to arrive and this was not the sort of business to stick around and answer questions about.

"They fired a hell of a lot of shots, a hell of a lot," said a worker in shirt-sleeves, looking for his glass of pastis. "Let's see, how many did they fire?"

"Two barrels," Amador answered, chewing. "Fourteen rounds."

"But wait, why didn't they get you?"

"Because they're a bunch of queers and they wouldn't

dare to come close," the Flea said. But when he was by the door, he rephrased himself: "Besides, I'm not much of a target."

And then he regretted having joked over the body of his dead little colleague. But it was too late by then.

The Man Who Interrogates Surgeons

I might go into Dr. Espinosa's consulting room, he being the only renal specialist to have publicly directed a successful transplant in Ciudad Juárez, on October 27, 1991. An interesting transplant, where the donor had been the patient's brother. An eight-hour operation.

The General Hospital is on the corner of Montes de Oca and 16 de Septiembre, a plain building with the morgue at the back. I might feel like Amador investigating in the cellars of the Barcelona Clinical Hospital, which I did visit once, but they were no longer what they had been, although they still had the same sordidness and damp walls.

A friendly hospital, full of voluntary specialists, run by the state of Chihuahua. Slightly mismatching yellow, gray, and bright green colored plastic chairs, families waiting outside the emergency room.

"Yes, in El Paso there are some hospitals that perform kidney transplants: the Providencia, the Sierra, they all have dialysis machines. The Sierra even has an outside unit in the west of the city. In Ciudad Juárez there is only one machine, that is only used in cases of acute renal failure."

I would take notes and promise not to lose them. Something has to come of all this.

More messages for myself: *List of patients who have used the dialysis machine.*

"A transplant operation could last four hours, the donor would need forty-eight hours in intensive care afterward."

Where did they keep her during the postoperational period? my notebook might say later on.

"The group could be made up of two teams, two surgeons in each one, one removing and the other transplanting, with two to four anesthetists, eight nurses, and a supervisor. They are two simultaneous operations. And there might also be a rejection, despite all the preoperative tests that have been done. A rejection and everything is useless."

Did they take the possibility of a rejection into account? What would they have done then?

"The donor must be identified through compatibility tests. It is not a simple matter; you have to identify the blood group, there have to be tests for the white corpuscles, tissue compatibility, a lot of things. The tests are usually done in Mexico City, they cost about a thousand dollars if you have them done over the border, much less over here. They take a few days, a week at the most."

Where did they do the preoperative tests? Who took samples from Karen? In the university? How did they know she would come to Juárez? They chose her a long time before the trip. It was an accident she was in Juárez. They're gringos, dammit! They're gringos and they've been following her since Austin.

"The recipient must have had vascular disease, glomerulonephritis, chronic nephritis. That must be the patient's case history."

I would take note, spelling the terms out: glo-mer-u-lo-ne-phri-tis.

And the amazing Boy Scout in the mutilations troop would listen very carefully to the technical details of how to perform a kidney transplant, and would be very diligent when it came to watching the doctor draw little diagrams showing where the sutures were made, what has to be cut and sewed and . . .

"Here, in Juárez, there was an unsuccessful kidney transplant a few months ago."

The doctor, with his arms folded, would refuse to give me the name of the private hospital where the unsuccessful transplant was performed and the recipient died. Something to do with ethics.

"And what about the possibility that they remove somebody's kidney and then take it to a recipient somewhere else? Far away, a thousand miles from here?" I would ask.

"You cannot remove a kidney and store it just like that. A kidney dies in twenty-four hours, and there are no cases of long-distance transplants with the organ being transported," the doctor would say.

They began to trail Karen as a donor before she wound up here to celebrate winning a game, but the operation was performed here or in El Paso.

"Anyway, nobody could have done what they said they did to the American girl. Nobody from around here. Please, it is impossible, not one of our people. For that they would have to have no professional ethics whatsoever . . . Motherfuckers," the doctor might say, changing his tone for once.

Motherfuckers, I would write down in my notebook.

Bombs and Searches

And then the petards and bombs began to go off, the explosions could be heard. More showy than harmful, with the damage done by sticks of dynamite visible to passersby, the explosions caused in the central neighborhoods clearly audible. Noise with meaning, the picaresque writer Quevedo would say. The bombs went off twice, one of them making a hole in a wall or breaking half a dozen windows, the second and much more powerful one going off in the newspapers the following day. On November 21, an awesome petard shook a house in La Diagonal; on November 23, a bomb blew up in Pelayo Street and three normal-sized petards made of dynamite went off (in the Captain General's office, no less), slightly wounding a driver and a soldier. Everything was blowing up. On the 26th a bomb exploded in a bakery on Boteros Street, and the press gave a lot of publicity to a student who had ripped the fuse out of a stick of dynamite and prevented the statue of Dr. Robert from being blown up. Two days later another petard went off, blowing up the outhouse in the Liberal Club and causing enormous damage to the bathrooms (Amador, in a piece for *España Nueva*, lamented the fact that no one was taking a crap at the time, which caused more proceedings to be taken against him for publishing offenses), and yet another one in a rubber factory on Recaredo Street, without causing any human damage. An unexploded bomb was found on the 29th, and on the 30th four more bombs went off.

The governor of Barcelona made a statement to the press: *We all have reason to believe another wave of terrorist violence is upon us. Bombs and petards are going off everywhere, every day. Murmurings, very much in vogue in a restless city, attribute this to anarcho-syndicalist groups. For this reason I have given the order to question everyone on their way out of workers' societies and newspapers and I deem not only questioning people leaving such clubs or offices to be appropriate but frisking people leaving such places also. After nightfall such frisking should be especially rigorous. I have also ordered extra watches to be kept on dynamite stores and quarries.*

But Amador, who was everywhere, found out from a servant that while Julio Amado, the governor of Barcelona, was writing this in public, in private he was asking the interior minister: *Are you sure this is the work of the labor unions? Are you sure that this is an act of savagery by the anarchists rather than by those who are interested in causing indignation within military and law-enforcement circles, those ready to come to the aid of the bosses' organization to eradicate the unions?*

With these arguments in mind and the word of a representative of the groups (whom he had met in a backstreet) that it was not them, Antonio Amador, while he confined himself to the bare facts in *El Progreso*, wrote a second report for the Madrid daily *España Nueva*, accusing the Barcelona bosses' organization of being behind the bombings. This report caused him to be called in to make a statement at police headquarters for having drawn attention to the suspicious coincidence that the student who was tearing fuses out of bombs was repeating himself; he had already done it twice, a very strange and suspicious stroke of luck. Amador's piece was received with scorn in other newspapers, the more so because he made the connection between the student César Campillo and a militiaman of the same name who, a week before, had been the victim of "an assault in Riera de San Miguel where they fired ten shots without hitting him."

But Amador wanted to dig much deeper in everything. While he continued to ask indiscreet questions about the disappearance of Angel del Hierro, he went into his newspaper at unearthly hours and in ways that were just as untoward, ate and slept badly, feverishly roamed the streets of Barcelona, getting to streetcorners where the echo of dynamite blasts still had not died down and the thick smoke of gunpowder hung in the air, when bits of rubble from the wall were still falling. Thanks to his multiplicity, he was right there, in the middle of the bloodstained debris, when a shady character called Juan Puig was detained, and when the remains of his ragman's cart were checked over after it had been blown to smithereens by a bomb going off prematurely. Amador, adopting the expression of a casual passerby, of an unwilling onlooker, of an idiot who had lost his way, took up the trail of that first investigation when the blood was still flowing and picked up the threads that turned into a rope and carefully listened to the rumors coming down the Vía Layetana, the leaks from the Central District commissary over what Puig had stated: admitting he was the perpetrator of the bomb blasts in Pelayo Street and in Granja Royal. It remained unclear who was responsible, or who was paying him, although he admitted he had done it for money—someone whose name he was covering up through fear or agreement had taken him by the hand to plant a few petards in return for a few pesetas.

And Amador, an old hand in this sort of skullduggery, walked around Barcelona with premonitions of the bullet with his name on it being halfway to his back already, stopping to drink a *café con leche* when he could find somebody to pay for it and asking questions here and there, in the shade of the bananas, under a sun that scarcely warmed him, getting into mysterious conversations in shacks and the corners of bars, in doorways where his friends the whores would make room for him to work, although he interrupted the interrogations with his deathly hacking cough. And he made notes in his little black notebook, writing things like how the bombs placed in Simón Aller Street that had caused damage to the Captain General's office had left a strange epilogue behind. Why, when General Milans del Bosch looked out to survey the damage, did Antonio Soler, alias the Majorcan, K's right-hand man, appear at his side, disguised as a policeman, accompanied by two men who really were policemen, and tell the Captain General that he was convinced that the bombs had been planted there by union members? What was the Majorcan doing there a few minutes after the blast? How did he know what he did not know?

So Amador went from one place to another, riding the streetcars for free, showing his CNT card to the unionized conductors and inspectors and hinting he was on a mission.

He kept on tracking down the strange things that were turning up, like the fact that a few hours before the bombs went off in the Captain General's office two women left their home in the middle of Chinatown and in the middle of the night, carrying bundles, reaching the Ramblas then crossing over the Plaza de la Paz and from there finding their way to the back alley . . . Who were the women? Were those bundles the petards that were to go off a short while later?

And he managed to get some bourgeois journalists who had some respect for him to tell him during dinner—and he watched them eat without being invited to do the same with his stomach tying itself in knots as it remembered his hours of doing without food—that the city had been inundated with anonymous threats of bomb attacks on bosses and government offices.

Amador could swear that König's band was behind the bomb attacks, that the threats and offers of protection came simultaneously from the same place, K's office in Rambla de las Flores. The Baron was trying to create a climate in which military intervention on behalf of the bosses' organization would be justified, and to a certain extent he was succeeding, because it was the anarchist groups who were getting most of the blame in the pages of the city's newspapers—regardless of journalists who were trying to break through the smoke screen set up by the conversative press in a city where tensions were getting more and more embittered.

The Aztec Karate Kid

So the Boy Scout of Nonexistent Cities just might smash the bottle of Cuervo Special Reserve Tequila with his cane to get the necessary silence, shutting up the trio playing *boleros* and even a distant jukebox in the bar next door, while he feels his bladder is about to burst with fright.

The pieces of glass and the liquor would be splattered down the guy's white shirt, and he would not be staring at a hopalong detective story writer one step away from schizophrenia and shitting himself with fright, but at the unrivaled, unbeaten and paradoxical, widely feared and slandered Aztec Karate Kid.

Which is the sumbitchest cantina? And who is the sumbitchest sumbitch in that cantina? My cooperative friends would point me toward La Perla and to the skinny guy in the white shirt, with the grim features and the elusive look and a kind of strange lump about waist-high, like the man himself.

And I might be on the edge of one of the clichés in the literature I write, that counterviolence has to be totally irrational in order to have any effect. I would have run through my previous characterizations (the Telmex Runaway, the E.T. of the Wild Frontier, the Boy Scout of Nonexistent Cities, the Man Who Interrogates Surgeons) to this one, which, for all its sins, is rather stale, and which seems to me will not do for very long. This version of reality would be called The Aztec Karate Kid, as could be plainly seen, because the hairs of my mustache would be standing on end, and my lips would tremble as I spoke.

"What's up?" the injured party would say, and with reason.

"I asked you a question."

"Pardon me, but I didn't quite catch it," the killer might answer, victim of a sudden attack of traditional Mexican good manners.

That means that it might work after all.

"I asked you if you knew a smuggler they call Jesús, Jesús Ronco."

"No, no way."

"Ah, what the hell, because I've just made him up . . . but I'm sure you know somebody who wants to tell me what happened to the gringas last month. The gringa they killed and the other one, the basketball players."

"And if instead of smashing bottles you'd care to pony up for one?"

"What would you like it to be?"

Here the killer might make a show of his sense of humor, shaking the bits of glass here and there, smelling the shirt and saying:

"Same again, my good man, Cuervo Special Reserve."

That would be enough for the noise in the cantina, which had died down for a few seconds, to rise again; for the onlookers who would like to have seen me dead to console themselves with a half-baked anecdote, and for the killer in the white shirt and the Aztec Karate Kid (your humble servant) to strike up a private conversation, well away from the bar.

"They'd told me about you, the goddamn asshole of a writer who goes around asking things, hobbling along hereabouts. You're really crazy, aren't you?"

"A bit," I might say with a smile.

"You see, you don't ask about things like that around here, my friend. Around here you don't ask anything. Did those gringas mean something to you?" And he would not wait for the answer. "Because you just don't ask. It's not that anybody knows a fucking thing, it's just that the one who does know sees others talking and gets to wonder and the one who doesn't know, what's he going to make an asshole out of himself for, just to get into problems he doesn't need? Now then . . ." And here he would open the bottle of tequila, pour a few drops into the cap, sniff it, and then taste it with his tongue.

"Much better than going around smashing it, my friend. And so, like I was telling you, the guy who doesn't know is best off staying that way, unless there's something in it for him, and if there's something in it for him, he'd be best off without it . . . S'good," he would end up saying, looking at the tequila.

"This guy talks to bottles," I would say to myself, overwhelmed with the things I come across without finding anything. And the guy would confirm my theory:

"That means you shouldn't ask and shouldn't answer a fucking thing, but while we're on it, I'll tell you there were four of them, the one in charge was a gringo, and the two they talk about so much, don't waste your time. They've gone. There was a lot of shit, a lot of noise. Romero and Mike have gone," he might say, looking at the crow decorating the label and raising his glass to drink to him. "I'm only telling you this because you're an asshole I've taken a liking to. Enough of an asshole to go around asking questions out loud and smashing bottles. And I'm a bigger asshole for going around answering them," he might say, this time to the tequila glass as he fills it, a little bit, before downing it.

"Thanks a lot, man, they told me you were a sumbitch, but . . ."

"I'm such a sumbitch that I told you what I told you; if I was less of a sumbitch, softer, if I was a wimp, I'd have fucked up your other leg with this," he might say, showing his .38, which he would take out from his waistband and put on the table. And I, within my characterization as the Aztec Karate Kid, which I like so much I'm thinking of taking it up permanently, might pick up the gun and stir the contents of my tequila glass with the barrel, put it to one side and knock the tequila back in one gulp. Just the opposite of a special reserve tequila.

And I would then say to myself: is this literature? There are those sort of novels that do not get written because they do not want to be written. So I would have gone to Ciudad Juárez to make a lot of trips, mostly to the inside of my panic, and then as a literary transvestite I would have changed my skin as the E.T. of the Wild Frontier who would be transformed into the Telmex Runaway who in turn would be revealed as the Chinese Detective, to turn into the Boy Scout of Nonexistent Cities and, in an orgasmic moment, into the Aztec Karate Kid.

And a short while later Karen might open her eyes and, contemplating my Pancho Villa–style mustache growing unevenly on both sides, ask:

"Who are you?"

"The Shadow, my dear," I would say. What the hell else can you say in crucial moments like that? Even so, she would just sink back into a comatose sleep, without giving me time to explain how fucking well it went, the great theatrical gesture of soaking the barrel of a .38 in a tequila glass and how all that craziness started when I saw her insult a referee.

The Dead Man

When the bombs started to go off, Angel del Hierro came back from the dead and turned up, in the middle of the afternoon, at the house of the woman who usually did his washing for him. The white sheets were shaking in the yard, throwing a party for ghosts in the breeze.

Without saying anything much, apart from commenting on the pernicious times they were all going through (Inés, the washerwoman, had a husband working in the Girona Ironworks who had been out of work for seven weeks due to a lockout), Del Hierro picked up two white shirts, three pairs of socks, a red and black handkerchief, and some greenish corduroy trousers with the knees very much worn out, and he gave the woman twice what he owed her. Because bad times were most likely on the way.

Inés, who had a hooked nose and elegant breasts, according to what her husband said, did not read the papers and could not tell Angel he was dead, that they had dumped him in a skiff in the middle of Barcelona harbor, leaving the body to be lost at sea. Inés would have liked to have borne witness to this resurrection story, but . . .

He looked serious to her, because life did not smile on Angel del Hierro Maillén, whose son would change his surname to Fierro on arriving in the Americas in 1942. Just the opposite. Moreover, for a long, long time he had not been happy, or he could not remember the last time he had been. Ever since Julia Goldman had died in his arms from tuberculosis in 1912 happiness had vanished for him, only stubbornness was left. Inés, however, did appreciate the habitual friendliness that in the case of sad people does produce pointless smiles and listless expressions. And Del Hierro was sad, although not because of the news of his death, because he had not read the papers either during the last eleven days that he had spent in the Modelo prison under an assumed name.

Del Hierro had been taken in after a raid organized by Inspector Más on a café in the Sarriá district, in which two guns (one of them his), had turned up on a table. Del Hierro had gone to the café to see a one-armed man who ran a like-minded group called the Sons of the Soviet, with whom he was interested in carrying out an operation aimed at one of the bosses' organization's collectors. The appointment was never kept, and he just about caught sight of a one-armed man among the people who watched him being taken away. They chained him to eight other workers and he walked through the Barcelona streets at nightfall toward the Modelo prison. Hundreds of workers had been arrested that day, and they had not gone through the usual procedures in the police stations, so he ended up in Workshop No. 3

under a false name and protected by a letter of recommendation he had forged himself, in which a boss from León recommended him to the boss of a marble works in Barcelona.

There was something sensational about his entry into Workshop No. 3. He realized then that it was not specially put on for them, that the same thing always happened when they welcomed new prisoners. A choir of old cons doing the prison chores began to sing the repertoire of revolutionary songs, like "Sons of the People" and "The Red Flag" and other lesser known ones that were little ditties currently in fashion, but with clearly subversive lyrics.

Del Hierro saw a few faces he recognized, but kept away from them. His comrades, realizing that he was not suffering from one of the attacks of craziness and isolation to which the sad and quiet motor mechanic was prone, but rather that he was up to something, let him be. But one of the more malicious ones, to confirm what was happening, asked him his false name and under the latter he received the food provided by money from the Pro-Prisoners Committee that was bought at the Collado tavern opposite the Modelo. In Workshop No. 3 there were about a hundred prisoners to whom the Barcelona organization paid full wages. Del Hierro refused to collect wages and sign up on the list, saying he was not a member of the Confederation with a wink to the man in charge of the Pro-Prisoners Committee, all for the benefit of the possible informers that might be around in the workshop. But there were more than a couple of hundred prisoners to feed and there were nearly 200,000 unemployed workers on the streets because of the bosses' organization's lockout.

As he was trying to slip by unnoticed, Del Hierro never knew what a few (at least half a dozen) fellow prisoners knew: that he was dead, and that they thought that was the main reason for his isolation. It is a well-known fact that dead people do not have social lives. This round of mistaken perceptions continued, because some did not know anything; because others thought that the dead man (who was not) wanted to stay that way; and the dead man wanted to also, so that the guards would not identify him and throw a very fat book at him.

For this reason, Angel del Hierro did not know that the Baron's gang had his house surrounded for four of those eleven days, that they had waited for him on the way out of Meneses sheet-metal plant where he worked (then they got bored and picked on another dead man, as they were anxious to collect the thousand pesetas the bosses' organization had put on his head), and finally, that the press had declared him dead, with a skull smashed by blows from a piece of piping. And that he had been officially dead since Tuesday.

For this reason, surrounded by his comrades' silence and cut off by the halo emanating from the story of his death, he went through the names of the main industrial cities in the world, trying to put them in alphabetical order: Glasgow after Berlin but before Orizaba . . .

Eleven days later, he was released just as he had been taken in, to make way for newly detained prisoners.

On getting out of jail and thinking these were not good times for going back to the works—he had to check his friends out a bit more, as somebody had blown the whistle about the meeting in the Sarriá bar—Del Hierro went to pick up clean clothes, to shed the smell of jail and fear. In his fresh white shirt and corduroy trousers, he walked down to the harbor. Some were saying it was to see his corpse, others, the rational ones, that it was to get a breath of fresh sea air. In Barceloneta he bought *España Nueva* and found out that Amador, alias the Flea, the journalist who was closest to his heart, was writing an article about the bombs going off all over Barcelona.

Amador was right in what he hinted at between the lines, that the Baron's gang was behind the bombings. Del Hierro could swear to it. He had found out a lot in the last few months that made him think so. And once he had come to that conclusion and remembered that he had two hundred pesetas saved, tied up in a handkerchief hanging at the top of a lamppost in the workers' neighborhood, Del Hierro set himself a task. A personal task that committed him until it was accomplished, or he died halfway through it. An obligation, a commission. A task worthy of a dead man who had come back to life. A task that, as could be guessed at by any reader familiar with dime novels or by anyone bound by ethical commitments, consisted in attempting to take the life of the mysterious Baron, the man who, without Del Hierro knowing it, had already killed him. He had decided to kill his murderer. A case of a metaphysical settling of accounts.

The Apartment-Block Housebreaker

It might be the music from the third LP, the one prosaically labeled with a Roman numeral *III*, the one on which Carlos Santana was portrayed wearing a *sarape* from Saltillo and sang "Nobody That I Can Depend On" in a pained voice, the one with congo player Michael Carabello and Coke Escovedo, which is in my head when I get to the scene of action. A special song for all Santana fans, for being simple, obsessive, and lucid, where the lyrics are rehashed to form the bilingual phrase: *No tengo a nadie that I can depend on* and the musical phrase tails off into a Hendrix-style guitar and a multiple base rhythm of kettledrums, congas, and other weird percussion instruments. Then Santana takes up the lead guitar line on the melodious phrase, and enriches it again and again.

The same record that put "Guajira" into the top one

hundred. An eclectic record with only nine tracks on it and that, among other things, gave thanks to the Zopilote Villanueva brothers for their affection. Album cover with flying pegasi and psychedelic colors. A record in which Santana was losing his way with his neurons, although he never lost that marvelous empathy with his guitar.

With the music of that record in my head, with the phrase *No tengo a nadie that I can depend on* repeating itself in the brain-box, I might go along to an apartment block on 5 de Febrero Avenue. The trail leading there would have turned out to be quite easy, a contact with a Ciudad Juárez policeman who badly needed to take his wife's sewing machine out of hock, who would have identified Mike and Romero for a few bucks; for a few more he would have handed over their files, with photos and all, and for a last few he would have checked with the traffic department to give the license plate number of Romero's old Mustang and an address, this very one.

I might have spent two days keeping watch from the taco joint opposite, using up all the Buddhist tricks of patience and concentration, all of it learned from watching a series of kung fu movies. A fixed stare, a cigarette every half hour, expressionless eyes homed in on the target, without the dust, traffic, or sun diverting their attention.

By the second day, the waiter might ask:

"Are you waiting for your wife to come out?"

But that would be the moment in which a drum roll can be heard and then the guitar slowly comes in, as though climbing up a cotton waterfall, and I will take my time over answering:

"My wife's a bitch."

This would be a good argument for him, enough to place another Coronita in front of me without asking, and even to give me some salted peanuts.

On that very afternoon, up to my ass in kung fu Buddhism, I might go to a hardware store, buy a crowbar, and go up to apartment 6, which would fortunately be out of the way of the neighbors, on a landing at the top of the stairs, so I could wrench the door to the absent Romero's (or whoever it belongs to) apartment open, having now become the Apartment-Block Housebreaker.

I would not even have to get the shotgun out of the canvas bag I would be carrying it in, because Nico Romero's apartment would be so empty that the dust would have settled on the television and there would be a pile of ants milling around a roll left there two weeks previously.

The bedroom wall would be covered with photos from *Playboy*. I might pick out a favorite, Samantha Fox, whose spectacular bust seems to threaten the photographer. Then I would fill up my canvas bag with every scrap of paper, photo, newspaper cutting, document, or used Kleenex that might appear in the drawers, on the kitchen table, under the mattress. Life, as all writers know, leaves a trail of paper behind.

I would say goodbye to the apartment by kicking the busted door shut. I would take a taxi. The Apartment-Block Housebreaker will go happily along to Camelia's with his loot, to write a novel and to check over a load of crap.

Back in Camelia's, I would spread my treasure all over the bed and the floor. The photos first. Nico Romero on a police ID card from Sabinas, Coahuila, looking up at me. If that was him, then he was also the one in the middle of the photo with two fat women, grabbing an ass with one hand and holding up a can of beer with the other. And while I would be staring at Nico Romero, other questions would come into my head: *When was Espartero's statue put up? Was that phrase already in use in the 1920s? Did the blue tram really go up near the Tibidabo hill, or did it just go to Valvidriera? Where was Valvidriera?*

Another photo: Nico Romero, ex-cop from Sabinas, while doing some target practice, a gringo about my age by his side, with a face like a detective story writer. Supermarket checkout receipts, mostly from the frozen food section, some shampoo and dog food (??). *Why did Antonio Amador never have any money? He earned half pay at* El Progreso, *didn't he?* Bank statements from October and November 1992, worked out on the stubs of a Banco Internacional checkbook. Four million and eleven million pesos paid in; a check for eight million in the middle of November. *He needed a good map of Barcelona from the 1920s.* Dry-cleaning bills. Love letters from a northern woman with bad spelling. A lot of them, so I would put off reading them until I had time to do it carefully. And I would wonder: how had he gone away and left all this behind? *And in Barcelona, an ornate style along the lines of Ponson du Terrail or Eugene Sue: descriptions and dialogues, backup information for the context, lots and lots of adjectives. Things are noisy, their sounds hurtful, everything is dismal and there is not a wooden floor that does not creak.* A phone number written on a Kleenex, a phone number on the back of a postcard, belonging to an insurance agent. *And wasn't good old Antonio "the Flea" Amador eating up my poor grandfather? It wasn't my grandfather, a shadow among shadows,* more of a shadow than this Nico Romero who had bought four cans of black cockroach spray on November 28 in a store in El Paso. *Four?* I would ask myself, abandoning the Apartment-Block Housebreaker to make way for . . .

Guests

The big old apartment was on the fifth floor, right on Paseo de Gracia, but the old money that had purchased it was long gone. There were damp stains on the wallpaper, running across the walls like scars. Iribarne had inherited it from an uncle, and his salary as a correspondent for *El Sol* in Madrid had not run to anything more than keeping the locks and windows in place. Even so, the mixture of old money and new poverty gave the place a decadent and exotic air that the bearded journalist did his best to keep up: lacquered Javanese furniture bought in the harbor off an English ship that had brought it from Turkey, a Russian samovar with steam billowing from it, a collection of well-thumbed movie magazines and a pile of watercolors by the best and poorest painters in Barcelona, given as payment in kind for meals and breakfasts, and that would make Iribarne rich as the years went by.

"He's an excellent fellow, he's so brave that at times it scares me. You know, that absolutely Spanish, almost suicidal sort of bravery. Do you realize that it's a national characteristic? Only the Russians and us make them like that."

"What would you say about the Afghans? The Armenians? The Peruvians?"

"I don't know."

"Well then, don't talk rubbish," said Francisco Madrid in a cutting tone. He was a permanently bad-tempered, dour journalist, whose head was covered with gray hair, despite his not yet reaching thirty.

"But Amador's got more balls than the horse on the Espartero statue," said the host, referring to the sculpted testicles on the horse bearing the general in Madrid.

"Yes, but you must admit he's a bit mad, around the bend, that he's lost his marbles a bit. Look at that article he wrote about why the lions in the Barcelona zoo never last long. The poor things used to die right away, and this ruffian comes to the conclusion that Barcelona is a bad place for wild animals, that here they die of boredom or disgust, getting up the backs of all the monarchists in Paralelo. It wasn't enough for him to be hated by the bosses, the monarchists, the police, the shipping line owners who have him on a special blacklist, so he can't get on a boat in Barcelona after the Taya Company business; as if that wasn't enough, he has to make all the nationalistic botanists and shopkeepers angry."

"He wasn't far wrong. The used to throw any old shit for the lions to eat, that used to do away with them."

"That's not what Amador hinted at."

Iribarne was dressed in a slightly frayed silk dressing gown that had too many tassels on it. The wages he got, as Barcelona-based editor-in-chief of a chain of Madrid newspapers that were liberal and flirted with republicanism, were enough to eat well on, but no more. His companion Francisco Madrid was a correspondent for the Madrid-based *El Socialista*, which meant he earned a bit less than half the other's wages. Both had been founding members of the journalists' union, along with Amador and Angel Pestaña himself, who had been editor six months previously of the now banned *Solidaridad Obrera*.

The doorbell made Madrid get up from the Persian sofa with the stuffing falling out of it and walk over to the hallway to open the door, making the floorboards creak as he did so. Antonio Amador was gasping for breath in the doorway.

"For Christ's sake, it's only five floors up. Next time we'll make appointments with you in the middle of the street."

"The street's no good for that," said the little journalist as he came in and took his jacket off. He threw himself onto the sofa and began to cough.

"We were just talking about you," said Madrid, trying to look to one side so as not to see how Amador's coughing tore his lungs apart.

"And what were you saying then?" asked Amador, once he had recovered.

"I was saying that you were mad. Iribarne, who likes you a bit more, said you weren't scared of anything."

"I'm only scared of Koch," said Amador.

"Who are we talking about?" Iribarne asked, somewhat confused, as he brought some cups in with him.

"Koch, the one with the bacillus," Madrid replied with a smile. "He's the only one this fellow's scared of."

"Aren't we being a bit bombastic? Even a bit pretentious,

I'd say, drunk with stories of mysterious gangs, where the chief is a crowned head, here where the bosses' organization is the monarchy's first line of defense, a pile of gutless dukes and counts who are no good even for looking after country estates."

"Laugh all you like," Amador answered. "König runs a network of blackmail, murder, and dirty tricks that would make Alfonso XIII blanch at the thought. He's behind the bombings. He comes and goes with the police turning a blind eye."

"They told us that's what you wanted to see us about, so we could tell you what we knew. But a nod's as good as a wink to a blind man. What are you up to? What do you know? Do you know who's planting the bombs?"

"Got anything to eat around here?" the little journalist asked the host.

"Nothing, the cat eats it all."

"Well then, do you two know anything I haven't got on that swine?" Iribarne laughed, and poured the tea.

"Don't look at me. You know as much as I do."

"I do, maybe something new. But first I want to know when we can print it."

"Next week. All together. I'll start off in *España Nueva* and then you two carry on."

"I think the attempt on Pestaña's life last week was their work. What's more, I can tell you who were the three who fired on him. Soler, the Monkey, and the Argentine. Pestaña just got in from Madrid and was in a house in Pueblo Seco. Don't ask me where or what he was doing, you must know that better than I do. As he was leaving the house, three men opened fire on him from the opposite pavement, but Pestaña's friends were no fools, and fired back so that the three men had to make a run for it in a car. As ever, he was saved by a hair's breadth. Six or seven shots. The rest is old hat, stuff I passed on to you last month."

"And what do you know about the death of Angel del Hierro? That story about how he was found in a boat, and there was nobody on it . . ."

Amador put six spoons of sugar into his tea, and began to tell his story . . .

A few hours later, Antonio Amador was wandering along the streets of Barcelona with his hands in the back pockets of his trousers. Foolish, because you could not have your hand ready to draw your gun if the need for it should arise, but as his friend Llarch said: "A worker's only horn of plenty is his ass, which is why you put your hands inside the lining of your trousers to warm them up." As he went along Rambla del Centro, a pigeon crapped on the sleeve of his jacket, whose elbows had been darned hundreds of times. It was not his day. It had been how long? Let me see. Breakfast the day before yesterday, supper in Susana's house . . . he had gone without solid food since supper two days ago, tricking his stomach with *café con leche*, tea with lots of sugar, and a gin that a Russian typographer had bought him, who told him Polack jokes and showed him a photo of the stairways in Odessa during the 1905 riots, and another one of his granddaughter, a little girl with ringlets in her hair.

When he took the tram that went up to Valvidriera, the blue tram, he thought he was going to have to steal a scarf for himself. The ice-cold wind came in through the broken windows. You could see the Tibidabo mountain in the distance.

From the top you could see Barcelona. A strange and peaceful Barcelona. He looked at the semi-deserted surroundings of the Tibidabo amusement park blasted by the wind, and then walked over to the hall of mirrors. The woman in charge knew him, and let him in. Amador looked for the mirror that made him grow and looked at himself for a bit before going out into the cold again.

In the middle of the promenade in the amusement park, opposite the coin-operated binoculars, with the church on the left and a few yards away from the café-restaurant. A tiny little world, on a mountaintop from which you could see the city, and make believe you owned it. He walked over to one of the binoculars, but he did not have any spare change to put in it. Even without optical assistance, you could see all of the Ensanche district and the old city right down to the sea, from here. The cable cars turned up quite empty. A bad time and a bad day.

A man wearing a corduroy jacket and rope-soled shoes approached him.

"Cheers, comrade. I was told to tell you that the bombings during the leather-tanners' strikes, the one in the San Martín neighborhood and the other one in the Rafael Turró works in Pueblo Nuevo, were nothing to do with us, nor was the one in the Captain General's office."

"There were no victims, the damage was limited," Amador summed up.

The man waited to see if Amador had anything else to say. Then he went on:

"It was said that we were the groups behind it, but I've been commissioned to tell you that it was not us. It wasn't anyone from the Barcelona groups. The organization does not control us, neither do we work for it. There are things that we do together, and others we do apart. Nearly all of us are with the Confederation, but the membership card doesn't oblige us to stay with the union. Other bomb blasts were ours, or done by others who think like we do, but not those ones, those were not the work of anarchists. I have spoken."

Amador looked at him warily, he seemed far too serious.

"Then who was it?"

"Ask whoever paid a lottery-ticket seller they call Snub-Nosed Rosie to plant them."

"What do you know about the death of Angel del Hierro?"

"Just that he's not dead."

Now it was the man's turn to smile at a disconcerted Amador, who started rummaging pointlessly in his pockets for a cigarette, to give him time to rephrase his questions. But by the time he felt like resuming, he realized that the man with the green corduroy jacket was walking over to the restaurant.

The journalist did not even try to follow him, he was exhausted. Tiredness had descended on him like a ton of bricks. Gathering up some strength from somewhere, he watched night fall over the city and took the cable car back down again. The dark night, the witching hour. On the Gran Vía, a little girl with braids dressed like a red checkered rag doll took him by the hand and led him off to a big ramshackle house that was broken up into lots of inner patios. She left him there and went off, skipping. The Flea wished he had a cigarette on him. He wanted one so much he did not realize he was suddenly in the company of Angel Pestaña, the most wanted man in Barcelona, who was washing his face in a sink.

Pestaña offered him some tobacco and cigarette papers while he dried himself with a white cloth. He then took

Amador along a maze of corridors between the patios until they came to a small room between floors.

"The house belongs to some friends," he said, as if he was excusing himself.

Angel Pestaña was so famous during those months, a bit before his spectacular escape and journey to the Soviet Union, that songs were sung about him in the Barcelona music halls with the lockout as background.

My man's got two pictures of Pestaña/hung up on the wall/ He reads the Nueva España*/and says Gorki and Soviet/They're saying in the neighborhood we'll get to Communism yet/that I owe him half of every penny I get/but when I talk of marriage/ he tells me through and through/It's the lockout, the marital lockout for you.*

The little journalist and the CNT leader went into the room with their arms around each other. There was a dismantled clock on the kitchen table, on top of an old newspaper. Pestaña sat down and picked up some tweezers and a jeweler's loup, which he placed in his right eye.

"I haven't even got any coffee."

They called him the White Angel, perhaps in contrast to Del Hierro, who was known in some union circles as the Black Angel. Amador could not be too formal with him, as they had been through a lot together. When Pestaña took charge of editing *La Soli* in 1918, the Flea had been his ace reporter. When Pestaña had started off the campaign to unmask Bravo Portillo, Amador was the man who searched for and found the documents, the one who risked his life to put pressure on Snub-Nosed Bellés and get Bravo's handwritten notes out of him—messages he sent to the German submarines about the departure of merchant ships. Amador was the one who drafted the articles together with Pestaña, cheering him on over his shoulder, urging him to give the screw another turn, to go for it. It was Amador who threw the scandal into the spotlight, that the head of the Barcelona police Special Brigade was a German agent.

"With Maestre Laborde as governor, there is nothing to do but wait before the backlash hits us. Not whether there will be a backlash, but when—under what real or contrived excuse they'll come down on us like a pack of dogs."

Maestre Laborde had been governor for a couple of weeks. The article Amador received him with in *La Soli*, during one of the rare moments in which it circulated legally, was simple and straight to the point: "A mediocre man, barely intelligent but headstrong, who brings with him the unenviable reputation of having pacified Seville at the cost of trying to destroy the labor unions." That resulted in more charges against him. If he stayed alive and his lawyers got no better, Amador had a few months in jail to look forward to when the trial was over and they came to settle accounts with him.

"We're under siege," Pestaña asserted. "The lockout's already affecting 200,000 of our comrades throughout Catalonia, and we're going to have to eat the soles of our shoes. There isn't a single legal union. They want to go back to individual contracts, the gangs and the police are attacking people collecting union dues. To go out and collect is to risk your life. Our comrades are going mad, they look toward aligned groups, but the answer isn't there. If we can't maneuver mass action, there will be an all-out war between armed bands, ours and theirs. And they'll do away with us like vermin, with starvation as well as gunshots. They're eating in makeshift soup kitchens in the streets."

"Where?" Amador asked him, frankly embarrassed at not knowing such an essential piece of information.

"Opposite Boquería, in the San Antonio market, in the waiters' union . . ."

Pestaña touched a gear and the clockwork began to move. He then lifted his eyes up from his task, as if it were inevitable that it would work, and went on to another topic.

"Antonio, you know more than we do. You're like a lonely vulture, you know more than the very organization that has put all its trust in us for this story," Pestaña said in that dry and friendly whispering tone of voice that was typical of his contributions, even his admonitions.

Amador felt overwhelmed. Pestaña, as ever, was right, but he was not going to tell the CNT's White Angel how to keep his anger in check, how to write journalism without biting your tongue.

"The organization is commissioning you to make sure all this information becomes public knowledge. I'll give you what I've got. If you can't get it to me in the next few days because of the way things are going, get it to Bajatierra in Madrid, he'll make sure it comes out in *España Nueva*, and apart from him get a copy to someone close to Bueso, he'll know how to get it around Barcelona. That's if we're all still alive in a week's time. If we're not, it makes no difference. If they kill you, or you die because you won't take care of that tuberculosis, because you take no damned notice of it, it makes no difference, you come here dead and run the story. You leave it to somebody and he runs it. Tell Nin, that kid from the market workers' union, or Iribarne, who's as crazy as you are and does us a favor now and again. It's the same difference."

Amador nodded. He'd run that story on the Baron dead or alive. Dead if he had to.

"Look, the first thing that came to us," Pestaña said, lighting up a cigarette and putting down the tweezers, "it's one of those things that low-life stiffs and stool pigeons do, the ones who will just as easily give a worker away, who will sell a comrade for a peseta, who are ready to sell information to the union organizers. It was a letter written about October 24, a letter that was delivered to *La Soli* signed by a Frenchman called André Penón, who had been an informer and was feeling guilty. I asked around and they told me he was a drunk." He took the letter out from inside a book and handed it over to Amador.

If it is necessary to provide some proof, I can affirm that I was in the service of the German subject Keniz, who hires Antonio Soler, aka the Majorcan, to spy on the unions and carry out attacks on them if necessary.

They got their money from a boss who I heard was called Miró, who used to meet with Keniz in No. 80 Paseo de Gracia, on the corner with Mallorca.

I can provide proof of all this, having infiltrated and knowing that they were definitely carrying out an attack on the workers.

"Miró, of course, is the bosses' organization's treasurer, Miró i Trepat. I've got Miró stitched up everywhere."

"There's more," Pestaña said. "Conrado Gimeno, a habitual drunk, also came up to the organization and offered to spill the beans for a glass of wine. Frankly, he's a shady character, we know he offered to be a gunman for the militia, and even they turned him down."

"He's an ex-policeman, and lately he's been going around trying to sell information to journalists," Amador said, who remembered the man.

"Anyway, there's another letter from him here, that confirms that the bosses' organization is paying König's band's wages. Fifteen pesetas a day, no less." He handed another crumpled piece of paper over, which Amador unfolded carefully.

"They pay me less at the newspaper, and they're killing me off more slowly," said little Amador with a smile.

"They want to declare war and get the military on their side. They're after a dictatorship where the generals and the bosses' organization are hand-in-glove with each other, and the unions liquidated. They're after provoking the hotheads among us, the kids in the groups, who are just itching to grab a gun and start firing back."

"Anything else?" Amador asked.

"A friend who's burning the midnight oil and is fed up with all the crap in the police has passed some information on to us. The band has a few high-level cops on its payroll: Inspector Serrano, with whom König has a deal going, so he intercepts and opens all the mail in the Francia railway station, and Inspector Luis León, who gets a complimentary payoff."

"He's just that sort of poorly paid policeman—or rather, poor policeman—who are badly dressed, with a threadbare suit held together by grease stains, who want to get into the news. It's nothing to worry about. What should bother us is the connection between the band and Arlegui. Will he let them get away with it?"

"Would you trust a colonel in the Civil Guard who is also the police chief in Barcelona?"

Amador shrugged his shoulders.

"It's urgent. Don't beat about the bush. Grab whatever you've got and go right ahead. And don't think of signing it. Don't even think about it. D'you hear?" Pestaña turned around to hug the little journalist in the entrance to the small room. The sad and lanky man from León was a head taller. "I think you should go into hiding. This is no time for being seen in the newspaper."

"I need the money, Angel."

Pestaña smiled with that sad smile that made him so well loved among the workers in Barcelona, who know that sad smiles come straight from the heart.

Amador began to cough, because he felt like crying. It was true, they were all going to get killed.

"You're going to die, Antonio, you should go to Castile, to the dry sunshine. The weather in this city's bad for you. You need to get some treatment."

"And where could I go where they want me more?" the Flea answered him.

"You're great, dammit, but I told you to learn a trade, that journalism's no good in times like these. We've got an organization with 200,000 men and we seemed invincible, but we just seemed to be. Do you remember, Antonio, just after the strike in La Canadiense?"

The Flea, however, had been lost in thought since Pestaña's first comment, in a dream, thinking about the tense afternoons in the newspaper office, when what *Solidaridad Obrera* had to say was bread and butter for all of Barcelona.

"Journalism's great, Angelito, the rest is just lies. I won't give it up even when anarchy comes, then I'll write about bullfights, the theater, dance, jails, I'll write dime novels about just what this shitty Barcelona was like for those with short memories," the little journalist answered, and then he went off without turning back. As opposed to other mortals, he got bigger the further away he went.

Doctor X

Mindful that I might need to adopt a pop cultural characterization to read the letters written by the northern girl with bad spelling, dedicated to Nico Romero, former secret policeman from Sabinas, Coahuila—and nowadays my prime and favorite suspect—I would opt for Doctor X, who, according to my poor memory, was a character from comic books who specialized in heart disease and parapsychology. I might have opted to be a young poet from Octavio Paz's *Vuelta* magazine, but frankly that would be a choice that would haunt my worst nightmares. It would only be after making this wise decision, in the womblike security of my room in Camelia's, where I'm not only looked after but liked as well (the man in charge came up to me yesterday, offering to let me pay by the month, which works out cheaper), that I would tug at my beard and, just as I did when I read Quevedo's sonnets to the Philosophy Faculty students in the late 1960s, speak out loud and hear myself in someone else's words:

Nico baby, you told me you were going to be with lola so i dident wate for you becoz i new i cant never wate for you like that.

You just see if i weight for you agen even if you ask a thowsand times becoz i dont trust you no moor i aint never gonna do it agen even if you say pleeze and go on yore nees you never shod up then you dont sho up never and thats wot im thinkin so come tell me im rong. Your Emilia, allwaze.

Reading this would be quite an experience for Doctor X, worth putting down the experiment for and taking an alcoholic break with rum and Coca-Cola from the Room 11 mini-bar where, as the days go by, I would have built up a supply of all you need to make the best Cuba Libres in Ciudad Juárez, including the ice, lemon slices, and Classic Coke.

And then, after the first letter, the second one:

Nico, i no you hang arownd with the reel bad guys and yore fuking yore naybor in number five and she dont like it becoz she likes chiks but sez cool baby and yore her man an jest so yore hapy and you give her dollers becoz yore an asshole like evry matcho and you dont no. Emilia.

And into a trance by now, I would go on to the third letter:

Nicolas im riting you a letta becoz i dont no wot to think no moor after yesturday, wen you sed i was reel sinseer but i was trying to run yore life and didnt let you do the things a man has to do but i dont see how on toppa it you can go around torchuring folks you fuk a woman hoo aint no woman. Emilia an im reel sinseer.

And I would think that Emilia was not far wrong, that sincerity is a fine thing, and it's best not to go around screwing your neighbors.

Enter the Beggar

The late afternoon's light was fading on one of those days in which, for Amador, the difference between night and day was beginning to lose all meaning, becoming like the restless and endless continuum in the quest for truth in a city that was watching its last hours drift away in an hourglass.

Worn out, he went around Chinatown, quickly then slowly, looking for someone who would give him a cigarette, or some woman who would let him share the armchair in her room, or the carpet by her bed. He had wandered over to the top of the Baja de San Pedro to see if he could find a face he knew around the closed-down woodworkers' union, when he suddenly found himself facing a beggar covered in sores, whose face could scarcely be made out behind a dirty rag. An organ grinder could be heard in the distance; following the sound with his eyes, Amador realized the street was dangerously empty. He tried to avoid the beggar, but the man lurched over to the middle of the pavement in eerie silence and leaned on a lamppost to stop Amador getting through the narrow alleyway. Antonio Amador knew he was close to death, and because of it he had that kind of mad bravery that few people are blessed with for long, that kind of absurd courage that goes with the best characters during the last few weeks of their lives. He raised his hands to make it clear he was not thinking of drawing his gun and smiled, expecting the beggar to pull out the hand he had tucked into a pouch, producing a huge club.

The beggar took out two cigarettes and gave one to the little journalist.

"You, sonny boy, are looking for the Baron von Shit, the monster, the Beast of Barcelona," he asserted, and lit his cigarette with a lighter whose flame illuminated his face in that lonely street.

Amador pushed his mouth up close to the lighter and lit his own. The beggar smelled of mildew. The journalist did not feel obliged to answer him.

"Tomorrow, at eight at night, I'll show you him."

"If I want to find the Baron I'll look for him in his offices on Rambla de las Flores. I'll walk in and put two bullets into him, fuckface."

"Yes, but you're not the sort who goes around shooting people, and others are. You're the sort who believes in strikes and newspapers, who looks on and talks about it afterward. If you want to see him, sonny boy, come with me to the front-row seats. Get a grandstand view of him, like the rich kids."

"I'm grateful, my friend, but if you want us to get killed

together, you'll have to call me something else. Men are measured by their balls, and in that case you're a long way behind, fleabag."

"Well look at that, a philosopher of life, *olé!*" the beggar said to him, before turning around and disappearing into the shadows.

The Traveling Irrationality Salesman

So I might walk along López Mateos Avenue, the other end of Lincoln Avenue, enjoying the neon glow on my face like the sun the rich enjoy in the tropics, the neon on the face of the frontier by night, when a beggar with leprosy will get in my way stretching out his hand to beg, and without giving me time to give him some loose change, he might suddenly say to me:

"You are trying to find out what happened to the gringas. Midnight cowboy, the bookhound. I've read every page of every one of your books, really cool . . . When I could still read."

"Did you like them?"

"A lot, especially the one about the secret policemen who eat one of their buddies without knowing it. Now that is the sumbitchest sumbitch of a book. Real ass-kicking realism."

Would I have written a book with that anecdote in it? I might wonder, stepping out of the beggar's reach a bit as I slip my hand into the canvas bag carrying my shotgun, which would have followed me faithfully since the day before.

"So what, then?"

"Nothing, just that I know about these things."

And then I would be transformed into the Traveling Irrationality Salesman, because this beggar in the real world (or *reel* world, as the case may be) would be far too like the literary beggar who crosses paths with Amador in the Baja de San Pedro. Too much for me not to feel uneasy, victim of a metaphysical scam, then, during that future night in Ciudad Juárez.

The beggar would have his neck covered in sores and abscesses, his pants torn at both knees, one end of his mustache eaten away by scabies, a baseball cap, and a blue canvas bag like mine over his shoulder.

"What sort of things?"

"That Mike killed one of the guys helping him and buried him along the Jiménez highway, at the 32 kilometer mark, next to a vineyard."

"Was it Nicolás? Nico Romero?"

"No, some other dude. Some drug scam, a few grams of coke here and there. They're pushers, friend . . ."

The intermittent sound of a police siren coming along would make the beggar scurry away and hide in the shadows, in the alley next to a toy store.

"That's it, Mr. Writer. Get out of here, make yourself real goddamn scarce. There's nothing in this for you. There's some bad shit going down. They kill for all kinds of bullshit here."

The patrol would go wailing along the avenue and I

would follow it with my eyes, watching its flashing lights. By the time I might have turned my eyes to look for the beggar, he would have vanished.

I would have to watch out for the shadows, for the shadows and metaphorical accidents in neon-lit Ciudad Juárez and over there in gas-lit Barcelona, where the Black Angel would be fading away and all the pieces would be coming together in a meaningless jigsaw puzzle.

You have to be overindulgent to think that a metaphor is something direct. An arrow homing in on a target painted in black on the wall. It is not. It is dangerous, double-edged material. It is an ambiguous resource. It is the writer who creates it, but it is the reader who reinterprets it, adapting it to his own very particular aches and pains. You do not even own the ribbon in the printer you use.

I would go back to the neon-lit avenue, hobbling along, the only pedestrian in a city full of cars, a firm believer in walking, in stubborn pedestrianism, a fervent admirer of miracles of will. Faithful to that adolescent musing that whenever you jumped into the void you would invariably end up somewhere, usually somewhere better than where you had started off from.

And I would turn my steps toward the hospital, knowing full well that she, Karen, would be outside this novel; a person, not a character. People play by their own hidden rules, their own fateful vocations; they are strange, they do not behave as they ought to. They turn around the wrong corner. They wake up when they want to, they open their eyes under the influence of melodramatic reasons, remote from life itself, which as everybody knows is perfectly recorded only in fiction. But just as I might be sure about Karen Turner's situation, I might not be so sure about the place that I, José Daniel Fierro, would have in this plot. I would not know myself as a person or a character. And if that is the way it is, and if there might be some kind of trick or trap, there would be some other sumbitch who would be writing a novel about me, who would be writing about me as a character: the E.T. of the Wild Frontier, the Aztec Karate Kid, by now transformed into the one and only, mixed-up and perplexed Traveling Irrationality Salesman.

The House of Death

The city had gone mad, and Angel Samblancat, perhaps its most careless and apocalyptic poet, was writing the following in *Vida Social*:

Following the cracks of gunshots in the crossroads one heard the popping of champagne corks in the cabarets.

On finishing the day's work and leaving the docks behind, the workers would sling their jackets and overalls over their shoulders, waving them around like flags during fevered discussions.

There is no end to the gunshots. The poor know by instinct or by what their hearts tell them which are the friendly shots, and they welcome them.

They arrested an old woman trying to make her way into the governor's palace. She was carrying a butcher knife hidden away in her sleeve.

They are refusing to sell food to policemen's wives in the markets.

Amador folded his newspaper and went into the Clinical Hospital. The morgue was down in the depths of the old sanitarium; he went staggering down metal stairways, leaving scraps of ideas on the white, peeling walls, craving a smoke. Maybe Angel del Hierro's body was there, incognito, without a tag on him. Another anonymous body. Maybe they had murdered him after all. He crossed his fingers and looked for wood to knock, but did not find any. Long live scientific thinking! It was far more rational to recite the Romantic poet Espronceda: *With a hundred cannons, wind astern, full sail, the sea is not to be broken, but flown over . . .* That was the best cure for fear.

An orderly with a blood-spattered apron turned up in the middle of a corridor, and gave a sign of recognition.

"How's the night doing, Manolo?"

"So-so, pencil-pusher, let's just say so-so. There's more than usual. We get bunches of gunshot corpses in here. It's two in the morning and we've got six already."

They went through the underground nooks and crannies in the hospital together. Amador felt as if he was in a war zone in that hospital, moving along trenches in a theater of the absurd.

A dozen occupied slabs could be seen in the faint glow of the low-watt lightbulbs. Bloody sheets and drainpipes down which the fluids of death trickled away. Dr. Ricart was performing an autopsy at the back. A few policemen were smoking around the slabs, cutting unmistakable figures with their waistcoats open and ties loose, traces of a cartridge belt and gun holster here and there. One of them had bought it that night.

"Would there be a John Doe around here?"

"Is he a friend of yours?"

"A stranger, some John Smith or other. What did I say? Did I say Jones?"

The orderly nodded.

"One, a Mary Jane, a woman, they found her in the street yesterday, she'd put arsenic in her coffee. Two coffees with arsenic sugar in them. She was pretty. What a shame . . . you got some tobacco on you?"

Amador said no.

Suddenly there was a whirlwind of activity, stretcher-bearers, a group of strangers, shouts here and there. Amador stood to one side, trying to blend in with the shadows.

"Shut yourselves up, dickheads! Don't fuck things up even more, we're trying to work here," Ricart shouted from his table.

Cross-eyed and bad-mannered, he was the best surgeon in Barcelona, and one of the best amateur violin players in Catalonia. He charged a fortune in consultation fees, and even so he was down here doing the night shift for free now and again. He must have liked corpses. He must have liked corpses a lot.

The Flea stopped the last two stretcher-bearers, who were tossing a new corpse onto the slab nearest to the entrance. A man in a suit, with a pair of red flowers in the false bib he was wearing instead of a shirt, and two gunshot wounds in his chest.

"What the hell's going on?"

"They attacked Graupera in the street. They riddled his car with bullets. Three dead."

"And what about him?"

"It seems he survived. They've got him upstairs, with a few wounds. The first bunch of flowers is already here.

Who the fuck are these bosses? What time do flower shops open for them?"

"Fuckin' hell, there were about fifty bullet holes in the car, just like a sieve."

The policemen had mobilized and were milling around the stretchers. They must have recognized one of the dead men, because their voices got louder and more embittered. Hands started hovering around guns, then they all went out together toward the ambulance entrance. Amador slipped along after them. It was really going to be something now. Graupera was the chairman of the bosses' organization. If the groups had got that one together, this was going to get serious. Big time. Barcelona was going to fall to pieces.

He wandered around the corridors trying to pick up more information, but the place was beginning to buzz with policemen and was not a good place to be in. Nowhere with the cops was a good place to be in. Quite the opposite. Your nerves were on edge, trigger fingers became itchy. Two of the dead men had been policemen; one was Graupera's bodyguard, the other had been his driver.

"Fifty or sixty shots. Riddled with them. When the car was turning into Baja de San Pedro, some handsome guy without a shirt stood in front and emptied his gun at them, although they were firing, too. There were more of them firing from the crossroads, and a few on a motorbike behind them. But this guy just stood in the middle of the street and riddled them with bullets, stood right there, watching them while the car ran him over . . . fuckin' hell."

That sounded like that madman Del Hierro. The dead man who had come back to life to have a go at the chairman of the bosses' organization. It was said that whenever he went after somebody's life, he always took his jacket off and walked straight at them, with both guns firing, and that he was a better shot with his left hand. That was the kind of shit going the rounds in whispers.

"Graupera took three shots, but nothing much, the sort of wounds you fix in two shakes."

Amador began to look for the way out of the hospital. It was cold, very cold. The dead were calling out for the living to come and keep them company.

He hesitated in the doorway. His weakness was eating away at him from inside. A huge worm was crawling through his gut. He walked away from the hospital, trying to leave the images of the dead behind him, covered in sweat despite the freezing night.

The Not-So-Lone Ranger

Someone who has good ideas is never alone, I mean to say that when I come to tell all this. I might be transformed into the Not-So-Lone Ranger, the better, Mexican version of the Lone Ranger, surrounded by really cold beer, two Cuban sandwiches with lots of hot, smoky chipotle chiles, and with the television switched on, showing dire video clips featuring a certain Lucerito.

So here's what's going on (I might say to my notebooks):

a) The shit had all started in the United States, probably in Austin. The guys had had access to Karen's medical file, or had had tests done without her knowing. Or did she know?

b) There were four of them who had kidnapped Karen and murdered O'Brien, who worked for a gringo. Their names: Nico Romero, Mike, and two John Does.

c) The operation had taken place in El Paso. The surgeon was in El Paso or nearby. The same went for the recovery room where they had held Karen for forty-eight hours.

d) Nico had a dog. Someone had a dog Nico had bought food for. There was a goddamned dog wandering around this story.

e) Mike was a tall, drug-pushing gringo, although he might have been other things also. According to the file, Mike Gardner had been accused of rape in Parral and been released six weeks later. Nico Romero was the short guy with the silver-tipped boots and Samantha Fox pictures on his wall; a former policeman from Sabinas, Coahuila, thrown out for having set fire to an agricultural tools store, for which he had spent six months in jail.

f) Why buy four cans of cockroach-killing spray? Why not just one?

g) The hospital where they operated on Karen had a significant infrastructure: at least four or five doctors and half a dozen nurses were involved.

h) The body of one of the John Does was buried at the 32 kilometer mark on the Jiménez highway, in a vineyard by the side of the road.

i) The kidney's recipient had a fat file that could not be hidden very easily, and a lot of dealings with hospitals on account of his kidney failure.

j) Two phone numbers: an answering machine in Austin that repeated an innocuous message: "Harry's Sporting Goods. If you want to send a fax, do it now. After the beep, leave your message. Leave me a list of orders and your address if you need something urgently."

k) When Santana recorded *Lotus* in Osaka in 1973, with the local engineer with the exotic name (for Santana fans) of Tamoo Suzuki at the controls, he was almost as much in the dark as I would be just then.

l) Why did Antonio Amador never have any money? What secret little story obliged him to be poor? Where did he blow the miserable salary he got from *El Progreso*?

m) The other phone number belonged to the chief of the Federal Judicial Police based in Chihuahua.

n) If you could take any notice of northern women with bad spelling, you could find out something about Nico by interrogating the neighbor from number 5, and ask her in passing why Nico had left Ciudad Juárez so quickly.

The light in the motel room at Camelia's would start flashing, and the Not-So-Lone Ranger himself, me that is, would look for the shotgun in the canvas sack, and check that the cartridges were in place. Having finished the Cuban sandwiches, I would go on to dessert: peanut butter sandwiches, the best thing going in the middle of so much loneliness and so much private-eye-style clear thinking . . .

The Plaza del Peso de la Paja

Sometime or other, in an act of revenge, Amador had described District V, Chinatown, his adopted home, and had done it in the style of all those kinds of strange fixations, as an act of simultaneous love and hate:

District V is the city's open sore; it's the worst area; it is the refuge for bad people. True, there are honorable families living there. That is the tragedy. In the deformed pile of rubbish and pain, of unawareness and sin that makes up District V, workers and sausages go together, the washerwoman and the peripatetic singer who looks like a princess in the cabaret and sleeps on a cot at home . . . Not even the worst areas in Genoa, not even the dockside in Marseilles, or Whitechapel in London, can compare with our District V, with the ambiguous air of our forbidden zone. District V outdoes them all. In an absurd and unique way, here you can find the strangest bedfellows rubbing shoulders with each other, the brothel alongside the dairy for workers getting up early; the shop where you contract killers and where music-hall artistes are lent money, and Count Güell's palace; Cal Manco and the Radical People's House; the Santa Cruz Hospital and the Mina tavern; the Ataranzas barracks and the little book market; the furnished hotel rooms and the attraction for outsiders . . . The good and the bad, civilization and Hurdism, which is a national political movement. The wretches from Los Moños drag their rags along and a few idiots dressed like tramps and whores smelling of Heno de Pravia soap make them sing grotesque songs to laugh at their madness. Night watchman Juan crosses the street and covers his face so that the petty thieves do not recognize him. A few bootblacks sell cocaine and the queers turn up in the middle of the street, showing their shame, their indecency, and their sin for all to see; the Gypsy women from Villa Rosa and a few moochers lying in wait almost violently attack them. The poor sleep in doorways, and a drunk, leaning on a lamppost, expounds a philosophical theory to the tune of "Black and Blue" . . . Below the unreal gaslight there are still some romantic and silent streets to be found . . .

Nowadays, Amador did the rounds of these streets endlessly, along the romantic and silent ones, which were not in the least romantic, but rather openings to tunnels of uncertain light that let you see the color of fear in their depths. He sat now and again on a bench on Las Ramblas, covering his face with a scarf that he had stolen in a bar. But it was not just the night that was dangerous, the day was on fire as well, and trucks full of Civil Guards with their snub-nosed rifles in the air often went past him.

The Flea had not dared to show his face in the newspaper offices, Governor Maestre Laborde having unleashed a wave of repression. Word was on the street and the omens were there to be seen. Civil Guards, policemen from the special brigades, uniformed and municipal officers had been making their way into unionists' houses during the early hours. There was a rumor on the street that Seguí, the CNT general secretary, had been arrested, the few unions that had carried on working legally were closed down, the deserted *Solidaridad Obrera* offices (even though the paper had been banned for weeks) were attacked along with the *Tierra y Libertad* print shop, where militiamen smashed up boxes of typeface with iron bars. More than a hundred unionists had been arrested by morning. The militias were out on the street, a state of war had been declared, and a group of soldiers were joking around a .50 caliber machine gun. The number of people arrested had gone up to four hundred by mid-morning. They had even gone after the unions' lawyers, Guerra del Río y Lastra and Companys y Ulled, who had been put under arrest and taken into the central police station. The prisoners were being taken to the Barceló steamship because the Modelo Prison was full up. Preemptive censorship had been imposed on all the newspapers and even dispatches from the Madrid correspondents were being monitored in the telegraph offices. The streets were paralyzed with fear. People were persecuted willy-nilly. It was enough to be a worker with a union membership card in your pocket to be arrested. Strikes were illegal. Life was too.

Amador had a rendezvous in his head, a permanent one arranged six months previously: if the local Federation was to fall, he had to go along to a streetcar shed in Sarría at nine o'clock at night, as vice-secretary of the journalists' union, and wait for a man with a bunch of flowers to put him in touch with the new local Federation. On the other hand, he had a rendezvous in the Plaza del Peso de la Paja with the beggar at eight.

Amador went wandering along the Ronda de San Antonio, heading toward the plaza, a bend in the street with a couple of bars and a second-floor whorehouse with a lot of revelry going on inside.

Amador felt the heat rise through his veins and settle in his face. His face was burning on a frozen late afternoon that was already turning into an early night. He felt like a smoke. A ragged hand stretched out from a dark doorway and offered him one.

Amador, not startled, accepted the gift along with the flame to light it. There were friendly shadows, not just enemy ones.

"They're about to come out of that door. Right now. They might be coming down this second," the hand said, pointing toward the brothel.

"And how do you know so much?" Amador asked, choking back a cough.

The beggar stood up and took off some of the bandages covering his face.

"You're Angel del Hierro," Amador acknowledged, and cracked a smile.

The beggar, transformed into the Black Angel, the Angel of Death, took a pair of pistols out from his pouch. A few voices could be heard coming out of the brothel doorway just before the people appeared. The Baron was wearing a frock coat and an astrakhan hat. Soler was in front of him with another man, who Amador, from the shadows, recognized immediately as the Monkey. A woman appeared in a window and emptied a washbasin into some flowerbeds. The Black Angel went out into the middle of the square with a Star pistol in each hand and jumped on top of an iron bench.

"Baron von Shit! Here I am! Now you can really kill me!"

Amador ducked back into the doorway as he drew his gun, bewildered by the melodramatic turn of events and the violence of the Angel's shouting.

Soler, who reacted faster, rushed into the square and took cover behind a fountain of a chubby statue carrying a jug on it, and fired the first shot, which took some chips out of the stonework of the house where the journalist was hiding. The Angel of Death fired at the Baron twice and hit him once: he slid down a wall and fell over sideways with one hand clutching his belly. Then, during a seemingly interminable moment, Angel del Hierro followed the Monkey with his gun as he ran up toward the north end of Ronda de San Antonio, and fired again. The shot must have hit him in the head, because the Baron's gunman began to wobble around unnaturally, like an ostrich with its head in the sand, before keeling over and twitching in an odd way.

Soler, the Majorcan, and another member of the band who was crouching beside the Baron, as if trying to protect him, sprayed Angel del Hierro with bullets, but the Angel seemed oblivious to it all as the fountain filled with holes, forcing the Majorcan to cower behind a clump of daisies just before he was finished off.

The shots lit up the square with instantaneous flashes that lingered on the retina; the sound of the shots ringing in the ears lasted longer. The fireworks of death. Amador found himself drawing his pistol, and that other me, the one who did believe in the Ballad of the Stars, shot at the brothel doorway twice before fainting from weakness, thinking that if the Baron was dead it might be just as well to go off and have a mouthful of sausage and some squid.

The air was filled with night watchmen's whistles and shouts from the police patrols and Civil Guards in nearby streets. But Angel del Hierro kept to his post at the fountain, firing both pistols and looking for the Majorcan, who was crawling away from him. Firing one round after another, while shouting disjointed and incomprehensible insults.

The Faraway Lover Comes Closer

"Didn't anyone come to visit her?"

"Just you. It seems to me that her family . . . she can't have any family. There were a few calls from someplace in the United States, from Oregon I think, but they didn't speak to me; I don't count for anything around here, they spoke to Dr. Estrada. Someone else came from the gringo consulate."

The nurse who reads my novels would be giving me another look of approval.

"Are you a relative? A friend of her mom and dad?"

"I came here . . ." I might say, feeling like a jerk, like a comic-book Mexican, like . . . "I came to Comala asking about a gringa basketball player who knew Pedro Páramo."

"I've read that novel, too, it's by Rulfo," the nurse would say, happy, having just convinced me that she deserves to have my next novel dedicated to her, if that book should ever happen to exist. I would write her name down on the back of a prescription sheet (Cindy Pérez) and get ready to prowl around the city and the night.

"Aren't you going to go in? She's awake. She woke up already, a few hours ago."

Karen would be staring at the ceiling, and when I go in she would give me one of those looks she normally saves for the coaches from the other team.

"Where am I?"

"The General Hospital in Ciudad Juárez, Chihuahua."

"And this?" she would ask, lifting up her sheets and pointing to a scar running across her abdomen.

"Undercover kidney operation. It's a long story."

"That's what they said." And for a moment she might seem overwhelmed, fazed. "You've been here before, right?" And each word would be an effort for the girl.

"For twelve days now. Every night."

"You a cop? The cops were here already," she would say, almost as a whisper.

"A writer."

"Shit. A writer. I wanted to be a writer, but first a firewoman, then . . ."

"Did you know you were going to score when you shot with your back to the basket from the corner? That game against Washington University, you were 27-27 . . ."

But Karen would have drifted off again.

So I would then get out the photo of the da Vinci bicycle, the photo that is my only legacy from the life of grandfather Del Hierro, and I would place it on the bedside table and fix it there with a thumbtack. It's a curious photo: it proves that Leonardo invented the bicycle four hundred years before the ones who say they did. A photo of a rough drawing that, for my grandfather, was the definitive proof that the Magus from Vinci had demonstrated the impossibility of the realm of the impossible, and had thereby thrown open the door to hope.

Looking into Arlegui's Eyes

Angel del Hierro must have looked into Arlegui's eyes and discovered that behind the fixed stare there was not, as might have been supposed from reading accounts of that time, a nest of vipers nor even the eternal flames of hell. He must have discovered that in the depths of Civil Guard Colonel Miguel Arlegui y Bayonés's eyes, there was merely a void.

Del Hierro, the Black Angel, must have been, at that moment, in that Barcelona that was half slaughterhouse and half pleasuredome, a cold, dry man intoxicated with ideas, and beset with nightmares and fear, above all with the fear of losing composure, of falling into the depths of degradation in front of the enemy's top man. As for dying, you could die many times, but you could only lose face once. Terrified by the fear of turning into someone else, he could not have hated anybody more intensely than himself, nor been as intensely afraid of anybody as of his own weaknesses.

It was because of this that when Arlegui had him right there, and uttered the sort of words that usually begin this sort of meeting, he remained quiet.

"Well, Hierro, finally we get to see each other, face-to-face."

Angel del Hierro stared fixedly, so that the colonel could look from the void he had hidden behind his eyes and see a glint of something in Angel's: fate. Perhaps Arlegui, who had a couple of bloodstains on his tunic, who would murder Evelio Boal, the general secretary of the CNT, by strangling him in a fit of anger, found a spark, a flicker or a premonition in the depths of Del Hierro's eyes, because he took a couple of steps back, took a gun from a drawer and began to shout that they should get him out of there, get him out of his way.

The Angel of Death, who had pissed in his pants on being kicked in the bladder by the colonel's assistants a few minutes previously, who had a swollen, broken nose and had been dragged into the colonel's presence with two bullet holes in his body, went away smiling.

As they were dragging Del Hierro out of the office, Antonio Amador, the journalist, who was stretched out on two chairs with his jacket torn and bloodstains (his own coughed-up blood) on his shirt sleeves, got up to shake his hand. As they were both cuffed he got no further than rubbing the anarchist's hands.

"Kill him. No one can charge us with killing a dead man," Arlegui's voice could be heard from inside his office, just as the door was closing.

Amador, just coming around after fainting, was perplexed by his own bloodstained shirt. He prodded himself, looking for wounds, not finding any. It was either the vomiting, or an internal hemorrhage if he had broken ribs, that was hurting him.

"Arlegui! Arlegui!" the little journalist shouted.

The policemen who were escorting Del Hierro stopped. One of them threw the anarchist against the wall and headed toward Amador.

The office door opened again and Arlegui came into view, wiping his glasses with a handkerchief.

"Aren't you going to kill me? Are you going to leave me as a witness, you queer bastard?"

"Kill the pair of them together," the Barcelona police chief answered.

SECTOR FOUR

The Deceitfulness of Desire

Our desires deceive us;
time is short, death laughs at
our concerns; a life beset by
restlessness is nothing.
—Leonardo da Vinci

Jerry in Manhattan (I)

In those days Jerry was sleeping in the Chelsea Hotel, a ten-floor ruin rising up from 23rd Street. It was a monument to the soldiers of survival in New York, to the dollar pioneers, with very mixed blessings as a hotel. Such people as Kirk Douglas had preceded Jerry on his way through New York when he was a struggling actor; General MacArthur had been there, too, as a promising young captain; and so had the young Dylan Thomas, who must have felt his ethereal bones shuddering at today's company, made up basically of punks with honey-colored or pink hair, and Jamaican prostitutes in halter tops.

It was a hotel crawling with cockroaches, which explained why it was reasonable to charge thirty-two dollars a night plus tax. You were allowed to take bicycles up in the elevator, the receptionist would accept messages delivered by hand, but not over the telephone, and there was a different make of television in every room, every one bought from thieves over various periods of time. The TV in Jerry's room was a black-and-white Motorola model from the 1960s with a fourteen-inch screen, which gave out an almost feline purr when it got hot. The hotel had, however, installed New York–style cable in a fit of modernization.

It was for this reason that Jerry was able to tune in to Channel 35 that summer night and see his mother in a 1940s porno movie. It was a brief two- or three-minute sequence used as an interlude between commercials announcing "companions" and triple-X videos.

He saw it and liked it.

First came the surprise. Just what do you do, and more particularly, just what would Jerry do, on switching on the tube and finding his mother (in a picture that seemed prehistoric in its washed-out black and white) taking her bra off and playing with a black kitten, her breasts wafting in the breeze? Obviously you smile. Make sure first, then smile. It was his mother, no doubt about that. He remembered the mop of hair cut to within a few inches of her ears, the straight nose, and the plucked, almost nonexistent, blond eyebrows.

The film was just another three-minute clip, with no direct sound, which they usually dubbed with music by Glenn Miller, and which was not very hard-core when compared with the rest of the porno stuff on TV. It seemed to satisfy the longings that a load of New Yorkers had to sleep with their mothers, their aunts, old friends of the family, or wet-nurses. These old movies, with women whose aesthetic qualities had faded over the years, who wore garter belts, nylon stockings, voluminous panties, and lacy bras that did not match the rest of their underwear; these women who had undressed forty years ago looking at the camera, with no sense of eternity, and whose lips you could see moving now and again as they asked for instructions, with their pointed breasts and huge, dark aureoles, seemed to be fulfilling the oedipal urge to fuck in a time machine.

The plot was very simple: an Illinois housewife goes up to a refrigerator (he remembered that white creamy Westinghouse, which was always full of stewed apple that nobody ever ate), takes out a Coca-Cola and gets her skirt caught in the door as she closes it. The torn skirt stays caught, in spite of her unlikely tugs at it (the hyperrational Jerry said to himself that nobody takes the trouble to tug at a skirt caught up in a refrigerator door, normal housewives turn back to the refrigerator and open the door), and she shows some baggy panties and stockings held up by a garter belt. The legs are shapely, but a bit on the heavy side.

The woman smiles at her nonexistent spectators after that little mishap and walks toward a bedroom, the camera faithfully following her and going out of focus at times. On entering the room the woman gets her blouse tangled up in a coat hanger that is hanging from a mirror for some odd reason. It then seems that things do not turn out too well, because the camera goes down to the woman's generous, meaty butt while she struggles, then rises again. The woman is now holding her torn blouse in her hands, allowing us to see a bra with ample cups to it, which armor-plate her breasts rather than exposing them.

Jerry wondered. When did his mother make these films? Who was the cameraman? How much did they pay her? The daylight that found its way in here and there seemed to indicate that it was sometime during the morning, when he and his brother were at school.

The woman goes up toward a bathroom at the back of the bedroom, picks up a black kitten as she passes the bed, and talks to it. Jerry cursed himself for not being able to lip-read. He did not remember the cat. The film director-cameraman-producer must have brought it along with him.

Jerry's mother enters the bathroom with the kitten in her hands and the camera takes exception to the excessive light. When the f-stop is adjusted, the woman can be seen staring at the camera in what is supposed to be a lusty look, but is more likely due to barely contained panic. The take opens up to show her slipping the kitten into her panties and licking her lips.

The film was thus far more or less disconnected, but with a certain primitive logic to it. But from that moment on it seemed to get really disorganized: there followed the first cut in a film so far shot straight from the top and without any sequential breaks. Probably because the cat had dug its claws in the confined space inside the panties, all hell had broken loose.

The following scene showed the woman with her panties a bit below her knees while she held the cat between her wobbling breasts and tried to explain something.

And then it was all over.

The film faded into a series of ads for S&M shows and escort services and, finally, to an excessively outrageous commercial: *Phone-in Golden Showers, dial 555-PISS*.

Jerry sank back into his bed and looked for a Pepsi on his bedside table. Nothing in this world was capable of shocking him too much, but curiosity could get hold of him. Why did his mother, a gentle divorced Chicago housewife who lived off alimony, a job in a donut factory, and the meager support of Jerry's grandfather (the owner of a hardware store in Idaho), have to earn money on the side by making skin-flicks? Who had shot the film? A casual friend? A "friend of the family"? A semi-professional? Jerry tried to remember what he was like when his mother was the age she appeared to be in the film. About what year would it have been made? What was going on in their lives? There was some quirk in his memory that covered all those years up.

Given his failure at reminiscence, Jerry reviewed his reaction to the film. It was absolutely normal. Which was abnormal. What would John Wayne, George Bush, or Angel, the elevator operator, have done had they seen their mother, forty years younger thanks to the magic of the cinema, in a porno movie? It was by no means certain. But he had liked it. He had been unaware of his mother's thespian talents until then. he remembered her as a sour-faced, graceless, boring, puritanical divorcee; a woman without men in her life, who played gin rummy with casual friends who never lasted, due to the bitter hatred that could spring from spending time together and the poor quality of the tea and cakes; a woman addicted to television, reading novels by Vicki Baum, Mika Waltari, and Mickey Spillane. Awful. She was much better in the movie, slipping a cat into her panties.

Jerry was about to pick up the phone and call his aging mother in Florida and tell her about it. He could tell her he was going to get a copy of the movie from the Manhattan Cable Company and send it to all the living relatives he could remember. Finally, he decided to leave things as they were, although he did call the TV station and ask them when they were next scheduled to show the movie. When they told him that they would broadcast it again eleven days later, at 1:13 A.M., he wrote the time and date down carefully on a scrap of yellow paper and stuck it in the middle of the TV screen. They also told him that they also had *The Shanghai Train* and *The Velvet Hen* by the same model, but that they were not scheduled. Nothing with the same black pussy in it.

Leonardo (VI)

When Leonardo arrived in Venice, in March 1500, the Adriatic port was in a state of terror and awaiting the next landing by the Sultan's forces. Hysteria was running rampant; the Venetian fleet's defeat made the Turks' presence seem ever nearer, and rumors already placed them at the outskirts of the city.

Leonardo was fascinated by the Venetian sights; he wandered among men who were packing up their belongings ready to flee, blacksmiths sharpening old sabers, women crying, and children running through the streets playing at being Turkish soldiers. There, then, was a city that had both the privilege to be a golden trading bridge between East and West, as well as being at one with the world of water that so intrigued him. His notebooks, nonetheless, make scant reference to these feelings, and it was the military predicament that seemed to do most to stimulate his deepest-seated ideas, the most obscure projects he had tucked away in the recesses of his mind in the last few years.

Leonardo offered his services to His Most Serene Highness's government a few days after his arrival in Venice, propounding the manufacture of a device with which a man might come close to the Turkish boats underwater and thereby sink them.

It was a matter of a diving suit, complete with a helmet, a special shirt, and trousers that allowed the wearer to urinate underwater. The latter item seemed vital to Da Vinci and, after a great deal of thought, he had found a way to solve the problem, so that having to piss would not be a formidable obstacle for the suit's wearer.

A good deal of space is given over in the drawings of the project to the key part of the device, which we would today call a helmet, a mask with glass windows and a mechanism connecting the mouth and nose to a large bladder filled with air and sealed with tiny rings, which would pump oxygen from the surface down to the diver. Leonardo drew several plans of the suit and wrote a detailed description of how to get close to the flagship of the Turkish fleet and sink it by boring a hole in its hull below the waterline, using a bit and brace. The submariners would then set fire to the rest of the galleys.

But there was no reason to confine oneself to that project, as the Magus had also designed a "small underwater boat," whose purpose would be to sail under the sea without being seen.

Leonardo spoke with naval architects, with Captain Alvise Simón and Admiral Antonio Grimaldi, but in the face of such marvels he could only have met with surprised expressions, mistrust, and incredulous replies, all signs that they considered his ideas to be fraudulent.

The Turkish peril faded away in the end, and Leonardo hid his drawings, leaving the following note behind on page 33 of what would later be known as the Atlanticus Codex: *Why do I not describe my method for remaining beneath the water while all the time I might be there, without coming up for air? I do not wish to divulge or publish it, due to the perverse nature of men, who would use it to commit murder at the bottom of the sea.*

Thus were his ideas concerning submarines cast into the oblivion of centuries.

He was in Florence once again by April 24.

Jerry in Manhattan (II)

The heat wave that had engulfed New York was having some terrible consequences: twenty-seven murders in just one weekend; an eleven-year-old Jamaican boy shot his sister, aged five, because she cried too much; a woman had committed suicide by hanging herself with the cord from a table lamp. The 101 degrees Fahrenheit were given as the explanation on TV. There were the usual shots of fire hydrants open so that the pariahs could play in the middle of the street, soaking themselves in the jet of water, lowering the pressure and bringing back fleeting folk memories of neighborhoods alongside the beach. And that was not all: the temperature went up to 105 by mid-morning, according to an electronic billboard in Times Square, which was roasting in the sun like a frankfurter. Two old people had died, burned to a crisp in the heat when the air-conditioning in an old people's home broke down, and their problems were only just beginning there, as a hundred other old people were refusing to leave the retirement home, come what may. Dying at ninety to be a smiling corpse . . . Taxi drivers too. Three dead taxi drivers. One with his throat slit, leaning on the steering wheel in his yellow cab, honking forever.

Jerry adopted a polyvalent attitude toward the madness that seemed to have taken over the city; on the one hand, the heat and humidity reminded him of other hot places and he liked that; going around burning up inside, building up steam to be let off by slapping someone or dripping with acrid sweat; on the other hand, he felt like a spectator rather than a participant. So far, New York was a show put on for him in which he did not take part. He could see and hear what was going on, without being seen or heard or run over, like the little genies in the movies.

If the sun also rose in Paris, if Bangkok was a brothel, Zurich a retirement home, Paris a piece of nostalgia, and Asunción a stage set for a nonexistent play, New York was a supermarket, a huge department store, as a Mexican writer once said in a fit of lucidity. Jerry moved around, went into the supermarket with the sole intention of looking for a bargain, cashing in his coupons, and filling his cart up.

But not now. He had stopped being the invisible man, although this was not the first or the last blind date in his life. A call, a description. *Mr. X wants to talk to you.* A place, a time, a date.

Jerry met Mr. X in an open-air mini-delicatessen next to the New York Public Library, a café that boasted about its Italian sandwiches. Two Venezuelan students were throwing screwed-up paper napkins at each other over the table next to them, and discussing their theories about oil, the Caribbean, and gringo industrial pirates. Jerry knew a lot more than they did about all of those issues.

He carefully approached the appointed place, the third table to the right of the stairs, and ordered a soda. Almost immediately a strange person sat down in the chair beside him and gave him his hand. Mr. X seemed absurdly formal in the intense morning heat.

"I know what I have to say will surprise you, Mr. Milligan, and the man who has hired me insisted many times that I appeal to your sense of humor, to your patience. I am, and he told me I should use these very words, a messenger from the past. Okay?" said Mr. X, making a theatrical pause, which he used to light a cigarette. He was smoking Benson and Hedges 100s. Very elegant.

"Okay, you've got my patience and my good temper. I acknowledge you as a messenger from the past," Jerry answered with a smile. At least he was sure that it was not CIA business, nobody from the Agency would have used that tone of voice or those kinds of words. He probably wanted to sell him insurance, or hire him as a mercenary for Africa.

"I bring you good news: Mr. C is on this continent and has requested me to tell you that he acknowledges his debt."

Jerry looked down the avenue. The traffic was getting heavier, the students had taken over the space by the steps between the two ridiculous lions to eat their sandwiches. Who was the guy working for? Was this some sort of trap? He looked around, taking all the time in the world, observing the people who sat close to them. Mulattos reading the *Sunday Times*, a redheaded girl carrying a bag that she never took her hand out of, were possibly suspicious. He was old and out of training.

"Mr. C?"

"Mr. C told me that perhaps your memory would fail you. It is about someone you had an appointment with, in Thailand, at the end of 1975, someone who unfortunately could not make it to that appointment."

Jerry stared at Mr. X, a black man whose skin was almost blue, dressed in traditional Nigerian costume. He might work in a record store, be a secretary from his country's legation at the United Nations, or a Ghanaian disguised as a Nigerian, or an Argentinean soccer player disguised as an elegant Cuban.

"Mr. Christo's come back from the past. Well, well. It'll take me a few seconds to come to my senses, Mr. X."

"He told me that . . . you may take all the time you like. It has taken me six months to find you."

Jerry slowly sipped his Hawaiian Punch and then drummed his fingernails on the aluminum can. Fifteen years. Fifteen fucking years. And now the Bulgarian shows up. Now, when he wanted, not when Jerry had been looking for him in every corner of the known world.

"You must understand my situation, Mr. Milligan. I do not know what Mr. C and yourself agreed to all those years ago, I do not know how Mr. C's debt to you came about, and I prefer not to know. I only know that I have to pass some messages on to you and give you a check, once you identify yourself . . . and then ask you a couple of favors."

"Go right ahead, Mr. X."

"Well, then, Mr. C asked me to tell you that he acknowledges his debt with you, that he regrets the lost time, that he had his own reasons for this delay . . . do you have some sort of identification?"

Jerry got his driver's license out and pushed it over to the black man with two fingers. Mr. X examined it carefully, looking from the photo to the man a couple of times. Then he opened his briefcase and took an envelope out of it, which was marked with a numeral "1."

"This is a check in your name for $200,000. Mr. C told me you could consider it as an advance payment on the debt."

Jerry examined the check, drawn on Chemical Bank of New York. It looked good.

"And the favors?"

"Mr. C wants you to visit him to arrange that personally."

"Where?"

"In Mexico."

"What for?"

Mr. X took a second envelope out, with a big numeral "2" marked on it.

"It is all explained in here."

Jerry took the envelope and put it in his pocket. He got up and was about to go when the black man pulled a third envelope out that, of course, had a large numeral "3" marked on it.

"Mr. C asked me to show you these photos. He wants to know what kind of money you would be talking about to become an owner. Perhaps you could find out the asking price of these movie theaters in Manhattan before going to see him."

There were some very low-quality Polaroid outdoor shots of several theaters, the Gramercy, the Regency, the Embassy multi-cinema on Broadway, and even a porno theater on 42nd Street.

"Tell Mr. C he'll be hearing from me very shortly," said Jerry with a smile as he got up.

"I will pass your message on, word for word."

Jerry walked off, went down the steps in three short hops, and disappeared into the 42nd Street crowd, going west. Mr. X resigned himself to picking up the tab.

Leonardo (VII)

We shall also describe how air can be pumped underwater to raise enormous weights, in other words, how to fill skins with air once they have been affixed to weights at the bottom of the sea. There shall also be descriptions of how to raise weights by attaching them to sunken ships full of sand, and how to remove the sand from the ships.

Leonardo wrote this in one of the notebooks he had on him during the summer of 1502. This comment, an adventurous proposal to rescue sunken ships at the bottom of the ocean that might contain important treasure, was not addressed to one of the Italian barons or a major figure in dramatic Renaissance Italy, but (as we were to discover 450 years later), it was in fact addressed to the Sultan of Constantinople, Bayazet II.

Leonardo had made so bold as to write the letter after

having been encouraged by the presence of an ambassador from the Turkish court in Rome, who was touring the peninsula in 1502 in search of Italian engineers to enter his master's service.

Leonardo's letter was destined to vanish from sight, like so many other things in his life, until a group of British academics came across a translation of the text in 1952 as they were rummaging through papers in the Topkapi Serayi palace with their customary scholarly zeal.

The description of a mechanical system to remove water from the sunken shell of a ship was, however, one thing that would never show up.

This text, along with the explanatory drawings that Leonardo usually enclosed with his texts, was doubtless part of the material that was lost in the diaspora that the Magus of Vinci's texts suffered after his death. Nonetheless, another comment on the method to rescue sunken ships would later turn up in what is known as Manuscript L, which can be found in Paris and contains some notes dating from the period 1502–3.

It would seem, however, that the idea was of no serious concern to Leonardo, and that he by no means confined himself to such a simple proposal destined to be cast aside, to become another example of da Vinci genius lost in the mists of time. There is more information to be found in the famous Madrid I Codex, which could be connected with this matter. Here, on sheet 82 verso, we have a proposal to make a personal life jacket and a diagram of a large pair of floating shoes, a pair of useful ideas when it comes to looking for sunken treasure.

Was the return to these maritime and underwater ideas that had cropped up in Venice at the beginning of the millennium connected to any definite project? Was Leonardo thinking of any type of boat in particular, or were his musings confined to theoretical planning? Was there something more in his missing notes than just descriptions of wineskins, bellows, piping, and diving apparatus for installing those skins that were to be inflated? Had he gone back to his design for a diving suit but not to use it for sinking ships? Would there be a map, by any chance? Would there be any information on a ship about whose fate below the waves the Magus was especially concerned?

Jerry in Manhattan (III)

Jerry had been in New Delhi and had felt as if he was in New York. Why would he not feel like that? All the local taxi drivers were Indians, just like in the Bronx, Brooklyn, or Manhattan. What is more, who was imitating who? Were the Indians impersonating the New Yorkers, or were they just the same? The Indians, after all, had the New York habit of stepping on the gas without taking their feet off the brakes, of spitting at the car next to them, and using the fancy power-driven steering wheel to move the car like a pan-galactic spaceship, and hog the road to produce a chorus of horns going off. They cursed just the same, enjoyed the passenger's look of terror as he got out just the same, and overcharged just the same if they could, too.

Jerry felt very, very happy that morning. He looked carefully at the driver's hack license, as he always did before giving the address, and learned that he was in the hands of another suicide-jockey called Singh.

"The Flatiron Building, down there, on Fifth Avenue," he said, lighting a cigarette and waiting for the driver to tell him he could not smoke, which would make for a good argument about the human rights of smokers. Not only did Manabendra Singh not complain, he even grumpily asked him for a cigarette.

Jerry was a fan of New York taxi drivers' stories. They were a unique breed, with wide social mobility; they were combative, talkative, informative, and racially diverse. Jerry may have been a man easily given to cynicism, but he had never allowed his scorn or his hate to cloud his vision, and for that reason he regarded taxi drivers as the eye of the racial hurricane that the United States had turned into. The most interesting types of hate and the most bizarre love affairs were to be found there, especially when they could be observed from a distance.

Jerry had spent the last three months cutting articles out of the *New York Post* that had to do with taxi drivers. It seemed that they were just as interested in taxi stories at the *Post* as he was. There were babies born in taxis, women who left their husbands' heads behind in yellow cabs, competitions between limo drivers to see who could get the most traffic tickets in a month, the biggest cocaine deal in New York history taking place in the back seat of a cab . . . Jerry also took note of conversations, names, rumors, stories of assorted mafias, strange closed circles that were more exotic than religious sects, groups who rounded off the month by holding barbecues with types of meat and sauces with unpronounceable names.

Jerry was particularly interested in languages. New York taxi drivers had developed a separate linguistic world. English was no longer even the lingua franca. They spoke over the radio as if they were part of a mass of mysterious cults, alarming their passengers. In a Grand Marquis hired to take you to Kennedy or La Guardia they spoke Portuguese, or an arm-waving Brazilian version of it. The unlicensed gypsies who drove gray and black cars linked by radio would speak to each other in rapid-fire Spanish, leaving out consonants as in Colombia and Honduras. Yellow radio taxis formed part of a linguistic world that was predominantly Farsi, Hindi, and Greek. The service networks on CB stations were the domain of even more exotic groups and cliques that spoke Iranian Pashto or Tojolabal from the mountains of Guerrero in Mexico, Polish from Gdansk, or told jokes in Ukrainian. A network of yellow cabs doing deliveries from Newark used Korean as their radio language.

He was particularly fascinated by the fate of the twenty-eight motorized gypsies murdered so far that year, the famous gypsies, nearly all of whom were Latin American, who made up a radio-taxi syndicate, driving sixty-foot-long limousines and Oldsmobiles in Brooklyn and the Bronx. They were often murdered for nickels and dimes on picking up a fare. Who had decided to turn them into New York's biggest victims at the end of the millennium, and how? Maybe the clue was to be found in the rabid xenophobia that boiled over in the city's hot stove of madness now and again.

Jerry gathered up articles, newspaper clippings, recorded tapes, and notes hurriedly taken on paper napkins. He knew these notes would come in useful sooner or later. That was how he found out that the Colombian surname Macías was like mud in the taxi world, that the Iranian taxi drivers were the ones who spoke the worst English, that the Ukrainians were the ones who got the most traffic tickets per day, that the experts in getting tips were the Hondurans, and that the ones who got lost the most in New York were the Nigerians. He had also located a dozen pizza parlors and hamburger joints that were meeting places for taxi drivers, a store selling amulets for Haitian drivers, and a factory making statuettes of the Baby Jesus of Prague for Czech drivers.

It was, after all, a better idea to worry about taxi drivers than the unhinged paranoid aberrations that the reappearance of Mr. C, that old dinosaur who had come back from the past, had thrown him into.

Singh, the Indian taxi driver, hit the brakes outside 175 Fifth Avenue, the Flatiron Building, turned the corner, and asked Jerry for another cigarette.

Following Mr. X was doubtless the easiest apparent way to get to the Bulgarian's hiding place, but Mr. Christo had lived through a lot, learned a lot, so he must have set up a whole network of trip wires around the Ghanaian that was complex and baroque enough from the point of view of a Bulgarian survivor, and that would then be incomprehensible, so Jerry, who was hardly innocent himself, figured that it would be easier to find the Bulgarian by going through all the hospitals in New York City one by one, than by trying to get to him by following a Ghanaian, a professional in the already professionalized trade of go-betweens or middlemen. Was he really in Mexico, or was he just sending Jerry on a hellish wild-goose chase?

The doorman on the morning shift at the Flatiron Building greeted Jerry with a smile, stopped sorting through the mail he had to deliver, and waited. He liked this gray-haired gringo who handed twenty-dollar bills around like someone who played high-stakes poker.

"Could you make sure this gets to Nicolás?" Jerry asked him, handing him a brown-paper envelope. "This, and a message. I'll see him in three days' time in El Paso, in the usual place, and tell him to come and find me in the hotel."

Vicente took the envelope, waited for Jerry to flash him a twenty, and sang the first line of an old Mexican bolero "La Nave del Olvido," without it having to do with anything.

"That's an Armando Manzanero song," said Jerry, who could rarely be fazed by anything anymore.

"No fucking way, it's by Carlos Lico and it's sung by José José," the doorman answered.

But maybe the gringo was right. Vicente watched him carefully. This goddamn gringo was full of surprises. Jerry turned around and went away.

When he got back to the street, he looked for a cigarette in his pants pocket. It was getting more and more dificult to find decent tobacco in New York. You could not get Mexican *Príncipes* or Argentinean *Parisiens* anymore, Spanish *Ducados* were hard to find, and you could only get Canadian *Gitanes* now and again.

He walked to his hotel room, where he reread the Bulgarian's letter carefully. He sat down to think, the TV on, without getting sidetracked by any of the paraphernalia scattered around his room.

Jerry had a collection of exotic beer cans and a huge mural devoted to taxi drivers. All the murder scenes from the past year were marked on a huge map of New York. No matter how hard he looked, there was no scheme, no pattern at all, but he had managed to single out a neighborhood, a type of taxi, and a behavioral pattern for the murderer. In the North Bronx, there was a series of seven gypsy murders that could be linked to a single murderer by his modus operandi. There might be something in it.

This taxi business had come about as a way of passing the time until something new dropped into his lap. But it gradually became a bit of an obsession. Jerry made himself a chicken sandwich with Dijon mustard while he stared at his mural.

Once he realized that thinking was not going to make him smarter nor know more than he did already, he put a selection of mariachi songs on his tape player. It was the only Mexican thing he had available. Well, he would have to retire from the taxi business for a while, a story that would get him on the front page of the *New York Post*: FORMER CIA MAN TRACKS DOWN NY TAXI KILLERS: NIGHTMARE OVER. Or something like that. But for now, it was Mexico and the Bulgarian. A meeting that was fifteen years overdue.

Nothing good could come of it, nothing at all; but he was $200,000 better off than a couple of hours before, and he might as well die in Mexico as in any other place.

Jerry remembered something spurred by the influence of the mariachis' trumpet: that it is a good idea to let yourself get fooled by your desires.

Leonardo (VIII)

The man who had invented a way to get sunken ships off the bottom of the sea, who we might call the founder of mountain climbing, who would invent the bicycle and reinvent the enigmatic female smile, wrote the following toward the end of 1503: *Our desires deceive us; time is short, death laughs at our concerns; a life beset by restlessness is nothing.*

What might have seemed an expression of contrived pessimism was in fact nothing more than a well-rounded complaint about the awful technological constraints of his time. Leonardo could give free rein to his ideas in the infinite realms of his imagination and invent just about anything on paper, but where were the craftsmen, the finances, the forges, the glass furnaces, the apparatus makers, the giant bellows, the skins, or the special cloth that could make the Magus's dreams reality?

Leonardo had once written:

If a man has at his disposal a tent measuring twelve cubits wide by twelve high and covered with a canopy, then he might jump from any height without harm to himself.

He did not confine himself to designing that thing, which would later be called a parachute, in his imagination. There is a marvelous drawing to be seen, of a man jumping with a parachute, a sort of dome made from sections of cloth with a man hanging from its framework, a cloth pyramid with a man hanging underneath it, and this can be found on the front of page 381 of what we now call the Atlanticus Codex, in the Ambrosiana Library in Milan.

To make the parachute, however, he had to experiment, to carry out tests, and even to find volunteers. Would he himself have been one of them? Life kept on pushing him from one place to another, from one job to another, from one commission to another, to a patron, a city council, or a noble who wanted a painting of his wife. Everything seemed to vanish into thin air, like his idea of writing a novel.

Leonardo seemed to have found the time, place, and money to do it when Cesare Borgia appointed him military engineer on August 18, 1502. Leonardo went from one end of Romagna to another following one of the Renaissance's darkest figures, as one of his retinue, drawing maps, doing calculations for towers, designing fortresses and walls, thinking up military wonders, almost without any of his plans coming to fruition in the turbulent times of that campaign.

Finally, in 1504, he came to rest in Piombino, where he studied the tides from the Porto Vecchio or Porto Falesia up to the Gulf of Baratta, with the old fortified Etruscan city of Populónia as a reference point. His notebooks were filled up with notes on the tides, drawings of little ships, and graphs of the sea bed, i.e. all sorts of observations on the sea. His wanderings around the area were occasion for tongues wagging and some amazement. What was he looking for? Why was he so keen on staring at the sea? Did he know something about it that the locals had missed? Did he know a bit more than just about tides? Did he have any tips about something hidden at the bottom of the sea?

SECTOR FIVE

Desperately Seeking Karen

The Ballad of the Stars
(Part Two)

A pair of (very muddled) novels by

José Daniel Fierro

My life is a barren field,
flowers I touch their leaves do shed;
along my fateful way,
someone sows evil
that I may reap it.

—Jorge Manrique

A Bouquet of Roses

Antonio Amador did not feel particularly immortal, quite the contrary. Death was lurking in wait, sometimes like a duty, sometimes like a debt, sometimes like a pain in the ass; but although he felt its closeness and could even smell it on bad days, he also knew how to move it away with a slight touch of his fingertips. Not to get rid of it altogether, but just to push it a few inches back so that his personal halo did not go out on him. It was just to do with keeping death at a comfortable distance. In that way, death gave life meaning. And from knowing this he reckoned that neither this or that would be the last time he saved his skin by chance.

As well as his usual conviction that he would meet death in his own good time and that he would not give up his prearranged program just to suit the plans of a mortal, vulgar policeman, Amador had two other more tangible things to count on; it was raining in floods and the Cuban magician Leonardo Padura Buenaventura was traveling with them in the truck that was taking them to jail. The magician could be a determining factor, but the rain also had a lot to do with it as Amador knew (and you might well wonder how he managed to be so sure) that he was not going to die on a rainy day, turning around the phrases penned by a little Peruvian poet he would get to meet one day, and ten years ahead of his time.

It was hopelessly raining cats and dogs, and had gone dark. The truck was driven by a uniformed man with two of Arlegui's gunmen by his side; it made its way slowly along the middle of the backstreets. The Black Angel was lying semi-conscious in the rear part, which was separated from the front seat by some bars, with one of his feet handcuffed to the little journalist, who was handcuffed in turn to the Cuban magician, who had also been beaten up by the policemen, as far as could be seen.

Amador was not paying attention to the policemen's chatter, as he was absorbed in thinking how he was going to be saved, what with the rain and the magician. The truck emerged from the maze of side streets and went down the Icaria Avenue toward some part of the harbor.

"My life is a barren field/flowers I touch their leaves do shed," Angel del Hierro said in a halting voice.

Amador got near to him, trying to listen to the words. He had to get right up to the injured man's face.

"My life is a barren field/flowers I touch their leaves do shed/along my fateful way/someone sows evil/that I may reap it."

Amador stared at the Angel, and then laughed. A half-assed crackpot, quoting Jorge Manrique.

"Don't you like it?" the anarchist asked him.

Amador wiped his bloody lips on the cuff of his jacket. "I love it, pal, just love it."

"Well, don't forget it then," the Angel said.

"Never."

The Angel tried to get up onto one of his elbows. "Did I get all of them?"

"You sent the Monkey on his way, you certainly hurt the Baron, and Soler got away. When you ran out of bullets, you kicked some other guy's teeth in," the little journalist summed up for him, digging into his memory: the baron crumpled up in a doorway, Soler running away from the Black Angel's shots as the square filled up with policemen.

"What's our friend here saying?" asked the magician as he emerged from his tropical reverie.

"He's reciting some verse by Manrique. The one that goes *My life is a barren field/flowers I touch their leaves do shed/along my fateful way/someone sows evil/that I may reap it.*"

"I like it, I really like it," the Cuban magician said, and then pulled his ankle out of the handcuffs without even taking his shoe off.

"Well fuck me sideways! How'd you do that?" Amador asked him in astonishment, remembering an expression from his grandfather, who no one came near to when it came to swearing.

"To smoke a cigarette."

"No, not why, but how?" Amador asked him again, stretching his hand out so that the magician could pass him the packet.

Leonardo Padura Buenaventura played around with the handcuff on Amador's ankle for a bit and then he drew the manacles away sharply. A flame ignited between his ankles instantaneously, and he brought it up to Amador so he could light his cigarette.

"I always wanted to have an anarchist magician in our ranks," Amador said in amazement. "And why do they want to kill you?"

"I took the Captain General's girlfriend's knickers off, brother, then I set a count's shirt front on fire, and, for an encore, I made a bodyguard's pistol vanish."

"By magic?"

The Cuban magician smiled, showing a few gold teeth. It was a cheerful, feline smile. The Black Angel was shaking in his feverish, wounded sleep.

"He's losing blood," Amador said, looking at his friend.

"Something has to be done," the Cuban magician said, drawing on his cigarette as if he wanted to finish it off in one drag. "Something outstanding, exceedingly beautiful, something really spectacular. None of your cheap magic, man, something like . . ." And he finished off by pulling a bunch of roses from out of his sleeve and giving them to the little journalist.

The Carrier of the Snow White Syndrome

Snow White wakes up when princes kiss her in her sleep. Or was that Sleeping Beauty? Was it both of them? Who went around eating poison apples? The fact is that she (and there is always a she) wakes up under the influence of a kiss. Walt Disney said this with music by Wagner, or Spielberg with music by Vangelis, or Amado Nervo with music by Carlos Santana, it is all the same thing, it does not matter. It is the same thing whether it was Vangelis, Beethoven, Santana, Borodin, or Marc Knopfler, because they would not let me kiss Karen Turner when the sympathetic nurse's shift finished. What is more, they would keep me ten feet back from her, as if I were the sick man, the carrier of death. Karen, meanwhile, would open her eyes and look at the doctors, with the tips of her toes under the sheets and with a bluish cloth folding screen separating her living space from that of the other patients.

"I want to see the man with the mustache," she might say, in English.

One of the nurses would know what was happening, and I would be in front of her a second later, bewildered and apprehensive.

"I feel like shit," Karen Turner would say.

"It's a long story," I might say, sucking my mustache.

She would keep on staring at me. Friend or foe? And I would then like to place bloody trophies at the foot of her bed, like her kidnappers' heads, but all I would have would be a bunch of roses to place on top of the sheets, a bunch I would imagine to be as bright and fragrant as the one the Cuban magician pulled out of nowhere in the truck.

I would try to see myself through Karen's eyes: the character with the ample mustache and the leg in plaster, a checkered shirt and a belt with the golden eagle from the national crest, chronic bronchitis, who might seem like something from another planet . . . but everything would be from another planet, even the bunch of red roses.

Then the E.T. of the Wild Frontier, faggot-asshole-cocksucker, instead of declaring his undying love for Snow White, would get a Philips portable tape recorder out and try to begin a criminal investigation, that the gigantic woman basketball player would wave to a stop.

"No, I'll ask the questions first," Karen might say, baring her teeth in a fairly bitter grin. "Who the hell are you? What are you doing here?"

And then the Snow White Syndrome Carrier, who would then remember, as I would remember, I would have to remember, that he has already turned fifty-three and that she is eight inches taller than him, I would raise my arm to my head and ruffle the gray hairs around my temples. I would then look around for some doctors and nurses to get me out of this jam, and in the end, I would get to feel like lighting a cigarette in violation of the hospital rules and opt for the direct approach.

"They let you smoke here?" Karen might ask.

"Yes, it's a Mexican hospital. They're very permissive in this country."

"You can tell."

She will look at me with bewilderment on her face and then she would wave me on to start my story.

"I had just turned really old and was watching a basketball game on TV in Mexico City . . ."

"Which one?"

And everything would seem so farcical, that I would try again.

"I am the E.T. of the Wild Frontier, a sort of literary alien, my girl. I'm a writer. I'm a vampire sucking the blood out of other people's stories. I came to Ciudad Juárez to write a novel."

"We won that one, didn't we? We creamed those bitches from Iowa, right?"

"Because if I didn't come . . ."

"Ninety-one to sixty-seven, and then Jackie O'Brien and I came down to El Paso to celebrate. They killed her, didn't they?"

"That's right. They killed her, they drugged and kidnapped you and you turned up here two days later, in Ciudad Juárez with a kidney missing, an illegal operation. But I've already told you that, they told you already. And I was waiting for the next game in Mexico City, and then when

I saw that neither you nor Jackie were on court, that your teammates were wearing black ribbons for mourning, I took a bus and . . ."

Karen would stare at me in the light of this new information. She would beckon the nurse who would be a few steps away from us.

"What does this man normally do?" she might ask, pointing an accusing finger at me.

"He writes novels, miss," Cindy Pérez would answer, in a fortuitous appearance.

Karen might reconsider everything based on the supposition that nurses do not tell lies. Novelists, on the other hand . . .

"You put that there, didn't you?" she might say, pointing to my grandfather's da Vincian bicycle.

I would nod. I would have told her that story, too, but would she have been awake? Leonardo's bicycle. A woman basketball player come back to life. Karen Turner would touch the old photograph with her fingers, as though looking for contours that do not exist.

"What do you write? Have you got a book of yours in English? Could you give me a book of yours in English so I can read it? My father said that you should read writers, not know them. That they were unbearable in person, that he once met Hemingway in a clothing store. Hemingway was trying a jacket on . . . I want one of your books. Now."

And then, the Snow White (or was it Sleeping Beauty?) who used to go around giving elbow jabs in the ribs would smile openly for the first time.

Salvation

The uniformed policeman was the first to run away as though he had the devil at his heels. Leonardo Padura Buenaventura had stared into his eyes and said:

"Don't you feel, sir, as if a snake is twisting itself around your neck? As if what seemed like your innocent tie is a poisonous cobra, a vicious asp? Can't you feel the rough scales on your skin? Don't you realize that . . ."

One of Arlegui's gunmen was on his knees trying to put out an imaginary fire that was running up his sleeves, while the other one, who must have been at least partially immune to hypnosis, drew his Star, aimed it at his partner's chest, then hesitated and looked around for the magician, as if trying to make things clear in a world where there were no longer friends or enemies.

"I'm going to fuck you," he said.

But the Cuban magician put his hand into the ragged pocket in his jacket, took his own pistol out, and shot the policeman twice in the chest before he could react, saying:

"This is our song, baby!"

Amador, in the back of the truck, pushed the doors open with his feet and cheered. Then he got down, a bunch of roses in his hand. It was still raining.

"Bloody hell, that was great. How do you do that last trick?"

"Trick my ass, it was a gun I'd disappeared from a policeman beforehand," said Padura Buenaventura.

A pair of beggars covered in newspapers came up to congratulate the magician. One of them kicked the shot policeman, who was lying on the pavement, in the head. The beggars shook the Cuban's hand very ceremoniously, and he thanked them for their compliments. The other policeman was still on fire, despite the rain.

"Give us a hand, let's see if we can still save Del Hierro," Amador said, grabbing the ragged sleeve on the Cuban's jacket.

"Who, me?" Del Hierro asked, as he dragged himself over the edge of the truck and fell into a puddle. The blood from his shirt ran into the dirty water lit up by the streetlamp.

Amador went up to the man and tried to lift him up. If Del Hierro didn't die from that, he'd catch his death of cold.

"I have to get on a ship," the Cuban said.

"Which one?"

"Any."

The beggars had prudently vanished, the policeman tried to roll into the gutter to see if the running water could put out the fire in his sleeves. The whole scene seemed as if lit up by the imaginary fire.

The two comrades disappeared up a side street off Icaria Avenue, dragging Del Hierro's unconscious body after them. In the distance, a grain warehouse offered a safe refuge. They could hear lonely sirens. A far-off lighthouse seemed to show them the way.

"Do you have a doctor you know, my friend?" the Cuban asked.

Amador thought carefully.

"There is one, but at the other end of Barcelona."

"It's on the way back then, and we'll take the truck. Then you can drive me to the harbor."

"Can you drive?"

"No, how about you?"

"Me neither."

Amador looked at the terrible magician holding the wounded Angel up by the shoulders. The little journalist could not do two things at once. Either he could think, or he could hold Angel's legs. Amador seemed to be criticizing the limitations of magic with his eyes. But journalists are usually resourceful people, so he turned around and walked up to the first doorway in the rain. He rang a bell that sounded raucous.

A man, who had probably been watching everything from behind a window, appeared in the doorway, in a vest and with a butcher knife in his hand.

"What can I do for you?" he said, very correctly.

Amador showed his hands were empty to make it clear he was not up to anything.

"Do you know how to drive a truck? We need a hand to get a friend to a doctor."

"Are you policemen?" the man with the butcher knife asked. He certainly had not shaved recently and had a strong smell of red wine about him.

"Just the opposite. Arlegui's henchmen were driving us off to kill us," Amador said, sensing that the fellow was on their side.

"Jesus, you should have said so before. I'm the best driver in Barcelona! Gervasio Menea," the man introduced himself, and without more than a firm handshake threw the knife into the house and went out into the street without being bothered by the rain that soaked his vest right away. As he went past, he gave the on-fire policeman, still dancing deliriously below the streetlamp, a hefty kick in the balls.

"You thought you were the only one who could do magic? This is Barcelona, pal," Amador told the Cuban magician. Then he lifted his hands and his face toward the sky, pointing to the stars, taking it all in, soaking his face, whirling his arms around windmill-like in an effort to lift himself up, in a triumphant gesture, looking for the sea, turning his body around like a compass. But the sea, as ever, was hidden by warehouse fences and the thick wall of rain.

Indiana Fierro on the Balcony

"You were sleeping with Nico Romero," he might ask the neighbor from number 5, without further ado.

"A glass of lemonade?" she might answer immediately, keeping the doorway blocked with her body.

A woman with very short hair, barely an inch long, so short that you could tell she had it cut like that so as to use a wig, dressed in the top half of a man's checkered pajamas and some scanty black panties, would be staring at me with a smile in the passageway of a building in whose upper floor I had already been the Apartment-Block Housebreaker.

"With two sugars."

The woman would leave the door ajar, and then the Indiana Jones of the Absurd would push past it to get into the apartment. The woman would give me a sideways stare as she moved glasses around in the kitchen and found a lemon squeezer. There were cushions thrown on the living room floor, ashtrays full to the brim, and empty glasses.

"Dolores, right."

"And why do you want to know about Nico? We were friends, but one day he was here, the next he was gone . . . he went away."

"Right," I would say, following an original line.

"And who might you be?" she would say, handing me a dubious glass of lemonade.

"I . . ."

"What do you want with him?"

"Everybody's looking for Nico."

"A girlfriend of his is also looking for him, that stupid bitch Emilia. But she doesn't like men, she likes women."

"Listen, what did Nico want four cans of cockroach spray for?"

"For the house they had in El Paso that was crawling with them. Goddamn cockroaches everywhere, you know. Wherever you wanted to go, the cockroaches got there first."

We might go over to the balcony. There was nothing to see, just a suburban desert with single-story houses and cars. It would be getting dark.

"How did you break your leg?"

"Coming out from the movies."

"Do you go to a lot of parties? We party all the time in Juárez. We have a really wild time, here and there, and we screw a lot."

"Well, down in Mexico City, what with the pollution, the acid rain, the flooding, the altitude, we screw less and less, you know."

She might look at me sarcastically. Then she would look at the street. I would lean on the balcony rail, not being sure how to throw the lemonade without anyone noticing.

"And what about the dog?" I would ask, to see if changing the subject might get me somewhere in this line of questioning.

"What dog?"

"Nico's. Didn't he buy a lot of dog food?"

"No, Nico didn't have a dog. Over there in El Paso they had a dog, you know, that foreign man."

"And did this foreigner screw a lot?"

"No . . . listen, just who are you? I mean, what do you do?"

"I'm a writer. I'm writing Nico's story." I would wave my arm, trying to take the whole world in. "It's really fascinating."

"Really?" She would raise her hand to her cropped, almost nonexistent hair.

"I also want to know about Nico's friend, that Mike Gardner guy. His partner."

"Well, Nico and his friends sort of scare me. So much that I think I'm going to go over the border," Dolores would say to me with a sideways glance.

"Do they party up there? Do they screw a lot in the North?"

The woman might then put her hand on the thigh I have against the rail. To hide her intentions, she would pick up the last of my cigarettes and I would be trying to light it just as she put both hands on my chest and pushed me.

"Shit!"

"Die, you asshole!" the woman would say as she ran out of the apartment. I would be hanging from the balcony, my good leg caught between the railings, with my hand clutching the rail and the rest of my body floating, inertia set to make me fall three floors headfirst.

My cap and cigarette lighter will be the first to go and

I would not be able to do anything to stop them, seeing the thirty-foot drop, the cars, some kids playing soccer on the sidewalk, and I might fall, I might almost fall, because my fingers could not . . .

And I would say, this is like out of a novel, not the other business, but this is reality and not dumbass conversations about other people's dogs, while a couple of taxis go past at full speed thirty feet below my head, which is looking at the world upside down.

And I might keep on thinking, as I try to get my good leg back into balance to counter the awesome weight of my plaster leg that is trying to drag me into space, but at the same time I would stop, stuck, that the Barcelona novel is spraying shit around with a fan, throwing questions up on every page that should not be there, because novels are not questionnaires, and I would not have a good library to delve in, but rather I would be scared to find the answers. But furthermore, dammit, my grasping fingers are losing their strength, it cannot be that way, it would be too much like real life and not enough like fiction, the characters will be following a broad scheme, an enormous rope, a cable that would be guiding the fate of anarchist Barcelona in the early 1920s, and not developing personal stories or building up enigmas. Amador would not have a twin brother who was the son of a count from Burgos, nor would mysterious characters cross its pages. Also, my grandfather, good old Angel, as ever, would be condemned to stay on the sidelines while the little journalist grabs the limelight. And if I don't die then, now, I might say, trying to make use of my plaster leg to swing back up again, to manage at last to get a hold on the edge of the balcony with my other hand and sweating profusely, I would have to seriously get into this novel. And I would come back to life by getting a shoulder onto the rail with a supreme effort, and all before finding Nico and Mike and well, at least, I would think while putting my leg back on the balcony, Dolores's glass of lemonade would have gone to shit and the Angel would still be alive in Barcelona.

Nun, sans Mustache

The government crisis produced the presumption that the governor of Barcelona would have to be changed; along with this presumption came a temporary lifting of censorship, and the story broke all over the place in fresh ink. Newspapers were being avidly read throughout Spain and particularly in the city upon which centered all the great events. Queues of workers would form on streetcorners in the early hours waiting for the newspaper sellers to show up. The news would be commented on in cafés and factory entrances, in offices, in queues for bread, and in front of counters in banks. Angel Pestaña was writing for the still illegal *Soli* from his hideout:

The Lion D'Or, the café where the most select high-fliers got together, has become the focal point, the meeting place for those that kill. Suppers are organized, banquets are thrown, wild orgies are held, and work goes on between one glass of champagne and another, between starters and dessert. . . . Sometimes a copious and sumptuous supper is interrupted so as to go out for a few minutes for a hit to be made, and when this has been done, the supper carries on and is peppered with tales of the particulars, incidents, and circumstances that took place during the operation. They speak of the way the attack was carried out, how the victim resisted, his cries for help, which one of the hit men gave the coup de grâce, *and other odds and ends that reveal the typical depravity and cynicism of degenerate and abnormal people. The job these people have is invariable, almost the same every day. The visit the police chief's office every afternoon, where the victim, or victims, for that day are pointed out. Afterward, they do some target practice so as not to miss and* get it over with *as they used to say, and in two shakes they visit the place the victim has to die in, and then there is the execution.*

Not everything took place in such a carefully orchestrated way.

A confused character turned up in the editorial offices of *El Sol*, claiming to be Bernardo Armegnol—Baron von König's right-hand man—in the middle of a binge and offering to sell his story. At first, after consulting with Madrid, he was given two thousand pesetas and two stenographers were sat in front of him, to whom he poured out eleven hours of delirium and confessions mixed up with stories of crimes and concierges' gossip, names of figures in the Barcelona bosses' organization involved with crimes committed by König's gang and their connections with the Captain General's and the police chief's offices. Once the material was put in order, the order from Madrid came to wait, to freeze the gangster's confessions like half-rotten fish.

It was Antonio Amador's long-awaited article that definitely blew the lid off the scandal just hinted at in the other papers. Amador fought for three days with pages of manuscript that were threatening to turn into an encyclopedia. The little journalist locked himself up in an attic belonging to Benito Melindres, the king of numismatists and well-known whoremonger, and on a diet of Indian tea robbed from a British cargo ship in the harbor with lots of sugar, and after using all known literary resources, including sucking his pencil, he came up with fourteen sheets that were worthwhile. They came out on the front page of *España Neuva*, from Madrid, which sold out a few hours after coming out on the street, as did three reprints that came on the trains that ran between the Spanish capital and the Catalan port.

Even so, the article, signed "Rocambole," held some information back that the organization circulated in a pamphlet entitled *Stories from the Dark Side of Barcelona* where the little journalist, writing under his own name in an act of suicidal audacity, revealed the mob's activities in detail and with spicy prose, full of anecdotes about König's lover's stockings, the meetings in Miró's offices, the relationships between the gang and the waitresses in the Apollo, the connection between the gunmen and the army Captain General's office, a compendium of crimes by Soler, the Majorcan, and the amounts charged by Inspector Luis León for selling false passports, the drug connections in the ballrooms, the addresses of the illegal gambling houses under police protection, and a list of murders committed by the mob. The pamphlet provoked an uproar all over Spain and went abroad by news-agency wires. Amador was the man of the moment and a photograph taken of him, ominously autographed and with him smoking, of course, and seated, to obscure his real height, was auctioned in the union office of a textile mill in Badalona, where there were lots of female staff.

The pamphlet went from hand to hand for the next three days among all the workers in Barcelona, a large part of the shopkeepers, all the journalists, the majority of servants, craftsmen, and almost all of the uncultured people in the city, and was reprinted six times. Amador was locked away by the police while he was picking up fresh copies of the pamphlet with the red cover from a secret press in Igualada.

"Try taking away the fun I've had," Amador said as they came for him, before disappearing into the arms of a Civil Guard, who somewhat unusually respected the law and prevented his colleagues from taking advantage of his fainting and beating him up.

A local doctor recognized the small body stretched on the pavement and diagnosed him.

"Consumption, this fellow is dying of starvation. He has not eaten for at least three or four days, and his lungs are in bad shape."

The police immediately drove him to the Modelo prison, to place him under the jurisdiction of the courts, a clear indication that times had changed, as otherwise they would have applied the "law of flight," shooting him while attempting to "escape," in some dark alley. Given that the little journalist had six censorship charges hanging over him, he prepared himself for a long, forced holiday in jail.

The bosses' organization felt obliged to deny the accusations on May 17, but the denunciations stepped up day by day. A campaign is something that goes beyond those who start it and even those who try to stop it. The other newspapers joined in the business and a day never went by without new accusations against the bosses' organization appearing.

Amador, who was safer inside jail than out and who, thanks to the Pro-Prisoners Committee, was eating three times a day, paced up and down his cell asking questions no one could answer.

"Why don't they do away with König? Now he's more of a hindrance than a help to them. The scandal is going to screw Colonel Arlegui. Is somebody going to catch the Baron off-guard now that the police aren't protecting him? Where's the Black Angel gone? What does Dolores think about me?"

He also coughed, drawing furious stares from his cell-mates, who could not concentrate on their games of chess or their copies of *Man and Land* by Reclus.

In the midst of Amador's bloody coughing fits—which took him to the infirmary on more than one occasion, where his fever did not seem to subside—a rumor reached the prison to the effect that the Black Angel was prowling around König's offices on Rambla de las Flores, dressed as a nun and with two guns under his habit, to settle accounts once and for all. Amador believed the story and even imagined his friend, whom he had dropped off a month before in a clinic with two bullet holes in his collarbone and his chest, now dressed as a cloistered nun and looking a bit like a penguin, with a habit going down to the floor to cover his rope-soled shoes and with his mustache faithfully shaved off.

And the little journalist paced up and down in his confined world, taking advantage of his short legs and the long cells to skip around the universe in seventeen paces and take a break to smoke a quarter of a cigarette (he always seemed to have one up his sleeve, even though his cell-mates hid their tobacco). He had learned something during his fleeting relationship with the Cuban magician, who had vanished into thin air just like the Black Angel.

In the middle of these perambulations, Antonio Amador heard the rumor that was going from cell to cell, that the Interior Minister had decreed the expulsion order of Rudi Colmann, German subject, better known in Barcelona as Baron von König, on June 1. And that four days later, the governor of Barcelona had carried out the order and taken him to the French border along with his wife, René Scalda, she of the black stockings (which he hoped were now full of runs).

Amador heard the news with a mixture of pleasure and despair. The character was going to get out of Spain alive. The Black Angel had failed in his hunt for him.

There was more news, coming at opportune moments. Halfway through his midday soup, at night during his first fitful nap, during the visit by the buxom sister of the cell-mate next door, who had been taken in for mugging a lottery-ticket seller to give the money to the orphans, bit by bit, he heard about the dissolution of König's gang.

As the days went by and the information about the breakup of the gang became more detailed, it became known that one of them had joined the Foreign Legion, another had died in front of a brickworks, and yet another, a police inspector, had requested a transfer to Guadalajara. Amador feared that his life would lose its meaning; faced with this existential dilemma, he devoted himself to impossible platonic love affairs.

Thus it was, as he was imagining Dolores rolling cigarettes and stroking her breasts in a suggestive fashion, that he heard the news about Soler, the Majorcan, while somebody read him the *Novela Semanal*. He was on a steamship bound for Havana, carrying tons of money and with two women in tow. He wanted to set up a casino and whorehouse in the Caribbean islands. The news gave further details as to how he fought with a Galician over some problem to do with women, and how they knifed each other. He died five hours later saying he did not want to take his secrets to the grave. It was rumored that the man who killed him was not the Galician, but a union man who lived in Puerto Rico and that the typewritten confessions were headed for Amador. Nothing about the whole business was clear.

Amador saw the long, just hand of Angel del Hierro in all of this, dressed as a monk, a womanizing Galician, or a Senegalese hunchback. And he celebrated by sucking the rickety bones of a bit of whiting they had been given for supper that day until they shone. Then he thought a bit harder about the business and came to the conclusion that the whole thing rather seemed like the work of Leonardo Padura Buenaventura, the Cuban magician.

The Dime Novel Supplier

Halfway through her reading a couple of paperback books that I would have bought for her in a bookstore in El Paso, Karen would want to know exactly what had happened to her friend, the O'Brien girl. I would then show her the photos in the newspapers of the body dumped in the hotel doorway and the funeral. She might look at them carefully, without shedding a single tear. She might ask for a telephone later and make a few calls, to the university basketball team coach and to a brother of hers who, so it seems, works in a bank in Alaska. Then, just as her curiosity seemed insatiable, it might disappear and she would want nothing to do with all of it, with her convalescence, with what had happened, the death of her friend, her missing kidney, the itch in the scar that was healing, with the information about what you can do with just one kidney (not too much exercise, do not risk giving birth, a permanent watch over your health, an almost normal life, you know?), with her kidnappers, with the dark tales she would be carrying inside her head, even with the author of the novels she was reading. She would devote herself to reading.

I would then be a bundle of nerves, because being thrown off of a third-floor balcony turns out to be kids' stuff compared with having your own novels read to you, face-to-face. There are tortures and accidents. Ever watchful for signs of approval, a smile at the end of a chapter, I might find signs of boredom, which I would not know whether to ascribe to the novel in her hand, or to the black angels that must be running across her imagination, or the friendly and inimical ghosts that are living with Karen Turner.

At times, Karen might sink into a moment of sadness, which would end up in a few tears as she gazes into the hospital garden, gradually transforming into a look of rage. That would be the Karen I would recognize, angry with everyone, going through a whole hierarchy, beginning with herself.

Meanwhile, I would be doing the rounds of the hospital, going around other wards, other consulting rooms in the hospital, where young and foul-mouthed doctors will be discussing whether having been suspended from a balcony will have improved the possibilities of the bone in my leg knitting back together, whether they should take the cast off or wait for the scheduled time, or whether they should recommend being thrown off a balcony as a method for treating broken ankles. Whether you live through all that, all of it and everything else, is material for a novel.

They might let us walk around the hospital corridors, five days after having observed how Karen Turner, the retired basketball player, had entered a new stage in her life: of being a furious reader, with her fingernails bitten down. Like a pair of peaceful old folk in convalescence. Shit, we would both think, the idea coming to us at different times as we walked down the corridor, where some pots would be full of withered, half-dead plants due to lack of water. I would see Karen in her white bathrobe, dragging a stand along with a drip on it, a full eight inches taller than I, twenty-three years old as against my fifty-three. Grandpa with a broken foot takes his post-op granddaughter out for a walk.

And Karen would keep on reading, almost ignoring me.

Karen might get her hand out from under the sheet on the seventh night after the Sleeping Beauty's comeback, carefully move the catheter feeding the drip into her arm, and say:

"I won't be able to shoot hoops with a kidney missing, but I might be able to become a writer."

Away at Last

If early 1920s Barcelona had something, it was not being condemned to standing still. Social forces were a whirlwind that moved swiftly, dragging small happenings along with them. One day, anarchist unionists were on the edge of a revolutionary general strike, with 300,000 members acting like one man, which would end the world as it was known and usher in a new dawn of collective paradise and industrial cooperativism. But after a week, the strike had drawn back and there was a state of siege. One day it was the bosses' organization's gangs who controlled the streets, and a month later it was the anarchist hit squads who attacked more than fifty bosses, and were filling up the Catalan bourgeoisie's graveyards. One day there was the splendor of wartime trade with the allies, and the next the factory warehouses were full of unsellable products. One month was given over to apathy and Gypsy women who read palms, and the next was seized by the predictions of Bakunin and Prince Kropotkin, by the rumors of the Bolshevik revolution and the sailors' uprising in Germany. Sometimes union meetings were held in bullrings, and even they could not hold everybody, and a few days later union offices were closed down and armed men from the secret police or anarchist hit squads lurked near their entrances. Life was lived to the limit, with the strange idea that everything was imminent, everything was possible, or impossible, everything, especially death.

It was just like that that the governor of Barcelona, Count Salvatierra, was dismissed on June 22, and replaced by a liberal monarchist, Josep Carles Bas, who decreed an amnesty. Antonio Amador combed his hair carefully, hugged his cell-mates, all those who were leaving or staying behind (because when it came to amnesties, you never knew who it would be next, due to the workings of the law, the ambiguities of the decree, bureaucrats' carelessness, or judges' shady dealings), and walked out of the Modelo prison into a sunny day.

Amador grabbed some words for himself, which would someday be written by a young and barely known novelist with an aristocratic name, Ramón María del Valle Inclán: *I am the torment of a bad dream*, and so as not to abandon his premonition, he said to himself in someone else's words: *How the sun shines on hearses, on the gilding!* These morbid thoughts went well with his character and his health.

He drew up a list of priorities: 1) work, 2) health, 3) the Angel's whereabouts, 4) seeing Dolores from afar, 5) lodgings. They made it clear in *La Publicidad* that they would not take him on again even if he walked right down the Ramblas on his knees. After being carefully examined in the Clinical Hospital, they told him they were neither a funeral agency nor a hotel, both of which he needed a lot more than medicine. But even if the journalist had insisted in staying, a bed cost two whole pesetas a day.

He bumped into Liberto Calleja in a bank on the Gran Vía de las Cortes.

"The comrades are a talkative mass where you can see the effects of isolation. It's just the time when the faint of heart give in."

Amador, who was hardly an optimist, but whom the street scene put in a good mood, did not go quite so far.

"Don't even think of looking around for work, they'll just spit in your face. Don't kid yourself, the bosses have come out of this stronger than ever, especially with the lockout. We're going to have to begin to operate in secret, there's no way the shop stewards can act openly."

"So?"

"You've got just one chance. *España Nueva* has opened an office in Barcelona. Maybe there. The pay's bad."

"They censor less, though," Amador said. The sun was increasing his optimism, drying up the malignant effluvia in his lungs and making him feel like having a smoke.

Amador put his hands in his pockets and found he had a dirty handkerchief, a pamphlet that had the words and music to "Man the Barricades!," a leaflet from a pharmacy where you could get a discount on condoms, his Federation card, a peseta, and two toothpicks. He got the card out and gave the peseta to Liberto, who put five twenty-centime stamps in the squares on his card.

The Unfailing Witness

And I would not give a shit what I might want to hear and what she would be ready to tell, because deep down I would be much more interested in knowing what she thought about Chapter 5 of *Pancho Villa's Head*, or if she liked the ending of *The End of the World*, when the guy gets on his motorcycle . . . But it might then seem that nobody can dictate Karen's pace, not even I, the Unfailing Witness, the UW, who would sound like a stupid version of the North American Free Trade Agreement in those fateful days, in dreary old Ciudad Juárez, where days would pile up on previous days and chains of gringo ice cream parlors would compete with a clear edge over the lemon ice vendors in the street.

Then suddenly:

"There were two of them, the ones who jumped on Jackie and me in the hotel entrance. One had silver boots on.

Silver boots? Silver tips . . . The other one was American, like us. He said something in English, I don't remember what. The car was black. That's it, I can't remember anything else about the kidnapping. The smell of chloroform that got me in the throat."

"But there must have been a house, then an operating room. Or did they do it in the same house? Well, if they took you to a hospital, they must have taken you back to the house."

Karen shook her head.

"Nothing? A house? A dog? A foreigner? Someone who was neither Mexican nor American? Cockroaches . . . conversations . . . it must be in El Paso."

Karen shook her head again.

"Nothing, until I ended up in here. I opened my eyes, felt I couldn't talk, that I'd been struck dumb. There was a guy with a mustache looking at me. You."

"Nothing?"

"Nothing . . . I'm sorry."

Karen's strange beauty would be there for whoever would want to behold it, for whoever might invent it. Her long blond hair would have grown over the days, and there would be her wild-looking mouth, perhaps because of that toothy grin she pulled now and again, her protruding chin, and devilishly green eyes.

"You know more than I do."

"Bits and pieces that don't even fit together. There were two guys with the pickup, just as you recall. I suppose the one we know as the guy with the silver-tipped boots is called Nico, an ex-cop from Sabinas, the one who kicked Jackie to death. The one who filled you with chloroform was a gringo called Mike Gardner. They were looking for you. Did you have a medical examination sometime in Austin?"

"I suppose so, I don't know. The checkups they give you every three months in the team."

"Did you ever have kidney trouble? Did you volunteer to be a donor? Did a relative of yours lose a kidney, something like that?"

Karen shook her head again. She was getting upset. The hands that did not have a basketball to play with were holding the sheets tightly.

"Were you in hospital at any time? Here or there?"

"When I was born, you dope. Then last year because of the accident . . ." Her eyes brightened. "A car crash, when we were coming back from a game."

"Did they carry out any tests on you?"

"Not on me, I just broke this arm here," and she would show it, "but they did to some other girls . . ."

A pause. A long one. Karen was racking her brains.

"What?"

"Is it possible they got it wrong? That they were after Jackie but they got me?"

"Did she have kidney trouble?"

"I don't know, but they did some tests on her after the accident . . ."

"We can check that out . . . you don't remember anything about the house, the operating room, nothing?"

Karen shook her head. Again. She was beginning to despair. I would light a cigarette.

"I don't know if I want to know anymore," she might say and then, after a pause, "Do they let you smoke in Mexican hospitals?"

Sad Angel

The Baron had disappeared. He had crossed the French border at Figueras, taken off his monocle to shed a smug tear, and vanished. He might be in Paris with a new name by now, or in Monte Carlo or Milan. The office on the Ramblas had been dismantled in a matter of hours. The Baron had gone out, taken a taxi, and disappeared, carrying a pigskin suitcase, which was probably full of pesetas. His band had completely split up. Its inheritors were toddlers, waiting in the wings. It might be that lawyer who was accused by the unions of having sold out to the bosses' organization and passing information to them from the booths in the Modelo prison, it could be the new gangs of gunmen from the Free Union. This last had begun to organize itself during the final weeks of the lockout and was made up almost entirely by traditional monarchists and strikebreakers with links to the church. Its hit squads were made up of grunts who were part of the huge underworld of Barcelona, which was built up and rebuilt every day in Chinatown. Or it might be that crazy scab whom the workers' wives spat on that day he felt like driving a streetcar during the strike and who suffered from delusions of grandeur, who thought he was the illegitimate son of a count, that life had not done him justice . . .

The Angel had to be very attentive, to observe all of them, to watch and listen while he kept up correspondence with anarchists in France and Italy, even in faraway Germany and Switzerland, while waiting for the Baron's reappearance.

Meanwhile, it was a vegetarian diet, open-air walks in the country on Sundays, an office job with a shipping line under an assumed name, living in a boarding house in a neighborhood where nobody knew him, and keeping his guns well oiled. There were no appearances in the union offices, and above all, few meetings with trustworthy people. Angel was a man of few words in any case, speaking with comic gestures, looks, and one-on-one friendships. He wasn't a man for committees, public speaking, taverns, parties, or even dances.

Was the Black Angel depressed? No, he was just lost in stagnation. Was he not in the thick of the fight? Was he mistaken when he took up the pistol as the great democrat, the great leveler of social differences? Was Angel Pestaña right when he said that those who had taken up the revolver along the road of individual attack were lost to the collective cause and would sooner or later be lost in the society that was being forged in the basements of the Barcelona bourgeoisie? Did the road to swift justice, justice by point-blank shots in a backstreet, face-to-face with the enemy, close off the road to long-term justice? Angel thought about these things now and again. He thought about whether social revolution had come an inch nearer because of the men he had killed: two gunmen from the Baron's mob, a textile boss who raided his workers' pension fund, a corrupt policeman, a stool pigeon, the bosses' organization's chairman's chauffeur . . . He thought about his dead men with reluctance, because they were his and would be with him forever. In this war, you did not fire on faraway objects in the shadows of trenches, on unknown people who were disguised in uniforms different from yours. You fired on men ten, fifteen, three yards off, facing up to them so they could see the poor people's Angel of Death saying farewell to them before going off to the rich people's hell. It was a war of vengeance, and killing was easy, but dying was easier still. The Black Angel thought about that and bided his time.

There were times for waiting, but waiting never lasted long in Barcelona, and less so in his case. Just as Angel del Hierro was getting over the two gunshot wounds he'd received in the shoot-out in the Plaza del Peso de la Paja, looking at their pink edges, getting his appetite back, and feeling stronger and stronger, he met the woman who was to be his wife in a meeting of the print workers' union, to which he turned up disguised as an organ grinder.

The Sèvres Porcelain Lover

My grandmother. He met my grandmother. I might think about that. And on a far-off morning, too.

I came to two conclusions that fall morning in Manhattan, when it did not want to rain: a) God was not Mexican and b) wind like that was wasted on New York. Both observations were tenuously linked.

I might think about all this in Ciudad Juárez, in the burning wind that moves loose dirt and scatters its heat. The plants would be turning yellow in the backyard. Karen would be snoozing, watched over attentively by the nostalgic Sèvres Porcelain Lover, a character I had thought to be buried beneath my deepest memories.

I came back, then, to my line of argument in New York, dodging the lunch crowd, whom I looked at with the disdain that a carnivore feels for salad eaters: if God had been

Mexican, then the wind would have blown strongly every day in Mexico City, with that same marvelous and brutal intensity, to wipe away the smog. Ergo: God was not Mexican, or maybe he was, but not from Mexico City.

Perhaps God was from Toluca, although God, before this journey and its sequence of absurd reflections, seemed to be a gringo. Not from New York, of course. If God was a motherfucker, as was proven beyond doubt by the last twenty-five years of personal and world history, he could not then have come from a city so full of ethnic groups, faces, and cultures. He had to be some poor son of a bitch who hated everybody else, a Texan, a shithead from Nebraska, a Muslim fundamentalist, a Catalan storekeeper, or a Serbian nationalist, someone convinced that anyone born more than ten miles from Mecca, Lérida, Montenegro, or El Paso was a poor cocksucking asshole.

Afterward, while watching over the sleep of my murderous basketball player in Ciudad Juárez, controlling the smooth flow of her breathing, I would recall the story of the Sèvres porcelain I had fallen in love with, a marvelous green plate, made by Maximin Doat (1851–1939), a person for whom no references are given in Webster's. A plate made around 1900, with very sketchy silhouettes of women and pixies encrusted, almost suggested, in it. A plate that the label in the Metropolitan Museum described as being of "porcelain with pâté-sur-pâté inlays."

"Are you all right?" Karen would ask me, emerging from her sleep. I would nod my head, because I would not be able to believe all of this. How on earth could I have fallen in love with a piece of Sèvres porcelain? Karen would go sink back into dreamland, and my wristwatch would show it was half past four. Karen was turning Mexican. Siesta. Siesta time.

A Sèvres porcelain lover. Careful, just some, not all of it! Was that incompatible with writing detective stories and having set up student solidarity committees with the railroad strike in 1958? Could you be a fan of Santana and Joyce? A fan of Wagner and Frank Miller comic books? Eclecticism carried a heavy dose of guilt with it. It's an effort to be impure. Guilt was all right, it was as good a motive as any other, just as long as it did not show too much.

And then, in the Ciudad Juárez hospital, I might conclude that God was with them, that God was a Texan, that . . .

"You have a call," a nurse would say in a whisper. I would try to get up without making too much noise, and I would hobble over to the pay phone hanging on the wall by the entrance to the emergency room.

"What the hell are you doing in there? It's taken me all day to find you."

"Who's calling?" I would ask, risking that the answer might be what it would be.

"God, you jerk."

The Pompeya

Witnesses would later recall, with hoarse, broken voices broken up by sobbing or plain distress, that a person of medium height, dressed like a worker, sat down on one of the extra seats placed behind the stalls in the Pompeya music hall at a little after half past eleven at night.

A few yards away from him, some students from Zaragoza were having a good time watching half a dozen feathered chorus girls performing titillating dances. The boys from out of town did not give a second thought when the young man with a tense-looking face put his cap down on the seat next to him, got up, and walked out of the room a moment later. One of the students had the vague feeling that the man had gone out to take a leak.

One of the students, called Antonio, who was in one of the cheaper seats, as he was a student after all, smelled an acrid odor like a burning fuse and noticed that there was smoke coming out of the cap. He got up from his seat, attracted the attention of his friends, lifted the cap up and saw a bomb with a burning fuse. His first reaction was to run away, and he had barely taken two steps when the bomb went off.

Along with the bomb blast in the back seats of the stalls, there was a bright flare-up and a dense cloud of smoke that filled the whole room. The student from Zaragoza tried to get near to where his friends were, and then realized that he still had the cap in his hand and that his left arm was bleeding heavily where a piece of shrapnel had nearly sliced his hand off. The audience was trampling each other to get out of the theater. A few tables were broken, black smoke had filled the hall, and chaos grew among the shouts and the flames. The floor was full of wounded people and smashed crockery. A few women had fainted, including one of the dancers, who had keeled over. A large pool of blood marked the spot where the bomb had gone off.

The survivors were huddled in the entrance along with a few hundred people drawn in by the blast. Indignation was rising. The Pompeya was a popular venue for workers. Who had planted the bomb there? The wounded were being taken to nearby hospitals on the shoulders of policemen, in taxis, or in ambulances. Nine men and a woman were taken to the Casa del Socorro in Barberá Street. Fortunately, Dr. Riera was on duty there, along with a few other practitioners.

Another eight wounded people had gone to a new hospital, five of whom had died on the way. Three people were dead on arrival at the emergency room, and five others were left in the stalls at the Pompeya. A few of them were young men in their late teens. Their jobs were revealed as they were identified: truck driver, officeworker, a working couple, laborer, two sailors, two students, colleagues of the young man from Zaragoza, a bricklayer, a dyer . . . There were at least eighteen critically wounded people.

Little Amador cropped up in the middle of the street, taking down names in his black notebook before the smoke had even died down, trying to get descriptions of the young man who looked like a worker and had planted the bomb. In that way he got a description of the cylindrical bomb, made from cast iron and full of shrapnel, out of the distressed student from Zaragoza.

"How tall was he? Like that?" and raised his hand well above his own head.

"Lower."

A stretcher went by carrying a woman with one of her legs missing. The crowd began to move down to the Casa del Socorro, beckoned by an imaginary voice. A demonstration full of whispers; passersby joined in, following on behind the stretchers and ambulances. Amador went along after them. A couple of comrades waved to him, leaning in the doorway of a bar on the corner.

"It was the bosses' organization. They want to provoke a confrontation," one of them said straight off.

The other one, who was cleaning his teeth with a toothpick, avoided his eyes.

"Who'd you see?"

"Nobody, just rumors."

"What rumors?"

"That Muntadas from the bosses' organization was offering fifteen thousand pesetas to anyone who felt like committing an atrocity."

A few hours later, Amador managed to get a name and a few contradictory versions of events: Inocencio Feced, an anarchist who had been tortured by Arlegui a few months before and had changed sides. The rumors said the bomb had been intended for the electricity plant where there had been some layoffs, but that he could not get past security, so he went into the Pompeya. That he had planted the bomb so as to ingratiate himself with the groups he had turned his back on. Other rumors were more exact: the bomb was intended for the music hall and was a provocative act by the bosses' organization to stir up a confrontation between the unions and the army.

Amador got to the newspaper office around three in the morning and typed his article in an empty office by candlelight, as the lightbulbs had all blown. Then he telegraphed the text to Madrid, describing the Dante-esque scenes, the horrible sights. He summed up some statements from the CNT leadership: "brutal, barbaric, anti-worker, a provocation by the bosses' organization." But he did not dare put the theory of Inocencio Feced's involvement forward, let alone his name. He had remembered seeing the sickly-looking young man from the metalworkers' union in a meeting once.

Thousands of workers surrounded the hospital into the small hours. The local chapter of the CNT had sent a call out to attend the funeral. Amador, his eyes tired from seeing so much, his throat dry from asking questions, watched the arrival of thousands of workers, who had left the factories at a standstill. He began to make some estimates from a rooftop facing the clinic. There were no fewer than seventy thousand workers.

The conservative newspapers offered their version of the events: an anarchist plot, with Angel del Hierro, the most wanted man in Barcelona, as the guilty party.

The crowd waited in silence, but the procession was not

going to get under way, as the civil government had banned it and delayed the funeral. A workers' delegation, including Amador, went over to the governor's palace. They arrived just as Police Chief Arlegui was leaving, and gave him a chorus of hissing.

Following negotiations, the funeral was to be allowed to take place the following day. Nearly 125,000 workers had gotten together when the procession started at three in the afternoon. They began arresting unionists several hours later.

Amador had spent those nights searching for two people: young Feced, whose description matched that of the one who had committed the crime, but who had also vanished from the boarding house where he had been living; and Angel del Hierro, who seemed to have vanished into thin air.

He could not find either of them.

The Midnight Novelist

Not only had Nicolás vanished into thin air, but Lola too, so there would now be two empty apartments in that building. The way things were going, my inquiries would soon depopulate all of Ciudad Juárez. And while I was waiting for Karen to get better, all my leads would be drying up. God, against all my wishes, would not turn out to be an anonymous informant but one of my publishers, asking me to fulfill my contract and send off a novel that did not even have a hint of existing, which did not seem to want to let itself be written. The dog and the cockroach fluid were leading nowhere, and the letter to the University of Texas in Austin had drawn a blank. Maybe there had been inquiries before the kidnapping, but all that came of it was a furious bureaucratic missive pointing out that records were confidential. So, if the information had come from there, they were not admitting to it. That would just leave me with the hospitals in El Paso and the missing link with Mike Gardner.

But by then, stimulated by God, I would have gotten into another personality, one who could not give a damn about running around gringo hospitals to conduct inquiries that would lead nowhere: i.e., my version of the Midnight Novelist.

I would write in odd moments, in spare moments, during sleepless hours, in the hospital café, in Karen's room when I found myself watching over her sleep. But I would also be writing in my dreams, in my watches, in my nightmares. I would write words in air, in my memory, words off the record.

It would be a novel about my grandfather and I would be pointlessly trying to resurrect a grandfather I did not know too well. Not a tight-lipped old grandfather eating jelly on toast, but one wrapped up in the pall of terrible times. My grandfather the magical, vanishing Angel del Hierro, the Black Angel of Barcelona.

Some other time some other me (apart from the Midnight Novelist, that essentially Ciudad Juárez character) had spent some time reading through newspapers and leaflets in the Barcelona public library, when a name suddenly came to me in the books full of notes. One Antonio Amador, known to his contemporaries as the Flea, a journalist who changed newspapers like he changed his underwear, the subject of dozens of arrests for "offenses against opinion," a founder of the press union in the CNT. The Flea came up again and again in the archives of the International Institute for Social Studies in Amsterdam, where they have the best collection of anarchist newspapers in the world.

His articles, which I read obsessively, took a real hold

of me, as the afternoon went by through the Romanesque windows in the Municipal Archives in Barcelona, or watching the snow fall on the canals in Amsterdam.

Hc risked his neck in every one of them; you could feel his anger, his manias, the healthy madness of Spanish anarchy at the beginning of the century. They challenged the powers that be, the murderers under police protection, the military, the bosses, the governors, the clergy's eternal wisdom, the encyclopedia compilers, writers of kitchen recipes, doctors, ministers . . . Amador did not only turn up as a writer, but also appeared as a character in leaflets written by other journalists and writers. Amador had been part of my dreams, as all that was irreducible and not negotiable, a space for burning principles. His instantaneous writing, his journalism, made me nervous; and if at times he verged on the baroque or on clichés, he was generally irritating, and cast doubts all over my writing. By now, in those days in Ciudad Juárez, full of dust that threatened the coming of the fall, he would be in the novel.

And just then, as the Midnight Novelist, for all that I threw theory at it, I was not happy with the manuscript and knew that there was something behind the keyboard that would be stopping the novel from coming out, smothering me with a dissertation that literally said: if novels were good for something it was to tell us what the others were like that we could not be like. It was not, as they thought in the first half of the twentieth century, a means of instruction, which entailed lectures, morals, advice, images to imitate and deny. They did not know a thing. Even less was it raw material for linguistic experiments. Naaah. Literature was a resource for the future, the stuff of premonitions: a book of schedules, a real proposed chapter for intervening in real life, basically in the arena of illusions and dreams; ergo, the best novels are the ones that are not read because they are written in deeds, which is written beforehand in real life. No bullshit, there is no such thing as fiction, just a rehearsal in fiction to be acted out in daily life. Well then, why write it when you can live it? Basically because you can live reality beforehand, but not foresee it. And even more basically, because things turn out better in fiction, as reality has its own particular way of ruining things.

And I would say to myself, fuck you, you got it, jerk? If it was like that, then it was not like that, because the distance between the Black Angel and his friend Amador, and the pastoral observer of Karen that I would have become, who wrote stumbling along at night, was getting bigger and bigger.

And the pages would come out in the middle of all these doubts, just as they always do.

Journalistic Encounters

Antonio "the Flea" Amador felt on days of certainty, on those days in which no mistake seems possible and everything is as clear as the Mediterranean on a lazy afternoon, that it was also a certainty that there were no certainties.

Amador discerned that the city had changed; he sat in the dump where *España Nueva* had its Barcelona offices, an attic that always smelled of damp, which he shared with a bookkeeper who worked by the hour, someone in charge of distributing the newspaper whom he never saw, but supposed that he did work, because the newspaper was all over the place. There were also a couple of telephones, a table with two typewriters on it, and an assistant who was on the street looking out for rumors. And a gray armchair with the springs coming out of it that Amador slept in, when he did sleep.

While whistling a ditty, Antonio began to give the couple of sheets he had for today some kind of shape. You could see something through the miserable little window that might be mist or just a longing to rain.

He had chosen a letter from one Lorenzo Lorente out of the huge pile of correspondence, due to its special language. The Aceros Hispania worker denounced the steelworks management not only for having sacked him, but also for putting a price on his head, said that they were the same ones who made the workers at the Santa Ana lead works tear up their union cards before coming into work, and finished off without pulling any punches, saying he was waiting for them and that ". . . I have got a pair of fists, a pair of b——, and one of the guns you gave to your stooges."

He had a series of notes from anonymous informants for the bottom of the first page:

Confrontations at the entrance to the Pujol textile mill when the strikers tried to picket the place.

Felipe Baeza, twenty-three years old, wounded in the thigh on the Montjuich road by unknown assailants who ran off.

Workers' emigration to France continues. "The destitute worker, two or three dozen a day leave the city." This was a report from his assistant, a young lad of no more than eighteen, whom he had chosen because he was a demon at editing notes, with all sorts of mistakes but with the maximum speed you could get out of a typewriter (162 characters per minute) and also because he was barely five feet tall.

He re-edited a strike call to the newspaper sellers, who had been denied a rise in commission—which had even gone down a centime—following a rise in newspaper prices.

He included an article by Amichatis that had the kind

of strident tone he admired: *There are piles of money, you can play the stock market from your bed, gasoline and silk stockings are running short, apartment towers that face the mountains are being built, the 30 & 40 is gaining popularity. Hospital beds are being cut back, the university chaplain is begging so as not to close the Clinical Hospital. All the high-street banks look like nighttime hotels. There are fifteen-year-old girls sharing lovers. A lot of theaters have closed their doors and installed gaming tables on their stages, clinics for social diseases abound, pimping is a recognized profession. The women from the Apollo Theater are known as "readily available pieces of skirt." Rumors of a general strike mean that security guards go around armed with carbines; union meetings have been banned for months.*

The untiring, frenetic Amador went straight from correcting his friend's article to taking a few of Arlegui's statements from the previous day's *Progreso*:

Journalist: *General, can you tell us why security guards carry carbines while on duty?*

Arlegui (hysterical and red-faced): *Because I damn well feel like it!*

In order to carry on with his review of the press, he included a little snippet with a spurious title ("Dogs Do Bark, Sancho") that had appeared in the previous day's *Publicidad: Never before has insolence reached such levels as in this age of unionism. Servants are rising up and waving their livery in front of their masters.*

He gathered together all the information he had on shoot-outs between armed gangs from the Free Union and unionists from the CNT and used statements made by Layret in the Chamber of Deputies in Madrid the day before to put at the head of his article (*The bosses' organization has never been so mean, they fine and coerce their members who hire unionized labor. These skinflints have set up a puppet union . . .*) He had at least half a dozen loose pieces of information, or bits of letters from factory correspondents that gave an account of how the cancer was growing. Something was rotten out there, not just the money from the bosses' organization and the bosses favorable treatment of scab unions; the workers' tiredness, their exhaustion after almost two years of struggle without a day's peace, had a lot to do with it.

But it was not just the scabs who were active, the squads were answering back, and most of the time they were getting the upper hand: a scab union was broken up by gunshots in the Sans neighborhood; Miranda, a gunman hired by the scabs who had put poison in the coffee in a collective soup kitchen, was chased at gunpoint . . . There was a shoot-out every day. Workers were dying, but bosses were going down, too. Bombs were planted in convents where the scabs met.

Amador then took a break, something he did not do very often and that he took as being the "sin of reflection," and thought that the polarization that was under way was dangerous.

The first page was ready. He stopped for a second to thumbtack a phrase by Valle Inclán on the wall over the table. Someone, before the place had been an office, had hung a hand-touched family photograph of an Inland Revenue clerk with his three marriageable daughters. So as not to be unworthy, Amador stuck a piece of paper alongside that said: *Journalism is as much of a prank as politics.*

He stepped back to look at his work. It was not bad. But there was something missing, the more so in a city where one of these days they were going to shoot dissident journalists. Go on with your pranks! A city where lies were told with sinister motives. Here you did not hide the age of an heiress or how many millions an industrialist had, here you pointed a journalistic finger at a man as being guilty, and that was like sentencing him to death.

Amador took up the second page while nibbling a crust of bread that one of the host of visitors had left behind. He had a juicy one here, he said to himself, as he wrote the lead: *There was a swordfight between Inspector Fernando Torner (who died) and Captain Del Toro, from the surveillance division, who was severely wounded. Arlegui's resignation has been called for, being the one who put them up to the duel, as they had previously exchanged insults and slaps.*

Just as he was enjoying finishing it off, he felt that another presence had come into the room; he had a vague feeling of not being alone. Ghosts in his nerve endings. He brought his hand up to his gun, caressing the butt, and raised his eyes. An Indian in a turban was staring at him.

"Can I help you?" the journalist asked him, slipping his gun slowly back into his pocket.

"They tell me that as well as being queer you are also an Orientalist," the Indian said in a voice with a strange accent, "and I have come to instruct you in the mysterious arts of mesmerism and resistance to pain, when they screw you left, right, and center. I think the best thing to start with would be a bite of sausage . . ."

The Indian placed a huge sausage on the table and pushed it over to the little journalist.

Amador stared at the character and hesitated as to whether to draw his gun again. The features beneath the disguise became recognizable again bit by bit.

"You're alive," he said.

"Absolutely. Thanks for having come to my defense over the Pompeya business. I would never have pulled such a dirty trick."

"I know. Have you got a smoke?"

The Santana-Loving Pistolero

A track called "Black Angel," with words and music by Carlos Santana, was recorded on October 14, 1982, during a jam session in the Automatt Studios in San Francisco, in preparation for an album called *Shangó*. Doubtless it was dedicated to my grandfather.

The track was jumbled up and incomplete, so it ended up in the archive of unfinished projects and it was not until November 1987 that the recording was finished. Five years had gone by. It was mixed by Jim Gaines in Sausalito the following year. In the final version, Carlos Santana played lead guitar and vocals, along with Alex Ligertwood, Richard Baker, and Gregg Rolie on keyboards, Graham Lear on drums, Orestes Vilato on percussion and vocals, just like Raúl Rekow. According to

Santana, it was Armando Peraza on congas who gave the song its texture, its meaning.

It went something like this:

Un ángel negro/que todito anunció/mi gente!/
la hora ya llegó./Y dijo temblando/la
libertad será/
la música es lo único/que el alma pedirá

(A black angel/who said it all/my friends!/
the time has come./He trembled when he
said/
we'll be free/music's all/your soul can ask
for.)

I might be thinking about these things as I go out of the hospital on my way to Camelia's to change my underwear, humming the Magician from Autlán's lyrics. It would still amaze me that Santana had guessed at my grandfather's existence. When did the paths of the musician from Jalisco state and the Barcelona anarchist cross?

The investigation into Karen's kidnappers would have eluded me, slipped between my fingers. The novel, on the other hand, was getting along nicely. Maybe it was because demons seemed to come up from the vasty deep when they were summoned in the novel, and in reality there was nothing more unreal than demons.

Holes in Boots

"Everything's about to go up in smoke and I'm in love with a blond girl with a little pale green jacket, a Polack," the Indian with the turban said, handing a cigarette over to Antonio Amador, who in the heights of bliss had forgotten that more than half the second page had yet to be done, and put his feet up on the desk.

"Isn't it always like that?"

"No," the Angel said, sitting himself down on the floor and crossing his legs.

"And now you're meditating, like you were a Brahman."

"No, fuck it, it's just that you haven't got a single decent chair in this office."

Amador turned his head around as if to confirm what his friend had said.

"There's always the armchair, friend."

The Angel shook his head.

"What's all this about dressing like a monkey?"

"Going from the sublime to the ridiculous always works for me. If you're going to disguise yourself you should be a priest, a bishop at least."

"When you're less than four feet tall, the best thing is to be a dwarf," Amador said in a philosophical tone.

"You only just got away, friend."

Amador lit a cigarette, got up onto the table, and trampled all over the articles as he danced a few steps of a *chotis*. "Yes, they'll kill all of us, and I'm in love, too. I'm always in love, and what's more, if they don't kill us, then the TB is going to get me," said Amador with a smile as he went back to his chair.

"There's a difference. You're the one who writes history down. I would have to die some other way. I've always thought that there must be something symbolic about dying."

"Dammit! Just look at how religious you hard-core anarchists are getting. And as for my just writing history down—away with your fairy tales! Writing history down, here in Barcelona, is just as useful as making it."

"I'll take back what I said," the Angel said, who was in tears by this stage of the interview.

"Fucking hell! This is serious," Amador said, and without pausing to think it over too much burst into tears, too, sat still in his filthy chair with a couple of crossbars missing, showing the soles of his boots to all the world, with two holes symmetrically placed in the middle, worn down after so many hours of pounding the cobblestones.

Hospital Departure

In 1990 Santana, with a headband covering his receding hairline, recorded *Spirits Dancing in the Flesh*, wherein he sent a little message dedicated to boxing champion Julio César Chávez: *People depend on money too much these days, on food, on gasoline, and this musical statement is a bridge to remind people that inner gasoline (the spirit) is what will get them to their final destination*.

It would be an effort to get into Santana's metaphysics, but I would doubtless need a lot of inner gasoline to get through the crossroads facing me at the hospital entrance.

Karen would be filling in pieces of paper, a stack of them, so that the Mexican hospital could file a claim for her American college insurance. She might raise her eyes from the pile of paper to smile at me now and again.

There would have been a mixture of intuitive communication and absolute lack of it between Karen and me during the last few days. I don't give a shit for those Muppet monsters and I don't suppose she would be too interested in Santana's biography or the terrible problems entailed in writing in the first person and in the future.

It would not have been easy to explain to Karen why Santana, without meaning to, was looking more and more like my memoirs of the comedian Tin-Tan. It so happened that according to my recollection, the rock artist had the same mustache. She had no problem in rationalizing my being a Santana fan, which she could more or less bridge the generation gap to understand, but it was almost impossible to explain to her who Tin-Tan was, or why it was important that, in the mists of our memory, we did not lose sight of Tin-Tan dressed as a sultan in a harem, giving a hard time to everybody in sight.

Cultural differences.

Karen would wander around the corridors with a bunch of papers in her hands. It would seem as if she wanted to run free, taking the ball off Dr. Suárez and scoring a basket before the amazed nursing mothers near the incubators. Karen without a kidney would be like a bird without one of its wings.

I would pick up the postcard with da Vinci's bicycle on it from the top of her bedside table, and would then put together a bundle of my novels for her.

The burning sun would come right at us at the hospital entrance. Karen would protect her eyes with her hand.

"What now?" I would ask, expecting anything except the answer, the goodbye, see you around sometime, each his own way, eavesdroppers on life, hustlers of looks, go fuck your mother . . .

"Well, we'll look for them, won't we? If I can't shoot

hoops, then we can play at being detectives. And if the game turns out well, so much the better," Karen Turner might say, and would try to walk on, but would stumble and then, holding on to my arm, we would cross the avenue to get a taxi.

But it would not be like that. Karen would mumble two or three things about having to go back to college, having things to sort out . . . and she would take the sliding pile of books and the picture of the bicycle from my hands. We would say our ceremonial goodbyes in the hospital entrance, with a very correct peck on the cheek. I'll give you one, and you'll give me one, the last one. A few words about Santana's inner gasoline in order to keep up the stubbornness and toughness. Myself, a reconditioned José Daniel Fierro, with no cast on my leg anymore, ready to investigate; she a retired basketball player, ready to cross the border and vanish into the mists of the nonexistant American Dream.

SECTOR SIX

Passion for the Tail

Convinced that passion that is not entrapped by the tail, and follows on to the head, will never show its face again and, instead, leaves an eternal emptiness in the soul.

—Carlos Fuentes

Jerry Leaving New York

Jerry was a worldly American, which for many people was a contradiction in terms; but he was worldly too in the sense of being cosmopolitan, a citizen of the world, or to put it more exactly, a citizen of no world at all. He did not have the same boundless narrow-minded nationalism in common with the majority of his fellow countrymen and women, and would have had a hard time with ten of the dozen key values that, according to Jerry himself, were the norms of the American way of life (apple pie, Hawaiian shirts, a love of remote-control devices, a passion for Japanese cars, belief in freedom of the press, fear of physical contact when greeting neighbors, free trade, the relative superiority of sex over Nintendo, the truth of opinion polls, and the superiority of housepets over the homeless) and agreed only with two: free enterprise and how wonderful the absence of a senior partner in your life could be. Being an exceptional person, he had little in common with the average American; he was not a woman either, although he was white; neither did he live in the suburbs of a big city; neither did he have two children; neither did he like shrimp cocktail; neither did he watch six hours of TV per day or read two books per year. He was not like the rest. Life and service had made him that way. He was not just worldly, though, he was disposable; wash and wear and use and throw away. He was a leftover. Did his cosmopolitanism have anything to do with the fact that he preferred Russian Pepsi to Detroit Pepsi, with the fact that he liked having his money in a Parisian bank rather than in Chase Manhattan, that he preferred Thai food from Nakhon Ratchasina rather than the pasteurized version in the Village, that he preferred reading *Der Spiegel* to *Newsweek*, or that as far as movies went, he preferred Sergio Leone's Westerns to John Ford's? In the end, maybe all this had to do with the fact that he did not give a damn for the fate of the United States.

Jerry left his room and went over to Chemical Bank, deposited the check for $200,000 into an account he opened in his own name. He made a few checks out to himself in Swiss francs and German marks, filled his pockets with twenty-dollar bills, and put another $8,000 of traveler's checks into an attaché case he had bought around the corner.

He then wandered down Fifth Avenue to look for a Mexican airline, the attaché case in one hand and a carryall in the other, into which he had dumped his passport, a couple of shirts, socks, a bathing suit, and a couple of paperback novels.

Maybe that was the best thing about New York. Taxis and walking. Urban landscape while you walk, instant sociology in a taxi provided by the man behind the wheel.

Maybe it was because although it was hard to find black tobacco, at least nobody would spit on you in a tobacconist's if you asked for something other than Marlboro Lights. New York was different from the rest of the United States, the land of highways, expressways, freeways, and superhighways. Here you walked. New York was a city of universal walking pariahs or subway users, yellow-cab children at best. A unique, unhinged, knowingly unhinged, city. Nowhere else was there so little space for normal people, nowhere else was the dollar sought after with so much passion, in no other corner of the world could you be so different.

It was a city in which virtually everybody felt partially exiled, and everybody generally foreign, if you left out twenty thousand secretaries and another twenty thousand male and female yuppie executives who felt the city belonged to them, eating badly when they thought they ate well and drinking Pepsi Light. The rest were part of his crew.

Jerry had lived in half a dozen countries in the last few years, and half a dozen cities in the United States, without including New York, that in his count belonged more to the list of foreign countries than American cities. He had lived alone, without cats or dogs, birds or hamsters, women or men, mothers or fathers or wives or cousins or children. All this had lent an enormous strength to his internal monologues. He went down the street making up unreadable novels, telling new stories or rehashing old ones, like a character from Joyce. Sometimes he went over his autobiography: he had been the proprietor of a sex shop in Spain during the post-Franco liberalization, a hotel owner in Thailand, and worked in a savings-and-loan in Alabama. He had gone back to Spain to work for the Agency, then Argentina, had lived in Paris on the money he got from a scam he pulled in the Southern Cone of Latin America. He had $6,000 in negotiable pesos in a Spanish bank and a daughter in Lyon. He had retired at forty and was now forty-three and was going to leave the only real city he had known. At least temporarily.

But all of this was just a bunch of anecdotes and cities, Jerry said to himself, as he crossed the Avenue of the Americas on the corner of 17th Street, passing by an office-supply store specializing in all sorts of envelopes, with his airline ticket in his hand.

Homecoming

The first thing he saw in Mexico City on opening his eyes, as the bus pulled up at a stoplight, was a pair of fat Santa Clauses kicking the shit out of each other. Onlookers were circling about the fight, duly lit up by neon light.

He felt like getting off the bus to join in, but he had only just woken up and his reactions were slow; when he tried to get up, the light had turned green and the affair was already a long block behind them. Things always seemed to be slipping through his fingers.

José Daniel Fierro smoothed his mustache, slung his canvas bag over his back, and took a taxi from the Northern Bus Station to his home in the Del Valle district. The building was in darkness, the lights were out in his apartment, and probably shut off at the main. What was he coming back to? To a novel that would not come out? To an apartment that was probably flooded? Had he left the faucets on, or was that just in his writing?

The taxi had turned around at the end of the block to get back onto División del Norte. José Daniel Fierro raised his hand to flag it down again.

"To the Northern Bus Station," the writer said.

"Forget something?" the driver asked him.

"Something."

The first three lights were green. The driver stopped because of a red light on the bridge over Insurgentes. José Daniel changed his mind. A pair of flower sellers drew up to the car.

"Just here, young fella. How much?"

"Are you sure, boss? Seems to me like you don't know which way you're headed."

He walked back home, opened the door, and left the flowers on an armchair. The apartment was suffering from the aftereffects of the flooding. The original puddle by the bathroom door had dried out, leaving the green carpet with two new original colors. The stereo turntable had broken down, the motor burned out from the constant replay of "Black Magic Woman."

Fortunately, there were some reserves left, like being able to put the *Europa* tape on at full-blast, the gig from 1976 with the suggestive subtitle, "Earth's Cry, Heaven's Smile," where Santana's talent was mixed with keyboard-man Tom Coster's. The biggest Santana fan (apart from José Daniel himself), Jordi Serra y Fabra, another detective-story writer, would describe it as a masterpiece.

Europa featured a very basic backing group, barely more than the bass and a keyboard hidden away somewhere, and all of it, absolutely all of it, was Santana's phraseology with the guitar. It evoked a series of questions in Chief Fierro regarding absent friends; asking about people who were no longer around. Questions that became more and more worrying as the track's high notes and riffs went by. He preferred the melodious and affectionate intro to the more way-out guitar riffs, but even they encouraged him and made him sit down and write things you just know about and cannot put in words.

José Daniel Fierro sat down by the computer and opened a new file, and the words *The Ballad of the Stars* slowly unfolded on the blank screen. He lit a cigarette and looked for a 35mm film can to use as an ashtray. *A novel by José Daniel Fierro*. Somebody was knocking on the door, probably the neighbors, who resented going back to normality after a month's break from Santana. *Chapter 1* and then the first line: "*Shit, don't setbacks just suck*," José Daniel Fierro said aloud, at the same time as he typed it out . . .

Jerry in Mexico City (I)

The Bulgarian had basically not changed in fifteen years, although his haggard features showed the signs of his illness. The dirtiness of his sweaty undershirt and suspenders covered in cigarette ash gave him away. Who used undershirts like that at the end of the millennium?

Jerry stared at him. Noise from traffic filtered into the room through a window with dirty and broken panes of glass, patched up with cardboard from milk cartons. There were two televisions and a fan in the room, a huge pile of *Playboy* and *Caballero* magazines, and full-to-the-brim ashtrays everywhere.

"Why do you live like this, Christo? You're not living like a Bulgarian millionaire. Are there any Bulgarian millionaires? Living in houses on the Black Sea?"

The Bulgarian was lying in bed connected to a machine

that made gurgling noises as it pushed fluids in and out of his body. The plastic tubes from the machine were hidden below the pink sheets. One of the gunmen handed him his thick glasses and the Bulgarian put them on slowly, to look Jerry over at leisure. The other one sat down on a rocking chair and moved softly, cleaning his fingernails with a penknife and lulled by the noise of the buses on Guerrero Street.

"Did you look into the movie theaters, Jerry."

"Yes, and you can buy two or three, no problem, if you've still got the little bags I gave you in Saigon," Jerry said, lying.

The Bulgarian sighed.

"I suppose I ought to tell you now why I didn't show up on time in Thailand. Or rather, why I turned up early and couldn't hang around for you. I'll also have to explain why I can't just go to New York and we have to see each other here. I'm going to have to explain a load of things . . . you don't work for the Agency anymore, right?"

Jerry shook his head.

"You just the same, Jerry?"

"And you, are you still the same Bulgarian cocksucker?"

Christo Mandajsiev burst out into hoarse laughter, shaking the bed. One of the gunmen diligently handed him a bag of peanuts.

"They won't let me into the States. They don't take in defectors from democracy now." The Bulgarian laughed. The machine beside him gurgled a bit. "Interpol is looking for me. I raided a luxury hotel on the Black Sea when there was a cardiologists' convention on . . . I kicked the ass of an ex-communist deputy who's now a Christian Democrat deputy. I ran over the U.S. ambassador's dog in Sofia."

"Just the dog?"

"One of his bodyguards, too. But it was an accident, my

friend. I swear. You never do stupid things like that on purpose . . . can you get papers for me?"

Jerry hesitated. "No. The ones that can would just love to get their hands on you. East European refugees are out now, especially ex–secret servicemen. It's all your fault for going around trying to kill the Pope. I don't think they could fix you up with anything decent, something to get you past any immigration official that can read."

The Bulgarian shifted around in his bed. Jerry could feel a tension in him he had not noticed before.

"Why don't you stay here? Don't you like Mexico?" he asked him.

"It's getting to be very expensive," Mandajsiev explained, pointing to the two heavies. "The same guy who charges me for staying here throws these two in. And I'm not too sure that one day he isn't going to be out of a job and charging me double. You want a drink?"

"A soda."

Mandajsiev said something in Spanish to one of the boys, who went to look in the refrigerator in the room next door. Jerry, who spoke Spanish well, added that he would prefer mineral water.

The two men kept staring at each other for a while.

"You owe me a lot," Jerry said at last.

"You're right . . . exactly four fifths of what I've got. Wait . . ." He got a little notebook out of the bedside table. "Almost two million dollars . . . I'm a good payer."

"I want certified checks, traveler's checks, and cash."

"Sure. It's your money."

"I know."

"But like I told you in the letter, I must ask you a favor," the Bulgarian said.

"The favor is for before you pay me what you owe me?"

"I guess so."

"I'll think about it," Jerry said, and he got up and walked out the door.

Leonardo (IX)

Leonardo da Vinci always wanted to write a novel, and in a certain fashion, he left indications of his ideas in his notebooks as the years went by. In the Atlanticus Codex, particularly, you can find the outline for a novel followed by an experimental chapter in the form of an illustrated letter addressed to the nonexistent Devatar of Syria, lieutenant to the even more nonexistent Sultan of Babylon.

Students of da Vinci have always been nonplussed by the text, trying to link it in a biographical way to Leonardo's known movements, thinking it was some sort of travelogue, and members of sects who studied his work thought that this literary testimony proved Leonardo's links with a splinter movement from the Order of the Temple and an imaginary secret journey to the Middle East.

Nonetheless, any writer could easily tell you that Leonardo's text belongs to the realm of fiction. It is an easy matter to unearth the fact that the letter forms a part of the fabric of a novel, and it is not hard to disentangle the plot that Leonardo was weaving.

The novel, which might have been called *Mount Taurus*, has an outline of twelve chapters set down in it along with three appendix chapters. The chapters lay down the story of a preacher who warns his listeners of an impending holocaust. A scientific preacher, so much to Leonardo's taste? It seems that the preacher's warnings mostly fell on deaf ears, and much as he warned them, they did not take too much notice of him.

The predictions are fulfilled and the area suffers a huge flood (Chapter 2), as a result of which the city is destroyed (Chapter 3), which makes people despair (Chapter 4), and go after the poor preacher (for having told the truth). As if the disasters were not enough, with the preacher free again (it is not clear how this comes about), there now comes the tale of the devastation that a mountain falling down will cause (Chapters 6 and 7), of an avalanche, the appearance of a prophet (the preacher under a new guise?), and the prophecy that he is now making (Chapters 9 and 10), and, finally, "the flooding of the lower regions in western Armenia, whose drainage was occasioned by cutting away Mount Taurus" (Chapter 11). Finally, science triumphs—the preacher demonstrates that what has happened and what he predicted came about naturally, and not through divine intervention or magic. What is more, natural events have causes and explanations.

In the appendix chapters, da Vinci, by now more concerned with Mount Taurus, natural causes, and comets than the novel's plot, outlines three descriptions: one of the Mount itself, one of the River Euphrates, and one of a strange phenomenon that brought about consternation among the locals when "the mountain shines brightly at its summit for half the night, or a third of it, that would look like a comet to those living in the west, after the sun goes down, looking just the same to those living in the east before dawn."

As for the novel's format, it would seem that da Vinci was inclined to let the plot unfold in a series of epistles, whence the letters to the Devatar of Syria or to his friend, Benedicto Dei.

But Leonardo did not leave it at that, and in other notes we find the idea of incorporating the story of a whale, then he flirts with the notion of inserting a giant from Lebanon into the story, who is showered with adjectives, who "was born on Mount Atlas and was black. He fought against Artaxerxes with the Egyptians, Arabs, Medes, and Persians, he lived in the sea among the whales, killer whales, and ships" and "had a horrific and terrifying face, swollen, ruddy eyes beneath fearful and dark brows, that could darken the sky and make the earth shake."

Perhaps he found that the story got shorter as he told it and that the outline was taking over the narrative; he also discovered that he preferred to describe a geological formation than tell how a character climbed up it. He got bogged down in the difficulties that go with the job of telling stories, or maybe he just got bored and wandered off toward another of his many fly-by-night projects.

Jerry in Mexico City (II)

Jerry decided to say yes for two million and one reasons. The extra deciding factor on top of the two million others was that he had bummed around for too long with no access to any of the corridors of power; the Bulgarian had reminded him of the stroke of good luck that was about to change everything, and then vanished into thin air and ruined the future. The Bulgarian's request, in a strange way, made him feel that he was still different, that he had been different all his life and would stay that way.

He had plugged in to his contacts in Mexico before the meeting and was building up a safety net to fall into from the flying trapeze, in case the Bulgarian wanted to play dirty. Was it worth it? Of course, if things were the other way around and he had millions of dollars, he would have played dirty with Christo. He would have kept all the money. Property is 99 percent possession. Just let the dead go and complain about it. Would he do it? Of course. The Bulgarian would disappear just as soon as he did not need him anymore. Jerry was convinced, then, that the Bulgarian was not inclined to pay up all of the Saigon money; probably just a part of it, to return the favor.

He ended up calling the contact number the Bulgarian had given him, from a suite in the touristy Zona Rosa where he had been staying.

"Come to a decision, Jerry?"

"Sure. Okay. What do you want me to do for you?"

"I want a good kidney transplant. No questions asked. The doctor who saw me said I need one urgently, that I'm not responding too well to dialysis treatment. I also want you to get my minders off my back, get me away from my baby-sitters."

"Are you going to trade them in for some of mine?"

"I've got stuff on you. That's my insurance, and besides, you love me, Jerry Milligan, you must have dreamed about me for years and you can't just let me die. I'm in a situation in which you're the only one I like. I don't care too much for current friends."

Jerry thought this over.

"A third of what you owe me when we start work . . . and money up front to get things moving."

Now it was the Bulgarian's turn to be silent.

"I sent you two hundred thousand bucks . . ."

"That's part of the debt. You knew that if it wasn't for that, I wouldn't have given you the time of day."

"I don't have all of it on me, I'll have to fix something up."

The Friend of the Man Who Lays Mines

Among the known stories about José Daniel Fierro was the one about how he had learned to lay anti-tank mines and defuse them. It is a curious thing for him to have acquired a talent so apart from his usual areas of interest, but it so happens that in 1989 he shared a hotel room in Prague with a unique Cuban called Ambarajá de Cuito who, apart from having seventeen Cuban and Angolan decorations, snored like a factory-elevator motor.

The story is so complicated that it could be told quite simply: José Daniel had gone to Prague for an International Association of Crime Writers conference to be held in Dobris Castle; the Mexican embassy in Madrid had said it would tell his hosts which flight he would be on; the communications room at the embassy took the weekend off and José Daniel got to Prague on a Sunday and found nobody waiting for him at the airport. After finding out about the black-market exchange rate, the taxi and prostitute business in the miserable airport, he got a cab and asked to be taken to the most centrally located hotel in Prague, to put off looking for his Czech buddies until Monday. There was no room in the hotel. The hotel bar served tequila at a dollar and a half a shot. He met a Cuban guy who was giving a course on mines to his Czech colleagues while drinking tequila. The Cuban had read a couple of his novels. He invited him to share his room after he found out about his predicament. José Daniel found his colleagues on Monday morning but stayed on in the hotel, because he was intrigued by the stories that Major Ramón Román Ruenes Rodríguez (obviously known as Four Rs) told.

A week later, José Daniel finished off at the conference. It had ended in a tense mood, as the IACW had moved in favor of freeing Czech dissident Vaclav Havel during a press conference whose content had not come out in the press, radio, or TV, but had done the rounds of Prague by word-of-mouth. The Czech authorities from the writers' union had thrown them out of the castle a day before the conference was officially over, and the Czech section of the association was in some danger.

José Daniel stayed on in Prague for a couple of days. In the end he knew a lot more about mines and how to translate Havana-speak into Spanish, at least theoretically in both cases.

Ambarajá, who was so called by the Angolans because of his fast-fingered card tricks, learned how to defuse mines in Cabinda in 1975, at the beginning of the war in Angola, and to assemble them in Cuito Cuanavale in 1987.

He told some unusual tales, like how the South Africans had experimented in Angola with new mines.

"No, man, it some bad shit; they got everything and from all over: South African case an' explosive, Japanese timer, an' Belgian battery. Bad shit, 'cause they go off when you touch them on top wit' a boot, they set them to go off sometime, o' they blow they up by radio. Same shit, man, they fuck o' they fuck you. Amazing, man. I got one an' took fessperiment, you know, essperiment. An' I knows, I knows they got two level' o' mercury, they run off together, close the circuit and essplode. I disarms and difuses it, and plays with the fuse when it go off in my face. Shiiiiit! Burned black, I was, man. They wanned take me to Cuba, fix me up, but not me, country boy with big balls, wanna go back to the place I find it an' tell the comrades why that shit essplode like that."

Then he drew diagrams, showed me some parts, made signs before the writer's watchful eyes. After the first night, he felt obliged to take notes.

"There was shit like that we see for the firs' time. So I finds one, looks like another, juss the same, suppose to deactivate with a li'l knob, an' then, no problem, man. Easy, man. I call the guys and say come here, an' when I press the li'l switch, the thing go tick-tick-tick, fly off an' go riiiiiing! Shiiiiit! Well, I running, right over other guy, like in that Mad Max movie. Fifteen minute later, no tick-tick-tick or riiiing shit, no essplosion, not a fuckin' thing; an I say to the guys, no, look guys, it's a joke."

José Daniel took notes, looked on terrified as the Cuban took sticks of dynamite, plastic explosive, and fuses from under his bed (José's that is, where he had slept so snugly before finding out) and disarmed mines from under his (the Cuban's) bed, just like somebody picking popcorn out of a pot, and broke into a cold sweat as the guy showed him the fulminate of mercury.

"I'm havin' a good time with you, man, but I goin' away," he would say, in the middle of a trial run, mixing Portuguese words in with his explanation and tossing a grenade into José Daniel's hands while he went into the bathroom to take a piss and fix his uniform.

Sometimes clouds of black smoke would come out of the room, terrifying the blond chambermaids, who hated the black Cuban major and the Mexican writer. They made their beds in the worst way they knew how, full of creases and with the pillows like rocks.

"Did you get a plate?"

"From the dining room?"

"No, man, you tied last night."

"With rope?"

"Shit, no, you sleep a lot this mornin', you get a plate."

"And what's that got to do with mines?"

"Nothin'."

Once they set the television in the room on fire when Major Ambarajá performed rudimentary electronics on it, trying to get some components out.

"Some shitty apparatus, that," he said, quite seriously.

Out of all the stories he told him, the most exciting was about one of the major's adjutants who found himself taking a crap on top of a mine in the middle of the bush, and who began to scream.

"And what did you say to him?"

"Cool, man, take it easy. You shit a lot, you fly a lot."

And so, between Belgian fuses and Turkish explosives, Major Rodríguez made the crime writer into his colleague and buddy. José Daniel tried to repay him by giving him a couple of his novels. It made the major fall right in love with his pupil and translator.

"And what did you use to do if you found a huge minefield? Did you set it off?"

"Nothin'."

"????"

"Just go for it."

"A lot?"

"Loads, piles, a stack."

"You mean shitloads," Fiero translated, appreciatively.

At the end of the week, Ambarajá confessed that José Daniel had been the best pupil of the goddamn course, better than the fuckin' Czechs, who could not tell the difference between a mine and their mother-in-law's ass.

Jerry Preparing to Leave Mexico City

Jerry got Romero on the move in El Paso, and met up with Mike in one of the many garbage heaps where the Agency kept the human leftovers from some of its aborted operations. But that did not solve anything.

The first thing was to get the Bulgarian away from his keepers and "friends," out of the clutches of some commander in the Federal Judicial Police who had started off by helping the Bulgarian for money, getting him an illegal residency, and then broadening the "friendship" so as to take him for everything he had. For that he had to get him out of Mexico City, a city in which Jerry operated badly, besides.

Jerry brought the Bulgarian a bunch of flowers for their second meeting. The bodyguards who minded him in the flophouse in the Guerrero district, full of whorehouses, tenement buildings, and sleazy bars to the north of downtown, had changed. This time, there were two fat beer drinkers there, wearing white shirts with .38s in shoulder holsters. Christo looked more lively, the gurgling in the machine seemed to be more regular.

"Can you disconnect yourself from that heap of shit?"

"A couple of days, three, four, maybe. It's a coincidence that you always see it here. I go around the city with friends. I'm not an invalid," the Bulgarian said, and handed him an envelope. Jerry took it and put it away in his coat pocket, making it clear to one of the fat guys that he was not hiding anything.

The envelope contained a pawn ticket for a necklace that Jerry sold for four million pesos, without any problems. He was sorry not to have seen the necklace close up. He spent most of his nights dreaming about it.

The second problem was to find a doctor, a hospital, a donor, all those things you needed for transplants. He rented an ambulance with the money. It was far from clear what he was going to use it for, or what part it was going to play in the scam he was setting up, but it could always come in useful and was much cheaper than traveling by taxi. The suspension was good, too.

Leonardo (X)

There are four aspects of Leonardo da Vinci's life story that are temporarily interconnected: undertaking the mural of the Battle of Anghiari, inventing the bicycle, the maritime surveys in Piombino, and beginning to paint La Gioconda.

The Battle of Anghiari was laid out and painted between 1503 and the first few months of 1506; at some time during that same period in Florence, Leonardo designed the bicycle; in November 1504 he went to Piombino, and, between 1504 and 1505, he began to paint the picture that would come to be known as the *Mona Lisa*.

Leonardo, master of the unfinished, was in his fifties by this time, had done fewer than a dozen paintings and murals, many of which were to disappear in the mists of time or fade away for technical reasons; was writing about countries he had never visited like Armenia or Hungary; invented things that would never be made, like the system of counterweights for the automatic lock in a door that he never made; and was creating landscapes he had never set eyes upon. He designed tapestries that did not get into the hands of weavers, like the one he did in 1479 in Mese Piero's workshop that was meant for the King of Portugal, *Adam and Eve in Paradise at the Moment of Original Sin*, that should have been woven in Flanders out of gold and silk and whose original painted design was to disappear. He painted pictures that were to suffer mutilations, like the one of Ginevra de' Benci, whose lower part was cut off, thereby taking away the proportions that Leonardo had given to it in its day, and which is now the only "American" picture by the artist.

He also went around promoting himself on his own recommendation for undertakings that no one commissioned him for, as when he wrote to Sforza pointing out his military aptitudes, among which was his ability to build bridges or cannons, saying, *I know how to get to a desired place along tortuous pathways and underground chambers, dug without making any noise, even if it were necessary to go beneath a ditch or river*.

The Gioconda was going to form a part of this enigmatic chaos in Leonardo's future, and would drive more than one art historian mad. The picture, now to be found in the Louvre, came to be there because it was "inherited" in a not very orthodox way by the kings of France on the Magus's death in 1519, and came to be known throughout the length and breadth of the planet as *La Gioconda* or the *Mona Lisa* (Madam Lisa), thanks to a very dubious identification made by Vasari, Leonardo's first biographer, in 1568. Vasari had never seen the picture, and could only rely upon a description of it. Those who followed down Vasari's road identified the woman portrayed with the enigmatic smile afterward as Lisa di Gherardini, the wife of the silk merchant Francesco di Zanobi di Giocondo.

Nonetheless other historians, following parallel trails, found records of two paintings—one of Il Giocondo, and the other not his wife but rather a Florentine lady, a lover of Giulio de Medici, painted at his behest. By persevering with this line of inquiry, they appear to have identified the woman as Pacifica Brandano.

But the doubts did not stop there, and a third woman could be the one portrayed, if we follow the line of inquiry leading to a poem by Enea Irpino that tells of how Leonardo painted his lover in those years, one Constanza d'Avalos, the Duchess of Francavilla.

Not content with this chaos of identification, and incapable of putting a date on when the portrait was painted, although the fact that Raphael copied it seems to clearly establish that the work was begun at least as early as the beginning of 1505, a new legion of "Giocondists" went back to the issue at the turn of the twentieth century, especially after the robbery in 1911 by Vincenzo Peruggia and the picture's return three years later. The analysts came up with the following contradictory hypotheses to add to the existing ones:

a) It is in fact a self-portrait in which Leonardo divests himself of masculine attributes and idealizes himself as a woman. This Gioconda-Leonardo theory, the most adventurous one, is not without reason. It is enough to study the few portraits of Leonardo that do exist.

b) It is a portrait of the artist's mother, painted from memory.

c) It has to do with a nonexistent woman.

The myth has been gone over in literature also, lending greater interest to the story: Is the landscape in the background from Lombardy or Tuscany? What happened to the three inches missing from each side of the original? Where did the pillars that bordered the picture go? Was the model pregnant? Is her smile voluptuous, as Théophile Gautier has said? Or was Oscar Wilde nearer the mark when he said, "Her head is the spot where all the ends of the world have gathered together"? Who painted over it, changing the original varnishing? What are the elements of mourning doing in the picture? Are they due to widowhood, to the loss of a child? Was Sacheverell Sitwell right when he said of the woman that her smile was like that of a cat that has eaten a canary?

Jerry in Mexico City (III)

This time the Bulgarian was not plugged in to the machine, he was sitting in bed eating huevos rancheros, in a bathrobe and slippers. The minders that time were a combination of the two gangs that Jerry had seen before: the fatter of the two fat guys, and the young guy who ate peanuts.

"Are you ready?"

"Whenever you like, if you don't mind me eating these eggs as I go, they're really good." He got up.

The fat guy seemed to realize something was going on. "The gentleman cannot leave, he's very ill," he said, raising his hand to his holster.

Jerry anticipated the move, revealing the .38 he had under the rolled-up newspaper he was carrying, cocked and ready to fire. The fat guy stepped to one side, but the young guy, the peanut eater, came out of the bathroom with a razor in his hand. Jerry aimed at his face and fired without hesitating. The young guy jumped backward but the bullet hit him in the throat. The Bulgarian threw the plate of eggs on the floor and collared the fat guy; he gently took the gun out of his holster.

"Don't kill me," the fat guy said to Jerry.

Jerry blew his head off.

Then he walked over to the bathroom. The young man's legs were shaking in spasms, his blood gushing out over the white tiles. Jerry aimed at his head and fired. The bullet ricocheted off the floor and smashed the toilet.

Christo Mandajsiev picked up a carryall from under the bed, put a gun into it, and smiled at Jerry.

"You didn't have to kill them. You Yankees are too bloodthirsty. It must be the influence of TV, along with the fact you weren't invaded by the Nazis in the 1940s."

"I don't want to leave friends of your friends around who can identify me."

Jerry put the young man's blade in his pocket. His right hand was beginning to tremble. He took the Bulgarian's bag so as to have his hands full and hide the trembling.

The ambulance was two blocks away from the hotel, buried in a maze of alleys smelling of pulque and rancid fried pork tacos. Jerry settled the Bulgarian into the back, took the wheel, and drove off looking for the Mexico–Tacuba road. He had memorized the quickest route out of the city. And that might have been the most difficult part of the operation.

"Who were your minders?" Jerry asked, as they went past the concrete slabs in Ciudad Satélite.

"When I came down here I didn't have any good contacts, so after hanging around, I got in through Veracruz thanks to a Swiss guy who had a friend in customs, to whom I sold a couple of those little bags you left me in Saigon. This friend had a friend who works in stamping out the drug traffic in Mexico City, meaning that he's the real dealer and that the Swiss guy's friend was just a cover. And the friend's friend, Fats Vera, the guy who chases pushers, not only offered to continue buying off me, but to get me some papers fixed up so as to hang around in this City of Palaces, and then he introduced me to a doctor friend of his, then he got some of his sidekicks to watch over me, and in the end the only thing missing were the bars in the hotel room. As they say in Mexico, there are some love affairs that can just kill you."

"You just can't trust friends," Jerry said.

The Bulgarian nodded dolefully and then burst out laughing.

"Do they know who I am?"

"They'll have figured it out."

"And Mr. X, the guy you sent to look for me in New York?"

"No, he's another old friend, from way back. Nothing to do with the fat guys."

"Don't tell me he used to work for the Bulgarian secret service?"

"It wasn't such a bad job," Christo Mandajsiev said, offended, and suddenly aware he had not shaved in five days. He then wrapped himself up in a blanket and dropped off to sleep.

A Love Letter from Austin

When Chief Fierro opened the door, he found himself facing two Hare Krishna devotees dressed in saffron robes and fresh out of the barber shop where their skulls had been cropped. He slammed the door in their faces.

He wandered around the kitchen, indignant at the intrusion that he regarded as a symbolic tearing down of his castle walls, and when the bell rang for a second time, he was on the point of attacking the postman with a pineapple he had been chopping up to make *tepache*, fermented pineapple juice. Fortunately, the postman handed over a letter with an Austin, Texas, postmark on it before José Daniel Fierro could hit him, and because of it he walked away with a ten-thousand-peso tip.

José Daniel stuck the letter to the bathroom mirror with some Scotch tape and went back to his computer and the novel that would not come out. Sometimes he wondered whether the novel was not progressing because he had nothing to say, because his ability for capturing passion on paper had left him. Perhaps the latest setback in his life, his absurd visit to Ciudad Juárez chasing after the romantic illusion of a gringa basketball player and her abductors, was proof that he had been left on the fringes of reality. After telling so many stories he had gotten stuck in one. He was a fictional character and he did not know it.

José Daniel smiled. If that was what things had come to, he would give the novelist writing about him one last chance. He was giving him just fifteen minutes, the time it would take him to go to the bathroom, open the letter, and read it. Because right after he got back, the novel would just have to come out, the story he wanted to tell would have to be told, different verbs would be utilized—refrigerate, trivacilate, subnormalize, unstudy, fraudulate, spear, interprefer, illustrate, prejuriate, phuck with a "ph"; Peter Piper would pick a peck of pickled peppers in Puebla. The lousy sparrows could come home to roost on your balcony and screw around in their nests and shoot the breeze in a city that woke up to the Acerina dance band; biting dialogue would come out, descriptions of canoes and Aztec masks; there would be passages with pedal-driven streetcars, characters that you had always wanted to meet, that blond girl would have one breast bigger than the other when the guy with the mustache eyed her plunging neckline as they drank horchata that would taste like horchata, thanks to the adjectives. Otherwise, he would curse the hell out of the writer who was using him as some fucked-up character.

The letter said:

To begin with, you are nobody in the United States. That is what education is about, to make you stay that way for a few years so you cannot compete in the flooded market of "somebodies." I had been an expert in being nobody until I discovered basketball. I took out all the hatred of the unperson teenager I was on it, because I was a teenager until a month and a half ago, until the day Jackie got murdered and I got operated on. Now I'm back to being nobody. Do you want a nobody, writer? You know what it's like to live with a nobody? A nobody does not know what she wants, says she would like to study anthropology but never enrolls in the program, wanders around town like a ghost feeling undressed and thinking she would like to go back to the womb, to the UT campus; a nobody spends hours in front of the TV and even though she has only got one kidney, she hangs on to sex as the only way of staying in touch with reality. A nobody soon gets tired of the people she loves and hurts them. A nobody is more dangerous than that green snake in your novel, because she does not even love herself. Are you sure, writer?

I told my brother I was going back to Mexico to sleep with a writer, to shack up with him for a few months, that the guy was over fifty. He told me he had better be a good one. Like Hemingway? At least.

Are you sure, sir? Even revenge does not matter to me very much anymore. I am more curious than angry.

Karen

When the doorbell rang, José Daniel was frightened to death, a picturesque panic, a teenage fear that everything would turn out so well he just could not believe it. The bell was a sign of things to come:

Could it be the Hare Krishna followers, the postman, or Karen herself? The absurd future in any one of its forms.

I'm not the pheasant plucker, I'm the pleasant fucker's son, I'm only plucking pheasants till the pleasant fucking's done. Doddamn dangerous dife. If he was a story, he badly needed a new scriptwriter.

Jerry on the Road

"Where are we going to do it?"

"In Ciudad Juárez."

"So far away?"

"So close to your Manhattan movie theaters you can almost touch them," Jerry answered him.

The ambulance went along as if it were floating in the middle of the plains of wheat and prickly pear, corn, and aloe in the state of Guanajuato; they headed north on the Pan-American Highway. Jerry liked Mexican highways and he liked the bright unfiltered midday light; he even liked the way the ambulance drifted along the asphalt like a big ship on the ocean current. He smiled. Then, seeing his smile in the mirror, he changed back to the dry expression he had had for the last few days, just so that the Bulgarian would not misinterpret his good mood.

The next conversation cropped up two hundred kilometers later, when Jerry was driving the ambulance into the forecourt of a motel in the suburbs of San Luis Potosí.

"I got to Thailand a week before you."

"I knew that," said Jerry, as he got his suitcase out of the back of the ambulance.

"But I was only there a few hours. A few very entertaining hours, you might say. They only tried to kill me twice."

"Long enough to sell the green Mustang."

"It was mine, wasn't it?"

Jerry nodded.

SECTOR SEVEN

Desperately Searching with Karen

The Ballad of the Stars
(Part Three)

A pair of (definitely nostalgic
and tear-jerking novels) by

José Daniel Fierro

"I sang in my chains like the sea."

—"Fern Hill," Dylan Thomas

He Could Not Make Himself Understood Because of His Cough

The firing of one governor and the hiring of another was typical. Amador confined himself to mentioning them without comment in *España Nueva* and splashing it across the page in forty-eight-point type.

Bas: "They are throwing me out because I will not be a killer."

Martínez Anido (on taking office): *"I have been in Cuba and the Philippines. I ought to be in Africa. The government has sent me to Barcelona and I shall proceed as if I were at war."*

Then he stood back to contemplate his work, sticking a finger up his nose. As he was poking around he came to the conclusion that not even a fool could escape the message. Barcelona was just like Cuba and the Philippines during the war, like the military/rich kids' war against the Moors in Africa. November was going to be bad. The cold came in through the broken windows in the hovel; he could feel death in his bones or the damp in his thoughts or the police treading on his tomb. You tell me. It was the same thing. He wrapped up his material and went out into the Barcelona night and headed toward the Sans station to put it on the midnight express so they would have it in the editor's office in Madrid by morning. He no longer trusted the telegraph, the telephones, or the mail. Modernity had been taken over by the state, progress was enemy territory; drums were safer, like the declarations of love carved into tree trunks, the messages inscribed on stones in the quarry, drunken songs in run-down bars.

He walked two or three kilometers to the station, hiding in the shadows, staying away from streetlamps and other people's footsteps on the cobblestones, one hand on the package and the other on his gun. Alone and unknown. Little Amador's face was covered up to his eyes with an English woolen scarf that went around three times and hung on both sides of him like a horse's reins.

He regarded himself as being in a ridiculous disguise, like a poor imitation of his friend the Black Angel. An angel who had vanished in a time belonging to demons. Where was he? Had he gotten together with the blond-haired woman in the green dress?

After he had left the package in friendly hands, and spent a couple of hours drinking cheap wine in the station bar with a couple of gamblers who had lost everything and were going back empty-handed to Lérida, he bedded down in the package depot, lulled to sleep by the sound of the trains, among the boxes of woolen berets the Catalan textile industry was sending to Castile, the cages of sparrows who did not know how to sleep in the dead of night, the blocks from a French printing press that was on its way to Madrid. It was an unusually peaceful night.

They started arresting union men just two days later. Following a timely telephone call, Amador closed the office, dismissed his assistant, and gave the cleaning lady a vacation. She may not have been the greatest as far as cleanliness was concerned, but she was the widow of a comrade murdered by the bosses' organization's gangs. He had decided to set up a movable office and live permanently on the run, to become an ethereal, invisible fugitive. Because as soon as they saw him they would fuck him over good.

A couple of days later the little journalist met with the general secretary of the Confederation, Salvador Seguí, inside a removal truck while it made its weary way around Barcelona. He would have preferred to talk with Pestaña, with his calm voice and his patience, but it was said he was on his way to Russia on an important mission. Seguí, the general secretary, was quite the opposite. He lacked for nothing in presence, stature, command, *sangfroid*, or leadership, but words did not come out of him as quickly as he wanted to say them.

"Those who can stand the pace will win. Take the strain without neglecting the organization. Spread the word. The hotheads have got to get the message not to get out of hand," Seguí said, sitting on a chair with his feet resting on a rolled-up carpet. Without realizing it, he was holding up a vase as he spoke.

Amador got down from the truck and watched it go off into the night along the Rambla de las Flores. He waved to two whores he knew who were going into a café to get away from the cold, and he went up to a smoky grill where an old man was roasting chestnuts. Everything was all right, but they were going to close the newspaper down any moment. They were going to gag them.

Because of the roasted chestnuts, because he was enjoying the warmth that soaked into him through his outstretched hands, he committed the unforgiveable mistake of not having his finger on the trigger of his gun. He was going to pay for it with interest.

At first he felt a hand on his shoulder, not a friendly one, then a kick in the kidneys, then two truncheon blows on his head as he keeled over coughing.

He woke up and before getting an idea of his whereabouts, he caught sight of his scarf stained by the bloody spit. Had he been coughing up blood? Had they broken part of him? He ran his hands over where it hurt. Antonio Amador knew a lot about pain, about a body that fell apart in spite of the will to keep it in one piece.

Under the faint light of a bulb that a fly was warming itself on, the little journalist put the pieces together. The place was known to him. He was laid out under a bench in one of the waiting rooms at the Modelo prison in Barcelona. *S'nothing, just like home*, he said to himself. From there he could see a calendar, advertising a brand of aniseed liqueur, covered in messages written with black and red pencils. A pair of boots stuck out from under the desk. Military boots. Bad news, bad news.

Amador crawled out from under the bench, and fresh pains reminded him of the kick he had gotten in the kidneys.

"Well, it was about time you came back to the land of the living," said Basterrechea, the governor's adjutant, who looked like a bad bit-part actor when he was out of uniform.

"Just one question, Captain, isn't your mother ashamed

of you? Does your wife kiss you good night? Aren't your kids scared that they'll be stained with your shit?"

"All talk, ass, and besides that was three questions . . . if there's one thing I'm here for, it's not to be putting up with the walking dead."

"To what, then, do I owe the doubtful pleasure of seeing a syphilitic sore with no balls like you?" said Amador, leaning on the wall for support. He felt faint inside and his lungs were pumping his throat full of bloody phlegm.

"I have a message for you from the civil governor of Barcelona, who has just declared a state of emergency in the province. It goes like this," the captain said, as he put some gloves on and walked toward the door. "To be an anarchist when you're a worker, well that's all right, but for a journalist, a man of learning, to be one, that's a sin. He's really happy you've been taken in."

Amador began to slide down the wall, grabbing his chest with one arm to hold back a coughing fit.

"Tell him I shit on his whoring mother," he said, but the words could not have been very clear in the middle of all the coughing, because the captain did not seem to hear.

The Reorganized Red Butler

It would be Karen. With dark glasses. Standing still with a suitcase at her feet and a sleeping bag and a basketball under each arm.

"I let the letter get here first . . ."

"What will you have for breakfast? I suppose you must be sick of hospital food and gringo university cafeteria food, too . . ." I would say, helping her to get her things in and thinking the apartment was in complete disorder, having not lived with a woman since 1989, and that the bed would probably be too short for Karen and her feet would stick out.

Love also tends to a practical thing. Fried or Mexican-style eggs? Should he shave every day? I would stroke the hobo's beard that had been growing in the days since I got back. And to celebrate I would put "Black Magic Woman" on at full volume.

Karen would drop into my armchair in front of the TV, would take her dark glasses off to reveal the bags under her eyes, with signs of having cried, and she would burst out laughing. A good mixture: Santana and Karen's loud, unrestrained laugh.

And then a wave of terror would wash over that poor disconcerted novelist with no novel. A sweeping glance, the worst kind, would take stock of the mess all over the room. Shit would shoot up around him as if he were the epicenter of all chaos. Beer cans would sprout up like mushrooms, along with old newspapers that would not be just piled up, but screwed into balls, ready to be blown away in an Arizona wind; plates with remains an archaeologist would love to identify, including Cortázar's fried egg; ashtrays filled for Sherlock Holmes; a dead chicken; sweaty undershirts from time immemorial; a Texan hat and the matching boot set out like a trophy in the middle of the table, uneasily balanced on a pile of *Motivos* magazines and two empty boxes of Spanish cigars. A bunch of black bananas (a new kind) between Ross Thomas's novels; a piece of rag garlanding the young Cuban novelists; three pebbles stopping Fallaci's books from falling on the floor; a vacuum cleaner pipe sticking out from Philip K. Dick, like a science-fiction apparition. Broken plates, lots of them, would be strewn around the room. Six rolls of toilet paper on top of the computer, a monument to the act of taking a shit; a puddle of water, dead flowers, six shoes, a gas tank in the middle of the room. Scenes from Ehrenberg.

Jesus wept! I might say, like that character from the Spanish comedian Sister Anguztiaz de la Cruz, who frightened people on their deathbeds in post-Franco Spain. And just as Karen stretches her long legs out, to make up for hours spent on the road, or on the narrow seat of a plane, or who knows what, I would be transformed into the Reorganized Red Butler, who is a version of one of Agatha Christie's novels, but one who quotes Lin Piao as he washes the dishes, and would begin a mega cleanup.

"What are you doing?"

"Making space for us to dance polkas."

Deported

Whether Basterrechea heard Amador's message or not, in order to pass it on to the governor, and moreover, whether having heard it he was disposed to repeat it, will never be known. His car was overtaken by a motorcycle three blocks from the Modelo prison, and the Black Angel of Death emptied his revolver in his face, getting away in the middle of a hail of bullets fired by the adjutant's bodyguards.

The Flea would not know about all this either, until much later. Neither would he know that six hundred union activists were taken in that night and the one after. Neither did he find out that press censorship was set up a few hours after the assassination, newspaper offices were closed, and people arrested by the government were not handed over to the courts but remained at the governor of Barcelona's disposition. CNT boss Salvador Seguí was one of those arrested.

Antonio Amador was in the infirmary at that time. He had suffered another attack of consumption and his throwing up of blood had terrified his cell-mates. His face was haggard, his lips swollen, he had a glassy stare and feverish hallucinations. The little journalist fought between life and death for a week, coming out of the crisis more dead than alive, but only just, with the feeling that nothing could kill him, despite the doctor telling him very seriously that if he did not look after himself he had only a few months to live.

"And if I look after myself?"

"A couple of years. I won't be optimistic with you, I can tell you're a man who enjoys looking death in the face."

"I'll take bets, then," Amador said, and rummaged under the straw mattress covering the bed, on the floor, among the newspapers somebody had put beside his bed, for a cigarette he had stolen from another patient.

The cigarette, however, had mysteriously disappeared. Amador slowly got up and started to shout insults at the top of voice at the civilian and military authorities in Barcelona, the King of Spain, his mother, all the Bourbon dynasty, the Catalanists, the textile mill-owners, a cousin of his in Valladolid he had not seen for some time, and a baker's wife who had told him some years that "I don't like doing it with shortarses." The Barcelona winter cold soaked into him through the gray floor tiles and went right through him, making him shiver.

"Put some slippers on, shithead, you're not going to die here. Get a move on, you're all being transferred," a guard in the doorway said, pointing his gun at him.

"We'll come after you even when we're dead, dickhead. A frozen hand's going to grab your balls at night," Amador said, very dignified, as he put on some worn-out socks. "Long live the dead, you bunch of faggots!"

A group of guards milling around the Modelo prison entrance, with their shiny three-cornered hats and rifles ready to fire, lined the way for them. Amador got a few pats on the back and greeted friends and others alike. The candidate for deputy and the unionists' lawyer were also there, and handcuffed, too.

Because of his curiosity about inconsequential things, his mania for trivia that went with the job, Amador memorized the numbers of the trucks from the army headquarters that were waiting for them: 54, 75, and 76. There were thirty-six prisoners. Seguí; Amador; Botella; Salvador the organ grinder; Piñon; Vidal; Arin; Meca, the best carpenters' organizer and hero of the two strikes that had been kept going with gunshots in each workshop; Albaricias; Dalmau; David Rey, the wizard from the underground press, who had driven the Barcelona police mad by printing *Solidaridad* every day during the Canadiense strike without their finding the press.

Amador wrapped his bloodstained scarf around him and hid from the cold that the feeble sun did nothing to get rid of. What a sight for sore eyes: a group of women behind the green mass of Civil Guards and secret police, cordoned off by police on the pavement opposite, shouted farewells and messages. Amador heard one that made him smile:

"The general strike's broken out, brothers! All of Barcelona's on strike!"

The harbor was occupied by the 21st Battalion of the Civil Guards. Amador, who was last into the second vehicle, alongside Albaricias, looked at the three-cornered hats through a crack in the white canvas that covered the truck. They made them get down really quickly, with a lot of pushing and shoving. The boat was nothing special and was called the *Giralda*.

A prison in the harbor? Were they deporting them? Where to? To Africa, no doubt, maybe to Guinea, one of the colonies, to Morocco. No, Morocco no, the rebellion there gave the military the jitters.

The prisoners went on board the *Giralda* in a long line and were led down to the hold, while the escort remained on deck.

"Well, we even get a chance to talk calmly, instead of going around the city in hiding and running from one place to another," Mena said to the little journalist.

The motors started up a little later and the boat steamed out of the harbor. Amador got a blast of pure freezing sea air through the broken glass in a skylight.

"Get away from there, shithead, you'll catch your death," old man Arín said to him, offering him a cigarette.

Amador got out a small notebook and the stub of a pencil, and began to walk around the lower deck where they had been locked in, taking notes and asking for comments.

"Where do you think they'll take us, Vidal?

"Do you think the general strike will be a success, Albaricias?"

The comrades smiled.

The boat, against all expectations, arrived at Mahón, on the eastern edge of Menorca, in the Balearic Islands, at dawn on the second day at sea. The unionists were kept on board for two days, without the local authorities knowing what to do with them. They were, without knowing it, hostages against the movement. If the general strike drove the Barcelona civilian government to its knees, measures would be taken against them; if the anarchist groups had unleashed another wave of attacks, the *Giralda* hostages would pay for it. The long hours of waiting took place on the quayside in Mahón. The news got through to the working community in Menorca bit by bit, and the workers went down to the dock, closed off by the civil guards. The prisoners did not have anything to eat, and a jug of water was passed around every four hours. A navy officer came up to Seguí and whispered something to him during the long hours of waiting. Seguí passed the message on, rather perturbed. In Barcelona they had murdered Layret, the invalid who was the lawyer for nearly all of them, the only man who had spoken in Congress against the persecution of the unions. The men looked downcast as they heard the news; the CNT groups, who had learned to survive the harshest blows, went down as if they had been hit with a mallet. Death was always close by, but there were deaths and then there were deaths, and out of all of them, this was the most unjust and foul.

At last, after forty-eight hours in which Amador saw his life slipping away from him many times in dreams and delirious attacks, they were all tied up with rope and dragged out onto the quayside. It was a gray afternoon, and the lack of sun gave a dismal cast to the proceedings. The journey was going on, but to where? At the end of the quayside, they were loaded onto some dinghies and taken to La Mola, a little cove with a tiny village dominated by a castle that was to be used as their prison.

I haven't got time, Amador said, regarding the castle's outline of reddish rock plunging into the sea. I haven't got time. The days are slipping away from me. It's better to die like Layret. The sun was going down, throwing up greenish sparks. Others might be able to lose a couple of years of their lives, but I can't. The waves were smashing against the rocks and foaming. I haven't got any life to lose. I haven't . . .

The Partially Reactivated Hunter

I would feel as if I am leaving faces from the past behind, faces that would not come into focus in my memory. Even faces that were once attractive to me will get mixed together, be superimposed, and go away. I would be in a time warp, without a past, without friends; lost in a space-time curve. Even so, there would be things that would not change. I would still have bad memories of telephones, and perfect ones of dates. This would probably have to do with the fact that sex with Karen would turn out to be gymnastically marvelous.

Juan Hernández Luna would turn up at the apartment with two kilos of Serrano ham and two melons he bought in Puebla with no guarantees. He would also have his new book, *Tobacco for Pumas*, hot off the presses. I would open it and smell the fresh ink. Then I would look at the cover with a knowing eye. Good, baroque, very colorful.

"Chief Fierro, the mortals in Puebla send you greetings. They miss that conference in which you insulted a governor."

"There you go," I would snap.

Karen might show up in the bedroom doorway, yawning, with one of my shirts covering her up, and the sleeves too short. I would feel obliged to do the introductions, faced with Juan's astonished expression.

"Karen, Juan."

"What, you're not a character from a novel?"

"In English, pal," I would feel obliged to interject. "And don't push it. Just leave it at that."

The ham and melon would help, but not much. Juan Hernández Luna, as good as he is at writing adventure stories, and for all that he may be my best pal, would not be used to gringa basketball players. Too many inches of leg dashing around the room for him.

I would tell the whole story badly, the prologues and the waiting, while Karen managed to find some beer in a closet. I would try a theory.

"From a different angle. Let's say a Colombian gangster who has kidney problems cannot get operated on in his own country. He sure as hell won't in the United States. He comes to Mexico. He sets up the business on the border with the drug-trafficking network he already has up there. That's why he does it from Juárez or El Paso. The deal cannot be legal, he can't show his face, he can't buy a donor because he's on the run, what with the FBI, the DEA . . . he's got the money to rent whatever he likes, but he can't get in . . . why Karen? Just a coincidence. But he likes the idea that it's an American girl. There's a certain poetic justice in going around the world with a gringa's—pardon me—kidney, when your name's González or Escobar. Something like that."

"And where are you going to begin with a story like that? You can't pick up any leads here in Mexico City. You've got to go back to Ciudad Juárez and get stuck into the plot there, haven't you? That's how they do it in novels."

"Thanks, maestro. And what are the leads?"

"The goddamn dog," Hernández Luna would say. Being skinny and with a desperado's smile by nature, he will always go for the most absurd option if he has to choose.

"Mike Gardner and Nicolás," Karen would say.

"The operating room. The hospital," I would say.

"The one who got the kidney and his story of kidney trouble," Juan would say.

"The strange dead guy they told you had been found by a highway," Karen would say.

"The woman I met and who then disappeared, the one who hated the woman who wrote the dumb letters," I would say.

"The house in El Paso where the woman said they were holed up," Juan would say.

"The cockroach-killing spray," Karen would say.

"I don't know," I would say.

Although it is certain that everything would be hidden in Ciudad Juárez, or that the trails that had so far been leading nowhere would go from there, it would be annoying that everything might seem so easy, that that false image of blunt clarity might cloud over the reality I had lived through. Going around and around on the treadmill, a foreigner without papers and without the language in enemy territory. Because it might be that everything could be found in Ciudad Juárez, but in that moment I would be convinced that all these points would lead to blind alleys, to trails going nowhere.

Juan would meticulously slice the melons. Karen would toss a napkin into the air. I would fiddle with the pull tab from a beer can.

Where did they say you had to begin?

Alone

While the news got around about how the general strike was falling apart amid police repression and the bullets from a new bosses' gang, and while they heard about the resurgence of another blackleg union under the protection of Governor Martínez Anido that broke up meetings at gunpoint, the prisoners at La Mola were facing up to the ugliness of life in the castle. For a bed, just four planks on a rusty metal frame, covered with a worn-out straw mat.

A depressing isolation began to wear them down. Amador spent most of the day lying in the pale winter sun, trying to dry his lungs out. Despite the information network that was being set up bit by bit and the liberal and union press beginning to get through to La Mola, and in spite of books of every point of view turning up everywhere, Amador hid away in a world of dreams almost like a functional illiterate; his every move was smothered in apathy.

Workshops, a school, and a series of lectures were organized by Seguí, who did not know how to keep still. The group came back to life while waiting for their legal situation to be defined. David Rey shocked some of the older men by singing a ditty that went: *I feel like a Bolshevik/Because I've got no bread/Coz if I had money/I'd feel like I was dead.*

On January 4, 1921, a month and few days after arriving at the La Mola lockup, Antonio Amador got a telegram in which a sister he had not seen for five years curtly told him his father had died. The little journalist got up from his bundle of rags and asked for an appointment with the head of the military garrison in the castle.

"We are not on trial for anything, nor are we accused of anything that we know about. Quite simply, we are locked up for our ideas. I therefore see no reason why I should not be allowed to travel, under any custody you like, to attend the funeral at Valladolid. I would like to bury my dead father while the government makes up its mind."

The captain offered profuse apologies. He was "under orders." If it were up to him . . .

Another telegram came the day after, from Arlegui, the Barcelona police chief, denying permission.

Amador met with the committee that the thirty CNT militants had organized and asked for permission to escape. The pros and cons were weighed up in a strange discussion, in which no one asked how the little journalist would get away, or what escape plans he had in mind.

If they were being kept as hostages against the movement, Amador's escape could cause all sorts of reprisals in Barcelona. The fact that the situation could get worse for the prisoners in La Mola seemed to be of no importance, but the fact that security measures around them could be tightened might set a dangerous precedent that could prevent a mass breakout later. The committee went over the matter while Amador, stretched out on his bunk in one of the castle's passageways, waited for the answer. Piñón, the steelworker, brought him the decision a couple of hours later.

"Permission granted, journalist. Forward your plan to the committee when you know how you're going to do it. And good luck!"

Amador left the castle four days later wrapped up in a bundle of dirty laundry that was going to be washed in the village. He went as far as Mahón in a barrel of pickled olives on a fishing boat, and got to Valencia a couple of days later as a kitchen boy on a Greek ship.

By the time he got to Valladolid by train and could dodge the police cordon that had been set up to catch him at the station, his father had been buried for two days. He did not dare lay any flowers on the tomb, but confined himself to looking at the place they had buried him from a distance, leaning on the graveyard wall.

The Aging Lover

Hormones and adrenaline would rise up the walls among the haze of tobacco and sweat. Flashes of skin in the glass covering the pictures. Reflections of close-ups. Long, orchestrated, and endless kisses, trying to break high school records; sloppy, wet, liquid, runny kisses. Teeth clashing or vaginal juices on my mustache. One breast that might look bigger than the other because Karen would go against the current and slip her thigh over my chin. Our feet suddenly interlocked, hers becoming platforms for mine, from where I can throw myself into the rhythm of repeated movements, that I will slow down to hold the orgasm back. Orgasm is one form of the end and here we would always try to start again, discovering our bodies. Licking underneath a nose, feeling a nipple hardening at the touch of a fingertip, or blowing in a navel to get rid of nonexistent fluff. Playing.

At first, Karen would have an impulse to be precise, a need to do things well. The first moments of lovemaking with her would be like going through a manual. She would be in a hurry. I am not smart, but I am old. There would be no hurry, but an eternity of staring into each other's eyes, intertwined as we break the rhythm of coitus. This woman is a woman, she is another woman, she is a woman. *Vive la différence!* There is the discovery of varieties in repetition, the climax, and tenderness.

Little by little I might feel a muscular pain coming on in my left shoulder, an old recurring lumbago. I might also regret losing a few hairs from my mustache, the worst form of baldness there is, and my broken leg would hurt from the cold getting into the mended fracture. An elastic Karen, meanwhile, would stretch until her feet stuck out, of course, at the end of the bed, with legs eight inches too long for it. For how long can you put off old age? Can you be young forever with just a sense of humor to help you?

After making love, the best thing would be to look out the window while smoking. Surprisingly enough, the city would still be there. It would not have gone away, neither would it have stood still. Love is inside of time, for all that you might feel to the contrary. You smoke so as not to do more ridiculous things, like dance tangos in the nude.

The Key

Gustavo Adolfo Bécquer, the poet from Seville, died in Madrid in 1870, two days before Christmas, when he was only thirty-four, convinced that life had passed him by somewhere along the way, and happiness along with it.

A group of his friends got together a day after his death, on December 24, and publicly appealed for "friends of the arts" to come up with some money to get Bécquer's poetry published. Some poems had already appeared in magazines and newspapers; many had never been published.

The manuscript of *Las Rimas* had disappeared when the monarchist interior minister Luis González Bravo's house had been looted three years before Bécquer's death, because the former was in possession of it after having offered to publish it. This obliged Bécquer to reconstruct the book in 1868.

Bécquer, while unemployed and with just his two oldest sons for company, began to reconstruct his rhymes from memory on his own in Toledo, in a thick notebook he christened *The Book of Sparrows*.

There, under cipher 41, although his friends would later publish it as number 60, the following rhyme appears:

My life is a barren field,
flowers I touch their leaves do shed;
along my fateful way,
someone sows evil
that I may reap it.

This was the fragment of poetry that Amador and Angel del Hierro had remembered on their road to death, and this was to be the poem Amador would remember once again a year later.

The Bewildered Novelist

Baroja once wrote:

Our libraries shall be scattered, the mice shall eat our papers. . . . People do not really need writers in Spain. As long as there are cafés and cinemas, they will be satisfied. In time, it would be possible to make writers disappear altogether. A good start would be to throw into jail anyone who had ever written a book.

But Don Pio was mistaken. Books have outlived their devilish competitors; they are eternal ghosts. As for throwing writers into jail, they had already done that to me and all they got out of it was that I wrote a book behind bars. The problem was not with *books* but, as ever, with the *book* itself, this one, the latest, the one that was on the way but did not want to get going.

A writer who writes a book that does not want to be written is like a dog that cannot bark.

I would think about this, looking out the window, trying to find the answer where it surely would not be, in the Mexico City rain, that soft rain that does not patter on windowpanes and that stains clothing hung out on rooftops.

It was easier to manage the *nos* than build up a single *yes*. It was turning out much simpler to dump on most of my graduation class's tacky yearning for eternity, every one of whom wanted their statue right on Paseo de la Reforma, much easier to make fun of culture snobs' scams, shadowy inventions, political and cultural complicity. It was much easier to get away from sold-out literary hacks, from the sinister and absurd power games surrounding literature, and all of it was much easier than writing a good novel. A good novel did not have to provide explanations or make excuses. Readers would not give a shit about the antediluvian debate on the novel's social function, the author's mental derangement, his preference for grapefruit sliced in half, vertically, or what he thought of crime in Detroit.

If he could not put all of that into the novel, there was no point in it being published. And if this novel did not work, there was no point in him having wanted for years to write a version of *Les Misérables* reset in Mexico City.

"It's not coming out, right?" said Karen, looking up from Lesson 17 in her Spanish course.

But nothing would come out in those days.

The two of us would go along to the Bonilla bookstore, in the southern part of the city, sharing an umbrella, to give a talk on the novel and Mexico City. What novel?

"Amin Malouf said: *Astrologers have proclaimed it since the dawn of time and they have not lied: four cities have been born under the sign of rebellion, Samarkand, Mecca, Damascus, and Palermo.* Why did the Arab writer leave out Mexico City, a city with more potential for revolt, social reaction, and mutinies than the ones he mentioned? If it is not going to get astrological recognition, then it ought to at least get historical recognition."

The argument would seem to go down well with the audience, sitting on the floor and spilling over into the passages in the little room at the back of the bookstore. I would be surreptitiously drinking a beer, leaving the can underneath the black cloth covering the table.

There might be a couple of insulting telephone calls in the night. It would be nothing new. Karen might have nightmares. I would fall asleep thinking of Ciudad Juárez.

Messages from the Dead

Antonio Amador had filched two large cigarette butts from the ashtray on the table next to his, and was skimming through a copy of *Vida Nueva*, the Madrid anarchist weekly the shoeshine boy lent him every Monday, when he received a message from the dead. There was a small box in the classified section saying:

Little brother:
My life is a barren field,
flowers I touch their leaves do shed;
along my fateful way,
someone sows evil
that I may reap it.
Look for me in the original.

A sudden trembling came over Amador's hands, to the extent that Mariano Morales, the shoeshine boy, came up to him, ready to take the little journalist in his arms, thinking it was an attack of tuberculosis.

The color slowly came back to Amador's face. A message from the dead. Bécquer sending his miseries across time and the Angel who had come back from the Barcelona slaughterhouse. For three months, the journalist had wandered around Madrid, carefully making contacts with the organization and keeping a safe distance from Barcelona, where the government's backlash, led by Martínez Anido, had gotten so severe that the unions were practically smashed while the Free Union gangs were making mincemeat out of the activists. Almost two hundred activists were dead.

While he woke up every day in Madrid at the end of the Castilian winter, with its dry chill air cutting through every nook and cranny, he dreamed of Barcelona. His days were Madrid, his nights were Catalan, full of dreams of chases and death. He had gotten some work that kept him in bread and butter while lying low, thanks to a friend. He was a copy editor for dime-store romantic novels; for a few pesetas he spent hours in the dreary Arco de Cuchilleros going over proofs of stories of misunderstood love, made impossible for social reasons, about marquesses who raped the servant's son or rag traders maddened by drink who kept knives close to their hearts, ready for vengeance. And all the while he waited for the bad news that would come with the newspaper. He had opened the pages many times, looking for an account of how the Black Angel had done this or that, or how they had got him at last and put half a dozen bullets into him. His friend, however, even if he doubtless had had a hand in some of the anarchists' more violent responses to the government backlash, had miraculously saved himself from raids, informers, and shootings. Or he could well be in an unmarked grave.

And now there was this voice with four of Bécquer's verses.

"I need a bite to eat to think clearly," Amador said.

"Anchovies or squid?" asked the waiter, who had prudently come over on seeing Amador's agitation.

"Whatever's cheapest."

"Spanish omelet, and at a local regular's price."

Look for me in the original. The original? A bar with that name? A clothing store, a boarding house? A street? Bécquer Street? Sparrows? A park with sparrows? Something original, origin, the first one. A book, an original manuscript. Bécquer's original? And where was the original manuscript for *The Book of Sparrows*? In the National Library, dammit.

The Ashbin of Closed Files

A friend of a friend might hand over two files from the National Human Rights Commission, a whole one on Nicolás Romero, and another in which Mike Gardner's name would appear by accident.

It wouldn't amount to much, mostly well-known stuff. But I would know more after reading them than before, even if I would not be able to get faces or real people to come out of the files. They were much closer to reality when the hit man in the Ciudad Juárez bar recalled them like the shadows in a story. Now they would be back: Romero, Nicolás, officer in the Federal Judicial Police, elementary school, originally from the state of Hidalgo . . .

A Retired Colonel

The Flea raised his eyes from Bécquer's manuscript into those of a Spanish army colonel wearing a monocle. A ghostly silence usually reigned in the Special Manuscript Room at the National Library in Madrid. Only the manuscripts slowly wearing away or an elderly retainer shuffling along in suede slippers broke the awful, deathly silence. Amador, thanks to a card made in the publishing house he worked in that identified him as Alfredo Argüello, Doctor in Philology from the University of Salamanca, had spent a week living in the lonely room, looking over manuscripts and reading through Bécquer's book. And now, suddenly, this military man with graying hair, a scar running across the eye under the monocle, and a goatee beard, was staring at him.

"I got married," the military man said. "Well, it was

not exactly a wedding, more of a friendly gathering. The way things are now, anyone throws a party.

Amador dropped his eyes, stared at an ancient Greek dictionary he was reading upside down. A mad colonel was all he needed.

"Aren't you going to congratulate me, dammit?"

And then he realized that the Angel had managed to surprise him again.

"You got away!" the little journalist said, hugging his friend. "How's Barcelona these days?" He dragged him over and sat him down next to him.

"Like a jungle. We've all gone mad. Even shadows shoot at you, and as much as you fire back, the balance is always tipped in their favor. I'm beginning to doubt there's any use in taking a life for a life . . . but if we don't do it, our people are just going to go under. I'm going to go under myself. I don't like it . . ."

"And your partner?"

The retired colonel got a wallet out, then took a photograph out, a smiling woman dressed in a loose blouse, with blond curly hair and glasses.

"She's Polish. She's in Spain on the run because she had a go at Pilsudski."

"With a gun?" Amador asked him, pantomiming shooting a revolver.

"No, with an incendiary bomb that blew up one of the Marshal's carriages. She spent three days crying over the horses she had gutted. That's the problem with these Tolstoyan anarchists, but she's a hell of a brilliant cook, pal . . . what about you?"

Argüello, the Salamanca University professor, smiled and got a photograph out. It showed him in his underwear, surrounded by books and papers, a broom lovingly clutched between his arms, and flanked by two women showing off their ample thighs up to their garter belts.

"I've got some of the most lovely whores for friends, from Asturias. They're cider drinkers and work the morning shift."

The Electric Brooder

Dark moonless nights, news of a confused era on the radio, neighbors organizing drunken get-togethers, a dead bird at the entry to the building, pictures skewed on the walls as though there had been an earthquake and only they realized it.

I would wake up early, but not early enough to find Karen beside me. She would have gotten up before dawn to walk a couple of miles out and a couple back, stopping off on the way at a juice stall on the bridge over Insurgentes Avenue. Headstrong Karen, one of those rare women who think that strongheadedness is the highest form of reason. By this time she would be taking Spanish classes with a group of Norwegian diplomats' wives and two Japanese engineers. Conversation. Good morning, Señor Suárez, would you sell me a newspaper? My name is María, and I come from Veracruz. Where are you from? I am Manuel, I come from Chihuahua, and I like going to the movies.

And why not from Zapotlanejo, Tzitzipandácuri, Ixtlán, or Miguel Herrera Station?

I would stumble over to the computer with a chair. It would be programmed to flash me a message when I start it up: *Good morning, Chief dumbass Fierro, what crap are you going to write today?* The novel would be in pieces, in separate files. I would drink canned peach juice, as sweet as possible, sugar is much better than caffeine, while the first file comes up, and put a tape on, for example, the one with "Promesa de un Pescador" by Dorival Caynm, where Santana makes inroads into Brazilian music for the first time. I would have to confess that I became a Santana freak because a few years ago (well a lot of them), I read an FBI report analyzing a thousand radicals from the 1970s and among the coincidences (ah, the offspring of statistics), it appeared that 13 percent were into the Wizard of Autlán's music. Ideology, goddamn ideology, pure and simple, Dr. Fierro Frankenstein, Ierro Ankenstein, Chief Fierro, chief of nothing.

Would you really be bothered about not solving the Ciudad Juárez riddle? Would vengeance not have worn you out? Would the idea of vengeance not have been the shortest way to that TV dream called Karen Turner?

Neither the novel nor reality would be turning out well.

Maybe you just had a limited number of novels inside you and once they were done they were done, the whole thing was just screwed up and there was nothing left to tell, no more stories, *finito*, baby. I would walk around the room, going around and around the table, faster and faster each time. Fierro the Electric Train, the Electric Brooder. French fries with mayonnaise and green chiles. Would the diet not do any harm to Karen, Karen with a kidney missing? I would be sweating by lap 27 and would flop down into an armchair.

Dark, moonless mornings. Birds dead from the smog in the refrigerator. Vague news of more electoral fraud. Friends with vulgar diseases, like asthma, bronchitis, cirrhosis of the liver, laryngitis. An unknown city suddenly surrounding you.

That morning would make thirty-one false starts for a chapter. Thirty-one screens full of crap that would get deleted over the hours, and I would come to the conclusion, after a few hours of thinking it over, that a "seagull flitting across the shore" is not the same as "a baby shitting across the floor." That would bring me closer to the truth than before.

Leonardo's Books

The Angel did not say where he was living with his short-sighted Polish woman, and neither did Amador ask him. Might she be in Barcelona? Was the Angel up to something in Madrid? The Angel did not want to know what the fugitive Amador was up to either, or the name of the boarding house he was in, or the names of the whores in the photograph, as there was an arrest warrant out for him following his escape from the La Mola prison. In spite of their reservations, the two friends began to see each other in the National Library reading room once a week, and it was during the third meeting that Amador dragged a leather-bound tome off a shelf, nearly killing himself as he fell from a rolling stepladder while grabbing hold of it. While Angel was helping him put it back in its place, his fingers ran into three other heavy books, side by side, that had been covered up by the rows of books neatly lined up in front of them. They were three ledgers with hard covers, bound in red cloth that gave off a marvelous smell of old must. He got them out very carefully. Although the discovery seemed inconsequential at first, it made Amador peer out from his vantage point, half hanging off the stepladder, searching for the elderly guardians of that room full of treasure, all of whom were retired Civil Guards whose temperaments were tinged with doubtful parentage.

"What the hell's going on? Get down, won't you!" the Angel said.

"Hang on, there's some amazing manuscripts here, full of sketches," the little journalist said, carrying his load down the steps. "You find all kinds of marvelous things here . . ."

The pair of them took the heavy ledgers over to the table where the journalist usually worked and put them down carefully, almost reverentially.

"Look, it's written in Chinese."

"What do you mean Chinese, it's Latin, but written back to front, like Hebrew. It's pretty odd Latin," said the Angel, bringing his exotic linguistic knowledge into play.

In magical moments, there are small details that acquire new dimensions when things are remembered afterward. Months later, Amador would see the reading room in his memory, the dust floating in the air, lit up by a shaft of sunlight coming in through the window; he would see the ocher color from the manuscripts creeping up the walls, and the old mahogany lecterns shining with the linseed oil they buffed them up with now and again, so the ants would slide down and the termites would be poisoned. And he would remember having three of Leonardo da Vinci's manuscripts in front of him, with their wrinkled paper and red covers.

"It's mirror writing. Did you never play at that when you were a kid?"

"No way," said Amador, who could not remember ever having been a child.

"No, it isn't Latin, it's old Italian, Renaissance Italian."

"And how do you know all this?" the journalist asked him, just as his friend took a small mirror out of his pocket and studied the mirror writing as if he were a lay expert. There was a certain sweetness to the Black Angel disguised as a retired colonial colonel, and looking lovingly, as he was now, at the manuscript. The Angel of Death transformed into the Wise Angel.

"It's left-handed writing, back-to-front; there is some suggestion of shorthand." He paused. "There's also some Florentine slang, Latinate phrases. Wonderful! Have they got a lot of this sort of stuff in here?"

"They must, but to tell the truth, apart from Bécquer's manuscript, a couple of rare dictionaries, and a Cervantes novel printed in the last century, I haven't looked around too much," the journalist answered, and went out to the yard to smoke a cigarette.

When he came back, Angel del Hierro was waiting for him, staring at the door. The manuscripts were partially covered by a military tunic.

"What do you think this is?"

"What?"

"It's a manuscript by Leonardo da Vinci. Can't you see the drawings?" Angel handed the drawings over to Amador—water-driven clocks, castles, beggars' faces, and poems.

"Jesus, and that's a bicycle, isn't it?" Amador asked all of a sudden, fascinated.

The Observer Observed

Karen would be graceful, agile, and awkward at the same time. Wonderful when she combs her hair naked before going to bed, and wayward as she wanders around the apartment in the morning, knocking over books that are precariously balanced on bookshelves until she goes by. After looking at her, I would no longer look at the street through the windows.

One day, I might find her watching her former teammates on TV.

"Was I like that?"

"Better, much better. You were wild."

She might be wearing a short T-shirt with a picture of Simón Bolivar on the front, which they gave me when I went to a book signing at the Central University in Caracas. There would be a scar on the left-hand side of her back.

"I was better."

"Much better."

"But I could never make it through a whole game."

"You didn't need to."

"Did you write about that?"

"Do you want me to read it to you, to translate it?"

I would read off the computer screen while she switched off all the lights in the room. Ghostly lighting for the story. It would take me a long time to unravel it. Lighting up the words is not a bad thing for Amador's and Grandfather's wanderings. I would stumble along. Karen would object to the Ciudad Juárez scenes, but would cry when I read about how I fell in love with her image on the screen. All very wayward and dubious. English does not really suit my own disheveled prose. I leave too many substantive nouns out. I would spend more time apologizing than reading.

My relationship with unreal reality would get itself together again in the mornings. I might visit a textile mill on hunger strike, protesting against a frankly criminal massive layoff, two rounds of negotiations with a TV producer that would get nowhere, an article about my friend Laura Esquivel, who is now getting into crime writing. The afternoons would be all for Karen and the novel.

Then at last:

"And what did they find?" Karen would ask, stretched out on the floor by the armchair. I would have finished reading page 382 from the first draft off the screen.

"Leonardo's bicycle," I would answer her, pointing to a wall where there would be a photographically enlarged bicycle. A layman's bicycling altar.

"Is that all?"

"You call that nothing, sweetheart?"

Karen would shrug her shoulders and lose herself in thought over the bicycle. A small postcard version had hung beside her bed all through her recovery in hospital.

"They also found treasure."

The Bicycle

Although they had carefully hidden da Vinci's ledgers behind other books, when Antonio Amador and Angel del Hiero, the two fugitives from every arm of the law, turned up the following day, they hoped they had disappeared. Unfortunately two of the guards and an elderly student of the Visigoth kings were pounding the beat, and they had to wait until ten, when everyone went off to have coffee, to get the books out again.

They had gone through all the catalogues in the downtime, and had found no mention of the three ledgers. Then they went through everything they could find in the catalogue of references to Leonardo's legacy, but there was no mention of any material in the National Library in Madrid.

At last, the hordes of spiteful gnomes went away and Amador climbed up the stepladder again. The ledgers were where they had left them. They sat at one of the tables like children going to the movies for the first time.

"Can you read it?"

"It's easier with a mirror," the Angel answered, getting a small mirror out of his pocket, and setting it up so he could read the reflections of Leonardo's writing.

"What does it say? What does it say?"

"It says: *A brightness that can only shine briefly in a word, in a phrase, in the space of a few lines, and even so makes a deep impression on the reader*," said Angel, translating the words syllable by syllable.

"What's he talking about?"

"Literature."

They went over the pages, enjoying the drawings and the games. They found some sketches of the Mona Lisa in the third book, along with proposals for the Battle of Anghiari mural, maps of Piombino Bay in 1504, with lots of side notes, and, once again, a design for a bicycle.

"Goddamn. Now we really know. It's a bicycle, for Christ's sake. I told you!"

"When was the bicycle invented?"

"I don't know, sometime in the last century."

"Incredible! If that can be done, nothing is impossible!" the Angel said, echoing what Amador was thinking.

SECTOR EIGHT

Love and Violence

It was the end of November and it seemed the world was going under.

—Lawrence Sanders

The Nursing Home

"Who are you?" the old man asked.

"José Daniel, your grandson."

"Whose son are you?"

"I'm the only grandson you've got."

"You should have children by now, and I should have great-grandchildren. I'm ninety-eight, nearly a hundred."

"You turned a hundred-and-two today, it's your birthday. I brought you a present."

"Raisins?"

"Chocolate covered."

"Well I'll be damned. Don't let the one in the corner see them, he's a tight-assed holy Joe who doesn't share with the rest of us—you get all sorts in here."

"Don't you get bored?"

The old man wiped his chin where he had drooled a bit.

His hands were covered in old burn scars, and he had a cutoff smile, like a grimace. He was in a wheelchair, with a navy blue bathrobe covering his blue-striped pajamas.

"Don't you feel like coming to the apartment for a few days?"

"I can't stand your mother, and I almost can't stand your father."

"They died a couple of years ago. I'm living with a gringa basketball player, who could be your great-granddaughter."

The old man thought it over while he ate chocolate-covered raisins by the fistful. Before speaking again, he carefully looked over the one who said he was his grandson. He seemed to go along with the idea.

"I don't like it very much in here, but I haven't been out in years. I don't know if I would dare, I can't even remember what it's like out there."

"It's not much better out there, but I would like it if you came home to us for a few days. I should have asked you over before."

"When was the last time you came?"

"Three months ago . . . I went away," José Daniel said as if in apology. It was cold in the room with white-tiled walls. "Do you feel like it?"

"Would they let me?"

"I don't know."

"Do we have any more relatives?"

"Just you and me."

"Is that all? What about the rest?"

"They all died off, Grandpa."

The old man stopped eating raisins, and his thoughts drifted elsewhere. José Daniel lit up a cigarette without the nuns seeing. The old man seemed to liven up.

"Can you smoke in your house?"

"All you want to, and you can read *Playboy*."

This was not too clear.

"I went over there a couple of years ago. You were in jail, weren't you? Weren't you married?"

José Daniel nodded yes to each question.

"What was jail like? I've been in a lot of them. They're all a pile of shit. Did they let you read books?"

"My life is a barren field,/flowers I touch their leaves do shed;/along my fateful way,/someone sows evil/that I may reap it," said José Daniel, reciting.

"That's by Bécquer," the old man said.

José Daniel threw the cigarette out the window into some bushes and held the old man's hand. They stayed quiet for some time.

"Dammit, son, I like the idea of smoking. What's more, I'm sure the food's better in your place than here."

"I wouldn't be too sure."

"I would. These nuns poison you . . . they can't even make fried potatoes . . . you haven't been for a while, have you."

"Three months."

"That's what I thought."

There was silence again.

"What about the treasure?" José Daniel suddenly asked.

"What treasure, the stuff on the island?"

"What island? Was there an island?"

"Treasure Island, idiot. Didn't you read that book? I could swear I gave it to you when you were a kid, although you, of course, never read a bloody thing."

"No, the treasure you and Amador found in Leonardo's books."

"We didn't find any treasure. You must be making that one up. Look, I told you everything straight. The only thing we found was a bicycle, one that Leonardo invented and that I then used as a calling card. I used to leave them on the bastards that I did away with."

The old man lowered his voice and looked around the room. He was looking for stool pigeons. It seems he did not find any, or that he dismissed them as being deaf, because he went on: "I used to leave a postcard on them, like a scapular on their chests, and then I crossed their hands over it."

"Didn't you see the Baron again? Didn't you run into him in Italy?"

"Come and sit on my lap, grandson, I can tell you like novels, tall stories. You're like that little Amador, who liked fairy tales," he said, without realizing the honor he was doing his grandson. "We never saw the Baron again. What more did I want? If I had seen him again, I would have shot the bastard. He must have ended up knitting like some old biddy, or looking after Auschwitz for the Nazis . . ."

Yes, that would have been just up his alley. So they never ran into him again. He gave them the slip.

"Look, I think I'll stay here. Maybe next time," the old man said, suddenly changing the subject.

"Sure you don't want to come?"

The old man shook his head. Just as José Daniel was going out the door, the old man asked him out loud:

"Did you know they have pictures of the Pope in here?"

Yes, yes, he knew about that. The first thing the nuns in the home had told him was that his grandpa was smashing the pictures and burning them with some eau de cologne he had stolen from the maternity ward.

A Misspelled Letter

Sum boddy I now gave me youre a dress and showed me one of youre buks with vampyres and a man breething lotsof fire on it and told me this real brave mother wonted to now lots about Nicolas so im gointa rite you to say that Nicolas Romero aint from sabina or Juares but from Pachuca Hidalgo, noless, and hides it coz nobuddy likes saying there from that shitty one horse town but he reely is from their and it reely is shitty and i tell you Nico was hangin aroun that jerry like the littel mouse in the comics and the weird guy and them kidnaped the gringas just to fuk them up coz there real bad men and they kilt sumbuddy in laredo in Texas and hes popin pils al the time and get shitfaced and smoak til theirs no trees left down their in Pachuca and thats why they fired him and they didit in Doc leivas hospitel and Mike hoos a faggot kiked the other one to deth coz he duz evrythink Jerry sez an keeps house for him and woshes dishes and gose shoppin and minds the fukkin dog and they make lotsof munny in dollers and pesos and on a motorbike with a siren jerri bowt them they killd livrado vasques in Jimenes who was sposed to be there frend so you see their not to be trusted, over sum drug scam coz he didnt like the saks the other guy had put it in an jerry wen around sayin fukkin mexican faggotts all the time and nikky dont even get woshed and they like dirty lodown hores like lola who isnt even a woman and dosnt even wash her cunt yors sinseerly Emilia Rodrigues Tena

José Daniel read the letter twice and said, "We're going up north."

Karen's Dreams

Karen dreams about a man. A roommate in a room with twin beds. An unshaven man about fifty years old, wearing dark glasses. Sometimes she tries to explain her dream to Chief Fierro, with all the difficulties we have when we try to put into words that which seems so clear and exact to us in our imagination. And she tells him how she feels that the man beside her is linked to her by a sort of umbilical cord that makes them like twins.

José Daniel pushes her into telling everything she can remember about her dream about the man and the room. The man is obviously the man who got the kidney, in the transplant operation, he and she both think. But only Karen can say if he is nearly as big as she is, that he wears dark glasses (at night, in bed?) and that he is from some strange country, where they have civil wars. Yugoslavia? José Daniel suggests. That is it. The Yugoslavian guy. Was it not Colombia? There is a civil war there every day, José Daniel suggests, sticking to his theory about the Colombian drug trafficker. No, from Europe, Yugoslavia. There. And what about his age? He is like my dad. How old was your father when he died? Fifty, fifty-two. Shit. Are you sure the man in the dream is not your father? My father was a wasp, dumbass, he would never have worn dark glasses in bed. Mustache, beard, scars? Dark glasses, unshaven. Sorry, that is all.

What is between the beds in the dream? A bedside table with a big jar of aspirin, books in English, and a subscription to *Rolling Stone* . . . you sure?

At Camelia's

José Daniel Fierro set up his headquarters in Camelia's, not out of perverse Mexican logic (that was surely of Spanish origin) that better the devil you know than . . . but rather out of thinking that he liked that motel with its plastic flowers in water jugs, the secret lovers who wanted their pals to see them, as his friend Belascoarán, the famous one-eyed Mexico City detective, would say about motels in the north of the country. The place did not seem to make any difference to Karen, she had probably known hundreds like it as a basketball player. She confined herself to buying six boxes of "Paint by Numbers" versions of all the van Goghs in existence, thereby revealing a facet of her personality previously unknown to the writer. She got to work putting on some ocher No. 26, yellow No. 29 with a bit of white No. 2 and green No. 35 to re-create the cypress trees in

Arles, the fields of wheat and the sunflowers, the solitary chairs and the billiard tables.

José Daniel bought a real coffee pot in the same self-service store, a cork pad and some thumbtacks to hang things on the wall. After a morning spent sleeping and sweating off the journey, he spent the whole afternoon pinning up articles, Polaroid snapshots, maps, and the page of the phone directory where he had found Dr. Leiva's clinic.

He and Karen walked around Juárez at nightfall, two strange bipeds in a city full of cars, until they found Nico's old apartment and his neighbor Lola's. The lights were off in both of them, and the taco man told them that two brothers from big families had moved in, with grandparents, dogs, children, and tricycles, but that they were on vacation right now.

They took a taxi and ended up at the Immaculate Conception Sanatorium, run by Dr. Armando Leiva. A plain building with more room for parking than for patients. The receptionist told them that the best time for finding Leiva would be between ten and twelve in the morning. José Daniel looked for some flash of recognition in Karen's eyes, but the basketball player walked along the corridors with an expressionless face, without any reaction at all.

They went straight to the doctor's consulting room the next morning. Leiva's office didn't look like it belonged to a doctor; it was filled with photos of American football players, Swiss chalets in glass gobes that scattered snowflakes when you turned them upside down, and a picture of the doc with a former governor who was shaking his hand. Leiva himself seemed out of place, despite the white coat—corpulent, coarse, and with burly hands.

"I suppose you know about Miss Turner's case."

"Sure, they talked about it a lot around here . . . can we help you at all? Is the recovery going well?"

Karen frowned. She was a lot less aggressive without a ball and dressed up in those endless gray jeans. She screwed her face up under the effort of trying to remember, making her eyes look smaller.

Leiva did not know who to look at, he was getting nervous; he plumped for talking to José Daniel from behind a smoke screen of professional courtesy.

"It was a disgrace to the professional community here in Juárez. A blot. If we can help you, young lady, in anything . . . naturally our services would be free of charge."

José Daniel looked at Karen. There was nothing.

When they went out, José Daniel could not stop telling himself that the doctor never asked them what they wanted.

"That's the one, isn't it?" Karen said. "But I don't remember anything. Nothing at all."

It was cold and Karen shivered.

Back in the motel room, José Daniel decided he was burning to write some notes, and Karen resigned herself to a peanut butter sandwich as the best supper she would get. Halfway through, with her mouth full, she asked:

"Are we really going to find them?"

José Daniel looked up from his portable computer and hesitated before answering.

"Maybe, with a bit of luck."

"But do we want to find them?"

José Daniel realized that things were getting serious, so he took a long swallow of beer and lit a cigarette. Karen came up to him and sat down by his feet, on the carpet.

"Do we want to find them or are we just writing a novel?" Karen said, insistently.

"Do you want us to find them?"

"Not really."

In the Night

José Daniel picked up the bag with the shotgun still smoking inside it, grabbed Karen, who carried nothing more than a hairbrush with which to defend herself, by the hand, and looked for the rear window, which led to a fire escape. A man stood in the middle of the room screaming with pain, blood streaming from his mangled hand. The knife was still stuck into the TV stand.

"There's more of them," Karen shouted.

José Daniel stopped trying to wrench open the rusted-tight window, shoved Karen into the minuscule bathroom, went up to the screaming man and hit him in the nose with the shotgun butt. The man, instead of falling over, grabbed his nose, also streaming with blood now, and sat down on the bed.

"Fuck you! That hurts, asshole!"

While José Daniel was reloading the shotgun, the window that looked out onto the motel parking lot smashed into pieces; the bullet continued through a vase and shattered it.

An alarm siren, worse than a fire truck, went off. The wounded man tried to get out, but tripped over the cover on the double bed and landed on the floor. José Daniel fired both barrels without aiming. The window blew up into glass and wooden splinters. The curtain started to burn.

Karen, eyes wide, had replaced the useless hairbrush with a putty knife. At least she was ready. José Daniel Fierro reloaded the shotgun. The sirens seemed to have multiplied. Chief Fierro looked at the man howling on the floor by the foot of the bed and hobbled over to the door, holding the gun in front of him. A terribly sharp jab in the kidneys doubled him over. It was fear. Karen went over to him and stood on the other side of the door. The novelist noticed she had only one shoe.

She shoved at the door while he aimed the shotgun. The fire had spread from the curtain to the bedspread behind him.

The motel manager stood paralyzed in the doorway, goggling at them like a greenhorn seeing an old Western on the big screen.

SECTOR NINE

Desperately Searching with Karen

The Ballad of the Stars
(Part Four)

A parallel novel full of stories and
totally lacking in common sense by

José Daniel Fierro

*dedicated to the living and lead-filled
memory of my grandfather,
the Black Angel*

You write against your own loneliness and that of others.

—Eduardo Galeano

Another Article

For a whole week, the Angel and Antonio Amador explored the labyrinths of da Vinci's work in the three ledgers. Although Amador tended to get sidetracked by da Vinci's diversity, bit by bit, and almost without meaning to, he concentrated more and more on the bicycle and the jigsaw puzzles over Piombino Bay. He also made his friend teach him how to read backward. Since when had this bastard learned how to read backward? How the hell did he know Renaissance Italian? Amador had a good knowledge of Latin and understood modern Italian, but the Angel . . .

While the journalist found himself facing another one of his frequent cases of love at first sight over the bicycle, that grew and grew when he discovered very elaborate designs of gears, the Piombino story, on the other hand, was full of references, codes, loose ends, hieroglyphics, and riddles that wore him out. However, with Angel del Hierro's help, he transcribed all the references to Leonardo's stay in Piombino to a notebook with white covers that he had acquired for that very purpose, with the serious intention of studying them later.

As the days went by, they both felt obliged to investigate why the books were not registered, but they set out about it in such a furtive and conspiratorial way that a rumor went around the librarians and guards that they were a pair of Jesuits trying to find in religious texts a basis for the end of celibacy.

The fact is that with all the running around they did, Leonardo's notebooks were there and were not there; like themselves, they did not exist. To be on the safe side, they hid the books at the end of every day in the place where they had stumbled across them.

A month after having come upon the strange find, when Amador's copybook was full of notes, Angel stared at him and said:

"I think I'm going to have to leave you for a few days, maybe more. I'm mixed up in something . . ." he added, as if apologizing. And without further ado he went out of the room. Amador watched his friend go off. The Angel wandered in and out of his life like an opera singer who puffed his chest up, sang an aria, and vanished.

Amador spent the next few days writing an article about Leonardo's bicycle for an anarchist monthly in La Coruña that, alongside fiery polemics about the workers' struggle, published articles of scientific interest, apologias for naturism, scientific explanations on the virtues of free love, and the rational bases for atheism. The article came out two months later and went by completely unnoticed, despite all the knowledge, technique, and love Amador put into his description of the bicycle and into the context of the Renaissance and the implicit magic of the whole business.

The article finished off with the phrase: *If this man could do this, then nothing is impossible.*

As well as surpassing himself with that article, Amador read and reread the notes he had taken from Leonardo's text, especially the ones having to do with his visit to Piombino Bay in 1504, but he did not write anything about that.

When the article came out, Antonio Amador felt he had come back to the journalistic life and was not just an idle fugitive, so he celebrated by eating petit fours on the Gran Via. As he was leaving the cafeteria where he had indulged in the marvelous, nearly forgotten experience of gluttony, he felt the Madrid cold go right to his bones and collapsed in a faint.

For those who do not believe in luck, and Amador was one of them, it so happens that Elena Iturralde, the prostitute in whose house he had stayed to sleep a few times, saw him fall over. Elena, whose real name was Rosa (with no surnames), and was a fan of the romantic dime novels that Amador called "twenty-for-rent novels upgraded to dime ones" as he checked them over tirelessly every day, said: "Dammit, the lad's dead."

Immediately, just in case, she got into a taxi and took him to Malasaña Hospital.

The doctor who treated him was paid in kind on the armchair in Rosa's room, while Amador, out of consideration for his frail state, occupied the double bed covered in green tulle. The doctor accepted the story that he was a relative and went to great pains to wake the journalist up and get the magazine with the article about the bicycle out of his tight grasp.

"You are going to die, sir."

"And is that what you call a diagnosis? It isn't even new," Amador answered him in a faltering voice, the taste of blood on his lips.

The Interrogator Interrogated

"Then why did you have a shotgun?"

"It's a souvenir from the old days. I also like target practice and I was told there was some real hellish competition up here in Chihuahua," I would say with a smile.

"I was given orders to treat you kindly, not to fuck with you, but don't go treating me like a jerk," the captain of Judicial Police Group II in Chihuahua would say; a sharp-featured, skeletal man with a mean-looking mustache.

"Nothing could be further from my mind," I would say, lighting up a cigarette and finding myself to be the interrogated interrogator, a character that would not attract me in the least.

I have been in places like that, smelling the rancid gusts of fear, in front of torturers in their Sunday best like this one. The little window above his head must look down on a parking lot, because you can hear the noise of cars coming and going.

"Do you know who you shot? You ought to know, you've been asking a lot about him recently . . ."

Romero. That was Romero? The man with the bloody arm who whined and cried was Nicolás Romero?

"Romero? What a coincidence! What a fucking coincidence!"

"And why were you looking for him?"

"Because they told me he was the guy who had kidnapped my friend."

"The big gringa."

"Karen Turner to you."

"That . . ."

"And what do you know about the attack on our motel room, officer?"

I might be able to see some round fluffy clouds through the little window, like in a childish drawing. I would carry on smoking, under the policeman's watchful eyes. He would seem to want a cigarette.

"You two must know a lot more. By the time we got there the room was on fire, Romero was on the floor half covered in blood, and you were standing in the doorway with a shotgun."

"We were asleep, they started shooting, one of them came in with a knife, I fired a shot in the dark, the curtains caught fire, and the one outside, or the ones outside, shot the TV to pieces."

"Is that all?"

The guy would stay silent. There were no chairs in the room, so I opted for sitting on the desk, leaving the cop to wander around the little space that was left to him.

"I will soon know more than you."

"Are you going to torture Romero?"

"To interrogate him. We don't torture here."

"That's not what they say in recommendations to the National Human Rights Commission, last year's Americas Watch report . . ."

"What have those faggots got on us . . ."

"Nothing. If you say so."

"Just so. The governor has asked me personally to get to the bottom of this business with the gringa. It's a shame for the whole state."

"That's a fact."

"We're going to solve the case."

"Can I keep my shotgun?"

"Sure. The governor has a special interest in your hanging on to it . . . as for me, I'd rather they killed you in Coahuila or Sonora, or better still, in Mexico fucking City."

"Can I see Romero?"

"In a while. Tomorrow . . . let's not kid ourselves, first it'll be your humble and obedient servant . . . this week sometime, when he's got over the lead you pumped into him . . . so you can see we really like you around here . . . shit, you should have filled the other guy's legs with lead . . ." the captain would say, to finish off the discussion.

"I tried, I sure as hell tried, Captain," I would say, so as to have the last word.

Assassination

At about eight o'clock in the morning, on March 8, 1921, the president of the Ministerial Council, Eduardo Dato, got into his car in the Senate building and drove off toward his house. A seven-horsepower Indian motorcycle with a sidecar, that had been following the car since it went past the Plaza de las Cibeles, drew up to it by the Plaza de la Independencia and began to zigzag across the road.

It was then that the shooting began. Two men, one of them riding behind and the other in the sidecar, fired eighteen shots at the car. They emptied their guns into the back seat on the right-hand side, where Dato usually sat. One of the shots hit his footman, Juan José Fernández, who was sitting in the front seat, and his screams made the chauffeur realize what was going on and speed up. The motorcycle kept up with them, however, at least along the twenty yards between Olózaga Street and Serrano Street. They used a Mauser pistol and a 9mm Bergman.

When they got to Serrano Street the motorcycle and the sidecar made a break from the scene, and one of the men shouted, "Long live anarchy!"

The chauffeur drove the car to Dato's house at No. 4 Lagasca Street. Once there, the policeman on guard duty in the doorway heard the screams of the chauffeur and the wounded footman, saw the president's blood-soaked body on the back seat, and immediately suggested that they go to the Buenavista Hospital. The car got to No. 2 Olózaga Street in less than five minutes.

It seemed that Dato was still breathing and was twitching, so the doctors who treated him tried to revive him with camphor injections, but the ministerial president was a corpse within minutes. He had two gunshot wounds in his head and one in his chest. The bullets had gone through his jawbone and his skull, with one still lodged in his chest.

The ministerial president's bowler hat was left on the back seat, with two bullet holes in it, alongside his blood-stained wallet.

Amador read all this in the newspapers, sitting in a small back room and on top of an empty jug, covered in a ladylike robe with flower patterns stamped onto it, while his friend Elena was "exercising" in the room next to him. He read and reread, picking out the bare bones, here and there, of the most important assassination that had ever taken place in Spanish history.

The facts came out bit by bit.

On the thirteenth, the Catalan steelworker Pedro Mateu got to the boarding house at No. 164 Alcala Street, where he had lived up till the day of the assassination, and half a dozen armed policemen jumped him as he entered the dining room. He tried to draw a pistol he had tucked into his pants, but a policeman hidden behind the door immobilized him and another two pinned him down during the struggle.

In his only confession, Mateu said that he had indeed been the perpetrator of the assassination, but quite by himself; he declared he was an anarchist and finished off with his epitaph: "All men are victims of their ideas. Dato had his and I have mine."

The second and third men continued to be missing.

One of them was the Angel, Amador was sure of that. That is what he was up to in Madrid. There had been a rumor going around that the Confederation was planning to strike right at the top, but Amador had always thought that the assassination attempt would be aimed at the butcher of Barcelona, Martínez Anido, who was guilty of murdering over a hundred union men in the last few months. But never in Madrid, and never Dato.

Amador read and read on, coughing away in the back room while ecstatic moaning sounds issued from the bedroom. Elena had a wide range of animal noises on offer, according to the client's tastes, from wolflike howling to the clucking of an electrocuted chicken, from heartrending theatrical screams to the syncopated cawing of a crow, with sheeplike baaing on the way. Now and again a client would join in with her, but what most disturbed the little bony journalist, as it went beyond mere irritation, was the rhythmic rustling of the wire-spring mattress. That was the sound of madness.

And facts continued to turn up. A motorcycle had been discovered in a garage in Ciudad Lineal that in its day had cost 5,100 pesetas. They also found two pistols that had not been used in the attack. And if Casanellas, also a Catalan steelworker, had really been the driver despite his notorious nearsightedness, and if Mateu had really fired from the sidecar, then who was the third man balancing on the rear who had fired the Mauser?

The raids in Madrid had produced a hundred arrests, mainly men accused of having formed support groups for the trio who carried out the attack, but they were also trying to silence the CNT. For this reason journalists like Samblancat, Torre Beci (who was not even an anarchist, but a socialist), Quemades, and Nuñez de Arenas were also arrested. The Security Office censored all information pertaining to Dato's assassination, and the Madrid press retaliated by boycotting the SO's bulletins.

Amador felt relatively safe, but thought that picking up material from the publishers would not be a good idea, even if they were drafts for romantic potboilers. He tried to go out in the morning, but his legs were not responding well to treatment and he balked on reaching the stairs, so he went back to his little back room where the very newspapers he had been reading and some moth-eaten blankets made up his bed. He had a small mirror with which he had tried to shave himself, but to no avail.

He was dying. The Free Union gunmen backed up by Martínez Anido were killing his comrades in Barcelona. The world was coming to an end. You could not read the newspapers, even the sports pages were censored. He picked up a gun he had stolen from a security guard who was a client of Elena's, an enormous .45 that wore holes in his threadbare jacket. He pointed it to his temple. He laughed a little. It looked stupid, the pistol was bigger than his head and he could scarcely see it in the piece of mirror he had. He would blow his head up and half the room with it. The brooms would be blasted to shit and the calendar with scenes of Paris would go up in flames . . .

If that damned, unmentionable illness was going to finish him off in any case, if they were going to kill him like a dog if they found him, or he was going to end up in a frozen, lousy prison (the cold had frightened him lately), then what was the rush? Who was in a hurry to die if the trees were beginning to fill up with leaves? The sun would warm his bones in a month's time. He could write something. He could take some of them with him before he went. He lowered the gun and put it away in a bag that he filled by throwing some scraps of bread on top. He could write a poem . . . who was in a hurry to die?

The Hunter of Murdering Doctors

They would give us a new room in Camelia's with a view of the parking lot, and a rear view of the highway. The same old plastic flowers, they seem to have survived the blaze. A blue bedcover, and a TV with a bigger screen. The manager would be grateful for having appeared in all the newspapers. It seems that people from Juárez are a morbid bunch, and Camelia's would have turned for a few days into a fashionable hot-sheets motel for secret couples, eager to be seen at the scene of the crime, illegally turned on thinking that the next-door neighbors might be shot at any minute. The same old orgasms, but with a controlled feeling of fear, savoring the anxiety.

Karen's hands would be trembling slightly, which is no good for shooting from more than ten yards, especially now as she would have improvised a basket in the motel parking lot. Periodic rebounds are heard as I type away. Basketball would turn out to be like my novel, the same old shit following you around.

"Who is in a hurry to die?" Amador would say. Dr. Leiva had raised the stakes. In whose way are we getting, this poor retired basketball player and this surly wayward writer? Why did they send Romero after us? Was there any use in my grandfather killing Dato? None at all; the repression got worse in Barcelona. The ball would hit the backboard and I would imagine how it would be going around the hoop, spinning. Karen would have an audience, because cheers would be heard. They would come from the bodyguards the captain had lent us, and the manager's children.

A second round of cheering. A more difficult shot, probably with her back to the basket. Leiva lowered his guard. The kidney's recipient would still be around here. A month after the operation. Amador with his .45 between his teeth. The beer would run out; time to go out, I would be thinking.

It would not be too difficult to get rid of the two bodyguards. Out through the motel back door, across the highway, and run against the traffic for a bit (Karen, with a kidney missing, would take six yards out of me after running twenty-five), to get a taxi on the corner. A café two blocks from the clinic. I would take my scorched canvas bag with the shotgun in it, my old friend and partner, along with me.

"You have any idea how to go at him?"

"On my own—or maybe I should just wait for him?"

"No. That would mean too much time just hanging around there."

"Should we just walk into the clinic?"

"No, there'll be guards on the door."

"Go look for him at home?"

"No. Where does he live? Who would we ask?"

Good for Karen. Cold and logical. She would give me a big toothy grin after every negative answer. Sometimes, so much youth gets on your nerves.

We would walk up to the emergency entrance, two hundred yards around the back. An ambulance turning up would make everything easier. We would walk in holding hands with a woman in labor, who would seem to appreciate the gesture. We would get lost in a maze of corridors, and would hide in a room full of drip-feed containers.

Looking around. Leiva's office is not guarded. Empty. He would have a private bathroom. I would reload the shotgun. Karen would take a foot-long kitchen knife out of my canvas bag. She would give me a malicious smile.

"I'm learning how to write novels," she would whisper.

I did not like Doc Armando Leiva, and I never would. Clumsy, too bulky. I would like him even less when he came in humming an awful song by Yuri, the Mexican Madonna.

"Put your hands on the table, Doctor."

"Shall I cut his balls off?" Karen would ask, mixing my novels up with Andreu Martin's, flashing her knife.

The man would blanch, slowly turning a gray color that would ruin his suntan.

"Don't waste your time, Doctor, we just want to know a few things: Who was the guy who got the kidney? Who's Jerry? Which surgeon performed the operation? We don't know now and I don't give a shit if we leave here not knowing and with you as a corpse," I would say, cocking the gun.

Arturo Tancredi on the Attack

"What a surprise you should ask me what my endeavors are all about. Are you a Mason, a Rosicrucian, a mystic of some sort?"

Amador shook his head. The only thing he wanted to keep a mystery in his life was the number of holes in his socks.

"That's good, because I am interested in da Vinci, the Magus; as a painter above all, as a harbinger of analytical methods, as a Renaissance man."

Amador nodded enthusiastically.

"Da Vinci's work is terribly scattered. Right here in Madrid, two manuscripts were lost in the National Library centuries ago, stolen probably. Not even probably! Stolen, certainly, by English collectors. They are like a plague, those sons of fair Albion, when they get involved in collecting things . . . everything they have stolen is over there: the three Forster Codices are in the Victoria and Albert Museum, and the Arundel Codex is in the British Museum. On the other hand, you can find most of Leonardo's work in Italy, in the Ambrosiana Library in Milan, the one that Pompeo Leoni set up in the sixteenth century. It is all bound together in a strange way, some four hundred pages of it, and this huge book is called the Atlanticus Codex. You can track down some more of his legacy in Milan, in the Trivulziana Library, where the codex of the same name is kept and, while still in Italy, you can see the famous *Book of Birds* in the royal library in Turin. The Italians are a mess, they cannot get their act together, they lose everything."

The old man dunked a handful of pastry in his *café con leche* and paused a moment to suck at it. Amador watched him hungrily, but the expert on da Vinci, who had crawled out of the catacombs along the trail in Madrid, did not invite him to join him. Amador had nothing but a broken watch and two cigarette butts in his pocket.

"The French have what Napoleon's troops misappropriated from the Ambrosiana Library, twelve out of the thirteen manuscripts they took. Awful! The French are a bunch of shits, a country full of thieves."

Amador nodded very seriously and repeated the last phrase. It seemed to achieve the desired effect.

". . . country full of thieves."

"And what is your interest in the matter, Mr. . . ."

"Tancredi, Arturo Tancredi . . . I hail from Castellón de la Plana and as far as I can recall, my family is from that neck of the woods, but I did find some notes from my great-grandfather saying that we were distantly related to Leonardo and now that I am in Madrid . . ." said Amador, warming to his story. He really liked telling stories, dammit. He was about to tell the man about a cousin of his who . . .

But Lara-Lastra, the da Vinci expert, did not give a damn. He was in his own little world.

"And that is just a small part of the sixty or seventy manuscripts he must have written. It is a librarian's nightmare, because the ones who collected the manuscripts ruined them or broke them up, they have fallen victim to carelessness, looting, theft, and, furthermore, they were in no order other than the chronological one fixed by Leo himself."

"Do you know anything about his journey to Piombino Bay in 1504? I am especially interested because . . ."

"But of course. You can find the relevant material in Manuscript A, in Paris, and then in the Ambrosiana Library in Milan, where . . ."

The Future Dog-Feeder

"A goddamn Russian. It's all because of some half-assed Russian," Romero would say.

"He says he didn't kill your friend, miss, that was some Mike or other. He was the one who grabbed ahold of you," the Judicial Police captain might say.

"You were wearing silver-tipped boots, right?" Karen would ask Romero, who would have a few days' stubble and swollen eyes surrounded by bruises by now, along with a dirty shirt with bloodstains on it. How old would he be: thirty, thirty-five? From Pachuca, too. He would be cold here.

"What were the cans of roach poison for?" I would ask, and for my misplaced curiosity I would get a poisonous glance from the captain.

"The gringo couldn't stand 'em, he said they would crawl

up his bed while he was asleep. The Russian didn't care, he didn't give a shit, he was used to it."

"How much did you get paid for the kidnapping?" the captain would ask him.

"Four thousand in all."

"Two for you and two for Mike, dollars that is . . ." the captain would say, in an insistent tone that would make me suspect he wanted some of the bread to find its way into his pockets.

"Would you let us speak to him for a moment, Captain?" Karen might say, with a big smile like a British lady.

"She wants to be sure, Captain, so she doesn't need to go raise hell at the U.S. consulate," I would say, affably.

The sharp-featured man would graciously handcuff Romero to his chair and walk over to one side, like shadows do in dreams.

"You were the one who killed Jackie, you kicked her with those boots of yours. I'll tell you all about it."

"No, miss, I just held you down."

"It was him," Karen would say.

"We want to know where the gringo and the other guy are, the one who got the kidney."

"In Chihuahua. They're in Chihuahua, in a ranch by the university. Mike's in my apartment, with the dog, but they rented a ranch . . . you can see it from the university, behind the . . ."

The captain would no longer be in his office. He would have gone out to have some tacos in the square. He would offer us a soda.

"We're going to give you a present, captain . . . the operation was performed in the Concepción Hospital, Dr. Leiva organized it . . ."

"Impossible. He's my best friend, and besides, he hasn't done an operation in ten years," he said, choking.

"And the recipient, the son of a bitch who's got my kidney, has a real nice name, he's called Christo."

We would walk off under a sun that left no shadows, kicking up dust as we went. Later, Karen would ask me:

"What was it Romero told you as we were leaving?"

"He told me to feed his dog, because Mike forgets these things."

The King of Spain

Antonio Amador knew only one way of getting to Milan: by the Barcelona express and from there by boat to Genoa. And he knew only one way of getting through Barcelona without being killed: disguised as the King of Spain. He had not worked it out too well, though, as Alfonso XIII was very well known, had a Germanic mustache, and was a good bit taller. There were other options, such as dressing up as the Pope, but as far as he could recall popes were usually fat; it was that or dressing up as something exotic, following the Angel's advice.

He needed money and connections either way. Where would he find good costumes, where would he find money? Costumes in the National Theater, money in the Bank of Spain. Robbery or fraud? Both were complicated affairs, he would have to spend some time on the matter.

Antonio Amador felt dizzy as he watched the lions in Retiro Park. Someone had told him that they ate donkey meat in copious quantities, supplied to them by Gypsies, which explained why they were so docile; that and the freezing cold wind that swooped down from the mountains along the Paseo de Recoletos and through the Puerta de Alcalá.

There was less of an air of death about Madrid, that is why things were difficult to work out. Amador missed Barcelona. His dizziness was due to hunger. He picked the remains of a sausage sandwich out of a trash bin and walked around, looking at the monkeys and zebras, and wondering if it would be just as good to be the King of the Belgian Congo and to hold up a dairy, or a restaurant.

He ended up traveling to Barcelona as an admiral, with a false beard and gray hair in his temples, having held up a Madrid tobacconist's shop at gunpoint.

Yearning for the Red Sun

Nobody has considered the virtues of the much-maligned smog in its shaping of the landscape in the Valley of Mexico, I would say to myself in this land of mesquite trees, here where the sunsets would not be red, and where there was no artificial fog to make the mountain ranges hazy.

Nobody has praised the artificial fog, which seen from the screwed-up side of things is on a par with the other urban monsters on the planet; but that on its plus side creates those shifting, prisonlike landscapes, with no horizon, those landscapes that are unique to Mexico City.

"I like being with you because you're never in a hurry," Karen might say, taking off her sweaty T-shirt and exposing her breasts. Those sorts of bodily visions would make my old wounds hurt again, where my leg had healed, and make my head ache.

"That's because I haven't the faintest fucking idea what to do next."

"In our hunt for the bad guys, you mean?"

"In everything, with you."

The motel in Chihuahua would be called the Guadalupe, not Camelia's, a sign that we were headed south, and would have a big-screen TV and a bed where Karen's feet would stick out a bit less than before. There would be a coffee table between the arm chair and a glass door leading to the pool, where I would set up the computer. An office with a view. Karen, naked, would test how long the bed is, its elasticity, its suitability for bouncing bodies. I would have dark forebodings brewing in my head, a bunch of anxieties not conducive to thinking about sex. Guys shooting through the windows, razor-slashers, rooms catching fire, have a way of making my balls shrivel up.

Karen would read over my shoulder, making the screen fill up with Ks and Ns, because I would keep missing the keys. My typing ability would go out the window as long as she went topless. Amador would journey through badly spelled da Vincian mazes.

"Mike or the ranch?"

"Flip for it?" Karen would say.

"Eagle, it's the ranch; sun, it's Mike."

The thousand-peso coin would spin through the air, and land with Sor Juana's portrait showing.

"Where's the sun? That's a woman."

"Mexican coins are tricky like that. They've always got an eagle on one side, but any old shit on the other."

A low, three-story apartment building two blocks from the cathedral. A hand would come up from the ground to grab mine. Is it the metaphysical beggar, or is it somebody else?

"Keep out of there, it's full of cops, about fifty of them, everywhere. They're about to move in."

"Who are you?" Karen would say, nodding to the beggar covered in dirty bandages and rags.

"I'm one of the gentleman's fans, miss. Not any old jerk, but a reader from the old days, when he was unknown. Stay here, all hell's about to break loose."

And things would happen just as he spoke. A window blown to pieces, gunshots, a policeman in the middle of the street firing on the second floor with an M-1, people running, screaming.

The beggar would push us back against the wall.

"These assholes cannot aim, and have a lousy habit of spraying onlookers with bullets when they're on a job."

Another burst of fire on the second floor, bits of glass falling onto the street like confetti. A group of men in bulletproof vests running into the building, shouting to raise their spirits, like a Speedy González cartoon. More shots, but separated, and smaller caliber ones.

"They've fucked him over now," the beggar would say, vanishing behind our backs.

An ambulance siren would shatter the silence, giving rise to rumors, shouts. Onlookers, such as Karen and I, would get closer. We would recognize somebody in the doorway, the skinny captain, the man who moves sideways, keeping a tight hold of a canvas bag in his hand. The loot, of course.

"Well, well, if it ain't Wonder Woman and her writer," he might say, showing his knowledge of 1940s comic books.

"Did you get him?" Karen would ask.

"There he is," the secret policeman would say, pointing to a stretcher carrying Mike's remains, with his blood-spattered face and his hand hanging down to one side.

"You can go in and feed the lousy dog, if there's anything

left of it. Mauro, take these people into the dead man's room, they want to see if there's a dog in there," he would say, as the stretcher went past us. The crowds would push closer and closer to get a good look at the dead man to check it was not a relative, a brother, or even themselves, or even the one that these shitkickers killed by mistake. Because they felt like it, because there was something in it for them.

The door would be hanging off its hinges, there would be blood on the floor. If the dog was in there, it wasn't barking. The guy would clear the way for us, kicking broken glasses and lamps as he went.

"Must be at the back some place."

The dog would be laid out on the floor in one of the bedrooms, stiff and bleeding. A little black dog.

"Look, there's the sweatshirt I was wearing when they kidnapped me," Karen would say, pointing to a green Texas Longhorns sweatshirt, with a number nineteen on the back, hanging from a nail on the wall.

The TV would still be on, and a red sun would come pouring in through the window to be reflected in the screen. A sun just like in Mexico City.

The Bicycle Killings

"What's the correct form of address for an admiral?"

"Your Excellency, at least," Amador said to the trashy Chinese emperor, who had dropped in on him in the empty first-class compartment on the night train. He had serious doubts about his friend Leonardo's sanity; only a mulatto Cuban magician would think of disguising himself as a Chinaman.

"We should have dressed up as Gypsy women."

"You'd be a danger even in that outfit, with your goatee and chocolate-colored complexion, my friend."

"My ass, you're an admiral. I suggest we get off the train in Pueblo Nuevo rather than Sans: the station's full of Arlegui's cops, and even magic's no good on those bastards, no way."

Amador was frankly offended that the Cuban recognized

him; all his time and effort to disguise himself as one of Spain's grandees had been worthless.

They walked around the Barcelona backstreets in their clownish outfits. Amador, given his short stature, kept tripping over his sword, and the magician kept getting tangled up in his Chinese silk robes.

"And what the hell were you doing on that train?"

"Coming back to Barcelona. I had a bad time in Zaragoza."

"But you're wanted here."

"You too."

"I've got to get to Milan."

They dropped into a guest house famous for serving an excellent Asturian fabada stew for thirty cents that would fill two people. It was full of transvestites, among whose sequined dresses and false breasts the admiral's three-cornered hat and the mulatto magician's robes did not look out of place at all.

"It's not a good idea to walk around Barcelona at night."

They shared a room and a single bed at the top of the boarding house. They slept in shifts. The one who was awake stood guard, read poetry by candlelight, played with the admiral's medals or the Chinese robes, and put up with the other one's snoring. The magician rehearsed a couple of tricks with colored paper that vanished into thin air; Amador recited Calderón de la Barca in a low voice.

They tried out some variations the next morning, with the magician dressed as an admiral, and the journalist as a Chinese emperor. No good. The magician had a white beard in his suitcase that, along with the affectation of a limp and an old hat, turned Amador into an old man carrying a box of grapes. Padura Buenaventura, the magician, changed his emperor's outfit right there for an old streetcar driver's uniform.

They went down to El Ensanche at nightfall. The dangerous thing about going around looking for old faces is that you might get seen first in a city full of informants, where the Free Union's gangs were wandering around. Spring had arrived in Barcelona, and a pale sun was warming up the street dogs. The trees were beginning to fill up with new leaves. Reading *El Sol*, the journalist found out that the two top men in the blackleg union and a police officer had been found dead in the Ronda de San Antonio. They had probably been shot during a rendezvous. Postcards were found on their bodies with crude drawings of a bicycle on them. "The Bicycle Killings" the journalist called them, and it seemed they were not the first ones, either.

"Leonardo's bicycle. The Angel," Amador said, throwing the newspaper onto the floor as if it were burning his hands.

Amador left the magician to do the rounds of the seedy nightclubs and wandered over to the harbor, looking for clues, old faces. He wanted to meet one of the organization's leaders and ask a simple question, but most of them were locked up in the La Mola prison. Quemades was in jail in Madrid, Boal locked up in Barcelona, Pestaña in Russia. He had read some of Martínez Anido's statements in the newspaper, saying that the crackdown was going to get worse. A few pages further on, he had read about sixteen union men being killed as they were being taken to jail. The law of flight was back in fashion. He retraced his steps the day after, with little hope of finding anything. Things were getting dangerous.

A taxi pulled up beside him as he was walking down Icaria Avenue. Amador's hand went to his gun and he quickly devised a plan of action: fire through the box of grapes at his head, empty all five bullets into him. Taxi drivers were well known for being police informants, in return for getting permits.

"Are you looking for someone?" the taxi driver asked.

Amador glanced up. There were two men in the back seat. Pedro Vandellós. It was him, with his mustache, and his forehead a bit more wrinkled than he remembered. Amador had written a few articles in a campaign to get him out of jail in 1918.

"Get in, dammit," Vandellós said.

Amador cheerfully jumped into the taxi, which sped away from the curb.

"You were seen in Pueblo Nuevo, although everybody thought you were out of Spain after your breakout from La Mola."

"I'm on my way to Italy. I've got some business to do there, but first I need to get in touch with the regional committee . . . what are things like around here?"

"As you see, we're killing each other. They hit at us, we hit back. The organization's been outlawed, they want to set up company unions in the factories. We shoot back where we can. One of these days, we'll all be dead . . . if they find you, forget it." Vandellós's voice did not tremble as he spoke, but he had lost his old sense of humor. The taxi pulled up near a big steamship in the harbor. "What do you want with the regional committee?"

"I might find a lot of money, treasure. What should I do with it?"

Vandellós stared at him. The organization's people were going mad; even he was not too sure about his sanity, sleeping in a different place every night, feeling the imaginary bullets. But Amador was a different sort of madman.

The journalist smiled. "Didn't you read Salgari when you were a kid?"

Vandellós sighed. Then he began to make a list.

"We need to buy weapons, Thompson machine guns, a new model from the United States with fifty rounds in each drum. Set up a newspaper in the south of France, in Andorra. That's it. I think that's it . . . the prison support committees need money, they're broke. We need to pay lawyers. Not only haven't we got the money to pay them, with nearly five thousand in jail, but they're shooting at them as well. Lastra the other day, Ulled and his assistant yesterday . . . how much money is in this treasure of yours?"

Amador stared at Vandellós, the steelworker. He could not be more than thirty. Twenty-eight. The bosses' organization had put five thousand pesetas on his head.

"A newspaper in Andorra," he said counting on his fingers. "Pay the lawyers, money for the prison support committees, Thompson machine guns from America."

The sea breeze blew in through the taxi window. How could anyone live away from Barcelona, away from all of this?

"You've got to get a move on, Antonio, we haven't got long."

"If my body holds up," the journalist said, shrugging his shoulders.

"Are you in a bad way?"

"I'm going to die of TB one of these days. If I die, a Cuban magician will finish things off . . . who should he look for?"

"The regional committee, which today is made up of me, Nin, and Ramón Archs. If they kill us before you get back, I don't know. Whoever steps into our shoes."

"Do you know where the Angel is?"

"He travels alone. I know he's in Barcelona, but he goes his own way. He doesn't meet up with anyone."

"All right, Pedro," Amador said, getting out of the taxi, leaving the box of grapes behind.

"Say hello to the devil, whoever gets to hell first," Pedro Vandellós said from the taxi window, his brown curls waving in the wind.

Pedro Vandellós was arrested three months later in the Sans district while organizing a collection for prisoners among some workers on a building site. Arlegui, the police chief, tortured him personally, burning his eyes out and putting a stiletto through his stomach. To hide the signs of torture, his body was thrown under a train on the outskirts of Bogatell. They had finished him off with a Mauser in the back of the head. The chief of police's office issued a press release saying he had tried to escape at four o'clock in the morning on June 24, as he was being taken to court.

Amador, who knew a lot about death, had the distinct feeling, as the taxi drove off into the shadows, that he would never see him again. That same night, after looking unsuccessfully for the Cuban magician in Chinatown, he went on board a cargo ship that would take him to Genoa. Among his luggage was a faithful reproduction of the sketch of Leonardo's bicycle. And in spite of knowing what they would do if they found it on him next to the pistol, he took it out to look at it in the starlight of Barcelona harbor, as if it were a good-luck symbol.

The Del Valle Fireman

"Is revenge as important as curiosity?" Karen would say, showing that she catches on real fast.

"Aha."

"I hadn't realized that; you don't get to know these things when you're just a college girl shooting hoops."

"What things?"

"That looking for justice is like wading through a swamp. In the United States you have a hard time picking up simple things like that."

"Could you hand me the fuses, the red ones," I would say.

By that time, Chief Fierro would have become a technocrat, concerned with technical details—or, to be more precise, a fireman exported from the Del Valle district. I will be a wizard with explosives. Three turns to the right, leaving the spring loose. If the car tries to get away from here, Booooom!

"If we find the Russian or the Turk who stole my kidney, what are we going to do? Are we going to tell Dr. Leiva to operate on me again and put it back?"

"Aha. Now hand me the black tin, carefully now, and without smoking."

"I don't smoke."

"But I do. It's just to remind me."

"Since when did you learn how to make bombs and mines?"

"Talk softly, little lady . . . a Cuban friend of mine taught me. I always knew I'd get to use this in a book one day."

Now, slowly coming together, a bomb that will go off on impact. Good, there you are. The ingredients were not first-rate, there was too much cheap black gunpowder from fireworks and shitty gasoline, the nonpolluting sort. The ranch lights in the distance would be on all the time, competing with the glare from the city behind us, and a few stars.

I would be barely halfway through the operation when the headlights of a black pickup truck would shine into the front yard of the ranch. I would scarcely have time to throw Karen into a ditch and hide myself behind a tree. The truck would suddenly speed up, as if it knew we were there.

The truck would hit the first mine, the one I planted in the middle of the narrow dirt road, but the device would go off a bit late, shaking the vehicle and smashing up the rear window. A second mine connected to the first one would go off, setting fire to two trees on the other side of the road. I would see barely more than a flicker from the unaccompanied driver, a flicker in which he twists his mouth, in the blink of an eye. The truck would zigzag every which way before crashing into some brushwood and throwing up dust. It would then clumsily straighten up and speed up to head off toward Chihuahua.

"Shit, I'll never make mines with black powder again. Shit, shit!" I would say, kicking the gravel on the ground between the burning trees and the loose dirt up in the air.

Karen would stroke my back as the rear lights from the truck went out of sight. The house would be there, waiting for us.

Milan, and Later la Ville Lumière

Antonio Amador spent five and a half days begging in Genoa until he got enough money to pay the train fare to Milan.

Antonio went through Milan as if he were racing against time, a city where strikers were clashing with mounted police and there were fruit stalls on the streets, and locked himself in the Ambrosiana Library for six days, having first forged a letter of recommendation from the Bishop of Burgos. He worked eleven and a half hours a day, as long as the library stayed open, examining Leonardo's Atlanticus Codex with the help of a mirror and Bruno Arpaia, an Italian comrade, itinerant photographer, and exile from life, who worked as his assistant. Then he met up with some comrades from the Fraternità group, with whom he had corresponded occasionally, who told him that Pestaña had definitely just passed through on his way to Barcelona. He asked them to lend him money and took the train to Paris.

Afterward, he buried himself in those notebooks of Leonardo's in the National Library in Paris, with the help of a French anarchist called François Guerif, who worked nights as a butler (and urinated in his bosses' soup).

A few days later, after a visit to the Louvre and under a sun that was beginning to dry up his bodily fluids, Amador put his discoveries in order, by now convinced that he held the hidden key to Leonardo. He set out the whole story as he understood it, in a notebook with purple covers. The story, taken from the manuscripts in the Madrid Library, the texts in the Ambrosiana Library, the French notebooks, and the copy in the Louvre, was quite simple for whoever wanted to read it in order and in context. Finally, after a week in whch he had spent the mornings walking through the Luxembourg Gardens around a large fountain where children would launch little sailing boats, and the nights in a boarding house where the lights went out at midnight (obliging him to burn the midnight oil with a paraffin lamp), and after throwing a dozen rough drafts away, he came up with the following notes:

Leonardo's treasure:

1) In the year 1500, in Venice, Leonardo offers to construct an underwater device for his Most Serene Highness, to attack the Turkish ships that were threatening the republic. It was a diving suit complete with a helmet, a special blouse and trousers that would allow the wearer to urinate underwater. He goes into great detail in his drawings of the helmet, a mask with windows and a device connecting the mouth and nose to a large air-filled bladder, sealed with rings. Leonardo makes several drawings of the suit in his

books, and they come with a detailed description of how to get close to the flagship in the Turkish fleet and sink it by making a hole in the hull, under the waterline, using a bit and brace. The divers would then set the rest of the galleys on fire. The plans include designs of a little "underwater boat" that can sail while submerged. The Venetian naval bosses treat him as if he were mad. The Turkish threat evaporates.

(N.B. He is just playing around with ideas, there is nothing behind the proposal.)

2) A short while later, feeling somewhat frustrated, he leaves a message for posterity on page 33 in the Atlanticus Codex: *Why do I not describe my method for remaining beneath the water while all the time I might be there, without coming up for air? I do not wish to divulge or publish it, due to the perverse nature of men, who would use it to commit murder at the bottom of the sea.*

(N.B. Meaning, they did not take him up on it.)

3) Two years later, in 1502, he goes back to the submarine idea, this time for a project that will never take place, to recover sunken ships from the bottom of the sea. He offers it to the Sultan of Turkey: *We shall also describe how air can be pumped underwater to raise enormous weights, in other words, how to fill skins with air once they have been affixed to weights at the bottom of the sea. There shall also be descriptions of how to raise weights by attaching them to sunken ships full of sand, and how to remove the sand from the ships* (Madrid Codex 1, sheet 82).

(N.B. It seems Leonardo could not care less who his employers were. He is still interested in submarines, although he has no one to finance his schemes or to apply them.)

4) At last, in November 1504, Leonardo comes to Piombino, to rest a while. There is a reference to a *mysterious secret* in the Madrid papers.

(N.B. Watch out, we are getting into interpretation. There is also a cryptic reference to a last fortune that, once recovered, will finish *all types of servitude*.)

5) Leonardo studies the tides in the region, from the bay in the old port (i.e., Porto Vecchio) or Porto Falesia, to the Gulf of Baratta, with the old Etruscan fortress city of Populónia in the middle. His books are filled with notes on the tides, sketches of dinghies, graphs of the sea bed, and all sorts of observations on the sea. He is annoyed that his wanderings around the region are occasion for whispering and curious glances (Manuscript L, to be found in Paris, containing part of the notes from 1502–3).

(N.B. It is doubtless here that he hears about the sunken ship that was carrying the payroll for the papal troops. See note No. 8.)

6) He makes more cryptic observations about searching for underwater treasure, and writes out a proposal to make a personal lifejacket and some enormous floating shoes.

7) December 1504. He makes a sketch for the portrait of Giacomo Mascarpone that can be seen in the Sforza Gallery in Milan. We know that Mascarpone was in Piombino with Leonardo. He is probably the one who shares the secret of the sunken treasure with Leonardo.

(N.B. Who is Mascarpone? A mercenary who works as a killer for the Borgias. The portrait shows a face with stern features, and a slightly cross-eyed look; Leonardo does not seem to like him, there is no nobility in the portrait.)

8) Leonardo writes what has been called a "novel," which is not found together with the text on Piombino due to Leonardo's papers having been scattered, but it can be seen

in the Trivulziana Library. He refers to sunken treasure in one of the appendices to the novel, and details are given on the ship that was carrying the Vatican soldiers' pay.

9) He designs Mascarpone's jeweled silver dagger, which can be seen in the Metropolitan Museum in New York. A famous dagger, as Mascarpone used it to kill Rodrigo Borgia in 1503.

10) In notes pertaining to his will that he wrote in 1518, shortly before his death, the following text appears, disguised as a fragment of poetry: *the helmet, the dagger, the ship, the map of the future* (Madrid III).

(N.B. It is abundantly clear that Leonardo discovered something in Piombino Bay, that he thought it was possible to apply all his unfinished inventions to hauling this discovery out of the water. It is clear that the key to finding the sunken treasure is hidden in the poem, and that he was referring to Mascarpone's dagger and helmet in the portrait.)

11) If the helmet in Leonardo's sketch of Mascarpone's portrait is observed closely, a whimsical, asymmetrical sketch can be seen on the left-hand side. If this whimsical sketch is superimposed on a drawing of a map of the Piombino coastline, a remarkable resemblance can be seen, and a spot on the coast is clearly marked with a tiny heart.

12) By looking carefully at the sheet the dagger is on, it turns out that instead of finding the signature of the craftsman who made Leonardo's design, we see the following inscription:

37 Br—Scg.

The only interpretation possible is "at a depth of 37 fathoms (*braccia*), on the reef (*scogliera*)." And there really is a reef at the spot marked with a heart on the map of Piombino.

And it really was, or really could be. And the treasure was either waiting there, or had been washed away by the tides and movements of the sea bed, or some German had grabbed it in the nineteenth century, and the little journalist didn't have the faintest damn idea what had happened. Suddenly, Amador realized that he was in the same situation as Leonardo, with knowledge that could not be turned into money. How could you get a ship up from the bottom of the sea in Italy, where fascists were killing anarchists? Would Leonardo's methods work? Where would he get the money to set up a large-scale operation like that? Maybe *37 Br—Scg* just meant that the dagger had been made by Bruno Scaglia, aged thirty-seven, and nothing more.

His distressing flow of ideas was interrupted by a coughing fit. It was then, as he lay huddled up, feeling as if his lungs were tearing themselves apart, with his eyes streaming involuntarily, that he caught sight of the only man who could divert his thoughts from Leonardo: Baron von König.

Leaning on a bench, trying to get his breath back, Amador saw the Baron, dressed for the spring in a gray three-piece linen suit and an astrakhan hat, going out of the gardens toward the Latin Quarter.

Amador rose, followed. What about his pistol? He had left it behind in the guest house. Nothing, not a thing on him. He would have to strangle him with his bare hands.

Amador slowed down a little, out of breath. The Baron was taller, and almost double his weight. His anger would have to augment his failing strength. The Baron continued along the Boulevard Saint Michel, turned left along Rue Racine; as he was about to enter a three-story building, he turned and saw the little journalist stumbling along, caught up in the chase. Although Amador felt as if his heart would jump out of his chest, he went on, to meet his fate. Recognition slowly flickered in the Baron's face. The journalist sped up as he approached and threw himself against the stout Baron, brandishing nothing more than his rolled-up notes on da Vinci. The Baron responded by hitting him with his walking stick, throwing him against the front window of a pastry shop. On any other day he would have enjoyed having fallen among caramel truffles and cream buns. The Baron drew a stiletto from his walking stick, glinting in the afternoon sun, and tried to impale the journalist. Antonio Amador dragged himself backward, between the cakes and the broken glass. The Baron picked up the papers that had fallen from the journalist's hands.

"You're that crazy journalist that has it in for me. This must be more of your unfounded shit."

He lit a silver cigar lighter and ignited the bundle of papers. Antonio, blind with rage, threw himself at the Baron again, using a piece of broken glass as a razor, coughing up blood, drowning in his own mucus, his ragged suit stained with meringue and chocolate cream. The Baron used his sword-stick to hold him off and stepped backward. The little man's eyes were a picture of madness; the Baron tottered on his feet. The chase started up again.

While running through the cobbled streets of the Latin Quarter, Antonio "the Flea" Amador felt that the coughing fit racking his lungs was the final one. He fell onto his knees and cursed. Seeing his adversary on the ground, the Baron brandished his sword-stick and went back to finish him off.

Amador was dying. He thought it was very unfair, contradictory and cruel, to finish the life he had led on his knees in front of the enemy. It was then, as his senses began to fog, that he saw a skinny character enter the scene, wearing a light cloak. An ethereal, magical vision who drew a revolver from his pocket and, without hesitation, shot the Baron in the face at point-blank range, killing him instantly, like a mad dog.

So Amador faded away, smiling at his friend, the Black Angel of Death, the taste of blood mixed with cream cakes on his tongue. Now he could die. Or perhaps not, perhaps the little journalist was immortal. This was probably not death, the cream cakes tasted too good for this to be the end, the end of everything, the last . . .

The Defeated Novelist

In the middle of the well-lit room, a man would be sitting in a chair with his back to us, or rather tied to the chair with a telephone cord. He would seem to be strangely still, or even stiff.

I would wave the shotgun to cover any possible entrances by the enemy through the kitchen door, the corridor leading to the back bedrooms, or even the patio door we had just come through. Karen would carefully approach the unmoving man in the gray pants and undershirt.

"Wait! Leave him to me!" I might say, now converted into a fortune-teller, a Cuban magician, a front-runner, a defeated novelist.

Karen would stand still at the other end of the room as I approach the body, the corpse. The dead, glassy eyes, beneath the thick glasses, in the strangely dangling head of a fifty-five-year-old man with stubble on his cheeks, would be staring at me.

A message might have been stuck to his chest with duct tape:

His name was Christo Mandajsiev, he was Bulgarian. I've left the kidney in the refrigerator for you. Sorry for all the trouble. J.

Karen would stare at the dead man. There was a gaping wound beneath the undershirt, a red stain at the spot where the kidney must have been. She would go out into the patio to throw up. I would look for the kitchen, convinced the note was accurate, convinced of the horror waiting for me at the end of the corridor in a big kitchen with white walls and Talavera-style tiles from Puebla, with a fridge and a kidney on a tray in it. The certainty of his macabre conclusion would slowly lead me to another one: that Jerry had gotten away. As much as we might look for him in airports and border crossings, he would be a long way by now from any chance of revenge, settling accounts, or justice. And accompanying this would be the awareness that the Bulgarian in the well-lit room would not be able to tell us the fucked-up story at the back of all this.

Karen would be sobbing in the patio. I would not even have looked in the refrigerator.

SECTOR TEN

In the Great Starry Night for Storytellers

In that great starry night
that happens elsewhere.
—Roberto Fernández Retamar

Jerry in Manhattan (IV)

Jerry Milligan conscientiously cleaned the small kitchenette table in his dive of a room in the Chelsea Hotel in Manhattan. He took checkbooks, bank statements, bits of paper, and bills from out of his pockets; a suitcase, his billfold, from a hole between the floorboards. It was a morning for getting his accounts straight.

He thought he had done the right thing in slicing the Bulgarian up, getting rid of him forever, closing the book on an old story. True, he had lost a lot of money, but the Bulgarian had been like a bird of ill omen, always drawing storm clouds. Deep down, Jerry thought, as he sorted through a pile of American Express traveler's checks, Mandajsiev's sad eyes thanked him for the deep cut and the end of it all. There were a lot of movie theaters in that great place in the sky for kidneyless Bulgarian former agents.

Two hundred thousand Swiss francs in Geneva, $11,600 in used bills under the Bulgarian's mattress in Chihuahua, and counting.

He would have to leave Mexico out of his future plans. The writer was a model of stubbornness. Just how did he get involved in the matter? Jerry, chased after by a writer looking like a Mexican Marlboro Man, a United Nations secretary who was one of Pancho Villa's grandsons, or a respectable southern citizen, accompanied by a kidneyless lady basketball player. Too much of Mexico for your dreams, he said to himself.

It was a pity, too, because aside from the complications, he used to enjoy his talks with the Bulgarian. Jerry recognized the value of nostalgia in life. He worked out the balance on his Chemical Bank account, which came to $100,000, clear.

He used to enjoy his talks with the Bulgarian.

"If you kill me, I'll never be able to own a chain of movie theaters in Manhattan, and you'll never be a carefree gringo, a universal tourist, a permanent foreigner, a bird on the wing."

Along with Vera and his fat guys, the Mexico City police were getting too close, and the Judicial Police in Chihuahua were ready to pounce on the ranch. The operation had not been successful and the Bulgarian was rejecting the kidney. He was not too sure if that hustler Leiva had done the transplant properly to begin with, or if Romero and Gardner had kidnapped the right gringa. It was all a mess, and the Bulgarian was pissing blood.

At least the flowers smelled nicer in Mexico than the roses the Pakistanis sold on the streetcorners. Mexico was not so bad, really. The Bulgarian was a nice guy.

He looked through the *Financial Times* to find the exchange rates for the Mexican peso and the Swiss franc. He had a carryall with a pile of pesos in it. New pesos or old pesos? What a hassle. Somebody was stamping on cockroaches in the next room. Time to count pesos. The Ciudad Juárez cockroaches had probably come along with the pesos. They would have to fight it out with the New York ones, there was not room for all of them.

Eighteen thousand six hundred new pesos, one and a half million old pesos, or another fifteen hundred new ones, if the paperhangers giving out financial explanations as he crossed the border had gotten it right. Divided by three, it gave him a good $6,000. More if he changed it in Mexico.

The whole affair had a sharp edge to it, he thought, remembering the Mascarpone dagger in the Metropolitan Museum, the jeweled dagger that had committed a hundred murders, that had sliced through muscles, looking for the heart. It was his favorite exhibit in the Met. The Florentine dagger and Dr. Leiva's scalpel.

It had been a clean job. He had only left one photograph behind him from Guadalajara, in the social column. He had asked for the newspaper a while later, and a news agency in New York had gotten hold of a copy of *La Jalisciense* for him. "Businessman Jerry Milligan Goes Home to the United States." How the hell had the reporter gotten hold of his real name? From the immigration department? What journalistic diligence. Who the hell cared anyway? Why didn't they publish a picture of the cheerleaders from Houston who were on the same flight? And he kept on counting. Thirty-seven thousand dollars in the Manhattan Trust bank.

Jerry quit. Beside his bed there was a photograph of the jeweled Mascarpone dagger, close by the address of the porno dealer who distributed his mother's movies.

He carefully put the Mexican pesos back into the carryall, bunched all the papers together and put them in his jacket pocket, and put the Swiss traveler's checks into a plastic bag that he slipped inside a box of fish-sticks in the freezer. They wouldn't steal something like that, not even in the Chelsea.

A faint knocking at the door; he checked the room over carefully. All the money was safely tucked away. He opened the door, expecting one of the Jamaican whores from next door, waiting to bum a couple of bucks from him for breakfast. Instead he saw:

A veal kidney, still bleeding, on the floor and opposite his door. Beside it, a copy of José Daniel Fierro's latest novel, *Leonardo's Bicycle*. Pinned to the door—just when had they pinned it?—a plan of something that looked, surely enough, like a bicycle.

He carefully checked over both sides of the corridor, and even went up to the elevator, but the doors were shut.

"Shit," said Jerry. He kicked the kidney.

Endings

Every city ends up looking like it is in a movie, especially the most photogenic ones, Manuel Leguineche, the Spanish journalist, said in Berlin, before the Wall came down. If it were true, then which one would ours, warped old Mexico City, resemble? Which fucking frame from the duel in the O.K. Corral would it be like? Which bit of celluloid from *Blade Runner*, with its Los Angeles with dripping walls? To describe this city, you would have to look for other ones. There are no paintings that can do justice to the pastel shades thrown up by the atmospheric pollution, there are no films that convey the sensation of chaos and fragility or the relaxed haste of Mexico City. Reality only competes with fiction in novels, reality always triumphs in reality. It bowls stories over without hesitating, it eats them up. Reality is odd, reality is unreal, José Daniel Fierro, that unemployed utopian, is thinking. He imagines he is imagining the ending to end all endings for the novel he says he is writing. And I imagine him typing away.

So he writes a novel where Jerry dies in a house-fire and a chapter where they force a captured Bulgarian to go through the operation again, only the other way around, giving Karen her kidney back; second-hand, but in good condition. And all of this under the kindly eyes of Leonardo da Vinci, with his treasure in Piombino Bay never having been salvaged from the sea. A mobile Leonardo da Vinci, riding his bicycle through Mexico Park, looking at the dirty birds, the polluted Mexico City sparrows drinking in the fountain, before going up the bridge over Nuevo León Avenue, dodging the transvestites and the nighttime rose-sellers, to go into the Del Valle district and chug a few beers, a six-pack, with his friend José Daniel Fierro, who has just hung up the telephone after talking to another friend, the Bear, who told him that they had just rejected a book of poetry for the tenth time, and one of his sons, whom he had not seen in months, since the divorce, went to live in Puebla because he had asthma, and writes to him about murdered peasants in their communities in the mountains, and he thinks, Fierro thinks, just what has this country come to, that they fought for so many times, that it is a real effort to catch a glimpse of it, confined within the four walls of a room, from behind the stacks of books he had promised to read, from behind the computer screen.

As the day draws to a close in inclement weather, it needs to be realized just how much grace and sweetness can be seen in the faces of men and woman, Leonardo wrote, in a book that would later be lost and found a dozen times until it ended up being known as Manuscript A and was deposited in a library in Paris. Well, there is always that: men and women and stories to tell, cities that crumble and foreshadowing barricades, thinks José Daniel, Chief of Nothing, with the keyboard boiling over and sparks appearing on the screen where the text is blue, italics red, and bold characters are green.

The Black Angel suddenly appears in the bathroom doorway, wrapped up in a black robe that looks like Dracula's cape, and says something like, "Son, I want to take a leak, but I can't find the light switch."

"On the right as you go in, about chin-high, Grandpa," says José Daniel, fascinated by the old man's ghostlike appearance.

"They hide things more and more. Fuckin' hell, I should shoot someone's ass off," the old man says, shuffling in his slippers.

"Hey, were you involved in the attack on Dato, when they killed the government chief?"

"The things you think up! Everyone knows that was Casanellas, Nicolau, and Mateu . . ." The old man spat on the floor when he heard Dato's name. A good habit that, spitting whenever you hear a head of state's name.

"And the treasure?"

"What treasure?"

"Were you ever in Paris, Grandpa?"

"No, only Marseilles. I never set foot in Paris, it's full of Frenchmen, that place."

José Daniel sighed. Was there no other way of improving history apart from literature?

"Does the music bother you?"

"Not at all. I even like it a bit. It's a bit odd, but . . . to each his own."

Life Is for Living, Santana's latest, booms out from the record player. Its weird lyrics reminding us that we live surrounded by fear.

So there was the novel that would not come out, and for which it seemed José Daniel would never find the ending he liked. A version that alters all previous versions. In this novel, Karen would be a volleyball player and would go home one day, she would go back to playing volleyball she would say, she would say as she left José Daniel the night before his fifty-fourth birthday, which he would say was his fifty-third, just to fool himself a little.

José Daniel would catch sight of an unexpected movement in his apartment window. Leonardo Padura Buenaventura, the Cuban magician, would be taking rabbits and streamers out of a bowler hat, floating three floors up in the air. His teeth would seem to light up the whole street, along with the streetlamp on the corner, lonely and rumbalike in the absence of starlight. The great starry night would be supplied by the magician's smile.

Jerry exists and is waiting, he knows I am watching him at a distance, José Daniel writes, *and one day I shall be back and I will kick his ass until one of his kidneys comes out* and then he finishes the novel off (although he is still missing two hundred pages in the middle) as he had always wanted to, just like the *The Shadow* radio plays used to, and as he had never dared to, until Norman Mailer had tried to a couple of years ago: *Tune in same time next week . . .*

And José Daniel is thinking that they, his enemies, think he is an anachronism, a dinosaur, an extinct species. But, he thinks, they are mistaken. One of these days, he thinks with a yawn, Spielberg will call him up from Hollywood so he can write him a script called *Old Reds Never Die*, with Oliver Stone as co-writer. He did not know if he would be bothered.

Da Vinci has not come back from his bicycle ride and José Daniel turns out the lamp beside his computer, saves the file, makes a backup copy, and strokes the switch before turning the machine off and lulling everything to its electronic sleep.

He shuffles along as he walks, through habit, because even if he no longer has a cast he still has the memory of it and sometimes limps by memory rather than due to any fractures. He switches on the TV. He does not need any sound to enjoy the program, he can supply his own inimitable soundtrack perfectly well. He goes by the record player and turns up the volume a bit more on "Flor d'Luna," which the ignorant know by the name of "Moonflower," a tune recorded by Maestro Santana that owed a lot to the keyboard genius of Tom Coster. The guitar sounds like a mournful old folk song.

On the right, next to the armchair, a six-pack of ice-cold Coronitas awaits. He flops into the chair and smiles. The images on the screen come into focus, becoming clear and bright, just as Karen Turner shoots from outside the area.

The ball wobbles around the hoop.

It is falling, falling . . .

Maybe it is not reality out of reality, maybe it is just a repeat of an old game, maybe it is just a dream made up by a tired crime writer. He leans out the window, Leonardo is parking his bike in front of the apartment building. He is chaining it to a lamppost, because there are a lot of thieves in Mexico City. José Daniel watches him doing this under the great starry night of storytellers.

On the TV screen, Karen Turner shoots again and smiles.

The ball bounces off the backboard.
It is falling, falling . . .
Tune in same time next week . . . flashes up on the screen.

Mexico City, October 1991–April 1993

Apart from the Novel

Books like this use information that only I am responsible for handling, but it does come from friends, colleagues, and protagonists. All books stem, directly or indirectly, from a series of stories you were told, a load of images and things you lived through, and a stack of books, some of which you did not give back on time. For all these reasons I wish to thank all the work by others that made my work possible.

El Jefe José Daniel Fierro started off in another novel called *La Vida Misma* or *Life Itself*; I would like all those who have not read it to get hold of a copy. José Daniel was three years younger then, and almost never doubted things.

Jerry Bauer the photographer told me the story of the kidnapping in order to steal a kidney that started all of this.

In his version, the story took place in Lima. I moved it up to Ciudad Juárez, a much more accessible city . . .

My friend Mariano Rodríguez, the journalist, helped me a great deal with Cubanizing Ambarajá's language. He has been treated as a fictional character here, although he is quite real. I found him in the pages of *Verde Olivo*, in an article about Major Rodríguez. I hope he forgives me.

Dr. Espinosa really did contribute by explaining kidney transplants in Ciudad Juárez, and my guide in that city was Gustavo Piyú de la Rosa, who helped me to find my way when I got lost.

The images of modernist Barcelona come from my own faded memories and from the marvelous library belonging to my father, Paco Ignacio Taibo I, who still seems to trust me to give him his books back.

Barcelona in the 1920s owes a lot of almost verbatim pages to that wonderful group of anarchic journalists who kept the fires warm and their passion for informing up in the most difficult times, especially Angel Samblancat, Francisco Madrid, Salvador Quemades, Francisco Iribarne, and Antonio Amador himself, with whom I took every license allowable in the realm of fiction.

Jim Adams gathered a lot of material together for me in the United States about Operation Phoenix, thanks to which I was able to construct Jerry's beginnings as a character, although his participation in that operation was not used in these pages and will figure in another novel. Jerry's steps through Saigon were guided by Frank Snepp's outstanding novel *Decent Interval*; by the French journalist Jean Larteguy's disquieting memoirs; and by Alan Dawson's history of the last days of the Vietnam War.

Unknown Leonardo contains amazing accounts of the da Vinci saga in its pages, especially a marvelous article on the story behind the bicycle by Milán Augusto Marinoni, professor at the Catholic University of Milan. Leonardo's biographies by Bramly, Palenque, Racionero, Clark, Berence, and Mercjkovski were exceptionally useful to me.

Chief Fierro's "Santanamania" is mine, it is all down to me, but apart from the complete set of his records, it was Jordi Serra i Fabra's noble essay that helped me follow the Wizard of Autlán's story through.

It hardly needs to be added that all the characters here belong to the realm of fiction, even those who have the names of pals and good friends whom I have slandered in a fraternal way.

My Italian friends ruled out the name Mascarpone, but even so I love it. I first heard it in a restaurant in New York and it seems to be some sort of a cheese. I hereby authorize Mascarpone to be called anything else in the Italian version.

PIT II